MOMO ARASHIMA

STEALS THE SWORD OF THE WIND

MOMO ARASHIMA

STEALS THE SWORD OF THE WIND

Book 1

MISA SUGIURA

LABYRINTH ROAD | NEW YORK

Text copyright © 2023 by Misa Sugiura
Jacket art copyright © 2023 by Vivienne To

All rights reserved. Published in the United States by Labyrinth Road,
an imprint of Random House Children's Books,
a division of Penguin Random House LLC, New York.

Labyrinth Road and the colophon are trademarks
of Penguin Random House LLC.

Visit us on the Web! rhcbooks.com

Educators and librarians, for a variety of teaching tools, visit us at
RHTeachersLibrarians.com

Library of Congress Cataloging-in-Publication Data is available upon request.
ISBN 978-0-593-56406-6 (trade)—ISBN 978-0-593-56407-3 (lib. bdg.)—
ISBN 978-0-593-65033-2 (int'l)—ISBN 978-0-593-56409-7 (ebook)

The text of this book is set in 11.3-point Adobe Garamond Pro.
Interior design by Jen Valero

Printed in the United States of America
10 9 8 7 6 5 4 3 2 1
First Edition

For Tai and Kenzo:
At last, the book you asked for

Happy Birthday to Me

Niko says I should have known something was wrong from the moment he appeared in my backyard the night before my twelfth birthday. But I disagree. Because look—I can guarantee you that most people who saw what I saw that night would've said to themselves, *I must be dreaming,* or, *It must be something I ate,* and gone right back to bed.

And back then, I was trying really hard to be like most people.

But I'm getting ahead of myself. What happened was, I woke up to a yowl and a yippy bark. I got up and peeked out the window to see the neighbor's cat streaking across the yard, which was not unusual—but trotting oh-so-casually after it was a fox, which *was* unusual. The fox stopped in the middle of the yard, sat down, and pointed its sharp, twitchy nose and bright black eyes directly at my window.

The moon was shining from somewhere above and behind me, bathing the fox in cool silver light and casting a magical glow on the entire yard. As the fox stared at me, I was seized by this strange feeling that it knew who I was. Like it knew I was watching, and it was waiting for me. And then—I swear I'm not lying—it nodded at me and patted the ground with its paw. *Yes, you,* it seemed to be saying. *Come out here at once. I need to talk to you.*

That was not just unusual. It was unbelievable. Like, literally not able to be believed. "It's just my imagination," I muttered to myself. I shut my eyes and tried to shake what I'd seen out of my head. I *couldn't* have seen it. That was the problem with having what my teachers called an "overactive imagination"—I tended to see things that no one else could see. It hadn't happened in a long time, and I was annoyed (and maybe a little afraid) that it was happening now. Because normal kids didn't see things that weren't real, and like I told you, I really wanted to be a normal kid.

I put my hand out to knock on the window. If it was a magical fox who was here for me, he'd nod again, or do something else strange and un-fox-like. If it was a regular old real fox, he'd run away. I tapped three times—*tap, tap, tap*—just as a cloud moved across the moon and helped break the silvery magical feeling. The fox looked startled and scampered into the shadow of a big pine tree at the edge of the yard.

Okay, whew, I thought. *Regular old fox, then.*

I could just barely see him huddled under the lowest branches of the pine tree, his tail covering him like a fluffy blanket. He stayed perfectly still for several minutes, and eventually I got tired of watching him and went back to bed. Like a normal person.

If I had bothered to go to the front of the house to take a look at that cloud over the moon, I might have seen why the fox had hidden so suddenly. And I would not have been able to go back to bed like a normal person, because I would have been completely terrified. Because it wasn't really a cloud, as you may have guessed by now.

Hovering several feet in the air above the house, wearing a ragged black ball gown, black stiletto heels, and too much makeup, was a shikome—one of the death hags who serve Izanami the Destroyer, Queen of Death. The shikome's hair hung in patches from her scalp, which was peeling off her skull. Her eyes were pure white under her false eyelashes and drawn-on eyebrows, and although her lips had caved into her toothless mouth, she'd done her best and smeared a bright red outline of lipstick around the gaping hole. When she breathed, it was with a rattling hiss that would make your skin crawl. I didn't know it then, but she had followed that fox halfway around the world.

And *she* was waiting for me, too.

Mom didn't mention my birthday at breakfast the next morning, which was odd. She forgot a lot of things, but she'd always done something special for my birthday: pancakes for breakfast, handmade jewelry, a drawing of the two of us.

"Um, are we doing anything for my birthday?" I asked her, a little annoyed.

"Oh. I—I'm sorry, Momo, I forgot all about it." She looked more nervous than sorry. She looked like she was lying, in fact. "Maybe we can do something tomorrow."

I should have realized right then that something was wrong. But instead I decided to believe that she was planning a surprise, and dropped the subject. I told her about the fox—without the waiting and winking part, because the whole issue with my imagination was kind of a sensitive subject between us. Still, Mom loves foxes, and I thought she'd get a kick out of knowing there had been one in the backyard. But instead of smiling with delight, or asking me reproachfully why I hadn't woken her, she went pale.

"What did he look like?" she asked.

"I don't know. Like a fox," I said impatiently. "Sharp nose, bushy tail . . ."

"Where did he go?"

I shrugged. "The last I saw him, he was hiding under the pine trees."

"Hmm." Mom stared into the air, and her eyes grew unfocused.

"What?"

She refocused on me and bit her lip. "Nothing," she said. "Nothing at all." Shivering, she pulled her bathrobe more tightly around herself before sighing and leaning back in her chair, eyes closed.

I forgot about the fox. "Are you okay?"

"I'm just a little tired. I think I might go back to bed."

She pushed herself up and left the kitchen, moving slowly, carefully, as if walking was causing her pain. As I finished getting ready for school, I wondered if I should make a doctor appointment for her. I was used to making them for myself—she wasn't the greatest at stuff like that. But how would I convince her to go? She hated doctors, and I couldn't remember the last time she'd gone to one. If she was sick, we probably wouldn't be able to do anything for my birthday, I thought with some disappointment.

I glanced at the clock. I'd have to think about all of that later.

I had more pressing things to worry about, like getting through the school day. I sighed and swallowed the low-key feeling of dread I always felt before going to school.

The thing is, I was not exactly what you would call well liked. Don't get me wrong—no one actively hated me or anything. But I was pretty much at the very bottom of the trash heap known as the seventh-grade social scene. How do I know? You know these things. But if you want proof, I've got plenty.

For example, Kiki Weldon had recently made a list that ranked all seventy-one seventh graders at Oak Valley Middle School in order of popularity, and it had gotten printed and posted on the wall at school.

Guess who was number seventy-one.

Even worse than my rank was the fact that other low-ranked kids seemed to think that associating with me might somehow jeopardize their sweet, sweet spots in the upper sixties. So Sunita Agrawal (#65) stopped answering my calls (forget about texts— Mom didn't let me have a cell phone). Eliza Lang (#67) rolled her eyes for all to see when she got partnered with me in Spanish class. Marina Fernandez (#68) turned her back on me when I sat down next to her at lunch. Literally no one wanted to be my friend anymore.

By the way, someone told on Kiki, and she was suspended and had to make an announcement on the PA system about how sorry she was and how wrong and cruel the list had been, etc., etc., but did that turn her into a better person? Did it lead to a kinder, gentler era where everyone in seventh grade was equally popular and nice to each other?

Hello, are you a citizen of Earth? Of course it didn't.

And then there was last weekend at the back-to-school dance. Normally I would have avoided that dance like the pit of vipers that it was, but Ms. Pérez, my language arts and homeroom teacher, had asked me to help with the decorations, even though I wasn't part of the student leadership class.

"It'll be good for you to get involved in school activities," she said. "Working together with the others will help you bond with them." Riiight. But I knew that Mom worried about me not having friends. If I went to the dance, maybe she'd think I had friends again. Maybe it would make her happy. So even though every cell in my body was screaming at me to stay home where it was quiet and safe, I said yes.

Unfortunately, the result was a viral video of me getting splashed with a cup of punch and making one of those weird *AAACK!* faces—all in super-slo-mo, so the tiny yelp that actually came out of my mouth sounded more like the bellow of a charging rhinoceros. But that's not all, folks. The real highlight came when someone pointed out a sign on my back that said, *Help! I'm on fire!* and I basically turned into a horror-movie monster. With a Godzilla-level roar and a face that would make Gollum look like a sweet little foster kitten, I rushed the boy who'd splashed me—and then tripped over my own feet and fell flat on my face. No one helped me up. But I was suspended, the school counselor recommended therapy for my "anger issues," and Mom spent two days crying in her room.

So, yeah. Going to school felt like going into battle.

No one brought me cupcakes or wrote *Happy birthday, Momo!* on the whiteboard for my birthday, but I did ace a quiz on the Greek gods *and* a math test on exponents. (I aced all my tests because the thought of being unprepared for anything made my stomach hurt.) In language arts we watched a video about a whale whose song doesn't match the song of any existing whale species, and it wanders the ocean all alone. *You and me both, buddy,* I thought. I didn't raise my hand when Ms. Pérez had us discuss how the video made us feel, though. Keeping my mouth shut and staying under the radar was lonely, but it was the one thing I could control about my social life: if I didn't talk, no one could make fun of what I said. If I didn't try to make friends, no one could reject me.

After school, everything fell apart. I was first in line at the bus stop, trying to ignore Kiki Weldon and her BFF Ryleigh Guo. They were standing right behind me, giggling and whispering with their heads together like whatever they were talking about was *super* funny but sorry, they couldn't tell you about it because it was kind of an inside joke. Meanwhile, Brad Bowman and Danny Haragan and a couple of other bro-bots were laughing and watching a video on Danny's phone. They were shouting things like "Ohhh, take the L!" and "Ow, that's gotta hurt!" and "Again! Let's see it again!"

The girls took a break from whispering so they could sidle up to the boys, and within seconds it was a giggling, guffawing comedy extravaganza. I tried not to care, but all I could think was, *What are they laughing at? Why are they so mean? Why do kids like that get to have all the power?* and as always, *I hope they don't notice me. I hope they don't laugh at me.*

I was still trying to tune them out when the hairs on the back of my neck began prickling, and I got the distinct feeling that someone *was* watching me.

I looked up just in time to see a fox exactly like the one from the night before. Except he was standing on his hind legs. And he was wearing clothes. He had on old-timey pants that stopped at the knee, a vest, and a newsboy cap, and he was looking at me as if he knew who I was—just like last night.

No, I thought. *No, this isn't real.* I shut my eyes for three seconds, then opened them again. *Please let it not be real.*

But the fox was still there, standing on his hind legs in his old-timey costume like he was pretending to be a human boy. And then he *tipped his cap and winked at me* before turning and running into a tree. Like, he literally ran *into* the tree and— *poof!*—vanished.

I gaped at the spot where he'd been standing. *That did not just happen*, I told myself. *It was just my imagination.* It had to be my imagination. Foxes didn't wear clothes. They didn't tip their caps. They didn't disappear like magic.

At the same time, my head was spinning with questions. Was it the same fox from last night? What was it doing here? What did it want with me? Why was it wearing clothes? And why was I even asking myself these questions when I *knew* that what I'd just seen was impossible? But if it was impossible, why did it feel so real?

I heard a muffled giggle and some whispering that made those hairs on the back of my neck start prickling again.

"What are you looking at?" It was Kiki, who I guess had finally gotten tired of watching a video of someone falling and hurting themselves thirty-seven times in a row and was looking for somebody else to laugh at.

If my standard rule was to not talk too much to other people,

8

it applied a hundred times more to talking about stuff like pants-wearing, disappearing foxes. But I couldn't come up with a good lie. When Kiki looked at me like that, like a cat looks at a mouse, I froze from head to toe—except for my heart, which began pumping panic into my body at full speed. It took everything I had to mumble, "Nothing."

"No, you were definitely looking at something," she insisted. "I saw you go like this." She did an exaggerated double take and opened her mouth and eyes wide, like a cartoon person seeing a monster. "Right, Ryleigh? You saw her, right?"

Ryleigh nodded. "Uh-huh," she said. "Totally."

"C'mon, Momo, whaddja see?" Kiki said in a fake-sweet voice.

I wanted more than anything to run away and hide, but I had just enough presence of mind to know that would mean certain death. So I tried again. "I told you I didn't see anything. You're making it up."

"I am not!" Kiki protested. "Swear to god!"

"Don't lie, Momo," Ryleigh said. "Nobody likes a liar."

The other girls hovered, watching like vultures waiting to swoop down on a dead body (which is to say, me). Even the boys, who normally didn't even seem to realize I existed, had looked up from Danny's phone.

I was trapped. My improvising skills were terrible even on a good day—and forget about situations like now, when a little worm of panic was burrowing its way around my brain, shrieking, *Help! Help! Help!* I had two terrible options: I could keep pretending I hadn't seen anything and get sneered at for lying, or I could tell the truth and get laughed at for being weird.

"Fine." I paused and tried to calm my racing heart. *Come on, Momo. Think.* "I saw . . ."

Kiki looked at Ryleigh and smirked. "Yeah . . . ?"

"I saw . . ." *Think, Momo. Think! THINK!* A drop of sweat began trickling down my forehead. But on the inside of my skull, my mind remained stubbornly blank. Finally, I blurted out the truth. "I saw a fox."

Ryleigh snorted. "I don't believe you. If it was really a fox, you would have just said so instead of pretending you didn't see anything."

To this day, I don't know what came over me. Maybe I was sick of pretending I hadn't seen what I'd seen. Maybe it was magic. All I know is that I heard myself saying, "He was wearing pants."

"Bruh, a fox wearing pants? Where?" Danny and I were both Japanese—he'd been adopted by white parents. A long time ago, we used to be friends. But now he was one of the cool kids, and he stayed far away from me, like he didn't want to remind people that we had a single thing in common. I missed him desperately—and at the same time, I hated him for abandoning me.

Now he made pretend binoculars with his hands and stared not just where I'd pointed but all over the parking lot, across the street, and up at the sky. He clearly thought he was being hilarious. Kiki shrieked with laughter. Ryleigh rolled her eyes, and for a moment I thought she might come to my defense—but she just cooed, "Dannyyy!" and slapped him playfully on the arm.

"He's not there anymore. He—he disappeared." Maybe everyone would think I was playing along with Danny.

"What, like, *poof*?" Danny popped his hands wide open. "Like magic?"

I nodded. "Kind of. Yeah."

In the silence that followed, I knew I'd made a terrible mistake.

Kiki's mouth curled. "Wow. Magic, huh? That's very . . . interesting."

Someone in the crowd singsonged, "Weeirrdo—"

I felt my face flame with embarrassment and anger. How come when Danny pretended he was looking for a magical fox, people thought he was funny, but when I talked about the same magical fox, people thought I was a weirdo? Okay, so I hadn't been joking like Danny, but I *could* have been. It was so unfair. I wanted to scream. I wanted to smack them all in their ugly faces and tell them to shut up and leave me alone, but I didn't want another suspension. So I looked away and focused on silently hating everyone around me so that I wouldn't cry. Happy birthday to me.

The bus arrived and the door whooshed open. I got on, found a seat, and put my backpack next to me as a barrier. That's when the tears started coming. I brushed them away angrily and looked out the window to hide my face. I found myself searching the neighborhood for a fox dressed like he'd stepped out of *Mary Poppins*. But I didn't see anything. Well, of course I didn't. Those kinds of things belonged in myths and fairy tales, not in real-life suburban junior high school parking lots.

Still, as we rolled down the streets, I couldn't help thinking about all the foxes in the stories Mom used to tell me. Foxes are tricksters. They get people into trouble all the time. If there were such things as magic foxes in real life, that is exactly what one would have done: revealed itself to me and laughed from some hidden spot while I made a fool of myself in front of my frie— My classmates.

We reached my stop first, and as I stood to go, Danny called to me from the back of the bus. "Hey, Momo!"

Don't fall for it. Ignore him. I put my backpack on without looking at him.

"Let me know if you see any more disappearing foxes, okay?" The whole back of the bus practically exploded with laughter.

He's a giant pile of toenail clippings. He's body odor come to life. He's—

The door whooshed closed and the bus roared away.

Why did people have to be so mean to me? What had I ever done to deserve this? I wished I was a wizard so I could curse them. *PIMPLIOSO EXTRANORMICUS!* I'd shout, and they'd all turn into a bunch of oozing zits.

Mom always insisted it didn't matter what people said about me, and that I shouldn't bother trying to fit in with anyone who didn't understand me. I agreed with her in principle, but, ugh, it made life hard sometimes. Because so often I felt like no one understood me.

I wished I hadn't seen that fox. Or at least that he hadn't been wearing clothes. I wished this didn't feel like it was connected to the fox in my yard last night—like that fox was tailing me, trying to get my attention. Most of all, I wished it hadn't felt so *real*.

I thought I'd gotten over seeing things that weren't there. Why was this happening again?

Not Developmentally Appropriate

When I was young, I loved to curl up in Mom's lap while she told me stories about the kami and the yōkai—Japanese gods and monsters: how Susano'o, the god of the sea, defeated an eight-headed dragon and pulled a sword out of its tail. Or how a fisherman named Urashima Tarō spent three days partying at a palace under the sea, and when he returned home, three hundred years had passed. There was something about the way she told those stories that made them feel real, like the characters were old friends. "Did that really happen?" I would ask, and she would nod. "Of course it did."

She'd point to the sky during thunderstorms and say, "Look! It's Raijin, playing his drum to make thunder!" Or she'd take me for walks in the woods and say, "See the kappa by the creek? That little green creature with the dish of water on his head? Stay away from him or he'll pull you in and eat you." I loved those moments. They made me feel like we shared something special.

One gray and windy autumn day in fourth grade, I wandered onto the field behind the school to get a better look at a tattered wood-and-paper umbrella sailing around the roof. As I stared at it, Mrs. Evans, my teacher, asked me what I was looking at, so I told her.

Mrs. Evans called Mom that very afternoon. She sat down with both of us and said gently, "Momo told me today that she saw an umbrella flying in the sky. Are you aware that Momo sees things that other people can't see?"

"Yes, I am," Mom said proudly. "She is very special."

"Oh." Mrs. Evans frowned. "Momo has quite an imagination, which is a wonderful thing. But you need to stop encouraging her to believe that everything she imagines is real. It's not developmentally appropriate." She cleared her throat once, and added, "I understand that Momo's father passed away last year. I wonder if perhaps this might be related to her insistence on—"

Mom looked confused, then angry; I saw something flash in her eyes so fierce that Mrs. Evans flinched and fell silent. "Her father is not dead. She is not imagining things. She saw a hone-karakasa. They appear in the sky before bad weather." As if on cue, it began pouring rain outside. "See?" Mom said, and smiled triumphantly. It would have been funny if I hadn't been feeling so humiliated.

Mrs. Evans did not return her smile. Instead she said, "Please give some thought to our conversation, for Momo's sake. I can recommend a therapist if you like." Then she lowered her voice and leaned forward, as if by doing this she'd created a magical cone of silence, and said, "Her peers are starting to ostracize her. You really need to address this before she loses all of her friends," before walking us out the door.

I felt like Mrs. Evans had nailed me in the gut with a red

rubber playground ball, and when I stood up straight again, everything was different. It all made sense now, why I kept ending up alone on the playground, why kids rolled their eyes or grinned at each other and slunk away from me when I pointed out what I saw. It wasn't that they couldn't see what I saw, as I'd been telling myself. It was because what I saw wasn't there. The umbrella in the sky wasn't real. Susano'o and the dragon, Urashima Tarō, Raijin, kappa—none of it was real. I *knew* where thunder came from—we'd learned about it in school— and it was definitely not the drum of a scary-looking giant in the sky. Why had it taken me so long to figure this out?

I had an overactive imagination, just like Mrs. Evans said.

"Just because Mrs. Evans can't see what you and I see doesn't mean it isn't real. It just isn't real to Mrs. Evans," Mom said to me as we walked home together in the rain.

"No, Mom," I said, feeling anger rise inside me. "It's the opposite. If no one else can see what I see, that means I'm imagining it. Stop pretending it's all real. I know it's not." I took a big breath. "And stop pretending Dad is alive. He's *dead*, okay? Just accept it and move on like a normal person."

I looked at Mom's face and immediately felt terrible. I'd crossed a huge line, and I almost hoped she'd scream at me. But she took a deep, trembling breath, nodded, and said, "Maybe you're right." I had to look away so I wouldn't see the anguish in her eyes—I always worked so hard to make sure she didn't get too sad, and now I'd made her sadder than I'd ever seen her.

Dad met Mom when he was exploring the coast of a little island off the southern tip of Japan, where she lived. She'd come down to the beach for a swim, and she saw him taking care of an injured crab—he was a marine biologist. According to her, she fell for him right then and there: "I knew that anyone who could care for such an ugly-looking creature had to have a kind heart," she always said. And Dad would always add, "But guess who actually helped that crab get better?" And they'd kiss and get all gross and embarrassing until I begged them to stop.

After they had me, they moved to California, where Dad kept working and Mom was a stay-at-home parent. Mom was the dreamer, the one who could see beyond our everyday life into a whole other world full of magic, and who brought me into that world with her stories. She could make anything bloom, and no matter what I brought home to her—a baby bird that had fallen out of its nest, a rabbit with a broken leg, even a half-squashed lizard that the neighbors' cat had been playing with—she'd nurse it tenderly back to health before letting it go like she'd done with that crab. Dad was the one who kept us anchored and who took care of the day-to-day stuff: the bills, house repairs, back-to-school nights, doctor appointments.

One day when Dad and his team were on a research trip off the coast of Alaska, I came home from school to find Mom sitting motionless on the floor, staring into space. The Coast Guard had called. The research vessel had been caught in a storm, and Dad had been swept overboard. Both of his parents were dead, and Mom's parents had disowned her when she married Dad, so Mom and I were completely alone.

Mom never really recovered from that day. "The Coast Guard is wrong," she insisted. "I can still feel his life force." She never even had a funeral or anything. In fact, every day that summer, she would drive me to the coast and we'd sit for hours together on the cliffs of Half Moon Bay. I would watch as she stared out at the Pacific, crying and mumbling to herself.

After a couple of weeks, one of our neighbors, Mrs. Fisher, figured out what was going on. She offered to take care of me while Mom went to the ocean on her own. Mom looked at me and said I could stay with Mrs. Fisher if I liked, but I said no, thanks, I didn't mind going with her. The truth was, I hated it— it was upsetting and also *really* boring—but I was afraid that if I didn't watch her, Mom might fling herself off the cliffs into the foamy waves below and I wouldn't have any parents left at all. So I would go with her and try to cheer her up by pointing out whales and dolphins, or by asking her to tell me about all the magical creatures who lived in the sea.

Mrs. Fisher finally had a talk with Mom and helped her find a job as a Reiki healer at a fancy spa in town. Channeling the energy of the universe to heal a bad back might seem more like a way to bilk money out of rich white ladies than a real thing, but as always, Mom insisted it was real, and, hey—it kept us from starving.

Of course, it didn't keep Mom from being sad. So on top of learning to do the laundry, and calling the dishwasher repair guy, and reminding her to buy me shoes when my old ones were too small, I learned to watch out for her moods—when she'd go to her room for hours and stare at our only photo of Dad, where the three of us are smiling happily on the shore of Mom's home island. I would peek in and remind her to eat, and ask her to tell me a story—it was the only way to make her look up and think of something else.

During those storytelling sessions, I felt like I could see the *real* Mom, the one from the old days who was happy, and who took care of me, instead of the other way around. But after that day in fourth grade with Mrs. Evans, Mom stopped telling me stories and pointing out kami and yōkai to me. And every time I thought I saw a kami on my own, I would remind myself that they weren't real. Eventually I stopped seeing them at all. I missed seeing them. I missed believing they were real. But allowing Mom to keep pretending that this giant world of make-believe was real felt irresponsible somehow. Because if I didn't stay strong and keep my feet planted firmly in the real world, who would?

Unfortunately for me, Mrs. Evans's warning had come too late. I was well on my way to becoming an outcast, and there was no going back. I thought about this on my way home from the bus stop. Really, it was all Mom's fault. If she'd just told me those stories were make-believe, I wouldn't have believed them and gotten in trouble at school, and she could have kept telling her stories. Kids wouldn't have thought I was too weird to be friends with. On the other hand, Kiki and Co. were the kind of kids who would use any excuse to be mean to kids they'd decided weren't cool enough. Ugh. It was so unfair, and it made me angry at everyone.

I felt angry as I passed under the torii that Mom insisted on having built over the front path to our house—a sort of gateway made of two scarlet pillars connected at the top by two parallel beams. I felt angry as I walked between Alfie and Meggie, the two carved stone koma-inu (short-legged bulldog-looking creatures with curly manes like lions have) who stood on either side of our front steps. Alfie's mouth was wide open in a roar, and Meggie's mouth was clamped firmly shut. They were saying "Ah" and "Un," Mom always said, the first and last letters of the Japanese alphabet. Open and Shut, Beginning and End.

I was still angry when I took off my shoes and dipped my hands in the bowl of water that Mom keeps in the front hall "to clean off the outside world." All of this was stuff that made grown-ups and teachers say, "How fascinating!" and kids say, "How weird!"

But when I saw her at the kitchen table, I forgot about my anger. Or maybe I should say when I saw *him* at the kitchen table, I forgot about my anger.

A strange-looking red-haired boy sat there smiling at me. His nose was weirdly long and pointy, and his teeth were oddly . . . doglike? And he was wearing the exact same clothes that I'd seen on that fox at the bus stop: the brown newsboy cap, the vest, the funny pants. I looked at Mom for some kind of clue as to what he was doing here—maybe this was part of my birthday surprise? But her mouth was shut as tight as Meggie's, and her expression was just as stony.

"Why, hello, Momo!" the boy said brightly. "How lovely to see you again. I'm Niko."

A Rabid Fox . . .
Escaped from the Circus

"Um." I looked at Mom again. "Hi?"

"I was just about to—" he started to say.

"You were just about to leave," said Mom. She got up, grabbed his shoulder, and practically yanked him out of his chair and steered him toward the door with a focused energy that I'd never seen from her. I couldn't help staring.

"No! No, please, my lady! My powerful patroness! My gracious goddess! Please let me help!" he protested, but Mom was immovable.

"Find another way," she said. "I will not allow you to put Momo in danger."

"What? Mom, what are you talking about?" I blurted.

Mom and Niko turned and stared at me. "You can understand me?" Mom asked, clearly shocked.

I realized then that she wasn't speaking English—or Japanese, which I could barely understand anyway. And I hadn't been, either. We'd been speaking something that sounded like water curling over smooth rocks in a stream: clear, fluid sounds that flowed up and down and around as

20

the sentences tumbled forth. I nodded, afraid to say another word.

She gave Niko a look of pure fury. "Get. Out. Now," she said in that strange language—this time, the anger in her voice made it sound like waves crashing on a rocky shore—and he slunk out the door. "And don't try any of your tricks, or I will be very upset with you. Is that clear?"

Niko nodded so sadly as he stood on the doorstep that I almost felt sorry for him. And I could have sworn that I heard some growling and whimpering—was it Alfie and Meggie? Or was it Niko? Or all three?

There goes your imagination again, I told myself. *It was probably just the neighbor's dog.*

Mom waited until Niko had walked down the street, around the corner, and out of sight before she shut the door. Then her body sagged and she shuffled toward the back of the house, looking more like her usual self, as if pushing Niko out had drained every last drop of that weird energy she'd had. I remembered that she was sick. "Can you bring me a glass of water, Momo?" she said, speaking in English once more. "That rude boy got me out of bed, and now I'm so tired."

When I entered the bedroom, Mom was propped up against her pillows, looking pale in the fading afternoon light.

"Who was that kid?" I asked, handing her the glass. "And, uh . . . did he remind you of a fox? Or was that just me?"

She looked startled. "A fox? No! Why would he remind you of a fox? He looked nothing at all like a fox! You're probably thinking of that fox you saw last night."

That didn't make any sense. I tried another question. "What was he doing here?"

She took a sip of water. "I've known him since he was a baby. He was here to . . . to . . ."

"He said something about helping you," I reminded her. "And you said something about not putting me in danger. In a language I wasn't supposed to understand." I felt bad about pushing her when she was so tired, but this was too wild to let go of. I had to know.

"Momo," she said heavily. "I promise I'll tell you more later." Then she seemed to cheer up. "But right now, I have a birthday present for you." She gestured at a little shopping bag on her dresser, clearly trying to change the subject.

"Why can't you tell me now?" I asked.

She shook her head. "It's too much."

"Am I really in danger?"

"Not if you stay close to home and do what I say."

This was hardly comforting. On the other hand, what could be out there that could possibly be a real threat? It reminded me of the way she used to scare me with stories about the kappa to prevent me from going to the creek by myself.

"Look in the bag," she said.

I opened it to find a straw rope of some kind, made of two thinner ropes twisted together. It was as thick as my wrist in the middle, and tapered as thin as shoelaces at the ends.

"Happy birthday." Mom smiled.

"Um." I held it up and looked at it. "Is this a family heirloom or something?"

"Tie it around your neck," said Mom, "and promise me you will never take it off. Wear it every day."

"What?" I couldn't wear this in public—everyone would laugh at me!

Mom nodded. "It's a shimenawa. It keeps away impurities and evil—for your protection."

I was about to argue that I was twelve years old and I didn't need protection—that in fact, if anyone was doing any protecting around here, it was *me* protecting *her*. Then I remembered what she'd said to Niko. I looked at her suspiciously. "Does this have to do with that thing you said about me being in danger?"

"No, silly girl. It's for everyday use. All you have to do to stay out of danger is stay away from that bad boy." She seemed to remember something. "Oh! And I . . . I heard on the news that there is a fox in the neighborhood. A . . . a rabid fox. Escaped from the circus, so it's wearing a silly costume. So if you see it, you must stay far away from it as well."

"I did see it! Today, at the bus stop after school." Maybe I wasn't hallucinating after all. Although that didn't explain the part where it magically disappeared.

She looked startled—scared, even. "Stay far away from it," she said again. "And always, *always* wear this around your neck." She motioned for me to tie the rope on.

None of this made any sense.

"Fine." I sighed. This was turning out to be a really rotten birthday. I started tying it loosely behind my neck. Maybe I could take it off and put it in my backpack when I left the house. But Mom made me turn around so she could check the knot.

"This isn't tight enough," she said, and set to work retying it.

When she finished, she patted my shoulders. "There. Now I can relax." I ran my hands along the string. The loop was too short to pull over my head, and she had tied the knot really tightly. I was going to have to spend a lot of time picking it loose.

Mom took another sip of water, then sank back into her pillow, eyes closed, her long black hair pulled away from her face and tied over her left shoulder. I felt another little ripple of worry. She'd never been this sick before.

"Are you okay, Mom?" I asked.

But she was already fast asleep.

Run, Momo Arashima!

Mom was too tired to get up before I left for school in the morning. Looking back, that should have worried me more than it did. And I should have been more concerned with the appearance of Niko, the Boy Who Looked Like a Fox (as well as the Disappearing Fox Who Dressed Like a Boy) from the day before. But to be honest—and I'm not proud of this—all I could think about was getting rid of that awful white rope around my neck before anyone got a good look at it. Mom had tied a *serious* knot, and after picking at it forever the night before, I'd finally given up and gone to bed.

Of course, the moment I got on the bus, Kiki saw it and called, "Ooh, what are you wearing, Momo, a dog collar?" and everyone started barking at me. The barking continued all day, and I picked at the knot every chance I got and wished that (a) Mom wasn't so weird, and (b) people weren't so awful. Mom had said that the rope would protect me—ha. It hadn't protected me from Kiki and her crew, and it never would.

At the very end of the school day, things finally got better. I thought I could feel the knot loosening just a little, and on my way to study hall, which I had last period, an office assistant

25

chased me down and gave me an envelope with my name on it. "Someone dropped this off for you," she said in a bored voice, and ran back to the office before I could ask who.

I opened it and . . . *what?* Inside was a stack of gift cards: Forever 21. H&M. American Eagle. Ten in all, worth hundreds of dollars. I could buy myself a whole new wardrobe!

I wondered for about two seconds who had given these to me. Maybe they were my real birthday present from Mom, to make up for this awful rope I was wearing around my neck—or maybe the rope was a joke present. But that wasn't like her. And anyway, we could never afford something this extravagant. Maybe they were from that Niko guy. Maybe he was a rich cousin or something. Sure, Mom had said he was dangerous—but she'd also said he wasn't.

I probably should have thought more about who they were from and why. But somehow, the idea of a shopping spree at the mall pushed everything else out of my head. I know, it's super shallow. But I'd never had enough money to buy cool new clothes before, and everyone knows that clothes are important. Maybe if I had some cool clothes, I thought, it would be easier to fit in. People wouldn't be so mean to me.

I decided to take a city bus to the mall as soon as school was over. I'd shop for a while and then hit the food court for an early dinner of fast food before heading home. I felt sorry for Mom alone and sick in bed, but then I felt defiant. After all the worrying I had to do because of her, and all the bullying I had to put up with, I *deserved* an afternoon off—no Mom, no mean kids, just me and my thoughts and my gift cards. I told myself I'd take some food home to her.

I went to store after store and bought myself outfits just like the kind that Kiki and Ryleigh and their minions wore. Once I'd made my purchases, I went into a dressing room and changed into a brand-new, totally on-trend outfit: jeans, a soft gray T-shirt, an oversized floral camo jacket, and pink Chuck Taylors. I actually looked . . . cool. Well, except for my giant rope. Filled with determination, I worked at it in the dressing room until finally the strands came loose and I was free. I shoved it deep into my backpack with only a tiny twinge of guilt and left for the food court.

Feeling reckless, I decided to go full-on junk food for dinner. I stopped at the Sweet Factory for a bag of peach gummies (my favorite), and then Auntie Anne's for a bucket of warm, fragrant cinnamon-sugar pretzel nuggets (my other favorite). I was sitting on a bench outside Macy's, blissfully savoring their cinnamony, buttery goodness when Danny, Brad, Kiki, Ryleigh, and several of their closest underlings strolled toward me like a pack of well-dressed hyenas, laughing and yipping at each other. The usual anxiety bubbled up like lava in my stomach: *What if I say hi and they laugh at me? What if I say hi and they completely ignore me? What if, what if, what if . . .* But I had on a cool new outfit, and it felt like a kind of armor. Plus, I wasn't wearing that ridiculous rope around my neck anymore. So I wiped my cinnamon-sugary fingers, summoned my courage, and smiled at them when they paused in front of me.

"I see you have a new look," said Ryleigh with a smile.

"It's *so* much better than your old look," said Kiki, and I could see the glances spread through the group like a disease— slowly, quietly, from person to person. Someone stifled a giggle.

"Where's your dog collar, though?" asked Ryleigh. "Because *that* was cool."

"Yeah, speaking of dogs, have you seen any magic foxes around?" Danny asked.

I realized then that my new clothes hadn't made me cooler at all. To these kids, I was just someone dressed up and pretending to be cool. I wasn't wearing armor. I was wearing a costume. And those girls had seen right through it and were tearing it off, like the ugly stepsisters did with Cinderella's dress. They would never see me as anything but a loser.

Suddenly my anxiety and hope were drowned out by rage—the same rage I'd felt at the dance, and yesterday at the bus stop. It surged from my feet through my stomach and into my head. I felt my hands curl into fists as I stood and faced Kiki—I felt like I could knock her right over if I tried.

"Go away," I snarled through clenched teeth. "I *hate* you."

Everyone took a step back. "Fine, whatever," said Kiki, clearly startled. "Come on, you guys." They left, whispering words like "she-Hulk" and "nutjob."

The anger was still pulsing through me as I watched the pack yip and yap their way toward Macy's. I hoped one of them would trip and fall. Or maybe all of them, like bowling pins.

Which was when an orange blur came tearing out of the Macy's accessories section and nearly crashed into Ryleigh and Kiki—who shrieked, lost their balance, and fell right on their butts. I felt a glow of satisfaction, but I didn't get to enjoy it because the blur skidded to a stop in front of me and panted, "Run, Momo Arashima! Your life is in danger!"

It was a fox—*the* fox, I was sure of it, because he was wearing a vest, suspenders, and funny pants, and he was speaking the same language that I'd heard him speak with—no, no, wait. It wasn't a *fox* who had been talking to Mom. It was . . .

"N-Niko?" I squinted at him, searching for the boy under the fur and the foxy snout.

"Yes, yes, hello, it's me," he said impatiently, twitching his ears. "But this is no time for pleasantries. Run!"

I hesitated. Mom had told me not to go anywhere with Niko; she'd also told me to stay away from rabid costumed circus foxes. Besides, I wasn't sure I should be taking the advice of *any* fox, even if he had just knocked over my worst enemies and told me that my life was in danger. But then I was hit with a blast of air that smelled like rotting meat, and the sound of people scream-ing from the depths of the store. A figure dressed in a ragged black sequined ball gown was flying—*flying*—over the crowd, its long arms outstretched. And it was heading straight for me.

If We Don't Die, We'll Be Arrested for Littering

Her cheeks were sunken and gray under twin spots of garish pink. Her milky eyes, rimmed with winged eyeliner and false eyelashes, stared, unseeing, out of their sockets. A thick slash of dark red lipstick opened to reveal a gaping, toothless mouth as she unleashed an ear-piercing scream that sounded like—well, it sounded like death.

"It's the shikome! Run! Run for your life, you nit-brained ninny!" Niko yelped. He grabbed my Auntie Anne's bag in his mouth and took off on all fours. I didn't need to be told again—the shikome and her death-cry were worse than anything I had imagined when Mom used to tell me about them. I ran.

I was at a flat-out sprint, but I had to weave my way through a crowd of people who could clearly see the monster behind me—they were pointing and shouting at the tops of their lungs—but for some reason were not fleeing in abject terror. And when I spotted Niko again, he was far ahead of me, waiting at the top of the down escalator. No one was paying him the kind of attention he should have been getting, either.

Niko dropped the Auntie Anne's bag and urged me on. "Faster!" he cried. "She's gaining!"

I didn't dare look over my shoulder. I didn't need to. The death hag was so close, I could hear her gown swishing and flapping in the air. As I neared the escalator, Niko tore a hole in the bag with his teeth and shook it. Cinnamon-sugar pretzel nuggets began tumbling out, one after another.

I snatched the bag from him before he emptied it completely; I was furious now, as well as terrified. "What the heck was that?" I demanded as we rushed down the escalator. "Dumping my Auntie Anne's isn't going to make me go faster! *And* it's a waste of food!"

"I wasn't trying to speed you up, you addlepated airhead. I was trying to slow her down!" Niko gestured toward the top of the escalator, and I paused and turned just long enough to see the death hag swooping down to collect the pretzel nuggets, snarling and clawing at onlookers as if to warn them away from her precious nom-noms. I wondered again why no one was running for their lives, but I didn't wonder for long because Niko tugged my sleeve and shouted, "Come *on!*"

We sprinted across an atrium and out a set of glass doors, where he ripped the bag from my hand. The remaining nuggets rolled around on the sidewalk as we ran toward the parking lot.

"Now what?" I asked, lungs heaving.

Niko trotted briskly ahead of me, muttering, "No time to lose, no time to lose," until he came to a little red Kia Soul. He touched the driver's-side handle and said, "Get in."

"Who—what—" I babbled.

"Stop jibber-jabbering and get in! Hurry!" He opened the rear door on my side and gestured urgently at it.

"No. I don't even know who you are. That's probably not even your car!"

"I'm Niko, and this *is* my car now," said Niko. "Get in!"

"That's not what I—"

"Hey!" I turned to see Danny running toward us, holding my backpack. "You dropped this!" He reached us and handed it to me, barely even breathing hard. "Bruh, did you see that witch thing? It seemed like it was after you."

Niko made a strangled yelping sound, and Danny pointed at him. "You're the magic fox with the pants!"

"How . . . ," said Niko, his eyes wide. Then, "Never mind. Momo, get in *now.*"

"And you can *talk*? Whoa. I'm getting in, too," Danny declared.

"What are you even doing here?" I asked.

"JUST GET IN THE CAR OR WE'RE ALL GOING TO DIE!" Niko shouted as a scream came from the mall entrance.

"Listen to the fox, Momo," said Danny, and he shoved me into the back seat ahead of him.

"Buckle up!" Niko was already in the front seat, buckling his seat belt. "Do you have anything to eat, by the way?"

"Oh, like maybe the bag of cinnamon-sugar pretzel nuggets you just threw away?" I snapped.

"Why are we talking about food? I thought you said we were about to die," said Danny.

"Can you even drive?" I asked. "Do you have a driver's license?"

"Of course I can drive! And of course I don't have a license—do you think they give driver's licenses to foxes?"

"Okay, then, can you at least shift into human form like you did at my house?"

Niko paused for a second, then said sharply, "No. Now tell me if you have any food."

"But I thought foxes were shape-shifters," I said.

"It's a long story, I don't want to talk about it, and it's rude of you to argue. More importantly, we are—and I cannot emphasize this enough—*ABOUT TO DIE* unless either of you aggravating adolescents has any more food for our pursuer, in which case our deaths might be ever-so-slightly delayed and possibly even avoided. So stop dithering about driver's licenses and shape-shifting, and tell me what you've got!"

I dug around in my backpack. "All I've got are these peach gummies."

"I have some grape Bubble Yum," said Danny.

"Good. Toss them out the window when I tell you," Niko instructed us, and we screeched backward, slammed into a white Mercedes, then lurched forward and stopped so hard, my head hit the headrest in front of me.

"You're going to kill someone!" I shouted.

"I will not," Niko said through gritted teeth, and we zoomed around the parking lot, narrowly missing pedestrians and parked cars alike before blazing through a red light and into traffic.

"You're going to kill *us*!" said Danny, who looked like he deeply regretted his choice to trust a talking fox to drive a car. *Serves you right for barging in,* I thought.

"I will *not*," Niko said again. "Now be quiet and let me drive."

A bloodcurdling shriek and a thud overhead told me the shikome had found us. I looked up.

There was a dent in the roof.

Thud. Another dent appeared, as well as a crack in the windshield.

We were now racing down Stevens Creek Boulevard. Headlights streamed by and car horns *BEEEeeep*ed as we wove wildly through traffic.

Thud. The shikome threw herself against my window, and I screamed and flinched toward the middle of the seat.

"I'm going to throw my gummies at her," I said.

"Not yet," replied Niko.

"But she's literally right on top of us!" Danny protested.

Thud. The roof again.

"NOT YET!"

Thud. The crack in the windshield spiderwebbed out. This time, the hag hung on, her gruesome face and gaping mouth hideously distorted by the broken glass.

"We're going to die!" I wailed.

"No one! Is going! To die!" Niko barked, and took a hard left across three lanes of traffic. The shikome slid off the hood and a truck veered away from us as we careened around the corner and nearly hit a telephone pole.

"Now! Throw your food out now!" hollered Niko as he lowered the windows from his controls in the front seat. Danny and I flung our gummy peaches and grape bubble gum out the window.

If we don't die, we'll be arrested for littering, I thought vaguely. But when I looked back, the shikome was on her hands and knees in the street, scrabbling at the gummies and Bubble Yum with her bony fingers and shoving it all into her mouth as cars screeched and banged to a halt around her.

I breathed a sigh of relief that turned into a croak when I saw where we were headed: straight toward a giant oak tree at the side of the road.

"What the heck!" Danny shouted. "Stop! Stop the car!"

"Never!"

The oak tree rushed at us, and my heart leaped into my throat, along with my stomach, which may explain why I didn't scream my head off. I'm not even sure I was breathing, to be honest.

I don't know exactly what happened next, because my eyes were squeezed shut. But at the very moment that I thought I was going to be smashed to smithereens, I realized I was falling, or maybe flying, through darkness punctuated by flashes of blinding light in colors that I'd never seen before: green-but-also-purple, gold-but-also-red. I heard the roar of wind in my ears, and my body felt electric and prickly, the way soda feels in your mouth, like all of my molecules and atoms had separated and were dancing around each other in the extra space.

And then they were mashing into each other like people in an overcrowded elevator. The pressure came from everywhere. . . . It was unbearable. . . . I was going to be squashed into nothing. And just when I thought I was going to have to spend the rest of my life as an infinitesimally tiny dot in space, the feeling disappeared. I felt myself expanding back into my normal self, gasping for air as I hit the ground.

No Offense, but How Does *She* Have Godly DNA?

I lay still for a moment, catching my breath and listening with my eyes closed as I waited for the world to stop spinning. The air was cool and quiet except for birdsong and the sound of wind rustling in the leaves. There were no cars, no sirens, no ghastly screaming hags with bad makeup and worse breath. The spinning slowed down and I opened my eyes cautiously. Above me was the canopy of a giant oak tree. Danny lay next to me, also breathing hard. I was glad to see that he looked as pale and wobbly as I felt. On my other side was Niko, looking like a proper non-clothes-wearing fox.

I sat up slowly. "What happened?" I asked Niko, who of the three of us seemed the least freaked out. "Where are we?" I squinted into the semidarkness and realized we weren't under the same tree we'd crashed into. Instead, we were under another giant oak in the middle of a park near my neighborhood, where Mom used to take me to play—wait a second.

The tree we'd crashed into?

An icy horror crept into my chest. "Am I . . . Are we . . ." I couldn't say it.

But Danny could. "Are we dead? Are we in heaven?" He

patted himself on the arms, chest, and cheeks experimentally. Then he reached over to pat *my* cheek, and I swatted his hand away. "Whoa!" he said. "Chill!"

"Of course you aren't dead, you panicky pip-squeaks. We've merely traveled through a spirit portal to a different location."

"That sounds an awful lot like 'dead' to me," I said.

"Yeah, me too. Is that 'different location' the afterlife, by any chance?" Danny added.

"We are very much alive and very much on the earth, thanks to my quick thinking and excellent driving skills," Niko said snootily. "Not that I expect a thank-you from you ungrateful urchins."

"Oh. I guess if you want to call crashing into a tree excellent driving skills—"

"I did that *on purpose*, young lady! To keep you alive! Which, if you check your vital signs, you will find that you are," Niko countered.

I decided to believe him. Alive was better than dead, after all. "Fine," I said. "Thank you. Though as long as we're thanking each other, you're welcome for distracting the shikome with *our* snacks." I thought sadly about the pretzel nuggets and peach gummies that I'd sacrificed.

"Shiko-what?" said Danny.

"Shee-koh-meh," said Niko. "A death hag. Who would never have appeared if you hadn't practically banged on a drum and called it to you," he added, glaring at me.

"I did not! How could I have called a shikome?"

"Hold up. Spirit portals? Death hags? Also, why am I talking to a talking fox? Can someone please explain to me what the heck is going on? Do I need to be worried?"

37

"I wish I could tell you," I said.

"I'll give you the big picture later, but to answer your question, Momo, you shed your mother's protection! The shimenawa she gave you. When you took it off, you broadcast your vulnerability, and now it's useless unless your mother herself reties the knot. Speaking of which, where is it?"

"*This?*" I reached into my backpack and pulled out the rope necklace. "But—but that protection thing is just superstition. It's not real." Though even as I said this, I began to doubt myself. Maybe it *was* real. We had just escaped a shikome by driving through a tree, after all.

"Superstition? Not real? How dare you! If that's not real, then what am I? A figment of your imagination?" Niko spluttered.

I shoved the necklace back into my backpack. "I don't know. Maybe you are. Maybe I'm hallucinating. Maybe I'm dreaming."

"Um. Excuse me," Danny cut in. "Not to be rude, but can we get back to the death hag for a minute? 'Cause even if we *are* dreaming, she's still after us. Can she, uh, follow us here?"

"Well said, young man. Back to the crisis at hand. We're safe for the moment. Shikome are always hungry, and they can't pass up anything they find to eat. And she won't be able to go through the tree, like we did; it won't let her. Still, we should move quickly. She is quite set on killing you, Momo, and it won't take her long to figure out where you've gone."

My mouth went dry.

Danny stared at me. "Sucks to be you, bro."

I'm not your bro, I said in the back of my brain, but there were a lot of other things I needed to say first. Namely, "Why is she after me? And how do I know I can trust you, anyway? My mom told me not to go anywhere with you."

"We are headed back to your house, so you don't need to worry. You'll be safe and your mother can restore her protection over you and you can ask her if I'm lying. Now come along. I'll explain everything while we walk." He trotted off toward home.

I couldn't see any flaws in his logic, and anyway, night was falling fast and I didn't want to be in the park alone, so I followed him across the grass and onto the sidewalk.

"Hey, wait up!" called Danny. "I'm coming with."

"Huh?"

Danny Haragan wanted to come to my house and hang out with me instead of going home or going back to meet his friends? That was almost as strange as the fact that he could talk to Niko—assuming this was all real and I wasn't dreaming. I eyed him suspiciously.

So did Niko. "Who are you?" he asked.

"I'm Danny. I'm Momo's friend."

Danny still considered himself my friend?

"I mean, we're not *friends* friends," he corrected himself, and my heart squeezed tight. *Oh*. Well, at least that part felt like my normal waking life.

"Wouldn't you rather go back to the mall and hang out with your *real* friends?" I asked. I found myself walking a little faster, like it would somehow get me away from that yucky feeling of betrayal I always got around Danny.

But he stayed right with me and said, "Nah. This is way more fun. You're cool with it, right?"

So he didn't actually want to hang out with me—he was just in the mood for adventure. And naturally he assumed that I'd be "cool with it." In fact, he was probably wondering why I hadn't begged him to come right from the start. Like I'd welcome him back into my life as if he had never left.

"Did you say you saw the shikome?" Niko said.

Danny nodded.

"How very interesting." He gave Danny a shrewd, appraising look. "Very well. You may join us."

I gave Niko my very best *Are you freaking kidding me?* look. "I really don't think—" I started to say, but Danny cut me off.

"How come I could see it? Everyone else thought it was a vulture."

Niko shrugged. "People are very committed to their version of reality. As for you, I'm not sure."

We walked in silence for a few moments. "So does that mean I'm special somehow?" Danny asked. I rolled my eyes. Of course that's where Danny's mind went.

"I told you, I don't know," said Niko impatiently. "Perhaps. But if you haven't already noticed, we have more pressing problems to solve than the conundrum of your capabilities."

Danny looked a little taken aback, and I almost laughed. Kids like him—especially boys—always expected to be at the center of everything. Though I was beginning to wonder, too— how *was* he able to do and see all the things I did, when apparently no one else could? It had to have something to do with our friendship in the past, but what?

"Okay," I said to Niko hopefully, "what about me? Weren't

you going to explain everything? Give us the big picture and all that?"

"Ah, yes, that's right. Well. Ahem. Momo. Your mother is not who you think she is." Niko looked over his shoulder and began trotting a little faster. "Come, come, children, let's not dilly-dally."

"What do you mean, she's not who I think she is?" I demanded. Who else could she be? A bunch of possibilities flashed through my head, each one wilder than the last: A criminal? A wizard? An alien?

"She is Takiri-bime-no-mikoto."

"Taki-what?"

"Takiri-bime-no—"

"Actually, skip the name. Who *is* she? *What* is she?"

"She's a kami. A Shintō goddess. The guardian of the Island of Mysteries and the daughter of the great and powerful Susano'o, Lord of the Seas, Master of Storms, and Ruler of Ne-no-kuni himself."

That stopped me right in my tracks. *"What?"* I shrieked.

"Ne-no-kuni, the Land of Roots. Leaping lizards, could you scream any louder? Do you *want* the shikome to find us? And keep walking! In fact, walk faster!"

"Sorry." I lowered my voice and started walking as fast as I could to keep up with Niko. "And I *know* what Ne-no-kuni is," I said in the fiercest non-scream I could muster. "I was talking about my mom! She's *what*?"

"You heard me. She is a goddess—a kami. The spirit and guardian of the Island of Mysteries."

Whoa.

"Hey, what if Momo and me are, like, long-lost twins or—"

"No. Definitely not." Niko snorted.

Danny looked crestfallen. But I barely noticed because my brain was busy going *Nope, nope, nopity-nope* about the "your mom is a goddess" part. There was no way that Mom was a goddess in real life. Wouldn't she have told me if she was? And besides, if I had divine blood, surely I'd be taller and prettier and, I don't know, have some kind of gift like musical or athletic talent, or being able to move things with my mind. Maybe this *was* all a hallucination. Maybe the shikome really *was* a vulture, and I'd fallen and hit my head, and maybe I was really lying unconscious in a hospital, having a very strange dream.

At the same time, my heart was whispering, *But maybe . . . ?* Maybe that would explain why Mom was so superstitious. Why she talked about all those gods and monsters as if they were real. And maybe I really *had* just escaped a death hag and teleported through a spirit portal with a pants-wearing fox who could talk and drive.

Danny was looking at me like he couldn't quite believe it either, like he was thinking, *No offense, but how does she have godly DNA?* I could hardly blame him. Unlike Danny, who was handsome, athletic, smart, and had charisma practically pouring out his ears, *nothing* about me was godlike.

As if he'd read my mind, Danny said, "But I don't remember you having, like, divine superpowers. You haven't learned how to fly or teleport in the last couple years, have you?"

I shook my head. Even if all of this was real and Mom was a

kami, I was still just a weird kid who got chased by monsters. I wondered if Danny would decide to go home after all.

Niko, however, looked completely unbothered. "She has what she needs," he said. Whatever that meant. We came to an intersection and crossed the street. "Please tell me you know what the kami are, at least."

Danny and I nodded. Of course we knew about the kami. According to Shintō beliefs, kami are present in everything in the natural world, as well as in human concepts like wisdom, music, health, and luck. Some of them have human or animal forms, with stories and legends about their lives, and some of them exist as nameless nature spirits.

"Your mother, Momo, is the guardian kami of the Island of Mysteries. I saw a photo of it at your house, so I assume you know about it. And you know that you were born there."

"I didn't know it had a name," I said, realizing guiltily that I'd never thought to ask.

"There is a cave on the Island of Mysteries that leads to an abandoned portal between the Middle Lands—that's your Earth—and Yomi, the land of the dead. Your mother was responsible for making sure nothing escaped from the cave.

"When your family left the island years ago, she put a shimenawa across the mouth of the cave as a protective measure." He looked pointedly at my backpack, which held the rope she'd given *me* for protection, and I felt another stab of guilt. "She also cast a binding spell to seal the island in case the shimenawa failed. That would give her time to return and send the spirits back to Yomi before they invaded the rest of the world."

Danny looked impressed. "Bruh. Your mom is a *boss.*"

He was right—she was kind of a boss.

"So something got past the shimenawa somehow, and you came to warn my mom?"

"Correct," said Niko.

"Was it the shikome? How did she get past it? And how did she break through the binding spell?" Danny asked.

Niko looked worried. "I really can't say."

"What do you mean, you can't say? Do you mean you don't know? Or do you mean—"

At that moment, the air around us did a kind of reverse flash: instead of a split second of light, there was a split second of total darkness, like a glitch in a video game. Niko looked anxiously at the sky as the streetlights flickered back on and the stars came back into view. "Another time," he said. "Now we need to hurry." He picked up speed, and Danny and I had to jog to stay with him.

A minute later, we turned the corner onto my street. I could see my house at the end, two blocks down, and I had just opened my mouth to ask if we could walk the rest of the way when a sickening screech sounded in the distance, like a saw cutting through metal. The odor of rotting meat wafted toward us. "She's coming!" Niko howled. "RUN!" He leaped forward and sprinted down the street. Danny and I started off right on his heels, but within a couple of seconds, I was staring at Danny's back as he and Niko pulled ahead into the night.

I tried to keep up, but I wasn't fast enough. My world became the sound of my feet pounding the ground in time with my panicked breath—in-out-in-out-in-out-in-out. Then there was the stench of death, so strong I almost gagged, and another blood-chilling scream—the shikome was catching up. I felt like I was in of those nature videos where a hungry lioness attacks a herd of zebras and that old guy with the English accent goes, "Alas, one of the zebras is too slow. Try as she might, she cannot keep up with the pack. [*pauses sadly*] She is in grave danger."

One more block. Danny and Niko had just reached the house and were passing under the torii. Danny turned and saw me. "Hurry! Run *faster!*" he shouted. As if I were taking my time, just tiptoeing through the tulips, tra-la-la. Ugh.

Almost there. Niko was at the front door, barking. I could sense the shikome gaining on me. In fact, I could sense her so clearly, I knew exactly where she was: ten feet in the air, her hair streaming out behind her, her arms outstretched, her toothless mouth open in a wide, red grin as she gathered herself and dove at me. Her arms closed around my waist, and she would have swept me right into the air if Danny hadn't rushed forward and grabbed my hand. The extra weight dragged us downward, but she recovered quickly, and a moment later my feet left the ground. If Danny didn't want to get pulled into the air with me, he was going to have to let go. "Niko, help!" he shouted.

Niko came bounding through the torii, snarling ferociously. He was flanked by two enormous creatures with faces like bull-dogs and manes like lions—Alfie and Meggie, our koma-inu statues come to life! Niko grabbed my pant leg between his teeth and pulled, while Alfie and Meggie hurled themselves into the air and closed their jaws on the shikome's ankles. But she was too strong. We kept rising. I twisted frantically, trying in vain to squirm out of her iron grip, and as Danny's hand slipped out of mine,

I looked toward the house. *I'm sorry, Mom,* I thought. *I'm sorry I didn't believe you about all of this. I'm sorry I took the necklace off.*

And then I saw a figure silhouetted in the doorway.

"Mom!" I cried.

There was a flash of silvery light, and the shikome screamed and let go of me.

Niko and I hit the ground with a thud. As the koma-inu and the shikome continued to struggle in the air, Danny helped me to my feet. On our way back under the torii, I was dimly aware of that same blinding silver light passing us going the other way; when we were safely through, I turned to see a woman dressed in shining white robes rushing toward the fight. Once more, the shikome shrieked and dove. But the woman stood firm. She stepped forward, swung her hands in a circle in front of her, and pushed a beam of light at the shikome. With a final scream, the death hag exploded in a cloud of black ash that spiraled outward menacingly before streaming back in on itself until it disappeared. The koma-inu both dropped to the ground, spitting out gobs of yuck. A single black high-heeled shoe fell out of Meggie's mouth and clattered on the concrete before crumbling and sinking into the earth. Then there was nothing. Silence.

The woman turned to face us. She was wreathed in a light that seemed to come from inside her. "Momo," she said, and smiled, though her beautiful face looked strained and exhausted. Then the light flickered out and Mom collapsed in a heap on the ground.

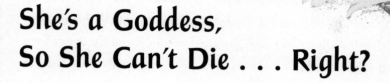

She's a Goddess,
So She Can't Die . . . Right?

Mom's face was pale, and her breathing was raspy and shallow. When I put my fingers to her neck like they taught us in PE, her pulse felt fluttery and weak. Alfie and Meggie had dragged her inside the house, and they helped her onto the couch before bowing and fading away like mist.

"She's okay, right?" I kept asking Niko. "She's a goddess, so she can't die, right?"

Niko cleared his throat nervously. "She used quite a lot of her energy sending the shikome back to Yomi. If she were healthy, it would be a different matter."

That was not the answer I'd been hoping for. I felt dread rise inside me, cold and black. "But—"

Niko looked sadly at Mom and said, "Think of Izanami."

"Oh." The dread reached my chest and closed its fist around my heart as I remembered the story of Izanami.

"Wait—who was that, again?" Danny asked.

"She's the goddess of death. But before that, she was the mother goddess who gave birth to the first earthly kami," I said dully.

"Oh, right. And when the god of fire was born, she got all burned and . . ." He trailed off.

"She died." Izanami wasn't *exactly* dead, but she ended up trapped in Yomi forever, and she transformed into the goddess of death—the cruel, dark goddess who, driven by vengeance and rage over her situation, dedicated her entire existence to making others die, too.

"When a kami's earthly form is destroyed, they must leave it behind and join Izanami in Yomi," Niko clarified.

"But her earthly form is—I mean, it was fine until a few minutes ago!" I said. "She just totally destroyed the shikome! She's just tired out, right?"

"Er, the shikome wasn't the only creature to make it through the portal."

"What? What are you saying?"

"She came with a bunch of oni." I did not like the direction this was taking. Oni are demons—vicious, bloodthirsty monsters whose energy pollutes everything they touch. "Your mother's life force is bound to the Island of Mysteries—she and the island are one. Once the oni emerged and began defiling it, that made her fall ill. If they are allowed to continue, the island will eventually die. And if it dies . . ."

"But I thought you said it was an abandoned passage," Danny said. "How come all of a sudden there's a band of oni and a shikome?"

Niko shook his head. "I wish I knew."

"They've never come up in large numbers like this. It's very troubling." It was Mom.

"Mom!" I turned to her. "Are you—how are you?"

48

She smiled weakly. "I've been better." Then she turned her gaze on Niko. "Thank you for watching over Momo. Though I still forbid you to take her anywhere." Niko looked grumpy.

"And I think I remember this brave young man," Mom said, looking at Danny.

"Hi, Mrs. Arashima," he said. I'd almost forgotten he was there, and now I kind of wished he wasn't. I didn't like him seeing Mom this way. Or me.

"Momo, did you thank Danny for saving your life?" Mom asked.

Technically it was Mom who'd saved my life, but she did have a point. "Thank you, Danny," I mumbled.

"You're welcome."

Mom smiled at him. "I'm glad that you and Momo are friends again," she said.

Danny opened his mouth, probably to explain that he wasn't here because he was my friend, but I cut him off before he could say it.

"Why didn't you and Mom go back to fight the oni right away?" I asked Niko. "Why are you still here? What's taking you so long? What's *wrong* with you?" I was suddenly furious with him. How could he have allowed this to happen?

"Do not be angry with Niko. It's not his fault that I didn't go back to fight."

"What?"

Mom looked at Niko, then at me. "Niko has told you who I am? Who my father is?"

I nodded. "You're Taki—Takiri-bime. The kami of . . . um . . ."

"The Island of Mysteries," she finished.

"And your dad is Susano'o."

"Lord of the Seas, Master of Storms, and Ruler of Ne-no-kuni," Niko intoned.

"Yeah. That."

Mom took a shaky breath and said, "I can't go back to the island. When I met your father, I kept him—and then you—a secret from Susano'o because I knew he'd be furious at me for falling in love with a mortal. When he did find out, I barely got the two of you off the island alive. He was so angry that he cursed me so that I would never be able to return. Even if someone like Niko were to hold my hand and lead me onto the shore, I'd lose my grip and be swept out to sea."

"But—but why? Why would he reject his own daughter like that? And his granddaughter? It's so mean!" Danny blurted, and I would have told him to please mind his own business, but I was too shocked that he'd said anything at all. Plus, he was right. I'd always thought Mom's father was a jerk for disowning her and forbidding her from returning home because of Dad and me. Sometimes I was glad that my grandfather wasn't in our lives: if he didn't want us, I certainly didn't want him. But sometimes I wished I could hunt him down and yell at him about what a jerk he was. And sometimes, in spite of myself, I wished he would hunt *us* down, apologize, and make things right again. But if he was a god, he could have done that anytime. If he was a god, he was an epic, monumental, unforgivable jerk.

"Susano'o is notorious for his rashness and his terrible temper. He cursed her without considering the consequences," said Niko.

"But what about your mother?" I asked Mom. She literally never talked about her mother, but if her father was Susano'o, maybe—

"I've never had a mother."

Okay, then. "What if you told him what was going on? Wouldn't he change his mind if he knew you were . . . ?" *Dying.* I couldn't quite say it.

Niko shuddered. "A preposterous proposal. Downright dangerous."

Mom added, "The kami can hold grudges for centuries, Momo. You should know this. And only one being has ever asked Susano'o for a favor and lived to tell the tale."

I looked at her, frail and wistful in her nightgown, and tried to wrap my head around everything. Those stories—the kami, the monsters, the magic—it wasn't as if I had stopped believing they existed, exactly. It was more like I'd stopped believing they existed in the world as I knew it, if that makes any sense. And now all of a sudden my mother was an ancient goddess— the spirit of an island, a spirit who'd fallen in love with a mortal man, had a baby, and been punished for it. And her island was being invaded by demons. And she was dying. And her father, the god of the sea, didn't care. Was that why she'd given me the necklace? To protect me after she died? If she was really dying, what would happen to me?

"Is all of this . . . Is it really true?"

Mom nodded.

But still, I thought. "If it's true, why haven't you ever told me about it?"

She gazed sadly at me. "Your father and I thought it would be safer. Easier. And as you grew older, it seemed less important for you to know. More important for you to be like everyone else."

I remembered how I'd wished so many times that she wasn't so strange, how I'd wished I didn't have to feel ashamed to invite kids over to play. How I'd wished I could be a normal kid who didn't have to babysit her own mother. And then I thought of that afternoon with Mrs. Evans, when I told Mom that her stories weren't real—how angry and mean I'd been about it. But I almost wished I'd been right. Because this awful problem wouldn't exist if Mom were a normal human being instead of a kami. It was all so much. I felt like I was at the edge of what I could handle.

"What if another kami went and fought the oni?" Danny asked as I tried to pull myself together. "Like, one of your friends from another island or something?"

I looked at Mom with desperate hope. I still wished Danny would stay out of this—or at least go to the bathroom—even though asking her friends did seem like a good idea. But she shook her head. "No one would agree to it."

"Remember the binding spell?" said Niko. "Any kami who comes onto the island to fight the oni will be bound there once they're finished."

"So no one thinks Mom's life is worth saving? Because if they succeed, they might have to spend the rest of their lives on a beautiful island? Doesn't anybody *care* about her?" I heard my voice rising, and I didn't even try to keep it down. Why should I? I felt so angry and so helpless—everything was just so *wrong* and completely out of control, and there was nothing I could do about it. I felt an anxiety attack coming on: my heart started pounding, and I couldn't seem to get enough air. My breath came faster and faster.

"Uh, you okay?" Danny asked.

"I'm fine," I mumbled through gritted teeth.

"Are you, though? 'Cause you don't look—"

"I! AM! FINE!" I screamed at him.

"Momo!" Mom said reproachfully, while Danny said, "Okay, okay, sorry!" He put his palms up in front of him. "Calm down. I was just worried about you."

"Yeah, right," I muttered. "That would be a first."

"What's that supposed to mean?" Danny's voice sounded like I'd insulted him somehow.

"It means I don't believe you. You're not my *friend* friend, remember? Why would you be worried about me? When's the last time you paid *any* attention to me?" I spat out. Danny looked at his feet—guiltily, I thought. I could hardly believe I was talking to him like this, but there was so much fear sloshing around inside me, and being angry at Danny felt better than being scared about Mom. "Plus, you're popular. Everyone wants to be your friend. Your dad isn't dead and your mom isn't dying with no one to save her. You don't have a clue what it's like to know that no one will stick up for you."

Danny looked stunned. "You don't know anything about me," he muttered.

Niko cleared his throat. I thought he was going to tell me to calm down and apologize, and I got ready to yell at him, too. But instead he said, "There is one person who can save her."

53

I'm Sure Niko Will Take Great Care of Me

"Niko," said Mom in a warning sort of voice.

"What?" I asked. "Niko, what are you talking about? Who is it? Where are they? Have you gotten in touch with them?"

"Ahem. Yes. Well—you see—the thing is—" Niko cast a sideways glance at Mom, who was now looking thunderous despite her exhaustion. "That person's mother has refused to allow her only child to travel halfway around the world to fight a band of demons on her behalf."

Wait a sec.

I blinked at Niko, who was still cowering under Mom's glare. "Did—did you just say . . . ?"

Niko nodded. "You'll be able to step onto the island because you're part kami. And if you survive, you'll be able to leave because you're part human. That's probably why the shikome was trying to kill you, in fact. To prevent you from going to the island and sending the demons back to Yomi."

"Okay. Um. Niko?" I quavered. "Did you just say the words 'if you survive'? And 'sending the demons back to Yomi'? In reference to me?"

"He did," Mom said softly. "And that is why you may not go."

"They're not big demons, and they can't fly," Niko said encouragingly. "Or swim," he added, as an afterthought.

"How big are they?" Danny asked.

"They're just, you know. Average sized." Niko stood on his hind legs, raised his eyes, and swept his paws energetically up and out, indicating something roughly the size of an NFL linebacker. "And there are only a few of them. Fifty or sixty, probably. A hundred at most. *Maybe* two hundred." He smiled hopefully at me.

My jaw dropped. I'd be toast. No—burnt toast. It was obvious what the right choice was. But if I chose it, how would I ever pull it off? What made Niko think I had even the slightest chance of success?

He added, "If you don't defeat the oni, your mother will eventually go to the land of the dead, and the binding spell around the island will die with her. And the oni will find their way to the rest of the world and bring their destruction and pollution with them."

Great. Like I needed any more pressure.

"If you go, you will certainly die," said Mom. "I will not let you put your life in danger. I forbid it." Her tone was commanding, but her voice was weak. Her eyes burned brightly, but the rest of her looked faded and washed-out.

If I didn't try to save her, she would fade away to nothing. And it would be my fault.

"I can't just sit here and let you die right in front of me."

Niko chimed in. "Momo has great potential. And I have a plan. I will be with her every step of the—"

"NO." Niko, Danny, and I shrank back as Mom rose from

55

the couch. Her voice had real power this time; the air around us seemed to vibrate with it. But it was too much for her to sustain, and I rushed to support her as she sank back down. "Take me to my room," she murmured.

So I held one arm and Danny held the other, and we shuffled to Mom's room together as Niko trotted in anxious circles around us. We helped her into bed, and I brought her a cup of tea. She sent the other two out of the room and sighed before closing her eyes and taking one long, slow sip, then another, and another.

"Oh, by the way," I said, to fill the silence. "Thanks for the gift cards for the mall. I bought this new outfit with them. You like it?"

Her eyes snapped open. "I didn't give you any gift cards."

Oh.

Mom closed her eyes again and murmured, "Someone wanted you to be at the mall, away from me. Someone was hoping the shikome would kill you there."

"Are you—are you sure?" I'd been hoping someone just wanted me to have nice clothes.

She lowered the teacup and fixed me with a gaze so intense, I shrank back a little. In a low, urgent voice, she said, "I told you—never before have so many oni found their way to my island. And the shikome is a bad, bad sign. There are forces at work that you do not understand. So you must not listen to Niko. Do not go to the island. In fact, do not leave the house. I will call the school tomorrow."

"*What?*"

"If you love me, you will do as I say and stay here with me."

"But I—why?"

"Do you promise to stay?"

"But, Mom, that's—"

"Promise!" Her eyes glittered like diamonds, and I knew there was only one thing I could say.

I sighed. "I promise."

I held Mom's hand until she fell asleep. All the while, I chewed myself up inside and wondered what I should do. Correction: I knew what I should do. I just didn't know if I could do it. If only I weren't so scared. If only I had something, some skill, some talent that I could rely on. If only leaving Mom and risking my life was actually the safest choice, as well as the right one.

By the time her breathing slowed and her grip loosened, I had made up my mind. I smoothed the covers around her and wrote her a note:

Dear Mom,

I've decided to go with Niko and fight the oni. I know it's dangerous, but if I am the only one in the world who can save your life, I have to try.

Please don't worry about me. I promise I'll stay safe, and I'm sure Niko will take great care of me.

Love,
Momo

I left the note on her bedside table, with my heart hammering and my stomach a ball of pain. When I thought about her waking up and finding the note, I almost changed my mind. Who would take care of her while I was gone? Not only that, but I knew that she *would* worry about me, and I hated to make her worry on top of leaving her all alone with no one to watch out for her. The only thing that kept me walking out the door and down the hall was the certainty that this was the only path I could take.

I went into the living room, where Niko and Danny were waiting. "Niko," I said. My voice was wobbly. "You said you had a plan?"

"Of course!" Niko sprang from where he'd been curled up on the couch. "So, she's granted permission? Excellent news!"

"Um. Not exactly."

Niko paused for a moment before waving his paw dismissively. "Never mind that. A little daughterly disobedience never hurt anyone, especially when it comes to saving lives. Now. I don't suppose your mother has any magical weapons or talismans stashed about the place? Or perhaps a snack that reproduces itself so we need never go hungry? Or a portal through which we may access any point on the globe at will?"

I shook my head, irritated. "I didn't even know she was a kami. How would I know about random magical stuff?"

"Good point." Niko looked around the room, lost in thought. "What about toys that come to life?" he asked.

"You had toys that came to life? That's sick!" Danny said. "How come I never knew about them?"

"I didn't," I said, feeling even more irritated—and also kind of sad, because toys that came to life *would* have been cool. So far, it seemed like the only things that being the daughter of a kami had blessed me with were social awkwardness and mortal peril.

"Are you sure?" Niko persisted. "What about toys that you remember playing make-believe with?"

Remember playing make-believe . . . Suddenly I saw an image of a black lacquer box of origami on a high shelf in the hall closet. When I was very little, Mom used to fold the colored paper into all kinds of animals—frogs, birds, butterflies, cats—and I would pretend they were alive and that they could run and jump and fly around on their own. Then she would unfold them, carefully iron out the creases, and return the paper to the box.

Was it possible that I hadn't been pretending?

I ran to the closet with a chair. Sure enough, the box was still there, high up on the top storage shelf, its shiny black surface dulled by years of dust and neglect. Niko instructed me to open it and take out a sheet.

"Do you remember how to fold a crane?" he asked.

"I think so." Carefully, I matched the opposite corners of the square sheet of silver paper to make a triangle, then folded the triangle in half again. It took a little trial and error, and I had to redo a couple of the steps, but in the end, I managed to fold the origami into a decent—if slightly lopsided—crane.

"Hmm," said Niko, examining it carefully. "We only have to get to San Francisco, so I suppose it will do. Now let's take it outside. Bring your backpack."

I felt my necklace shift in my backpack as I stood up. It was too bad I couldn't go back to Mom and ask her to fix it without arousing her suspicion. I would have liked a little bit of extra protection.

"Hey, you want me to come with you?" Danny asked. "I'd be down to fight some oni."

This again? "This isn't just some fun adventure, you know. My mom's *life* is at stake. Maybe you don't care about that, but I do."

Danny looked embarrassed. "I didn't mean it that way. I meant . . . I want to help you."

That caught me off guard.

"Why?"

"I dunno. I just think . . . well, your mom's dying. And you can't save her all by yourself."

What the . . . ? "I can and I will. I don't need you to be my hero." *Or my friend,* I thought. I spoke with more confidence than I felt, I admit. But seriously. Of all the bigheaded reasons he could have given me. Just because he was popular and good at sports and apparently had access to the spirit world (which, by the way, how infuriating), why should he get to play the superhero? He could go jump in a lake. And anyway, so what?

"Actually, we could use the help," Niko mumbled out of the side of his mouth. "He has proven himself able to survive the portals. And he did fight quite bravely against the shikome." I glared at Niko. I mean, he was absolutely right. I just hated giving Danny another reason to feel superior.

"I could totally help you," he said. "I got a black belt in karate this year. And I've been learning about ninjutsu. Remember? Ninja martial arts."

"I know what ninjutsu is," I muttered. Danny had been obsessed when we were little, before he got cool.

He chuckled nervously. "It's kinda nerdy, I know. I'd actually appreciate it if you didn't tell anyone."

I rolled my eyes. Mr. Popular didn't want anyone to know about his secret nerdy interest in Japanese stuff? Shocker.

On the other hand, ninjutsu might come in handy.

"Anyway, what I really meant was that you shouldn't have to do it alone," he said. "And we've gotten this far together, right?"

"I suppose you did try to save my life earlier," I said reluctantly. And it would be nice to have a friend—wait, not a friend. A companion. Company.

"So that's a yes?"

I sighed. "Fine."

"Sick." Danny nodded like it was no big deal. So very cool. So very annoying. I hoped I wouldn't regret my decision.

"Perhaps we should ask your parents?" Niko said. "Or at least notify them, so they will have some idea of what's happened if you don't return?"

"Oh. Um." Danny picked at the hem of his shirt, suddenly hesitant and awkward. "Nah, that's okay."

"Are you sure?" I asked. Maybe he thought they'd say no. Or, more likely, that they wouldn't believe him. "You don't have to tell them everything."

"No, it's fine, really." Danny looked back down at his shirt. "I mean, they . . . they're out of town anyway, and they think I'm staying with my aunt. I'll just text her and tell her I'm staying with Brad. I do it all the time—tell her I'm at Brad's and then just stay home by myself. She's pretty busy, so she never checks up on me." He whipped out his phone and tapped at it.

"What do you mean, 'all the time'?"

"My mom travels a lot for work now, and my dad can work

remotely, so whenever she goes somewhere cool like New York City or Hawaii, he goes with her and they take a couple of extra days for vacation. Oh! Speaking of which."

He tapped at his phone again, cleared his throat, and said in a deep voice, "Hello, this is Mike Haragan, father of Danny Haragan in Mrs. Rasul's homeroom. We will be taking Danny to Paris for a week beginning Monday, so he will not be in class during that time. Please email or post any relevant assignments so that he can keep up with his work. If you have any questions, you may reach me at 555-0983. Thank you." He grinned at me. "Boo-ya! A week is enough time, right? That's when my parents are coming back."

"But aren't you worried that your parents—"

"So, let's get on with the mission, huh?" he said, a little too loudly. "Let's go! What's our next step, Niko?"

Think of It as "Borrowing in a Time of Great Need"

"No way. Nuh-uh. Absolutely not."

The three of us stood in the backyard in a little triangle and watched the origami crane, which flitted around our heads. I would have been super excited to see something magical like this, but Niko had just told me to catch it, put it on the ground, and sit on it. As in squash it under my butt.

"Trust me," said Niko.

"I'll kill it!" I protested.

"It is not properly alive," he said. "The only thing alive is the magic, and you cannot squash magic with your butt."

"You cannot squash magic with your butt," Danny repeated under his breath, and snorted with laughter. "Can you suffocate it with a fart?" He snickered at his own joke. Ugh.

Finally, I agreed to try. I caught the crane in my hands and carefully set it on the grass, where it sat obediently, gently fluttering its wings. I put one foot on either side and lowered myself slowwwly to the ground—and suddenly I wasn't standing on the ground anymore, but sitting on the back of a silver-feathered paper crane the size of a giraffe. At least, its neck was as long as a giraffe's. I couldn't tell how tall it was, since its legs were tucked under its body. I wasn't sure I wanted to find out.

"Whooaa," said Danny. "That is *dope!*" He scrambled up next to me without being asked—and without asking, I noticed. Typical. Niko murmured something into what I guess was the crane's ear before springing up to join us, saying, "Lie down and grab some feathers, children! Crane travel can be quite . . . exhilarating for first-timers."

"What exactly do you mean by 'exhilarating'?" I started to ask, but it came out more like "What exactly do you mean by [*shrieks unintelligibly*]" because the crane chose that moment to lurch to its feet, spread its enormous wings, and take off into the cold, black sky.

Once I got up the courage to open my eyes, I peeked over the crane's left shoulder and saw the entire valley spread out below me like a carpet of twinkling lights between the dark masses of the Santa Cruz Mountains to the west and the Diablo Range to the east. Niko was stretched out next to me on the left, and Danny was on my right, peering over the crane's right shoulder.

"W-w-where are we going?" I shouted over the wind, through chattering teeth—not only was I terrified, but it was freezing up there in the sky.

"The San Francisco Asian Art Museum!" Niko shouted back. "As luck would have it, this is the first day of Dōjigiri's world tour, and—"

"For real?" Danny's mouth dropped open and his eyes lit up. "We're going to see Dōjigiri right now?"

Niko nodded and Danny gave an excited whoop. "I asked my dad to take me for, like, a father-son bonding thing, but he says he's going to bring me to hang out with him at his company's booth at a Forty-Niners game instead." For the school super-jock, he didn't look as happy about it as I would have thought.

"What's wrong with that?" I asked.

Danny shrugged. "I mean, it's fine, but I've done it before, and he always spends the entire game drinking and talking to his work friends." He rolled his eyes like he thought his dad was such a dork, but I could see that being ignored by his dad hurt him.

"What's Dōjigiri, anyway? A J-pop band?" I asked.

"A *J-pop* band? Are you freaking *kidding* me? What am I, some kind of loser? What is wrong with you?"

Coming from someone who'd spent years making me feel like a loser, this was too much. My sympathy evaporated, and I narrowed my eyes at him. "You know what? Maybe you should go home after all."

"Will you two stop your surly squabbling!" Niko growled. "Or I'll bite your noses off!"

I seriously doubted that he would follow through with his threat, but I clamped my mouth shut anyway and glowered at Danny.

"Dōjigiri is the sword that defeated Shuten-dōji," continued Niko more calmly. "Do you remember that story?"

"Ohhh, right." It was coming back to me. "The demon king." There were plenty of demons in Japanese legends, but accord-ing to Mom, the most powerful demon of all was Shuten-dōji—a giant shape-shifter who feasted on human flesh in his moun-tain fortress. The hero Minamoto Raikō cut off his head, and Raikō's sword became known as Dōjigiri, or "Demon Slayer."

"*Ohhh, right,*" Danny mimicked me. "It's only one of the greatest swords of all time! In the entire world!"

"So what? So it's on tour or whatever. What does that have to do with us?" I asked Niko.

Niko nodded. "Precisely. Dōjigiri will be a useful tool with which to fight the oni, considering our, ahem, collective lack of training in the art of hand-to-hand combat. And our lack of any other weapon whatsoever."

"You mean we get to take it with us? We get to *use* it?" Danny said.

"Momo gets to use it."

I could practically feel Danny's ego explode next to me. "Niko, you have to let me have it," he pleaded. "I'd be so great with it. You can't give it to someone who didn't even know what it was, for crying out loud."

"Excuse me for not remembering the name of *one sword.*"

"Plus, Dōjigiri is super long and heavy. Which is another reason why I should get it. No offense, Momo, but there's no way you'll be able to handle it."

I clenched my hands around the crane's feathers so I wouldn't punch him.

He kept going. "What if Niko got you, like, one of those magic bow-and-arrow things instead, with arrows that always hit their target? What about that, Niko? That way she doesn't actually have to—"

"Will you please shut up?" I snapped.

"Sor-ry. I was only trying to help," mumbled Danny.

"Only the greatest heroes, the strongest magical beings, and those with divine blood can wield Dōjigiri," Niko said. "And, Momo, the sword has such a reputation that if you walk into battle with it, I'm sure that half of the oni will run away, craven cowards that they are. And with a couple of days' training, you might even be able to slay a few of the ones that don't."

Danny looked grumpy, and I could tell that he still thought he should be the one to have it. The worst part was that I knew he was right. The last time we did softball in PE, I lost control of the bat and almost gave the catcher a concussion. How was I going to swing a sword without accidentally cutting off Niko's tail, for instance? If I had to pick between me and Danny to handle a magical sword, I'd pick Danny, too. Still, if I were really going to battle a band of demons, a sword named Demon Slayer would be nice to have.

It didn't take long for the city of San Francisco to come into view. I could recognize the tall, skinny pyramid that was the Transamerica building, as well as the swooping curves of the Bay Bridge leading out of the city to the east, and the lights of cars crossing the Golden Gate Bridge to the north. Patches of fog covered the tops of the highest hills in the city. The dark expanse of the Pacific Ocean loomed on the left.

We dipped lower as we closed in on the downtown area, with its tall office buildings and extra-bright lights. "Won't people see us?" I asked nervously.

"If anyone bothered to look up, perhaps," said Niko. "But remember what I said about people being committed to their version of reality? Even *you* stopped believing your own eyes once you decided that what you saw wasn't real." He had a point.

"And here we are!" he said a minute later. He gestured at a big concrete building with fancy Greek pillars and a giant banner across the front announcing the GRAND OPENING of a new pavilion. We flew directly into it at top speed, just like with the tree—right through the O in OPENING. This time, I screamed, not that the crane cared one bit.

My atoms came apart and smooshed back together, and the portal spat me, Danny, and Niko out onto a cold stone floor.

I groaned, rubbing my elbow. "Why do we have to keep crash-landing everywhere? Why can't we just glide to a gentle stop?" As my eyes adjusted to the darkness, I saw the crane next to me, normal-sized again, and I put it carefully in my backpack.

"Oh, my portal piloting isn't perfect enough for you?" Niko said. "You would perhaps prefer a ninth-rank fox as your guide?"

"You have ranks?" Danny asked. "Of what, magic? What level are you?"

"Shhh! Must you shout everything?"

I didn't think that was fair, since Danny hadn't been shouting. Niko was probably just feeling sensitive about his rank. (There are nine ranks, I remembered Mom telling me, and foxes get an additional tail with each one, so Niko, who had only one tail, was clearly at the bottom.) But our voices did seem to carry and bounce around in the silence.

"Is that why you can't shape-shift?" Danny asked. "Are you still a—"

"Shhh!"

We followed Niko down a long, open gallery overlooking a wide staircase on the left and an atrium on the right, up to a set of double doors. A banner hung above the doorway; I could just barely make out the words SAMURAI STEEL: THE LEGENDARY SWORDS OF JAPAN. Niko whispered at the lock, which clicked quietly, and the door swung open. I heard him mutter to himself, "Thinks my magic isn't good enough, does she? Cheeky little chipmunk."

The exhibit hall was like an old-fashioned ballroom—huge and square with high ceilings and marble columns everywhere. At the center of each wall were giant multipaned windows sheltered under tall marble arches. The exhibit consisted of a bunch of swords and some other samurai military stuff, each in their own glass display case. Inside the cases, which were arranged around the room so visitors could see them from all angles, the swords glinted and sparkled in the light.

Wait a second. Actually, wait two seconds. *Light?*

As we walked farther, the source of the light came into view: a sword displayed on a silk stand inside a case at the very center of the room. Its long, slender blade tapered down from a ridge that ran along its length to a razor-sharp edge etched with a wave pattern, and it curved elegantly from the hilt to a terrifyingly sharp point. And it was glowing, casting a soft golden radiance all around it.

From the way Niko's eyes glimmered when he saw it, I knew that this was Dōjigiri, the sword we were here to—haaang on.

"Are we going to *steal* it?" I couldn't believe I hadn't figured this out until now. But of course that's what we were going to do. There certainly wasn't anyone in charge of lending it to us, with papers to sign or forms to fill out, or . . . I didn't know what I'd been expecting, but for some reason it hadn't occurred to me that snatching a thousand-year-old legendary sword out of its case and absconding with it into the night was, in fact, theft. We were about to steal a precious artifact from a fancy institution. It was probably a federal crime. Maybe even an international crime.

"I wouldn't call it *stealing*," Niko said. "Think of it as 'borrowing in a time of great need.' Also, here's the thing. Dōjigiri has never left the protection of its shrine before. Only the gods know why, but it's here, now, exactly when we need it. That's incredibly good luck for us! And it's bad luck to ignore good luck. You could even say it would be a bigger crime *not* to take it."

"It's still stealing!" I said. My voice came out louder than I meant it to, and Niko and Danny turned to me and went, "Shhhhhh!"

"Anyway, what are we going to do, smash the glass and run away? What if security comes? What if the police show up? Wait—are there security cameras here? Do they have pictures of our faces?" My stomach twisted as a little movie started playing in my head: Me getting arrested and put in handcuffs. Mom having to come and pick me up. Me going to jail forever. Mom being all alone. Or dead. No. Stop. I couldn't do this. It was wrong, it was risky, and it could end up with Mom dying at home, sad and scared, and I wouldn't be able to help her or take care of her or even say goodbye, and . . .

Danny rolled his eyes. "This is an *adventure*," he muttered. "Be adventurous!"

"This is *not* 'an adventure,'" I shot back. "This is a very scary, very important mission to save my mom's life! I can't risk getting arrested because you want to play action hero. I need to know we have a safe, legal plan that's been carefully—"

"It's not as if we're taking it to sell on the black market or anything," Niko cut in. "Not yet, anyway."

I groaned. "So, not legal, then."

"Listen, Momo. We're taking it because we need it. *You* need it. It's full of magic that is meant to obliterate the oni, and it will be a humongous help to you, I promise. And besides, in a way, it needs us, too. We're allowing it to fulfill its destiny instead of wasting its life away in a case." As if it could hear us, Dōjigiri began to glow with even more intensity.

"Uh, Niko? Why is it glowing like that?" asked Danny.

"The oldest and most illustrious swords have their own kami," Niko explained. "Even normal humans can feel their energy, though not everyone can see it."

"So, like genies in a lamp?" Danny asked. "If I picked it up, would, like, a big blue dude come out and grant me three wishes?" He gasped. "Would I be the master of Dōjigiri's kami?"

Niko scoffed. "Absolutely not. You are not a hero. And anyway, kami are spirits. Only the most powerful ones can take the shape of a physical body beyond the vessel that they inhabit. And only a fool would presume that they could be the master of a kami—especially the kami of Dōjigiri, you hubristic hellion."

I couldn't help smiling at that insult, even though I wasn't quite sure what "hubristic" meant. Or "hellion."

Danny looked upset and even sad for a moment, but another pulse of light from Dōjigiri was enough to shake him out of it. "Look, Momo—Niko's right! It wants us to liberate it!" he said. "It's okay," he murmured, addressing the sword as he began walking toward it. "I know you want to join us. We're here for you. We're here to set you fr— AAAHHHH!!!"

71

A deafening *BOOM* at the far end of the room was followed by the crack and crash of walls and windows shattering. We dove behind a nearby display of battle flags just in time to avoid being sliced to pieces by flying shards of glass—and just in time to avoid being seen by two giant winged creatures who barreled through the newly opened hole in the wall. They somersaulted to the floor and stood up, dusting themselves off and folding their soot-black wings.

They looked like giant humans with bat wings; one was bigger and burlier than the other, but they were both easily eight feet tall. They had long black hair pulled into ponytails, and mostly human faces: wild, hairy eyebrows and goatees, and sharp, menacing beaks instead of noses and mouths. Both were dressed in red patent-leather motorcycle outfits that said TENGU across the chest and down the legs.

Tengu. I stared at them from the behind the battle flags, barely able to believe my eyes. (I know, I know, I'd just crash-landed through a cement wall on the back of a magic paper crane with a talking fox as my guide. I'm not great with change, okay?) I used to search the skies for tengu all the time when I was little, before that fateful day with Mrs. Evans, and I'd only seen one once (or so I'd thought), zipping behind a cloud. At the time, it was thrilling—like seeing a gorilla on safari, I imagine. But now, faced with not one but two tengu, up close and practically in my face, it felt even more real—and way scarier—than when I was a kid. Some wise tengu have been known to train great warriors, but mostly they're violent oafs who love chaos and have no loyalty to anyone but themselves. Which might explain why they hadn't bothered with spirit portals but had literally crashed through the wall and left a very real hole. They each carried a long metal staff topped with a ring, from which hung more rings that jingled as the tengu strode toward the display case that housed Dōjigiri. I held my breath. They did not look like the kind of tengu who would offer to train me to be a great warrior.

When they reached the case, they raised up their staffs and brought them down in one swift motion—*SMASH! CRASH!*

Niko, Danny, and I watched in horror as the larger of the two tengu pulled Dōjigiri from the pile of splintered glass and swished it around, laughing as he shattered the display case to his right, and then his left. His laughter sounded like gravel in a blender.

"Hey, Goro, give us a turn," said the smaller tengu. His voice was nasal and whiny, and he was speaking the same language that Niko and Mom had used in the kitchen.

"What, and have you kill me with it so you can deliver it to His Lordship and get all the glory for yourself? Ha! Not likely, Gara," said Goro, in a deep, gruff voice.

"I wouldn't," said Gara. "And how do I know *you* won't try to kill *me*?"

Goro lunged at his partner and held the sword to his throat with a menacing grin. "You don't," he said, "so you'd better watch yourself."

Gara snarled furiously but said nothing. Then both tengu turned, leaped through the hole they'd made, and flew off into the darkness.

This Is Not an Emergency

"The crane!" shouted Niko. "What did you do with it? Where is it?"

I reached into my backpack and pulled out a slightly squashed and crumpled crane. I smoothed it out as best I could and lowered myself cautiously onto its back. The magic still worked, thank goodness, although the wings were bent at funny angles and the feathers had some pretty intense bad-hair-day energy. Danny and Niko jumped on beside me. "After them!" I shouted, hoping it knew what I meant. The crane staggered to its feet, flapped its wonky wings, and launched itself out of the building as Danny whooped and yelled, "Let's gooooo!"

We plunged downward for a sickening moment before the crane steadied itself and began climbing. I relocated my heart, which felt like it might have left my body, and held on to the crane's papery feathers.

The tengu were visible in the distance, flying toward the Golden Gate Bridge. Miraculously, despite the bumps and wobbles, we were gaining on them—and they didn't seem to realize they were being followed. By the time the rust-red towers rose up ahead of us, the tops peeking out of a thick cloak of fog, we'd closed the gap to a bus-length; I thought I could even hear the tengu shouting at each other. They dove into the fog, and we followed right behind.

But the fog was so thick, we lost sight of them instantly. All I could see was mist and the bright orange smudges of the freeway lights below. I heard the distant sound of the traffic, the hum of the wind through the suspension cables, and the *whoosh-whoosh* of the crane's paper-feathered wings. But no tengu.

"Where are they?" I whispered.

Niko said nothing, but looked worried.

The wind gusted, pushing us sideways—the crane seemed to be having a tough time battling it. Tiny droplets of fog had begun to collect on my skin—even my hair was damp. I shivered and clenched my jaw to keep my teeth from chattering.

Another sudden gust tilted us like we were on some kind of amusement park ride, and I gasped in horror as the feathers in my left hand began to pull loose from the crane's back. I glanced at Danny, who looked like he might throw up, and then at Niko, who didn't look much better.

"Up!" Niko cried, suddenly energized. "Up! The moisture is weakening the paper! We need to get out of the fog!"

The crane tried to obey, but it was now struggling in earnest as the wind buffeted us back and forth. We clipped a suspension cable, leaving a little blob of wing stuck to it like a wet paper towel.

"I don't want to die!" Danny croaked.

"UP! UP! UP!" Niko shouted again.

A blast of wind sent us wheeling to the left, but instead of straightening out, the crane kept tipping, tipping, tipping. . . .

I screamed and scrabbled at the feathers, but they uprooted themselves wetly in my hands. My body slid sideways. Niko's feet kicked at my face as he struggled to stay on the crane's back. And then the crane tipped over completely and I fell into the darkness.

Oof. I landed almost immediately on something hard and metallic. And from the sound of it, so had Niko and Danny. Thank goodness. I lifted my head just in time to see the crane spinning away from us. I watched it fade into the fog, realizing that the last thing it had done in its life was make sure we were safe—kind of like Mom had done for me with the shikome. I swallowed hard so I wouldn't cry. A couple of hours in and I'd already let her down. My best hope of keeping *her* safe was now in the hands of a pair of flying chaos monsters on their way to who knew where.

I took in my surroundings; we'd landed on a platform that wrapped around one of the northern towers of the bridge. Safe, for the moment. And stranded. "What do we do now?" I asked Niko in despair. "How are we supposed to get Dōjigiri back?"

"And who are those tengu taking it to, anyway? Who is 'His Lordship'?" Danny added.

"How should I know? Do I look like I know everything?" Niko sniped. But then he sighed and said, "I am just as surprised as you. I have no idea where those brutal beasts came from or why they took the sword, or where they've gone." His ears and tail drooped.

"You mean we're done? We have to fight the oni without Dōjigiri?" I squeaked. "I can't do that! We'll die! There has to be some other way. Some other weapon. *Something* . . . Hey, what about your wishing jewel?"

"My wishing jewel?" Niko's whole body twitched.

"Yeah. Don't all foxes have a wishing jewel?"

"Ah, yes." Niko cleared his throat. "Yes, clever you for knowing about that. Unfortunately—"

"So where's yours? Can we use it?" Danny said.

Niko shook his head. "No, I'm afraid I can't tell you where it is. In any case—"

"Why not?" I demanded. "Because you don't know? Or because it's a secret? Can you even get to it?"

"Of course I know where it is! Why wouldn't I know where it is? It's just—yes, it's a secret, that's all. And as I was going to say, it's only for emergencies. If I told you where it was, you'd take it and use it for a non-emergency, and then where would we be?"

"Um, I hate to say it, Niko, but this"—I swept my arm around at the bay and the city below us—"seems like a pretty big emergency to me."

"I'll be the judge of that," he sniffed. "You clearly have no idea what a real emergency is."

"I think I do."

"Nonsense! *You* are a novice, and *I* am an expert, and *I* say this is not an emergency," Niko insisted.

"Why are you being so weird about it?" Danny's eyes narrowed at Niko. "Do you not have a wishing jewel?"

Niko's whiskers quivered and his fur bristled. "How dare you suggest such a thing! I do have one. It is in a safe place, and as I said, I will use it when I see fit."

Danny and I looked at each other. Niko was *definitely* hiding something, and it wasn't just his wishing jewel.

I tried a new tack. "Is there someone we can ask for help, then? There are tons of kami, right? Even if they don't want to come with us to the island, maybe they can give us something to fight the oni with."

"Hmm." He looked around and whined softly to himself before heaving a sigh and saying, "I suppose we don't have a choice. Follow me."

Niko led us onto an iron catwalk that clung to the outer wall of the bridge tower. I could see the city far below, and the main cable swooping down like the track of the world's tallest roller coaster. The wind gusted hard, and I closed my eyes and pressed myself against the tower. I could hear Danny muttering to himself, "Pretend we're on the ground. Pretend we're on the ground." At least I wasn't the only one who was scared. That was comforting.

I opened one eye to see Niko reaching through the guardrails; the horizontal bars were so far apart that he could easily have fallen through them, and I almost fainted. "Aha!" he said. "Right here." He looked back at us and gestured grandly at the empty air. "A portal to the Sea of Heaven. Accessible from most bridges that cross over ocean water." He stuck out his paw again and waved it slightly. A thick vertical line of soft pink light appeared a couple of feet away, as if he'd cracked open a sliding door.

"Once we go through," Niko explained, "we will board a boat that will take us to the Seven Lucky Gods."

"That sounds cool," said Danny. "Um, who are they, again?"

I stared at him. "How can you remember Dōjigiri but *not* remember the Seven Lucky Gods?"

He shrugged. "I dunno. I think weapons are cool. So what?"

Whatever. To each their own. The thought of having seven lucky gods on my team actually sounded better than having a demon-slaying sword, which I probably wouldn't have been able to use anyway. "Why didn't we do this right away instead of wasting all that time trying to steal Dōjigiri?"

"Because one doesn't just drop in unannounced on the Seven Lucky Gods and ask for favors. With the exception of New Year's Day, they are very stingy about granting wishes and giving gifts."

"Then why are we doing it?" I asked.

"Because we're desperate."

I'd Say We're over Denver, Colorado

Niko slid the door all the way open. "Follow me," he said. "And hurry!" With that, he hopped through and disappeared.

"You go first," I said to Danny.

"No, *you* go first."

"I thought you were all strong and brave and I wouldn't stand a chance on this mission without you," I said. "Are you scared?"

"I'm not scared," he said angrily, which I knew was a lie, but whatever. "And you *wouldn't* stand a chance—you won't. But this is your mission, so you should go first." If that wasn't the emptiest excuse I'd ever heard. But fine. Maybe I wouldn't be able to wield a sword, but I could step across two feet of empty space.

Over a 746-foot drop to certain death.

Easy. No problem.

It took everything I had to wrap my arms around the top guardrail and ease myself under it. The whole time, my eyes were squeezed shut and my legs shook so hard I could barely stand. Carefully, I inched my foot over the dark nothingness below and was pleasantly surprised when I felt solid ground right away. Keeping my eyes fixed forward, I straightened and stepped into the rectangle of light. When I looked down to find that I was still in the air, I almost stumbled backward, which would have been the end of this story. Luckily, I didn't. I saw that I was standing on a tiny wooden platform above a rowboat in the middle of a choppy sea—and surrounded by sharks, from the look of it. Their fins churned the water, making it froth and bubble.

"Hurry!" Niko called from below. "The longer you wait, the bigger the jump."

He wasn't kidding. The platform was rising slowly, like a helium balloon.

"Hurry up and jump, for crying out loud!" Danny said from behind. He sounded frantic. He'd made it through the portal and was crowding behind me, his fingers digging painfully into my shoulders. The longer I waited, the farther *he'd* have to jump, too.

"I'm worried about the sharks," I said nervously.

"What sharks?" Niko asked, looking around.

"Those are *sharks*?!" Danny's fingers dug in even harder, and his voice cracked into a squeak. "Oh man. I was hoping they were dolphins."

"Look at their fins!" I said, pointing. "Those are definitely shark fins."

"JUST GO!" Danny practically screamed in my ear.

The fear in his voice got me moving. I took a deep breath, focused on the bottom of the boat, and jumped.

"OW!" No, it wasn't me landing on the boat. It was Danny landing on me. He'd barely waited after I'd jumped, and now

I was facedown on the bottom of a wildly rocking rowboat in the middle of shark-infested waters, with banged-up shins and probably a broken back. "What'd you do that for?" I said angrily. "You couldn't have waited two seconds for me to get out of the way?"

"Sorry," said Danny. "I didn't want the door to go any higher. I'm not a good swimmer, and there were the sharks, and I was . . . I was . . ."

"You were scared," I finished. "Just like earlier."

"No, I was mad because you were taking so long, and I want to hurry up and meet the lucky gods," he said. "We need to get us some weapons so we can go kick some oni butt." *Liar.*

"You were scared out of your skull," Niko cackled from the little platform at the front of the boat. "Admit it."

Danny clambered onto the bench that spanned the middle of the rowboat while I rubbed my back and checked my shins. "I'm sorry I landed on you," he muttered, ignoring Niko's remark.

"Whatever." I got on the bench next to Danny and glanced nervously at the fins that kept poking up from the water around us. This was definitely a scary situation. *I* was scared. Why couldn't he just say *he* was scared? Who was he trying to impress?

"How are we supposed to go anywhere? There aren't any oars in this boat," Danny said crabbily, clearly trying to change the subject.

"We're going there already," said Niko, who was now facing forward, sniffing the wind. "Can't you tell?"

"Oh." To be honest, I couldn't tell right away. There was nothing to compare our progress against—it was just sapphire-blue water and sunset-pink sky all around. But when I glanced over the back of the boat, we did seem to be leaving a wake behind us. "Where are the Seven Lucky Gods, then?"

"On the *Takarabune,* of course!"

"Ohhh!" Of course. "I didn't know they *lived* on it."

"They don't," said Niko. "Not permanently, anyway. It's more of a vacation residence."

"Um, what was the *Takarabune,* again?" Danny asked.

"The *Takarabune* is the Ship of Treasures. It brings the Seven Lucky Gods through the Sea of Heaven and down to Earth so that they can grant wishes and spread good luck for the first three days of the new year," explained Niko.

"If we're in heaven, does that mean we're in the sky right now?" Danny asked.

"In a manner of speaking. The Sky Kingdom of the spirit dimension overlaps and intersects with the human sky. The great bridges of Earth serve as bridges between the two."

"So San Francisco is right below us?" I asked.

Niko looked thoughtful. "It's not point for point—the Sky Kingdom is not a blanket that covers the globe. But if I had to take a guess, I'd say we're over Denver, Colorado."

"That is very weird," Danny said.

"*Very* weird," I agreed.

"Speak for yourselves," Niko sniffed. "Narrow-minded nincompoops."

"*You're* a narrow-minded nincompoop," I countered, irritated with Niko's superior attitude. "I can't help it if I don't know everything about how the spirit world works. No one's ever explained this stuff to me before. Not in a way that—" I'd been about to say, *Not in a way that was real*, but it occurred to me that Mom had explained a lot of it in a way that was real. I just hadn't believed her. I wished I could talk to her about it all now. But I didn't want to be sad, so I said, "Anyway, who showed up in our world looking like he raided Great-Grandpa's closet?"

"It wasn't as if I had time to gallivant around the globe, researching human fashion trends, you know." Niko sulked. "I've been on that island for a hundred years. *And* I had to learn how to drive."

"You're a hundred years old?" Danny's mouth fell open.

"Maybe more," I said. "Are you older than a hundred?"

"Maybe he means in fox years," said Danny. "So, what is that, seven dog years for every human year?"

"Are dog years and fox years the same?" I asked.

"If he's a hundred fox years old, that would be about fourteen human years," Danny said.

"But his fashion is about a hundred human years old," I pointed out.

"Stop it, you blithering buffoons! You're making my head hurt." Niko curled himself into an orange floof on the bow and refused to look at us.

"Okay, sure. You can dish it out, but you can't take it, huh." Danny snickered.

"I was trying to educate you," said the floof. "You don't have to mock my fashion choices."

"I think we do, though," said Danny. "People who wear clothes like yours deserve to be mocked." He grinned at me. But I couldn't grin back. Yeah, Niko had been mean at first, and maybe he deserved a little teasing, but now it felt unfair. I hated it when kids like Kiki and Ryleigh made fun of my secondhand clothes.

"No, they don't," I said. "He was probably doing his best. Right, Niko?"

"I was," came the muffled response.

Danny rolled his eyes, and I took it as a reminder: he was not my friend.

For the next few minutes, Niko continued to sulk in the front, Danny and I fell silent in the middle, and our boat drifted on toward wherever the Ship of Treasures was. The sky grew lighter on the horizon. It was eerily quiet—no seagulls, no wind, just the water making those little lapping sounds on the side of the boat. Oh, and the shark fins swirling around us, cutting through the water and circling, circling, circling. I almost thought I could hear them muttering to each other in low, silky-smooth tones. Hopefully they weren't talking about how yummy we'd taste, or arguing about when would be the best time to leap out of the water and eat us whole. Something bumped against the side of the boat, and I jumped. Carefully, I edged closer to the center.

"How much longer till we get there?" I asked, trying to keep my voice light and steady. "And why aren't these sharks going away?"

"How much longer depends on where the ship is. And these sharks aren't going away because they're taking us to it. And they aren't sharks, my nervous novice. They're dragons."

"Dragons?" This time, Danny shifted closer to the middle of the boat—but I moved back to the edge. I remembered now.

"The prow of the Ship of Treasures is carved in the shape of a dragon's head!"

"And these dragons"—Niko flicked his tail at them—"are part of its spirit. They're guiding us back to their home."

I leaned over and looked carefully at the sharks—oops, dragons. They did have shark-like fins on their backs—but what I'd thought were multiple sharks were actually multiple fins on the long backs of only two dragons. Their heads still looked kind of shark-like, too, but with huge, round green eyes and looonnnnng skinny noses. One paused just for a moment to look up at me, and I felt like I could see everything it had seen, from the beginning of time itself—a wide, empty ocean, the birth of the land and mountains, and everything since then, all the way up to the present moment. I would have looked into those swirling green depths forever, but the dragon blinked and dove, and I snapped back to reality.

"They're beautiful," I breathed. Mom used to talk about dragons with a special sort of awe and wonder in her voice, and I wished I could tell her that I understood now, that I'd seen for myself what she had tried to tell me. I thought of her doing her best to share the magic and beauty of the world she knew, and how she must have felt when I told her it was all a bunch of baloney. It must have felt like I was turning my back on her, as well as her stories—no, her world. *My* world. I was fully in it now.

"I'm sorry I stopped believing, Mom," I whispered to the water. "If you just hang on while I'm gone, I promise I'll come back and you can tell me even more. I promise not to give up until everything is okay again."

Under the dragons, in the depths, I thought I could see twinkling lights. Or were they stars? Or fish? Or fireflies? There was so much I still didn't know. As I watched the dragons and wondered about the lights swirling in the darkness below us, I felt my eyelids grow heavy. I must have dozed off, because the next thing I knew, there was a *THUNK* and a *yip,* and I jolted awake to see Niko leaping into the air, having just barely escaped being skewered by a giant spear.

Foxes Like Pepperoni Pizza?

"HA, HA, HAAAAA! Look lively, rodents! I'm bringing you aboard," a deep voice bellowed from high above. It was hard to see who it belonged to, because he was backlit by what looked like his own personal sun as he gazed down at us from the deck of a wooden ship.

"Heard you lazybones snoring from miles away," the man continued as our boat began levitating out of the water. "It's about time you arrived."

As we drew level with him, our boat pitched violently and tossed Danny, Niko, and me over the ship's railing. I ended up sprawled facedown on a wide wooden deck, blinking dazedly at a pair of huge black army boots.

The boots were attached to bright yellow-and-green camo fatigues; shading my eyes, I looked farther up to see one of those black bulletproof vests, decorated with a jeweled mosaic of demonic faces that looked ready to leap out and bite anyone who got too close. The man had yanked his spear out of our boat and was holding it upright in one hand, tapping it impatiently on the deck. His scowling face was in shadow—that sun I'd seen before was a ring of fire that seemed to be strapped to his back. And yet despite the fire, the air that swirled around him was cold enough to make me shiver.

"O great and mighty Bishamon, sir, we beg your mercy," Niko began. I breathed a sigh of relief. Bishamon was one of the Seven—the god of warriors and the guardian of the North.

"Silence! On your feet!" Bishamon barked.

We scrambled up.

"Attennnn-tion!" Bishamon slammed his spear onto the deck, which made me literally jump to attention.

I straightened everything I could straighten and glanced nervously at Danny and Niko. Niko looked like a dog at a dog show, with his chin and tail up. Only his nose and whiskers were quivering the tiniest bit. If Danny was scared, he wasn't showing it.

"Eyes forward!"

I snapped my gaze to the front.

"Whiskers and noses still!"

I almost checked to see if Niko's nose had stopped quivering, but caught myself just in time.

"I've never seen a more raggedy, undisciplined little band of bugs in all my—"

"Bish, please. Chill. They're just children," said a very . . . well, a very chill voice.

"Children who don't know how to stand at attention," grumbled Bishamon, which I thought was unfair. It wasn't like I'd ever been in the army or anything.

"Dude. You'll ruin our image. Honestly, when you're around, I get confused: Are we the Seven Lucky Gods? Or the Six Lucky Gods and One Drill Sergeant? Don't listen to him, kids. Relax. Take a look around."

I let out a quiet sigh of relief, but Bishamon had me nervous enough that I only relaxed verrry slowwwly.

The laid-back voice belonged to a big, bald middle-aged guy wearing flip-flops, surf shorts, and a loosely belted bathrobe that hung open at the waist to reveal a solid, round belly.

"You're a *god*?" Danny said, staring. And then, "Ow!" when Niko nipped his heel.

But the guy in front of us laughed as if Danny had cracked the funniest joke he'd ever heard. "Whoo!" He wiped a tear from his eye. "I sure am, little buddy. Hotei, the god of contentment, plenty, and happiness at your service. Here," he said, rummaging around in the ginormous rucksack at his side. "What's your favorite candy bar?"

"Twix," said Danny right away, with a nervous glance at Bishamon, who was stamping his feet and making irritated noises.

"Ta-da!" Hotei produced two gigantic packets of Twix bars. "And how about an In-N-Out 4x4 burger, Animal Style fries, and a soda to go with it?" My stomach growled as he pulled an In-N-Out bag from the same sack and handed it to Danny, along with one of the Twix packets. "This one is for my hangry friend." He tossed the second packet to Bishamon, who accepted it with a grunt, tore the wrapping open, and crammed both bars into his mouth. Talk about ill-mannered and undisciplined! "It's his favorite, too," Hotei whispered with a smile.

Just as I was starting to feel jealous that I hadn't gotten anything, Hotei reached deep into his sack and pulled out a bucket of Auntie Anne's cinnamon-sugar pretzel nuggets, saying, "Heard you had to feed a nasty old shikome, so this is for your loss. Oh—and a fried-chicken sandwich from Starbird . . . and an Oreo cookie milkshake. I believe those are your favorites?" Finally, he laid a large slice of pepperoni pizza at Niko's feet.

"I didn't know foxes liked pizza," I said.

"Dish foksh doesh," Niko answered, chewing enthusiastically.

I popped a pretzel nugget into my mouth. It was warm, buttery, and sweet, with just the right amount of spice—perfect. I wondered how long it had been since I'd eaten.

Danny must have been wondering, too, because he pulled out his phone, saying, "What time is it, anyway?" He frowned and tapped it. "What's wrong with my phone?"

He turned it toward me. Where it should have said something like 8:25 p.m., there were four spinning disks, alternating silver and gold.

"Time has no meaning here," said Hotei, seeing our confused expressions. "A moment here could be a hundred years in the human dimension. Or the opposite could be true: a moment there, a hundred years here. I mean, what *is* time, anyway, right? Just a human invention. An attempt to measure and control the immeasurable and uncontrollable nature of—"

"And that is why you are not in charge of this ship." A tall, imposing woman strode out of the cabin at the far side of the deck. She was wearing a charcoal-gray pin-striped suit with a vest and black oxfords, and her sleek black hair was pulled into a neat bun at the nape of her neck. On her head was a jaunty black fedora with a couple of golden stalks of rice stuck into the hat band. She pulled one of those old-timey watches out of her pocket—the kind attached to a gold chain strung through a buttonhole on her vest. A tiny golden mallet dangled from the other end of the chain.

"Ah, Daikoku. Nice of you to join us," Bishamon said a little peevishly. "Kind of ironic that you're late, isn't it? Considering your specialty."

"I had other business to attend to, and I'm exactly on time," she said. She smiled, but her eyes flashed with something dark and scary, and I wasn't surprised when Bishamon backed down, grumbling, "Yes, ma'am."

"Daikoku? But I thought you were a man." Every picture I'd ever seen of the Seven Lucky Gods had shown Daikoku as a male. He was the god of wealth, farmers, and merchants, and protector of the home—although now I remembered Mom saying that he also had connections to ancient, nearly forgotten goddesses of time and destruction.

"Man, woman, god, goddess." Daikoku waved a dismissive hand. "Such limiting terms when the possibilities are limitless. For the first eight generations, before we came to the Middle Lands, we kami didn't even have genders. Do your research, child, and be open to the infinite, because I am one and I am all—though for now, I am female, so I will thank you to refer to me as such." She took a look at her pocket watch, put it back in her pocket, and said briskly, "The other Luckies are busy at festivals and whatnot, and I myself have loads of work to do elsewhere, so let's get started, shall we?"

"About time," muttered Bishamon, thumping his spear on the deck.

"Ah, yes. Speaking of time, let's begin by addressing Danny's question. According to my watch, it's been exactly eight Earth hours since you left the Asian Art Museum in San Francisco, and at that moment, it was precisely eight o'clock in the evening, Pacific Daylight Time."

"What? You mean it's tomorrow already?" said Danny.

"Today, in fact. But what *is* today, really?" Hotei murmured to himself.

Daikoku rolled her eyes before turning her attention back to me. "Bishamon tells me that you and Niko are trying to send a group of oni back to the underworld in order to save your mother's island and thus her life, and that your plan to use Dōjigiri was foiled. I assume that's why you're here? To ask for help? To beg for weapons and supplies?"

I looked at Niko, who bowed low and nodded at me and Danny to do the same.

"We humbly beg Your August Magnificences' favor," Niko said to the deck.

"That is a bold move, my friends," Hotei chuckled. "High five." He held his palm out, and Danny instantly straightened up and slapped it.

"Insolent is more like it," growled Bishamon. Danny shrank back, but over Bishamon's shoulder, Hotei grinned and gave Danny a thumbs-up. It was comforting, but ugh. The last thing I needed was a Danny-Hotei bro-bonding moment.

"Ms. Daikoku?" I said, my voice trembling. "Do you, um, have any idea how my mom is doing?" I had to ask—she did seem to know quite a lot. Though I almost didn't want to hear the answer.

Daikoku looked at me with her dark eyes. "The oni and the encounter with the shikome have weakened her, but she's fine for now, child. She's a fighter. She's a survivor."

I nodded and said nothing. It was nice to hear that Mom was a fighter and a survivor, but "fine for now" wasn't exactly reassuring.

"Um, so . . . if it pleases Your Wonderful Worship-fulnesses, perhaps a token or two of your most benevolent beneficence . . . ?" Niko said, bringing the conversation back to its alliterative point.

Hotei obligingly opened his rucksack and began rooting around inside, but Daikoku held up her hand. "Wait. Before we proceed further, Bishamon has news that you must hear regarding the Island of Mysteries. It is in far graver danger than you think."

This! Is Not! Funny!

Bishamon cleared his throat and spoke. "You came to us because your attempt to, ahem, *steal* Dōjigiri"—he paused to direct a fiery glare at Niko, who lowered his head and tail—"was thwarted by a pair of tengu who arrived just after you. We now believe that the theft of Dōjigiri was part of a larger operation being carried out by a very dark, very dangerous enemy."

I thought of what Mom had told me about forces at work that I didn't understand, and felt a chill creep over me. "Who?" I asked.

Instead of answering, Daikoku waved her hand, and a curtain of black smoke appeared before us. It swirled up and fell over us in a dome, and suddenly we were in a forest, standing in front of a tiny dilapidated shrine no bigger than a closet. It was nighttime, and the darkness felt alive somehow—brimming with menace that seemed to pluck at my hair and drag its fingernails across my skin, like it wanted me to know that it could destroy me anytime it wanted, but it was restraining itself for now. I took a step closer to Danny and felt Niko pressing himself against my legs. He was trembling.

"Where are we?" I quavered. "What's going on? I don't like this!"

"Don't worry," came Daikoku's voice. "This is only an illusion. I just want you to see why we are so concerned."

"You couldn't just tell us?" asked Danny.

"Shhh. Watch."

The trees blotted out any moonlight, and the darkness continued to press down on us. Just when I thought I couldn't take it anymore, a flash of lightning illuminated the forest for a brief second and revealed four figures crouched on the roof of the shrine. They were vaguely humanoid, with scrawny limbs, scraggly fur, and pointy ears like cats.

"Kasha," Niko whispered. Monster cats that eat human corpses.

They leaped down behind the shrine, and suddenly we were there, too, watching as they pawed ferociously at the ground. Eventually they dug up something large and round and covered with long black hair: a humongous severed head. Its eyes shone like a pair of yellow lanterns, and a snake slithered out of its half-open mouth; when it blinked and pulled its lips back to reveal a set of bloodstained fangs, I almost screamed in terror. Then it spoke in a voice so full of evil that it seemed to permeate the air and seep into my skin. "Return me to my body so that we may all rise together."

The kasha cowered and bowed low. "My lord," they hissed, and sprang into action. Each one grabbed a hank of hair, and with another flash of lightning, they leaped into the sky and vanished. The scenery around us turned back into smoke and dissipated, and we were standing on the deck of the Ship of Treasures once more.

"What . . . was that?" Danny asked in a shaky voice.

Bishamon answered him. "Surveillance footage of an event that took place at the same time as the theft of Dōjigiri. We have agents planted in sensitive security areas for this very purpose."

"But what *was* it? What just happened?" I asked.

Daikoku spoke. "You may recall that after Minamoto Raikō cut off Shuten-dōji's head, he buried it in the mountains and built a shrine to prevent it from rejoining his body and allowing him to rise again."

"I've collected intel that the demons of Yomi are gathering," said Bishamon. "The theft of Dōjigiri and the recovery of Shuten-dōji's head seem to confirm it, and I suspect that Shuten-dōji himself is their leader. With his head back on his shoulders, and Dōjigiri in his possession, he and his troops will be virtually unstoppable." The tengu's words came back to me: *His Lordship*. They'd meant Shuten-dōji. I remembered the feeling of evil around the burial site, those gleaming yellow eyes, the teeth, stained black with blood; that horrible hissing voice. My stomach started to twist and tighten.

"In the spirit dimension there are three realms: Yomi, or the land of the dead; the Sky Kingdom, where we are right now; and the Middle Lands—that is to say, your Earth. It is my belief that Shuten-dōji intends to rise up from Yomi and launch an attack on the Middle Lands. He and his army will travel to the surface through a recently compromised portal." Bishamon stopped and looked at me.

"My mother's island," I whispered.

"Affirmative. Dōjigiri's world tour created a unique incentive and opportunity for Shuten-dōji to attempt an attack on the portal; unfortunately, it was successful. And now that he is in possession of his head and the sword that killed him, all he has to do is wait for the binding spell to fail, and he can lead his army off the island."

My heart squeezed as I thought about what this meant for me personally. It felt selfish—the fate of the world was at stake, and here I was worrying about Mom. But I couldn't help it.

Niko looked miserable. "I'm sorry," he said. "If only I had been stronger . . ."

Poor thing. "It's okay," I reassured him. "It wasn't your fault—it was the shimenawa that failed, obviously. At least you got out and warned everyone, right? And you've been doing everything you can to turn things around."

"Yes," he said, nodding reluctantly. "I suppose that's true."

"And we aren't alone anymore. Now that the whole world is in danger, I'm sure we can get the kami to help," Danny said.

He was right, I realized, and I immediately felt better. Okay, so the fate of the world was at stake. But at least we weren't alone in this fight anymore. "The Kami vs. the Demons of Yomi" felt like way better odds than "Momo, Danny, and Niko vs. Two Hundred Oni."

"Right, guys?" Danny turned to Bishamon, Daikoku, and Hotei. "Right? You'll all be there, right?"

Bishamon cleared his throat and said, "If I were planning an attack on the Middle Lands, the best time to do it would be Kami-Con."

"The one in San Diego?" Danny said. "Why, because they could pretend to be cosplayers?"

"No, not Comic-Con, you blasted fool!" Bishamon roared. "*Kami*-Con. Otherwise known as Kami-ari-zuki—the Great Assembly of the Kami. Beginning on the tenth day of the tenth month, all the kami, from the smallest tree spirit all the way up to Amaterasu, Great Goddess of the Sun and Queen of the Sky Kingdom, gather for a few days to discuss the fate of humanity for the coming year. It would be the perfect time to attack, as the Middle Lands will be left more or less undefended."

"But . . ." I did the math. If we'd left the house yesterday, then . . . "That's in six days!"

"Indeed," said Daikoku. "And now that we have all the information, it's obvious that Shuten-dōji and his minions must have planned this quite deliberately."

"What do you mean?" I asked.

"When it was in Japan, Dōjigiri was protected by charms and spells. Last night was the first time it had ever been overseas, outside of that protective magic."

"So?" Danny said.

Bishamon sighed impatiently. "Consider the timing, rodent: the Island of Mysteries falls and the binding spell begins to crumble. The following night, the moment Dōjigiri becomes vulnerable, it is stolen. At the same time, Shuten-dōji's head is unearthed and, we believe, delivered to the Island of Mysteries. In a few days, Kami-Con will draw all the kami away from our posts."

"And Shuten-dōji will lead his army out of Yomi, launch an attack from the Island of Mysteries, and take over the earth unopposed, because he now possesses the only weapon ever to defeat him, and anyone who could stop him without a weapon is at Kami-Con," Hotei finished sadly.

"Which is where you come in," said Daikoku. "Without your intervention, the earth will fall to Shuten-dōji and his demons."

"Without *our* intervention?" I said. The panic that had started squirming around in my brain ballooned and combined with outrage to crank my voice up to a screech. "What about *your* intervention? Why is it all up to us? You're gods, aren't you? *You* intervene!"

"We would if we could," said Hotei. "But we're contractually obligated to be available to humanity, right? That means we can't go to your mother's island to get rid of the oni and reseal the portal, because the spell your mother cast would bind us there for all of time—every kind of time—and we wouldn't be available to humanity anymore."

"But—but what if she undid that spell from home? She can do that, right?" Why hadn't this occurred to me before?

"You forget that your mother draws most of her power from the island itself. If she's not on the island, she can't summon the power she needs to undo a spell as binding as the one she cast. And you know Susano'o cursed her to be unable to return there."

"Can one of you undo it, then?"

"No kami can undo another kami's magic without erasing their own spirit," said Niko.

"So you see, child," said Daikoku, not unkindly, "it has to be you."

"But if I can't defeat the oni and close the portal in time, you'll have my back, right? I mean, Bishamon, you're the god of warriors. Daikoku, it's your whole job to protect human families. So, you'll be ready to fight, right? If . . . you know . . ."

"If they attack during Kami-Con, I'm afraid we'll be unable to help," Bishamon said.

"There is Ebisu," said Hotei, scratching his beard thoughtfully.

"The god of luck?" Maybe there was hope after all.

Bishamon nodded. "Affirmative. It's his job to babysit you humans while we're gone. But he's pretty hard of hearing, and frankly you'll need more than luck to defeat Shuten-dōji's army, so I wouldn't count on him."

"Can't you skip Kami-Con for once? I mean, how many thousands of times have you gone?" Danny protested.

Hotei made a regretful face. "That's also a contract thing. We've tried to unionize and get out of it, but . . ."

"But that's not fair! If no one's there to help us, we'll never succeed!" This was bananas. How did they expect two kids and a fox to defeat an entire underworld demon army?

"Which is why. You need. To stop. Your lily. Livered. Belly-aching. And. STEP . . . *UP!*" Bishamon bellowed, thunking his spear in time with his words so hard that he actually punched a hole in the deck on "UP!" and lost his balance as the spear fell through.

"*Fall down,* more like! Bwaaa-ha-ha-ha-haaa!" Hotei laughed so hard at his own joke, he fell over. Danny and Niko and I started giggling, too, and in a couple of seconds, we were crumpled up on the deck, completely overcome with laughter. It was like my fear had eaten up my self-control. Plus, it felt good to laugh.

"PULL YOURSELVES TOGETHER, RODENTS. THIS! IS NOT! FUNNY!" Bishamon roared and thunked his spear once more—but this time, the *thunk* was accompanied by a flash of lighting and a boom of thunder so loud that I felt it ring right through me, and when I looked up, he had grown so tall, his head appeared to touch the sky. That got our attention pretty quick. "Shuten-dōji is no joke. He is evil to his very core; he is said to live off the joy of murdering others. He is the second-most-dangerous and hate-filled being in our universe after Izanami herself, the literal Queen of Death. You must not take this lightly. You must not fail."

"Wow, dude," Hotei said grumpily. "Way to ruin a good time."

"All right, then, are we finished with the shenanigans?" Daikoku checked her watch and drummed her fingers on her arm. "Because we're running out of time—Don't. Say it." She shot a warning glance at Hotei, who made a zipping motion across his mouth and shook his head.

"As I hope I've made clear, Momo, if you don't protect the Island of Mysteries, there's not much we can do about the invasion that is sure to follow. Of course, we will fight Shuten-dōji and his army as soon as Kami-Con is over—and I have no doubt that we will win—but they will likely have destroyed most of humanity by then. So, if you value your earth, your only option is to clear the island and close the portal before he breaks through during Kami-Con." She looked at me sternly.

My mind was reeling. "But . . . but I can't—"

"You can. And you will have help. Niko is bound to the island and to you, and he will fight with you. As for your friend here . . ." She studied Danny, who shuffled his feet self-consciously. "Try as we might, we have been unable to discover why you are with Momo or how you can have broken into the spirit dimension. Neither of your parents is a kami."

"I was adopted," he explained. "Apparently I just showed up in a box with a name tag at the fire station. No one knows who my birth parents are."

"Yes, we understand. But your blood shows no signs of the spirit world. It's quite puzzling." Danny's face fell, and I couldn't help feeling a little impatient. Sure, it was cool to be part kami, to learn that I was connected to these amazing, magical beings and all the stories and the history. But in a practical sense, what had having a kami for a parent gotten me? Superpowers? No. Amazing self-esteem and confidence? No. It had only given me more to worry about. Meanwhile, in spite of not having kami parents, Danny somehow got to connect with the spirit world and understand and speak the spirit language. Not only that, but with his athletic ability and good looks and tons of friends, Danny wasn't an average, ordinary human. He'd been special all his life.

"In any case, he's with you for a reason. That much is clear. I can only assume that it is his role to help you. Exactly how, of course, remains to be seen," Daikoku continued. "But you will not be alone. And you'll have a weapon even more powerful than Dōjigiri."

More powerful than Dōjigiri? I liked the sound of that.

"If you can get to it and survive."

I did not like the sound of that.

You Go, Humans!

Danny's jaw dropped. "Not—"

"Kusanagi," Daikoku finished.

My jaw dropped when I heard that. "But . . . but . . ."

Kusanagi was the most powerful sword in the world. Mom called it the Sword of the Wind because in addition to your standard awesome magical fighting power, it also gave its user the power to control the wind and call up huge storms to destroy its enemies. And it was one of the Three Sacred Treasures of Japan (the other two treasures being the Mirror of Truth and the Jewel of Kindness), supposedly sent to Earth by Amaterasu herself (Great Goddess of the Sun and Queen of the Sky Kingdom, remember?) as a sort of official goddessly stamp of approval: *You go, humans! We're rooting for you!* Which meant that—

"There's no way," scoffed Niko. "We'd have to break into one of the most sacred, most heavily guarded shrines in Japan. They'll have so many priests and protections—"

"Silence!" roared Bishamon. "No one asked for your opinion."

Hotei leaned forward and whispered, "The sword in the shrine is a fake."

As he spoke, the story came back to me. "The Battle of Dan-no-ura," I said.

All three kami grinned and nodded.

The Battle of Dan-no-ura was one of my favorite stories that Mom used to tell, even though it was about regular humans and didn't involve the kami at all. Almost a thousand years ago, during one of the many wars between different factions of the imperial family, the Taira faction fought the Minamoto faction in a bloody sea battle. For reasons I will never understand, the six-year-old Taira boy emperor, Antoku, was on one of the ships with his grandmother, Lady Tokiko, her ladies-in-waiting, and the Three Sacred Treasures. (Talk about putting all your eggs in one basket!) Someone betrayed the Taira and told their enemies which boat the emperor was on, and as the Minamoto closed in, Lady Tokiko and her ladies-in-waiting collected the Three Sacred Treasures and lined themselves up on the deck. Lady Tokiko picked up her grandson and held him in her arms while her ladies-in-waiting held the sword, the mirror, and the jewel— and everyone jumped overboard and sank beneath the waves in their heavy silk robes rather than surrender to the Minamoto.

I'd always thought that was a *bit* over the top. And poor, poor Emperor Antoku! Technically he was the most powerful person on the boat—and a little boy, for crying out loud—and I'm sure he was not in favor of leaping to his death on the count of three, but his grandmother and the ladies obviously didn't listen. He must have been so scared—and not a single bit of it was his fault or his choice.

Anyway. They say that the mirror was snatched out of the hands of one of the ladies-in-waiting at the last second, the

105

jewel was found floating in its wooden box on the waves, and the sword washed ashore and was returned to the imperial family by local priests.

Except apparently it wasn't.

"I *knew* it!" Danny exclaimed. "There's no way that a huge metal sword like Kusanagi could have just washed up onshore."

"Yeah, I bet that's the reason why no one's allowed to see it except the emperor and the high priest," I agreed. There was even supposed to be a curse on it: if anyone saw it who *wasn't* the emperor or the high priest, they'd die a terrible death. Which would have been exactly what you'd say if you were a priest or an emperor trying to cover up a fake sword.

"So if the one at the shrine is a fake, where is the real one? How do we get there?" I asked.

"Where do you think?" Daikoku asked. She looked at Niko and added, "Yes, Niko, you're right. So be a good boy and stop your whining."

I realized that Niko was moaning quietly to himself, "We're as dead as doorknobs, slaughtered as sea slugs, flattened as flapjacks—"

"Silence! You chose this path. You came to us for help. You will accept what we set before you without moaning and groaning," said Bishamon severely. Niko bowed his head and stopped talking. Bishamon turned to me and Danny and said, "The last known location of Kusanagi is the Taira palace."

"The . . . but I thought they all drowned," I said.

"They did, poor things," said Hotei. "But their desire for revenge and a return to power has kept their spirits on Earth." He sighed. "It's really too bad."

Daikoku added, "They built a palace at the bottom of the sea, and they've been planning to overthrow the Minamoto for the last thousand years. They're trapped in a sort of time loop, and they'll never escape until they've let go of their need for revenge." She took her hat off and adjusted the rice stalks in the hatband.

"To get back to the point," Bishamon growled, "they do not trust outsiders, and they will never willingly give up Kusanagi for any purpose other than to restore Antoku to the throne."

I gulped. "So, you're saying that we have to sneak into a palace at the bottom of the sea, somehow find Kusanagi inside, and steal it from a bunch of angry ghost warriors with trust issues?" My stomach started doing its thing, and I could feel myself starting to hyperventilate.

"And quickly, because of the time loop," Hotei said helpfully (not). "The passage of time in the Taira palace is even more unpredictable than it is up here."

"But how are we supposed to keep track of time if it's not the same as real time? What if it takes years to find Kusanagi? What if we get caught?"

"Not to mention, how are we supposed to breathe underwater?" Danny added. "I—I'm not a good swimmer."

"Calm yourselves," Daikoku said. "We will wrap you in magic that will protect you underwater."

"Can you wrap us in magic that will make us invisible?" I asked.

"Not to ghosts, unfortunately," said Hotei. "But don't worry. We won't send you empty-handed." He reached into his rucksack and pulled out two backpacks. "Ta-daaa!" He presented them to me and Danny with a bow. "One for each of you. You can put anything you need inside, no matter how big, and it won't weigh anything. Not only that, but whenever you reach inside, it will provide you with whatever you need."

I opened mine and looked in. It was like looking into a well—nothing but black, empty space. I reached my hand in and felt nothing—no side, no bottom.

"You should put your shimenawa in there," said Daikoku.

"It won't get lost?" I asked nervously.

"If you need it, you will find it," Hotei assured me.

So I transferred my shimenawa from my old backpack to my new one and watched it fall until it disappeared. It was weirdly scary. "Where does it go?" I asked.

"To the Aum," said Hotei. He pronounced it "Ohm."

"The who?"

"The Aum. Where all things begin and end. Or open and close, if you prefer. Like your koma-inu Alfie's and Meggie's mouths. People sometimes like to say the word when they meditate, to connect themselves to the vastness of the universe."

"Can—can people fall in there?" Danny was peering into his own backpack.

"Portals pass through the Aum, but I wouldn't recommend a free fall," said Daikoku. "The problem is that people often think they need something—or someone—when in fact they don't. Socks, for example, often end up in the Aum by accident. And while you might *want* that sock, you rarely have such a great *need* for it that the Aum will return it to you on demand. So if a person—or even a kami—should go into the Aum without being tethered to a specific destination, there's no telling when or where the Aum might decide there is a need for them to emerge. It might be never."

"Remind me never to crawl into my backpack," muttered Danny, zipping his shut. He looked a little spooked, and I felt the same way.

"Don't worry about it for now. Just know that when you need a thing, your backpack will provide it," Hotei reassured us.

"And now for a few items that we will leave up to your own judgment," said Daikoku.

She held out a small bronze disc. "This is a mirror that will reveal the actions of anyone you hold in your mind. It will help you plan your attack on the oni, and learn their weaknesses ahead of time." She saw Danny looking at it curiously and dropped it into a little leather pouch, which she tied around Niko's neck. "I suggest you and Momo stay away from it. Unless the viewer can focus their thoughts, the mirror itself will not focus correctly. Niko has a long way to go in his training, but he is still more skilled than the two of you."

Niko looked so bashful that I was almost surprised the white fur on his muzzle didn't turn pink. He bowed deeply to Daikoku. "I will not fail you, O greatest of the great."

Then Daikoku turned to Danny and held out her hand. "Give me your phone."

Danny reached into his pocket. "Do I have to?" he asked. "My parents will kill me if I lose it."

"I'll give it right back," said Daikoku. "I just need it for a moment."

So Danny passed it to her, and Daikoku waved her hand over it, like she was doing a magic trick with cards. Then she held it out to Bishamon, who tapped it once with his spear before giving it back.

"The battery is now permanently charged, and I have calibrated the clock so that no matter where you go, you'll know how much time you have left before Kami-Con begins. In addition, the flashlight will always point you to where you need to go. Keep the phone in your pocket so you can consult it even when the need is not dire."

"Sweet!" Danny said, and pressed the power button. He frowned. "Five days? But you said we had six!"

My chest went cold. "You mean we've already spent *a full day* here?"

"Time," said Hotei, shaking his head. "Such a wild concept."

"We have to hurry! We need to go!" I said. I thought of Mom at home alone, worried about me and getting sicker by the minute, and my stomach gave an especially sharp twinge.

Bishamon banged his spear on the deck. "Calm yourself! Panic will get you nowhere. Stay focused on the mission, Momo. Don't let fear steer the boat."

"Oh, one more thing!" Hotei reached into his rucksack, pulled out a spool with no thread on it, and tossed it to me.

I inspected it. "What's this?"

"A plan," said Hotei. "It's symbolic. Put it in your pocket. Because it's always nice to have a plan in your pocket."

Bishamon closed his eyes and muttered, "Why, why, why must I put up with this nonsense?" Daikoku sighed and shook her head. Hotei just chuckled to himself and winked at me. I wished he'd given me something more practical—an *actual* plan would have been ideal, or a map of the Taira palace marked with a big X where Kusanagi was. But I didn't want to complain, so I smiled weakly, tucked the spool into my pocket, and tried to ignore the fact that my heart seemed to be trying to jackhammer its way out of my rib cage.

Bishamon banged his spear. "Attennn-*tion!*" This time, I snapped to attention, standing perfectly still and keeping my eyes forward. Bishamon nodded his head approvingly. "You will now depart for Taira territory."

The rowboat was still hovering next to the ship, exactly where it had been when it tossed us out. Bishamon pointed at it with his spear. It edged obediently closer to the deck; Niko hopped in, and Danny and I clambered after him. Another stab in the air with Bishamon's spear sent us wobbling to the water, where the dragons coiled and curled around themselves near the surface. The moment the boat touched the sea, we began gliding away from the Ship of Treasures.

"Good luck, little dudes!" Hotei called from the deck, waving. "Look out for each other!"

"Focus on the mission and don't let fear steer the boat," added Daikoku, repeating Bishamon's earlier words.

Bishamon said nothing, but he saluted against the bright fiery ring on his back.

The dragons were carrying us far and fast, and it wasn't long before the Ship of Treasures slipped under the horizon and we were in the middle of a huge, empty circle of water—which began to spiral around us.

"What's going on?" I asked. I tried to keep my voice calm and steady.

The dragons had left the side of the boat and were swimming

in a circle around us; the water was moving slowly with them, and instead of moving forward, we were now rotating at the center of the giant watery swirl the dragons had created.

"They're opening a portal," said Niko.

The boat began spinning faster and faster. I gripped the side with one hand and the seat with the other.

"They're opening a *whirlpool*," I said.

"Ughh," Danny groaned, closing his eyes. "Make it stop."

"I wish I could." Niko was curled up in the bottom of the boat and had wrapped his tail around himself. Lucky him.

We're going to drown, I thought. The boat kept spinning. I felt like I was getting flushed down a giant cosmic toilet. My eyes were squinched closed now, too, and when I finally unsquinched one, we were at the bottom of a ginormous funnel of water; the dragons were above us, at the rim, undulating and shimmering like ribbons of bejeweled silk, the pink sky glowing softly above them—and then the water closed over us and I got one last breath in before we were sucked down into the Sea of Heaven.

The boat seemed to zoom through a tunnel, careening around corners and free-falling down sudden drops, like we were in one of those covered slides at a water park. At the same time, everything I saw seemed to move in slow motion while the lights I'd seen from the surface darted and flickered around us, like curious fish.

Souls, said a voice in my head in answer to my unspoken question. *In between lives, waiting to be born.*

Before I could think of any more questions, there was a

whoosh, and the world went dark as we disintegrated, re-integrated, and shot through the other end of the portal.

But instead of tumbling onto the ground somewhere, I was floating downward in the dark. It was weirdly silent: no wind rustling through leaves and grass, no birdsong, not even lapping waves. I could barely make out Danny and Niko next to me, their shadowy shapes dimly outlined by the faint silvery glow from above. My feet touched the ground. Sand. We'd reached the bottom of the ocean.

That's Not a Plan

I looked up at the surface, where fractured moonlight crackled and danced before filtering into the water and fading as it reached the depths where we stood. An octopus scuttled into view and then just as quickly whooshed away; a glimmering school of mackerel darted to and fro, and a sea turtle glided lazily over us like a blimp before it melted back into the darkness.

A low, echoey groan floated through the water, so low that it was almost more vibration than sound.

"What was that?" I whispered.

"Whale song," Niko replied. I thought of the lonely whale we'd learned about in school and imagined him singing that deep, majestic song, hoping for an answer that never came.

"Sounds more like a fart," Danny joked, and I curled my lip at him. He ruined everything. He probably had no idea what it felt like to be lonely.

We let the sound wash over us for another moment, and then Niko said briskly, "That's enough soaking in the atmosphere, I think. Let's go, shall we?"

"Where, though?" There was no path, no signs, no landmarks

(seamarks?), nothing to give us the slightest clue what direction we should take.

"Try your phone," Niko said to Danny.

Danny pulled his phone out of his pocket and tapped the flashlight button. A bright beam of light shone on his shoes. "Yessss!" He pumped his fist, and then immediately groaned when the light went out. He shook the phone and held it up. Still no light.

"It's supposed to point us to where we need to go," I said, remembering Daikoku's words. "Try a different direction and see what happens."

Danny held the phone out and turned in a slow circle. Suddenly the light went back on, and a tiny bit of the dark ocean revealed itself. "Whoa," he said. "That is some seriously sick magic."

Seeing the phone reminded me of something: "Won't your aunt be super worried right now? I know you told her you were at Brad's house, but it's been two nights. Shouldn't you try to check in?"

Danny's expression shifted into something I couldn't quite read. "Nah, she'll just figure I'm still at Brad's. She trusts me. She never checks up on me."

"But won't your parents have called or texted?"

He shrugged. "I don't think they think very much about me when they're gone."

"Oh."

"It's cool, though. 'Cause on the days when everyone thinks I'm with someone else, I get to do whatever I want. I can stay up late playing video games, I can eat Takis and ice cream for dinner—anything!"

"You're so lucky." I kind of wished I could trade lives with Danny. I was so used to being responsible for both me and Mom. It would have felt nice just not to worry about *her* bedtime, let alone my own.

"Yeah, I am." Danny grinned. But I noticed that the grin didn't quite reach his eyes.

I had a strange thought: maybe Danny's life *wasn't* that great. Sure, his parents gave him tons of freedom, but what was it like to be that sure that they didn't care what he did or where he was? Mom was weird and had turned me into a loser, and I got so tired of having to take care of her all the time instead of living my own life. But it was kind of nice to know she'd miss me and worry about me if I wasn't around. I felt a pang of guilt. She was probably worried right now.

I was glad she didn't know where we were at that moment, though, or she would really have been worried. The light had led us onto a path through a kelp forest, where thick, leafy ropes hemmed us in on the left and right, and I had this very creepy feeling that we were being watched—like there were creatures hovering in the darkness just beyond what we could see. Every once in a while, I'd hear a crackle that made me think of claws against rocks, or I'd catch a glimpse of something gray and menacing at the fuzzy edges of the little parabola of light that the phone cast in front of us.

"I don't like this," I whispered.

"Me neither," agreed Niko, his ears swiveling. "I can't smell anything down here in this blasted barnacle bath."

"We have to trust the phone," Danny said stoutly. "It knows where we need to go." The light flared appreciatively, and I jumped—I'd definitely seen something large and monster-like scuttle away into the gloom.

"I still don't like it. There's something out there, and I don't think it's happy we're here."

"Stop being such a wuss," said Danny. "You're going to have to be braver than that if you want to beat the oni."

"Thanks, Danny. Way to be supportive," I shot back.

"Hey, all I'm saying is—whoa."

It felt like someone had pulled back a curtain. The dense kelp forest had ended, and we were standing at the edge of a wide-open space lit with hundreds of lanterns full of fireflies— no, bioluminescent plankton. They glimmered in the water a few feet above the sandy ocean floor and cast soft blue-green spotlights all along a low white wall that stretched from one end of the clearing to the other. Beyond the wall rose a bunch of those curved tile roofs you see on old Japanese castles. Except for the bobbing lanterns and the swirling plankton, nothing moved.

"Is that the Taira palace?" Danny asked his phone. It shone brighter.

My heart picked up speed. "I think we should make a plan before we go," I said.

"Why? All we have to do is knock on the gate and tell them we're here to help them regain the throne, but we need Kusanagi to do it," Danny said.

"That's not a plan, that's an idea—a bad idea. Look at us. We're kids! There's no way they'll believe that we're ready to lead an entire army against their enemies. And we're wearing the wrong kind of clothes."

"Clothes? Seriously?"

"They're in a time bubble, remember?" I turned to Niko. "Can you really not shape-shift? I know I saw you at home in the form of a boy. . . ."

"That was with the help of your mother's magic," he said crossly. "I tried to shift at the bus stop, and again at the mall before the shikome appeared, and what did you see?"

"A fox wearing clothes."

"Exactly. I lost nearly all of my magic not long ago, and hardly anything works anymore." He sighed a gloomy sigh.

"Why? What happened?" asked Danny.

Niko shook his head. "It was an accident. I don't want to talk about it. It . . . it was terrible. Traumatic. Tragic."

We were not off to a great start. But before I could start worrying, Danny said, "Why don't we check our backpacks?"

Oh. Of course.

After a lot of confusion about what went where and plenty of irritated instructions from Niko, Danny and I were each dressed in white kimono-style tops and wide-legged white trousers gathered at the cuffs like size XXL sweatpants. Over the kimono tops we wore huge black silk crewneck tunics with extra-wide kimono-style sleeves. Even though they were generously bloused over a long sash, the bottoms hung all the way down to our knees. On our feet, we wore black leather boots with big round toes. "Look at my clown boots," Danny said, and started jigging around like a big dork.

I tried to breathe through my irritation as I reached into

my backpack in search of helpful items and hoped that Danny would take the hint. But Danny didn't take the hint, and there was nothing in my backpack: not a map, not a guard schedule, not even a set of magical walkie-talkies. I hated that he refused to take this seriously. It felt like when we did group projects at school, and I ended up doing all the work while everyone else spent the entire time goofing around—except with this group project, the only two grades were life and death.

Finally, Danny finished dancing and grinned at me. "Okay, plan girl, now what?"

"Why do I have to come up with the plan?" I said.

"Because you're the one who wanted one."

"Because we need one!"

"Then come up with one!"

Ughhh! He made me so mad. I found myself playing with the spool in my pocket and praying for inspiration, since it was clear that Danny was going to be no help at all. But the best I could come up with was for Niko to do the talking, since he knew more than we did. Also, I was a terrible liar, and I didn't trust Danny not to screw things up. "And maybe they'll sense that Niko's, like, a native of the spirit dimension," I added, "and they'll trust him. Just tell them we're allies. Be really subtle about it and try to get them to talk about Kusanagi and maybe give us some information about where they're keeping it. Once we figure out where it is, we can put it into one of our backpacks. And Danny's flashlight can lead us back out, hopefully."

"Awesome plan. Very detailed."

I scowled at Danny, because I knew (and so did my stomach) that it was a terrible plan. It had more holes than a screen door.

"Look," he said, "the way I see it, we have no idea what to expect, right? So no matter what you plan, something will probably screw it up. So I think we should just wing it."

"You're saying my plan stinks." *And he's right*, I thought miserably. But not having a plan at all made me feel like a balloon being blown up and released—I'd have zero control, and there was no telling where we'd end up.

Danny just patted me on the back. "Don't worry. I'm a great improvisor."

Great. Now I was even more anxious.

We walked toward the palace, kicking up puffs of sand that drifted and swirled silently around our feet. Nothing else stirred or made a sound. Whatever had been following us had disappeared—not that this made me any less nervous. We stopped in front of a set of massive wooden doors in the center of the wall. The planks looked old and weathered, but solid.

"Ahem! Er, pardon our intrusion, honored residents," Niko called. His voice sounded thin and small.

No answer.

"Hello?" I tried rapping with my knuckles. "Hello, um, honored residents? Is anyone home?"

"No, not like that! No one'll hear you if you do it like that. Here, watch me." Danny stepped back and shouted, "HELLOOOO! IS ANYONE HOME?" He banged on the door with his full fist. "HELLOOOO!"

"Quiet, you bumbling buffoon!" Niko scolded him. "Show some respect!"

"Seriously. Why can't you just knock like a normal human being?"

"Hey. No one answered either one of you. I don't see what's wrong with taking it up a notch. How are they gonna know we're here if we don't make some noise?"

"That's not the point," I said. "You have to be *polite.*"

"I'm sorry, but I was trying to be *friendly,*" he muttered irritably. "We're supposed to be their allies, aren't we?"

"'Allies' are not the same as 'friends.'" Kind of like us, it occurred to me. I glared at him for the entire next minute as we stood and waited for an answer.

Proving himself to be the least patient person I'd ever met, Danny eventually whispered to Niko, "What if you did your lock-whispering thing?"

Niko's eyes practically bugged right out of his head as he answered, "Have you lost your mind? If we are allies, breaking and entering would *not* be a good—"

The doors swung open slowly, and we all took a step back. Now that we *could* enter, I wasn't sure I actually *wanted* to.

We stepped through the gate into a broad courtyard. On the far side was a sprawling building. It was raised up and surrounded by a wooden walkway, and the tall, tiled roof we'd seen from outside extended over all of it. Wings and outbuildings were connected to the main building with more covered walkways; they seemed to stretch back forever. As we crossed the courtyard, I felt exposed and vulnerable, and the feeling that we were being watched returned and multiplied until every hair on the back of my neck was standing up.

Finally, we reached the bottom of the wide wooden steps leading up to the palace door.

"HELLOO—"

"Silence!" Danny was cut short by Niko. "There is no need to keep shouting your lungs out, you yodeling yahoo."

"Shhh!" I was sure I'd heard something . . . not human. Something that made my skin crawl and my insides turn to ice. "Did you hear that?"

We fell silent.

"What?" Danny whispered.

"It sounded like . . ."

There it was again—a scuttling, scrabbling, clawlike sound, the same one I'd heard in the kelp forest.

"Like a giant bug," Danny finished. I shuddered. I hadn't known how to describe it, but once Danny said it, I realized he was exactly right. But every time I squinted or turned to get a better look at whatever was making it, whatever it was moved quickly out of sight. And whatever it was didn't move like a human. Danny tried to aim the beam of his flashlight into the shadows, but of course it only shone when he turned it straight ahead, at the door of the palace. I took my backpack off and felt around for a weapon or at least another flashlight, but found only empty space.

Following the flashlight's guidance, we took off our shoes, climbed the steps, and made our way through a maze of rooms and covered walkways. The palace was completely empty and silent except for the giant buggy shadows and that creepy scuttling sound, which was now accompanied by occasional rattles and scrapes. In every room, golden sliding doors were painted with elaborate battle scenes: a battle in front of a temple along a riverbank with a torn-up bridge; another battle against a dark sky, with Raijin the thunder god banging his drum above the clashing soldiers while one general hid inside a hollow tree; an army on horseback charging down an impossibly steep hill.

"It's all war, war, war," I whispered.

"Right? It's like they're totally possessed," said Danny.

"You mean *obsessed*," I corrected him.

"'You mean *obsessed*,'" he parroted back at me. "Can't you ever just loosen up?"

"Speaking of possessed and obsessed, I think I've figured out what those noises are," Niko said in a low voice as we crossed the threshold into yet another cavernous, empty room dimly lit by bioluminescent plankton.

"What are they?"

Niko stopped walking. His ears pricked up and his nose twitched.

Doors on all four sides of the room slid open, and a wave of creatures poured through—not giant bugs, but crabs as tall as my shoulder, with shells as big as my kitchen table at home. The joints of their spindly, spidery legs moved nightmarishly up and down as they scuttled forward, and the sound of their crabby feet tapping and scraping softly on the woven straw mats made my scalp prickle. Within seconds, they had surrounded us, and they clacked their enormous front claws menacingly and stared at us with beady black eyes.

"Heike-gani," Niko whimpered.

Nobody Wants to Watch People Getting Hit on the Head

When the Luckies had said the Taira samurai were ghosts, I'd assumed they meant samurai-shaped ghosts. I'd forgotten all about the heike-gani. And also, "I always thought they were *little* crabs."

"Looks like you thought wrong," said Danny.

But they *were* little crabs, at least in the human dimension— Mom had even shown me pictures online after telling me the story one time. Anyway, whatever size they are, heike-gani are crabs inhabited by the ghosts of the Taira samurai who drowned in the Battle of Dan-no-ura. Their bitterness is so great that it's etched itself into their shells, which look like faces contorted with rage.

Niko planted himself protectively in front of me and Danny, but I could feel him shaking. Danny lifted his phone and moved it in a wide arc in front of us, the way you might swing a lit torch in front of you to keep wolves or tigers at bay.

But the light went out and my heart lurched. The clacking claws seemed to get louder, and I realized how safe that tiny circle of light had been making me feel.

"What did you do? Why did you have to swing it around like that?" I hissed.

"I was trying to scare them off! How was I supposed to know it would go out?"

"It only goes on when it's pointing to where you're supposed to go next, remember? Did you think it wanted us to charge these guys?"

"Why must the two of you always argue?" Niko's voice was a low growl. "We are under threat! Focus!"

"She started it," Danny grumbled.

I was about to remind him that *he* was the one who'd started swinging his phone around, when the plankton turned up their glow levels and a woman's voice echoed through the room.

"Who dares trespass in the hallowed palace of the most august emperor Antoku, the head of the Taira clan?" At the sound of her voice, the crabs dropped to their—well, I guess you could say their knees. Now the shells were all lined up in front of me, so that even though the samurai weren't facing us, it felt like I was being confronted by an angry mob. One of the crabs extended a claw and swept my feet out from under me; another did the same to Danny. Niko was already lying facedown on the floor.

I raised my eyes just a little bit and saw an older lady enter the room. She moved so slowly and smoothly, she looked like she was floating—come to think of it, maybe she *was* floating. She wore a flowing black kimono, and her hair was covered by a long white cloth, just like an old-fashioned nun. *She must be Lady Tokiko,* I thought—Antoku's grandmother. She'd become a nun late in her life, after her son took the throne. Lady Tokiko was now followed by five younger women in long, heavy, brightly colored robes embroidered with kelp, coral, and exotic fish. Their straight black hair streamed all the way down their backs. They walked along the wall, stopped in the center, and knelt on the floor, facing us.

"I ask you again," said Lady Tokiko. "Who are you, and what gives you the gall to think you can traipse into these sacred halls as if you own them? Why are you here? What do you seek? I should warn you that if you lie, you will be instantly beheaded."

I suddenly became very aware of how exposed my neck was, and how much I really liked the way it connected my head to the rest of me. I looked desperately at Niko.

"Your Most August Imperial Highness," Niko began, "we humbly beg your most merciful grace for our inexcusable impertinence as we—"

"Yes, yes. Get to the point," she said impatiently, evidently not the least bit concerned that she was being addressed by a fox. On the other hand, she was in command of a thousand-year-old ghost-crab army. "No, wait. Not you. I don't like the look of you. There's something shifty about your eyes. You. Boy with the shining jewel." She pointed her fan at Danny.

"Me?" he squeaked.

"Yes, of course, you. Do you actually think that I wouldn't have been notified the very moment that you and your jewel appeared at the gate?"

Danny cleared his throat. "Well, Your Most August . . . Augustness. This, er, jewel led us here from far, far away. And the gates opened on their own, so we figured we were welcome. Probably because we're *allies*." Danny hit the word hard and

126

grinned at me. I glared back. Niko covered his eyes with his paws and groaned softly.

Lady Tokiko said nothing, but one eyebrow went up.

"We have been chosen by the gods to prevent a terrible tragedy," Danny continued, gaining confidence. He swept his arms out dramatically. He was actually enjoying this! "Your mortal enemy, the Minamoto, have overrun the world. And we, your *loyal allies*"—he paused to let it sink in—"would like to stop them for you."

"Indeed."

Was she buying it? I couldn't tell. Lady Tokiko's face was an expressionless mask. *Please let her believe us,* I begged silently.

"Yes. Indeed." Danny grinned his most charming grin, the one that made so many girls (and probably some nonbinary kids and boys, to be honest) go gaga over him—the one that got him out of trouble at school, and that used to make old ladies say "What a charming young man!" and give him a piece of hard candy.

It used to work on me, too, but now I just felt annoyed. Having a person betray your friendship will do that to you.

"Well, young man, any enemy of the Minamoto is a friend of the Taira. How many of my soldiers would you like?"

"Oh! Uh . . ." He looked at me and Niko. "The thing is, the battle's probably going to be on land, so unfortunately we can't use your soldiers."

"Indeed," Lady Tokiko said again.

"Uh-huh. All we really need is Kusanagi."

Seriously!? I wanted to shout at him. *Do you not know what "subtle" means?*

"Aha!" Lady Tokiko stabbed her fan at us, and her eyes flamed. "I knew it! More usurpers of the throne!"

"But we're allies!" Danny protested.

"The Taira have no allies. It is us against the world, both dead and living. Seize them!" The angry samurai crab army leaped to its feet with a shout, and I felt myself being lifted from the ground and both of my arms being clamped from behind.

"No!" I called out. Danny had ruined our plan, so I might as well be honest and appeal to Lady Tokiko's mercy. "No, you don't understand! That's not why we want it! We don't want the throne! My mother is the kami Takiri-bime, and I just need to borrow—"

"Liar! The living never come to borrow. You only come to steal, to use Kusanagi to help you rise to power. But Kusanagi is ours, and unless you are one of us, you shall never have it. Kill them!" she screamed. "Off with their heads!"

That wasn't very nun-like behavior, if you ask me, but I was in no position to point that out to her. Danny looked at me, wild-eyed, as he struggled against his crab-captor. Niko was snarling and snapping, but in the grip of the heike-gani, he was as helpless as a toy. "Please," I called to Lady Tokiko. "Please listen to me! I just want to save my mother's life!" But my voice was drowned out by the roars of the angry ghost soldiers, and the rattle of their claws against their shells. I felt myself being dragged backward.

"Grandmama! Grandmama, what's going on? What are you doing in here with my soldiers?" A high, whiny voice pierced the chaos around me, and everyone froze. Danny, Niko, and I were pushed to the ground again, although this time, each of us had our neck in the grip of a giant crab claw.

"Oh, Antoku, darling, you're up from your nap! Grand-mama's just ordering an execution, that's all."

"Ooh! Who are you going to execute? Show me!"

The sea of crabs parted to reveal Antoku. He was dressed in a heavy scarlet kimono, and his shoulder-length hair framed an expression of shock on his face.

"But they're just children! They're not much older than me!"

"Yes, dear. But they're here to steal your throne, you see, and we mustn't allow them to—"

"Don't kill them."

Lady Tokiko looked taken aback. "But, darling—"

"This is the first time we've ever had anyone fun come down here, and I want to play with them. Make them stay and play with me."

I looked at Danny, and then at Niko. I could tell that we were thinking the same thing: being Antoku's captive playdate friends was better than being beheaded. Maybe he knew where the sword was. Maybe if we were nice to him, we could convince him to tell us.

"We know all sorts of games—new ones that you've never played before," said Niko.

"I can teach you how to play soccer. And basketball," Danny said.

"Basket balls?" Antoku looked puzzled.

"And stories! I can tell you stories you've never heard be-fore," I added.

"I like stories," he said slowly. "I am quite sick of the ones my aunties always tell. They're so boring." He glared at the ladies, who said nothing but bowed deeply. I saw a couple of them rolling their eyes, though.

"Ooh! And guess what! I have this, um, this magic . . . this magic jewel that you can see videos—I mean, you can see moving pictures on it." Danny wriggled a little bit. "I'll show you if I can just get to my pocket . . ."

"Don't say that! You don't know if it works!" I hissed at him, but he ignored me.

"There's one I downloaded the other day that's just people getting hit on the head. It's hilarious!"

I said loudly, "Nobody wants to watch people getting hit on the head. Especially not the kind and benevolent emperor."

"I *do* want to watch people get hit on the head!" said Antoku. "Show me. Guards, I command you to release the prisoners at once!" The crab behind me loosened his grip just the slightest bit. The other crabs glanced uncertainly at each other.

"But, Antoku, my sweet dumpling—"

"Release them! I am your emperor and I command you!" Antoku stamped his foot and balled his hands into fists. He did not seem like a fun kid to play with. He was probably the kind of kid where you had to pretend to lose every game you played so he wouldn't have a tantrum. Even if I hadn't been frantic to get out of there and find the sword and save Mom, I wouldn't have wanted to spend a single minute babysitting this spoiled little rug rat.

Still. It must have been hard for him, all alone down there for a thousand years with no one to play with except some ladies-in-waiting and maybe a few crab-ghost soldiers and some fish. It couldn't have been much fun. And they'd clearly poisoned him with their own bitterness and resentment. It was kind of sad, actually.

"Very well." Lady Tokiko sighed. "Guards, release the prisoners. But do not let them out of your sight!"

Within a couple of minutes, we were being marched to the front of the room so that we could properly thank Lady Tokiko before we were sent to play with Antoku. When we reached her, we got down on our knees and put our foreheads on the floor.

"Rest assured, you traitorous worms, I will have you executed the moment he tires of you," she murmured, and she smiled sweetly, showing a mouthful of blackened teeth. Mom told me once that high-class ladies of Lady Tokiko's time period used to think that was beautiful. I thought it was horrifying.

We were jerked away and shoved through so many more rooms and walkways that I felt sure that even Danny's trusty phone wouldn't be able to find a way out. Finally, we stopped and one of the crabs tapped on a door and announced, "Prisoners to entertain the emperor."

The door slid open and we stepped through. Two of the crab samurai bowed and stepped back outside, and I heard them clicking off down the walkway. The third one remained inside to guard us. Darn. Antoku sat on a cushion in the middle of the room, smiling. "Show me the magic jewel with people getting hit on the head!"

Danny dug in his pocket and brought out his phone. "Okay, so . . . it might not work," he warned Antoku, who glared first at the phone and then at Danny.

"You said I could see magic moving pictures," he said. "I want to see them."

"Ahem. Wouldn't you rather play a nice game of tag instead?" Niko said.

Antoku pouted. "That's not a new game. You said you were going to teach me new games. Anyway, I don't want to play games. I want to watch people getting hit on the head!"

"What about a story?" I jumped in. "How about 'Jack and the Beanstalk'? I bet you don't know that one."

"That sounds stupid!"

"Hey! That's rude."

"I do what I want," he said, and folded his arms. "I'm the emperor."

Ugh, this kid was just like Kiki, I thought. He thought he could treat people however he wanted and no one would complain or push back.

Then I had an idea. This was a kid who liked to make his own rules—just like Kiki. That meant—just like Kiki—he probably liked *breaking* rules, too. I lowered my voice to a whisper. "You could take us to see Kusanagi. I bet your grandmother never lets you do that." The guard shifted behind us. I could feel his beady eyes on me. I hoped crabs couldn't hear very well.

Antoku frowned. "That stupid sword. It's not even here anymore. Someone stole it ages ago, but Grandmama's so obsessed with revenge that she keeps pretending we still have it. Killing anyone who comes looking for it is the only interesting thing that ever happens around here."

What? We'd come all the way here, and it was *gone?* Despair howled into my chest like an icy wind. "Where is it? Who stole it?" I asked.

"How should I know? Anyway, I don't care about that sword. I want to see people get hit on the head in the magic jewel. Hurry up and show me!"

And now I felt a little spark of anger. Because first of all, I didn't care if Antoku was an emperor—he was a spoiled little twerp! Second, if the Taira ghosts didn't have the sword, that meant that Danny and his darn phone had led us into this mess for nothing. I felt the spark burn a little hotter.

Danny had his phone in his hand. It wasn't working. Of course. "Uh . . . how about we save it for later? Lemme show you some bangin' dance moves."

"Hit! On! The head! Hit! On! The head!" Antoku shouted. "If I don't get to see people hit on the head, I will have you killed."

That's what pushed me over the edge. No one deserved that kind of power, especially not this kid. Antoku was acting just like Kiki and her friends—and Danny and his friends. Like it was no big deal when other people got hurt. Like it was funny, even. Like no one else's feelings—or lives—mattered. I bet he would have laughed at that video of me getting splashed at the dance and turning into a rage monster.

"What if *I* hit *you* on the head?" I burst out. I had a smile on my face, but inside I was steaming mad. "I could use that cushion you're sitting on and just bop you. I could bop you and Danny both, in fact. What do you think? I bet that would be hilarious!" *Ha!*

Antoku's eyes went wide with shock—I doubted if anyone

had ever spoken to him like that, and for one sweet moment, I felt *great*—and then his whole face squinched up into a tight little knot, except for his mouth, which was open and yelling, "Guards! Guards!"

The guard in the room sprang forward. He grabbed me and Danny around the waist, and with another one of his feet he dug into the fur on Niko's back and dragged us out of the room. Danny and I thrashed and kicked while Niko snapped his jaws at the crab's remaining legs. We'd been helpless against the crabs before, but it was three against one now, and I could tell that he was having trouble hanging on to us. Once we'd cleared the doorway, the crab was forced to drop us, and we ran.

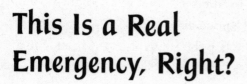

This Is a Real Emergency, Right?

The sounds of shouted orders and rattling swords seemed to come from every direction. We reached an intersection, and Niko, who was in front, turned left. I went skidding after him. But Danny's sash had come loose, and his now floor-length tunic got caught under his feet, and he went sprawling to the floor.

The heike-gani guard leaped over our heads and landed directly in front of us. I flinched away as he reached out and snapped one of his claws, missing me by inches. By that time, Danny had gathered up his tunic, and we spun around and ran the other way.

We'd almost made it to the end of the corridor when the floor dropped out from under us. We went screaming down a steep and slippery slide and landed in a heap at the bottom as the trapdoor swung back up and shut with a *clack*, leaving us in total darkness.

"That crafty crustacean," wailed Niko. "Now we're dead for sure."

"Ugh, I *hate* this outfit!" I heard Danny struggling to take off the layers of silk. "I don't know why you thought it would be a good idea to wear this thing."

"Oh, right, because it was the *outfits* that got us in trouble," I muttered as I worked off my own. (It *was* cumbersome, though I definitely wasn't going to admit it.) "Not you straight-up announcing that we wanted Kusanagi."

"Or you threatening to bop the emperor on the head with a pillow," countered Danny.

Tsk. He wasn't wrong.

"Shhh!" said Niko.

From the sound of it, a platoon of heike-gani was rushing down the hallway right toward us. The wooden planks above us began to shake with the force of all those feet.

"General!" It was our guard, still standing above us. "Sir! Over here!"

"We're doomed," Niko moaned.

"I saw them go that way! They're headed toward the south wing!" The soldiers thundered past.

"Wait, did he just—"

"Shhh!" Niko said again.

We stayed quiet for what felt like forever. The only sound was the *taka-taka-taka* of the guard's feet as he paced back and forth above us. I felt around in my backpack—nothing. Danny did the same—nothing. Niko took the opportunity to slink and sniff his way around the room.

"I can detect no exit except through the way we came."

"Try your flashlight," I whispered to Danny.

"It won't turn on," he said.

"It has to! Try again."

"You think I haven't? I've tried, like, a hundred times already, and I'm telling you, it is not turning on."

"You can't possibly have tried a hundred times."

"We really *are* doomed," Niko groaned. "And since that is the case, will you two please stop your incessant squabbling so that I can pass away in peace?"

I rolled my eyes, not that anyone could see it in the dark. But I was quiet again—which was when I realized that I *liked* arguing with Danny. It kept my mind off how scared I was.

"Maybe our guard guy is protecting us," said Danny, and suddenly—just like that—I felt a flicker of hope.

"Unless he's putting us aside to eat us later," Niko observed.

"He would do that?" The flicker of hope went out.

"He might. They're a bloodthirsty bunch."

"Hey!" I sat up. "What about your wishing jewel? We're trapped in a cellar and you're telling us we're about to be crab food—that's a real emergency, right?"

"What?"

"The wishing jewel. You said you'd only use it in a real emergency. Which is now."

"Oh. Yes, quite," he said. His voice sounded oddly nervous. "The wishing jewel. Indeed." Then he took a long pause, cleared his throat, and said hesitantly, "Ah. Ahem. So about that . . . you see, the thing is . . ."

"You don't have one, do you," I said, my heart turning cold as I realized why he was acting so weird.

"Err . . . no." Niko cleared his throat again. "Not exactly."

"Not *exactly*?" said Danny. "What does that even mean?"

"It means no," said Niko in a small voice.

"I *knew* it! I knew something was off before, when you wouldn't use it. I knew you were lying!" Danny said what I was thinking, and he sounded as disappointed and as angry as I felt.

Niko said nothing, and I couldn't help feeling bad for him. It wasn't like he'd hurt anyone by lying, and you could tell he felt terrible about it.

"Not that it makes any difference now, but why did you lie to us?" I asked.

"I wasn't lying, exactly. I mean, I do have a wishing jewel—it's still mine. I just . . . I lost it. It was an accident."

"The same accident where you lost your magic?"

"It wasn't my fault, but I feel like a failure every time I think about it." He sighed miserably. "I suppose I didn't want you to lose faith in me. So I lied." A noise that sounded like a combination of a moan and a whine escaped his mouth. "I'm sorry. I really, truly am. Please, can we not talk about it anymore?"

I heard Danny sigh. "You better not lie to us anymore," he said sternly.

"No, no! Never! The truth, the whole truth, and nothing but the truth henceforward. My mission, my dearest desire, is to help you defeat the oni, Momo. Please believe me. I've sworn it to your mother, and I swear it to you. I will protect you with my life."

At that moment, the trapdoor opened above us, and a shaft of watery blue light slid around the silhouette of the guard. The ramp lowered; the crab slid slowly down to the end and jumped off just as it bumped to the ground, which caused it to rise back up again. As the light from above faded, another light flickered to life. It was coming from Danny's phone. In its glow, shadows danced across the crab's ghoulish, craggy face. I wondered if the phone wanted us to become dinner. The crab lumbered across the room and loomed over us. It stared at me with its beady black eyes. I shrank back. Niko, true to his word, moved in front of me.

"If you want to eat her, you'll have to go through me," he said fiercely, and even though the crab could easily have crunched him down in a few seconds, I appreciated the sentiment.

But the crab paid him no attention. "Daughter of Takiri-bime," it said to me, "I'm honored to meet you. I apologize for scaring you earlier, but speed was of the essence." His voice sounded like a pair of chopsticks tapping against each other. "I had to get you to go in the right direction."

I stared at him. "Do you know me?"

"You tried to tell the queen lady about your mom in the great hall, remember?" said Danny.

Oh, right. "Yeah, but—"

"My name is Takamori. Years ago, I was caught by a fishing boat when I was out patrolling our perimeter. I managed to escape but was injured and thrown by the current onto the shores of the Island of Mysteries. Your father rescued me, and your mother healed me." He turned to the side, and I saw now that one of his legs was missing and his shell looked like it had been cracked in half and glued back together.

"You—you're *that* crab?"

"And now I have the opportunity to repay my debt. If you will please do as I say, I will help you escape and find what you seek."

Takamori went to the wall, raised his claws, and muttered something under his breath. He tapped three times, two times, four times, and a chunk of the wall swung open to reveal a long, dark corridor.

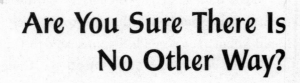

Are You Sure There Is No Other Way?

"No escape route, huh?" Danny said, but Niko looked away and pretended not to hear.

"You know where Kusanagi is?" I asked.

Instead of answering, Takamori swept a claw toward the tunnel and said, "Quickly. I will enter last so that I may shut the door behind us."

"So you can eat us in private?" Danny muttered.

"So we will have another wall between us and my fellow soldiers. And since you are carrying a lantern, perhaps you can lead the group."

Danny peered into the tunnel. "There are human bones in here," he said, recoiling. I peeked around him. A skull grinned at me on the ground a few feet in.

"I owe a debt to this girl's mother. I vow on my duty and my honor as a Taira samurai that I will not harm you," said Takamori. "But my friends up above have no such debt and will not hesitate to tear your limbs off and pass them around like rice crackers. If you would prefer to stay behind and take your chances, I will not stop you. But if you value your life, I suggest you hurry."

"C'mon, Danny, what happened to your sense of adventure?" I prodded. I hoped that made me sound brave instead of terrified. I was just glad *I* didn't have to go first.

"I will lead with you," Niko offered, which made me feel both guilty about not offering and worried that Danny would think I was a hypocritical coward. Which I was, I guess. I trusted Takamori, but I wasn't exactly excited about walking into a pitch-black tunnel full of human bones, either.

"I'm fine," Danny said irritably. "I don't need help. I'm not a baby." He took a deep breath and plunged ahead—with Niko by his side.

"Fine." I went in and tried not to look too closely at whatever it was that rolled into the shadows when I accidentally kicked it with my foot.

The glow of the flashlight seemed to intensify as the door shut behind me and the darkness grew darker.

"So, uh. You said something about helping us find what we seek?" I said, to keep my mind off what I couldn't see.

"You seek Kusanagi, do you not?"

"Do you know where it is?" Danny asked.

"I know who took it."

I waited a few seconds for him to tell us more, but he was silent. Finally, I asked, "So who took it?"

"Before I tell you, are you sure there is no other way to save your mother's life? Are you sure that finding Kusanagi is the only way?"

"Daikoku told us to find Kusanagi, so I'm guessing it's the only way."

"Ah." The crab clicked his claws thoughtfully behind me,

and a little shiver zipped down my spine. "Well, if Daikoku sees fit to send you looking for it, then I suppose that is what you must do."

"Yes, I suppose it is." I was beginning to get the sense that Takamori really didn't want to help us find Kusanagi.

Danny spoke up. "No offense, Takamori, but can we skip to the part where you tell us who has Kusanagi?"

"Very well." He heaved a gurgly, bubbly sigh. "Several centuries ago, Lord Susano'o stormed the palace and demanded the return of his sword. It was his originally, so he had a right to it, and Lady Tokiko had no choice but to hand it over."

That didn't seem good.

"So we just have to find Susano'o and get him to give us the sword," said Danny. "Are you going to take us to him?"

"I am bound to the seas that once belonged to the Taira, so I cannot accompany you. It will be just you two human children with your soft exposed skin, and your furry friend here."

"I am much more than a furry friend," protested Niko. "I am a guide! I am . . . I am a mentor! I have magic!"

"Ah. Have you, now." Takamori made a clicking noise that sounded a lot like doubt to me. "In any case, I cannot take you beyond our borders. But I am taking you where you'll find someone who can."

"Who?"

"Taxi."

"What?"

"You'll see."

Finally, we reached the end of the tunnel. Takamori moved ahead of us and tapped on the wall, which slid open to reveal a narrow ledge that dropped off into water so deep, I couldn't see the bottom. With a bow and a sweep of his claws, he ushered us onto the ledge.

"I have fulfilled my duty. It has been my pleasure to serve the daughter of Takiri-bime." Before we could reply, he bowed again and backed into the tunnel as the wall closed over him.

I looked around. The ledge stretched to the left and to the right, like a border between the trench in front of us and the huge coral reef that rose up behind us. I wondered what would happen if we stepped off—would we fall, or would we float?

"Now what?" I asked.

Danny moved the flashlight until its beam lit up the ledge to the right. "That way."

Whooo Are Youuu?

A few minutes later, the ledge widened in both directions and my mouth dropped open. We were standing at the edge of a broad, flat area bustling with sea creatures. When I say sea creatures, I don't mean just fish. There *were* actual fish, but there were also sea dragons, a shark-headed warrior-looking guy with a human body, and a brown-skinned mermaid dragging a suitcase behind her. A group of white people in fancy old-fashioned dresses and tuxedos laughed loudly together. "Ghosts from the *Titanic,* I think," Niko whispered to me when he noticed me staring at them.

"Attention, passengers." A woman's melodious voice floated through the water. "Welcome to the Western Pacific Transportation Terminal. Passengers for all Pacific routes, please go to Terminal A. Passengers for Atlantic routes, please proceed to the lower level for sub-sea passage access. Passengers wishing to travel to impossible locations, please form an orderly line at the taxi stand. Thank you for your cooperation and have an excellent voyage."

Niko left us for a moment to talk to someone behind a window. "Just sending a message to the Luckies to update them," he said when he got back. Then he led us to the taxi stand, which consisted of two lines. One was a line of sea turtles the size of cars. They were queued up along the edge of the station, just over the drop-off into the trench, and they wore caps that reminded me of police hats—stiff and black, flat on top, with a short, round brim on the front. The second line had all kinds of creatures in it, including a kimono-clad man with a squid for a head; a giant shrimp with a golden belly and a face like a cat's; and a seal with beautiful black eyes. ("That looks like a selkie!" said Danny. "I've seen pictures in my parents' Irish folklore books.")

We got in line behind the funniest-looking creature I'd ever seen. It had a beak like a bird, and big starry eyes. A pair of little blue fins stuck out the sides of its head like ears, and long hair flowed down its scaly body to three big fins at the bottom. It didn't seem quite solid—you could kind of see through it in the same way that you can kind of see through Jell-O—and its outlines shimmered and blurred a little. It eyed us with mild curiosity. "Hellooo," it said in a voice that seemed to come from far away, like an echo. "Youuu'd better hurrry. The worllld drawwws ever closerrr to a diverrrgence poinnnt."

"What? I mean, I beg your pardon?" I asked.

"Hmmmm?" it said.

"What did you just say about a divergence?"

"Twooo paaathsss. Twooo directionnnsss. Lefffft, riiight. Goood, baaad. Liiife, deaaathhh."

"Oh. Um." I glanced nervously at Danny and Niko. "You weren't talking about us specifically, were you? Or . . ."

"Oh, graaacious meee, child, I haven't the foggiessst. I

sssimply sssayyy whatever comesss to minnnd." It peered at me and said "Hmmm" again. And then, "You mustnnn't trust evvverything you seee."

Well, that was confusing. And a little troubling.

The creature swiveled around to look at Danny. "Ahhhh," it said, and sighed. "Yourrr path is clearrr. You will finnnd what you seeek. You will nottt finnnd what you seeek." It turned away from us and gazed at the line of taxi turtles in their little black hats, humming softly to itself.

"Hey! Excuse me, what does that even mean?" Danny said.

"Hmmm?" it said again. It looked slightly surprised to see us. "Helloooo. Do I knowww youuu?"

"Um, sir—er, ma'am?" I started.

"Ma'ammm."

She was already staring at Niko, so I spoke extra loudly to get her attention. "Could you please tell us what you—"

"Hellooo, foxxx." Too late. Niko jumped and accidentally knocked into a disgruntled-looking creature that reminded me of an alligator.

"Oh, sorry, sorry! Oh, dear me, I beg your pardon," Niko babbled. The alligator harrumphed and glowered at him, but that was it, thank goodness.

"Youuu will not finnnd what you seeek withouuut grrreat sacrrrificcce."

Niko looked around and said, "You mean that guy, right?" He pointed at the alligator.

"III meeeaan youuu." She waggled her ear-fins at him.

"EXCUSE ME!" I shouted.

She drew back and looked at me. Now that she was paying

attention, her eyes kind of freaked me out. They seemed to look straight through me.

"Uh, m-m-ma'am?" I stammered. "I was wondering . . . Could you please tell us what you meant by 'divergence'? And more about what we're seeking?"

"Is it a sword, by any chance?" Danny added.

"What you seeeek . . . ," she murmured. She cocked her head and lowered it, and I stared into her eyes, almost spellbound. It was like looking through a telescope into space. "I see betray-alll," she whispered in my ear. "Despairrr. If you want to suc-ceeed, you mussst . . . givvve uuup. . . ."

I backed away in terror. "Stop! Stop, that's enough, thanks!"

"What? I couldn't hear her. What did she say?" Danny asked.

The creature raised herself back up and shook her head and looked at the three of us as if she hadn't expected to see us in front of her. "Hellooo. Whooo are youuu?"

"Next!" We'd reached the front of the line. The creature smiled at us, then turned and climbed onto the back of the waiting turtle-taxi. They glided off, leaving a dim trail of light behind them.

"What *was* that?" Danny said.

"That was Amabie," said Niko. He pronounced it *ama-bee-eh*. "She and her kin, the amabiko, predict the future of whatever they look at. Though mostly they come out of the sea, look at the land, and predict harvests and plagues and things like that."

"Are they, um, accurate?" I didn't really want to know the answer, to be honest. But I had to ask.

"They are nearly always correct."

"Well, she pretty much covered all the bases when she said I'd find what I seek and not find what I seek. It's kinda hard to get a prediction like that wrong. I say she's a fake," said Danny.

"Yeah, you're probably right," I said. It was easier than believing what she'd said.

Niko shook his head. "Amabiko are nearly always correct."

"But she made no sense!" Danny protested. "Right, Momo? What else did she tell you, anyway? More mixed-up stuff, probably."

"Uh." The prophecy rang in my head: *Betrayal. Despair. If you want to succeed, you must give up.* I looked at Danny. *What if . . . ?* I swallowed. "Yeah. Just nonsense."

"Do not be so quick to dismiss Amabie's divinations, my scurrilous skeptic. Just because you don't understand her doesn't mean her words don't have value."

"Whatever," I said with more courage than I felt. "I say Danny's right. Even if she's not betraying us or, like, deliberately faking, she made no sense. We know it's going to be dangerous. We just have to be careful, that's all."

Danny nodded in agreement. But despite my own advice, I couldn't stop thinking about her final prophecy. *Betrayal. Despair. If you want to succeed, you must give up.* Who was going to betray me? What was I going to have to give up in order to protect Mom? What if giving up meant that I had to give up saving her in order to defeat the oni? That thought made my stomach twist into a scared, homesick knot.

Don't let fear steer the boat, Bishamon had said. But it was hard to follow that advice when everything was so scary.

. . . Skyscrapers?

A sea turtle pulled up in front of us. "Fare!" said the octopus dispatcher.

"In your backpacks!" Niko said. The backpacks came through ("Finally!" muttered Danny) and produced two sand dollars and a Spanish doubloon, which we handed to the octopus.

"Destination?" the turtle asked once we'd boarded.

"Ne-no-kuni, please," I said.

The turtle blinked. "The Land of Roots? Susano'o's domain? You're sure that's where you want to go?"

"We don't want to go there, but yes, that is where we're headed," said Niko.

We passed silvery tuna and giant sunfish. A squid the size of a jumbo jet streamed by like a rocket ship with tails, and we even hitched a ride in the wake of a sperm whale whose song wasn't anything like the eerie, lonely *ooohhh* we'd heard before, but a bunch of deafening clicks.

But for long stretches of time, there was nothing but the darkness of the ocean, and eventually Danny and Niko dozed off. Not me, though. It was like my mind, which had been super busy either absorbing new information or helping me to survive, had decided to take advantage of the peace and quiet to worry about all the things that could go wrong and all the reasons why I would fail.

What I had to do felt so huge—it felt big enough to fill my infinite backpack. We'd already failed twice to get what we needed to fight the oni. What if we failed again? What if Susano'o didn't have the sword, or what if he didn't recognize me and refused to hand it over? What if he *did* recognize me and refused to hand it over? What if we didn't even make it out of his fortress alive, like Mom said? Even if we did, how was I ever going to defeat two hundred oni from the land of the dead?

Bishamon, Daikoku, and Hotei seemed to think we had a chance, but what were our chances, really? One in a million? I thought of something I'd learned in math: one million pennies stacked up is as tall as four Empire State Buildings. It weighs as much as a hippopotamus. I was one tiny little penny against an entire hippo. Against four skyscrapers. It wasn't fair that I had to do this. All I'd ever wanted was a mother who would take care of me. And friends. Not to feel so alone all the time. Instead, I got to save the world.

Suddenly I felt exhausted. I closed my eyes and thought miserably of Mom. She'd tried to warn me, but I hadn't listened. Why hadn't I listened to her? My need to save her had taken over, like it always did. And now her life depended on me. The whole world was depending on me. And I would most likely fail. For a brief moment, I was furious at her for being so weak—and then I felt awful, as usual. It wasn't her fault. I imagined her lying sick and alone in bed and tried not to cry.

I rubbed the tears from my eyes, then stared in shock. I

was with her, in her room! No, wait. Not her room. At the very tippy-top of the Empire State Building. Murderous demons danced around us in a circle as lightning tore through the night sky. The demons were joined by a giant with wild, storm-whipped hair and a cruel smile; he was riding a stampeding hippopotamus, and he held a gleaming sword made of pennies. Susano'o—I knew it was him, somehow—swung the sword in a wide arc, and the pennies scattered and transformed into an ocean wave that swept me over the edge of the building. He laughed as I fell screaming toward the sidewalk far below. *I'm dreaming,* I thought frantically. *This is a dream. I have to wake up.*

But just before I hit the pavement, something dark and cold broke through and cushioned my fall. It swept me up toward the sky. *Shuten-dōji,* I thought. I strained to see Mom, but it was now too dark to see anything—even the lightning had been blotted out. I could still imagine that giant head, though. I could practically feel those yellow lantern eyes turning their gaze on me. I heard him inhale and blow a stream of air at me, like he was blowing out a candle. But I didn't disappear. Instead, I was enveloped by a cold mist—it burned my skin; it buzzed in my ears and stung my eyes; when I inhaled, it filled my lungs and choked me. I felt like it was alive—like it saw me. It knew my thoughts and feelings—everything I loved, hated, wanted, and feared. It knew where I was going and what I intended to do. It was . . . expecting me. And then it was gone and I was falling again. I woke up with a start to find myself safely on the turtle's back, with Danny and Niko still snoozing away next to me.

It was a dream. It was just a dream. I was pretty sure that even in the spirit dimension, Susano'o would not ride a hippopotamus to the top of the Empire State Building. That part had been all me—all in my head. Of course it was a dream.

That sense of being infiltrated and observed by something horrible and evil was harder to explain and harder to shake off. But Shuten-dōji was still stuck in Yomi, and I was here. It couldn't have been real. And anyway, what could I do about it if it was? Nothing. Just wait and worry.

I had no idea how much time had passed when the turtle finally spoke. "Passengers, we're approaching the Pacific Portal. Please buckle your barnacles. That is to say, grab the edges of my shell and hang on tight. That's a little joke, by the way. Haha. Because barnacles always hang on tight."

"Haha," I said politely.

"Nice one," Danny agreed.

An undersea canyon loomed ahead of us, and a few feet in, I could see a silvery circle of bubbles. "Is that it?"

"That's it. Are you ready? Are you hanging on tight?"

Thank goodness I was, because he didn't wait for me to answer and dove right through the circle. When I opened my eyes, we had washed ashore on a broad, sandy beach that stretched lazily along the water.

The sky was pale blue, and the light was the warm gold of late afternoon. The air was crisp—cold, even. I looked around to get my bearings. Beyond the sand was a walking path and a low line of trees, and beyond the trees, far off to the left, were . . . skyscrapers?

"Where are we?"

"Chicago. North Avenue Beach, to be precise. Please disembark. That is to say, please get off my back."

Danny looked at me and Niko in bewilderment as we slid off onto the sand. "What? Why Chicago?"

I shook my head. "I'm just as confused as you."

The turtle explained. "The only way to get to the Land of Roots is to pass through a portal here in Chicago. I have brought you as close as I could." He began slowly turning himself around.

"But I thought Susano'o was the god of the sea. Chicago is in the middle of the continent."

"Susano'o does not enjoy the company of his family. That is to say, Amaterasu, Great Goddess of the Sun and Queen of the Sky Kingdom, and Tsukiyomi, Prince of the Moon, and their father, Izanagi the Creator. So he has buried his fortress underground and closed all the portals except this one, which is located in a city full of humans. The celestial kami do not like to mingle with humanity, so they stay away."

I remembered then that Susano'o's family had kicked him out of the Sky Kingdom for being a rude, inconsiderate, brawling oaf—but eventually he'd decided he liked it down here, after all.

"But why Chicago?" Danny wanted to know. "Why not New York, or Tokyo?"

"He likes Chicago. That is to say, he's like Chicago. That is to say, it has a bit of an inferiority complex, and it brags and blusters to make up for it." Which I guess was as good an answer as any.

"Why doesn't Susano'o's family like humans? What's wrong with us?" I asked.

"It's not that they dislike humans on principle," said the turtle as he shuffled back into the waves. "They just don't like being around you. Humans die. The three celestial kami revile death. That is to say, they cannot stand the smell, and humans reek of it. No offense, of course."

"None taken . . . I guess?" I resisted the urge to sniff my armpits.

The turtle was fully in the water now; the waves washed around him and over his shell as he floated into the surf. Then only his head and neck bobbed above the surface. "Farewell, children. That is to say, good luck," he said, and ducked his head and submerged with a tiny *plip*.

We stood for a moment, shivering and watching the spot where he'd disappeared. "What does death smell like, anyway?" I wondered out loud.

"You've smelled it. Remember the shikome?"

"Oh." I shuddered. Heavy and sludgy and slimy, but also hollow and empty. Orangish-brownish-purplish black, bitter and sour and a tiny bit sweet. Like rotting meat. Like rotting leaves. Like sadness and loneliness.

"That's how we smell?" Danny wrinkled his nose. "Really?"

Niko shrugged. "Not nearly as much as a shikome. One gets used to it."

"Speaking of death," I said, "we should get going. How many days do we have left?"

Danny checked his phone. "What? No." He shook it and looked at it again. "No! That can't be. We couldn't have spent two whole days down there!"

But apparently we had. On the screen there were three tiny suns. I couldn't help thinking of what Hotei would say: *What is time, anyway?*

Three days. Three days until Mom died. Three days until the evil I'd felt in my dream broke loose and began destroying the world. Whatever time was, we didn't have much of it left.

I could feel a stomachache coming on. But I said bravely, "I guess we'll just have to hurry." I had to be brave, even if my stomach couldn't—and it seemed to work. But then I remembered something. "We forgot to ask where the fortress is." I turned to Niko. "Do you know where it is?"

He shook his head. My stomach gave a twinge. *See?* it seemed to say. *I told you this was bad.*

"No problem. We've still got this!" Danny pulled out his phone.

It was close to sunset, but still too bright for a flashlight to be useful. "How's it going to work?" I asked.

"I dunno. Let's just see if it does. Why do you have to be such a downer all the time?" Danny pressed the power button and turned in a slow circle, pointing the flashlight at the ground. About halfway around, a little red dot danced on the sand.

"Ha!" Danny gloated. "It's a laser pointer! Hey, Niko, chase the dot!" He jiggled the laser dot around and grinned at Niko, who pounced on it, and then stopped himself and gave Danny a furious look.

"I will not be toyed with," he said coldly. "If you do that again, I will send you right home."

"It was just a joke," Danny complained.

"But I am *not* joking."

"Okay, okay. Sor-ry."

"Why do kids like you have to be so mean to everyone all the time?" I asked, annoyed. We followed the red dot toward the jogging path.

"What's that supposed to mean—'kids like me'? I'm not mean. I was just messing around."

"You know. Popular kids. You and your friends. Like Kiki. She's super mean, and she always says the same thing you just said: 'Oh, I was just messing around.'"

"Ha." Danny laughed one short laugh. "I admit Kiki's a you-know-what. But mostly we really are just messing around. You get used to it, I guess. You know people are joking, so you don't get all sensitive and hurt about things."

I didn't buy it. "That sounds fake. Hurting someone's feelings and calling it a joke is just weaseling your way out of an apology—it's a mean kid's way of not having to feel bad about being mean."

"Okay, sure, whatever." Danny shrugged and kept walking.

We'd reached the jogging path; Danny moved the laser pointer around a bit, and it pointed us south, toward the sky-scrapers. As we turned, he said quietly, "Hey, Niko, I'm sorry I teased you with the laser pointer. I won't do it again, okay? And not just because you said you'd send me home if I did. I . . . don't want to hurt your feelings."

I stared at him in surprise. That had been a real apology. Popular kids didn't apologize for real.

Niko kept trotting and looking straight ahead. But he mumbled, "Apology accepted."

Danny looked relieved.

"Though I reserve the right to send you home anytime I wish," Niko added.

"Aw, don't send me home. We're such a good team! Come on, you know you need me." He grinned, back to his cocky, confident, popular-boy self.

Niko rolled his eyes and said nothing, but Danny didn't seem to mind.

"Hey, I have a question," I said.

"What, like why am I so awesome?"

I groaned. Just when I'd started to think he might not be the worst. "How do you handle being around kids like Kiki and Ryleigh and Brad? How can any of you stand each other if you're mean to each other all the time?"

"I told you. It's not like that. You just accept that people are joking, and you move on."

"You mean you pretend it's okay with you, even when it's not?"

He shrugged. "I mean, it's kind of a game you have to play sometimes if you want to be part of a group. Which I do. You know, fake it till you make it."

"That's not a game I know how to play."

"I'm not saying you have to play. I'm just saying that's how it is if you want to fit in. My dad says if you want to be a winner, you can't sit around whining about how things are unfair. You have to adapt. You have to accept group norms. That's what he called it."

"Oh, so like peer pressure? Like if they all wanted to play tag on the freeway, you would, too? Because of the *group norms?*"

Danny rolled his eyes. "No, of course not. He meant, like, learning to take a joke. Or, like, having the same interests."

"So your dad . . . made you change your interests?"

Danny looked uneasy. "He taught me how to get along with people."

"What do you mean, 'get along with people'? What people?"

"You know what I mean. People."

"*Which* people?"

"Ugh. *Cool* people, okay? I mean cool people."

Cool people? More like mean people. People who acted like they were better than everyone else, who were only cool for reasons I couldn't figure out.

No, that wasn't true—I knew what they had in common. Nice clothes, athletic ability, pretty faces. What else? The newest phones. An air of confidence, like they expected to get what they wanted. And it was weird, but even though half the kids at Oak Valley were Asian, most of the popular kids were white. I was sure that everyone would say that it had nothing to do with race, but . . .

What was it that Danny's mom always used to say? "We don't see race. It's simply not an issue in our family. To us, Danny's not an Asian kid or a Japanese kid—he's just our son." Which meant . . . what *did* it mean, exactly? Could Danny have stopped being friends with me because I reminded him—and other kids— that he was Japanese? If race wasn't "an issue," did that mean he'd left me behind because of my personality? That was almost worse. Or was he really shallow enough to ditch me because of my clothes and klutziness, and because I wasn't as pretty as Ryleigh or Kiki (whatever *that* meant)? Or was it all of those things?

He would never admit to any of it. He'd tell me I was making things up and overreacting. So I just said, "I can't believe the Luckies think you're supposed to be on this thing with me."

"Maybe I'm here to help you learn how to have friends," he replied.

"Not if they're friends like yours."

"What are you talking about? Everyone wants to be friends with us." Danny now seemed genuinely confused.

"Not me." Though if I was being totally honest, that was a lie. Because okay, sure. Kiki, Ryleigh, Brad—their whole crew—were despicable. I would never forget how they set me up at the dance. I would never forgive whoever posted that video. But at the same time, I *did* want to be friends with them. Or I wanted them to like me, anyway. Why? I kind of hated myself for it.

"You don't even want to be friends with *me*?" It was like he was reading my mind.

Of course I want to be friends with you, I wanted to say. I knew from when we were little that Danny understood how to be a good friend. I liked that Danny a lot. I missed him so much it hurt, and I would have given anything to have him back.

But I knew that *this* Danny didn't really want to be friends with me—not if it meant giving up being part of the popular crowd. Maybe he'd apologized to Niko, but he still couldn't be trusted.

So I said, "Nope."

Danny staggered backward and clutched his heart, laughing—back to his good-natured self. "Oof."

"Sorry," I said, and smiled, playing along. I'll admit, I was tempted to believe that he really was low-key asking to be friends again. But he'd already thrown away our friendship once, and I wasn't about to make the same mistake twice.

Roasted, Toasted,
Fried, or Raw

As we trudged along the path and the sun sank behind the city, we passed a couple of white wooden buildings that looked like they were snack bars during the summer, but that had been boarded up for the fall and winter.

"I'm starving," Danny said.

"I could use a sustaining snack," agreed Niko.

"Me too," I realized. "I guess technically it's been three days since we ate."

Danny and I opened our backpacks. Mine was as empty as my stomach. Danny's must have been, too, because he looked up and frowned. "What's the point of having these things if they don't have snacks when we want them?"

"What about that food cart over there?" I pointed at a little cart ahead of us. "The backpacks gave us money for the taxi. Maybe they'll help us buy something to eat."

The cart stood by itself, a sad, lonely reminder of summer in the autumn twilight. The vendor was a short guy with bowed, skinny legs. He wore a funny straw boater hat and sunglasses, and he had one of those white face masks over his nose and mouth. Pinned to his shirt was a little tag that read KAPTAIN

ALFREDO PICKLEBARREL. The menu on the side of the cart promised made-to-order churros and fried pickle chips.

"Scrumdillyicious snackies today!" The vendor's eyes shone as he called out to us. There was hardly anyone around, and he was clearly glad to have customers. "What a nice little doggie. If you buy a snack, Uncle Kappy will give you a doggie treat for free!" He leaned over, patted Niko on the head with a heavily bandaged hand, and winked at him. Niko looked furious, but he didn't say anything.

"We'll have three churros, please." I was already reaching into my backpack. There was something off about this guy, and I wanted to pay up, get our food, and leave as quickly as possible. But the backpack was empty. I looked at Danny, worried.

"Ooh, bad luck, kiddy-iddy-ola. We're fresh out of churros. Just sold my last one to that guy over there." Uncle Kappy waved toward a man walking away from us in the distance.

"What happened to your hand?" Danny asked.

"When you work with burning-hot oil, sometimes you get splish-splashed," Uncle Kappy replied, and he showed us his other hand, which was also bandaged. "Ouch-a-million, am I right?" He cackled to himself. "But what say I serve you some fried sardines and pickle chips? Dilly-dally-delicious!"

"I'm sure they're great, but I think we'll pass, this time," I said quickly. "Anyway, I'm afraid we don't have any money." I was almost glad we were broke. I was getting more freaked out with every second that passed.

"Yeah, thanks anyway," added Danny. We turned to go.

"No! No, wait! Come back, you nibbly, noshy nom-noms! I mean, you chunky, chewy children—I mean . . ."

We were walking away as fast as we could now. "Can we call the police on your phone?" I asked.

Danny started tapping desperately. "It's not going through."

"I *told* you to come back. I'm so sick of silty, salty sardines." Uncle Kappy's nasal voice was right behind us—how had he caught up so quickly? His bandanna had come loose, and I caught a glimpse of a mouth full of sharp, pointy teeth. Terror shot through me. I flinched away and started to run.

But he was too fast. Before I'd taken two steps, he shot out a skinny arm and grabbed my wrist with one of his bandaged hands. He began waddling down the beach toward the water, jerking me behind him and singing cheerfully:

Munchy melty marrow meat,
Oh, it is so good to eat
With a spoon or with a straw,
Roasted, toasted, fried, or raw!

Marrow meat . . . as in bone marrow? I fought as hard as I could, but he was incredibly strong. He dragged me along the sand beside him as easily as if I'd been a bag of groceries.

"Leave her alone!" Danny caught Uncle Kappy and me in a flying tackle. Uncle Kappy didn't fall, but he did stumble and loosen his grip, and I managed to wrench myself free and scramble away.

"Nyarrghh! Dirty, delusional little human!" Uncle Kappy's voice came out in a snarl. "Think you can take me, you piddle-paddle pip-squeak? Think again!"

Danny and Uncle Kappy were circling each other like wrestlers, crouched and ready to spring. The old man's hat was knocked a little askew, and his pants were falling down. When he edged around so his back was turned to me, I understood just how bad things were. Peeking out between his shirt and his sagging waistband was a strip of greenish skin and the bottom edge of a turtle shell. It confirmed what I had begun to suspect.

Danny was about to try to fight a kappa—the water yōkai that Mom used to warn me about. They seem harmless because they're so short and stubby, but they're freakishly strong, and one of their favorite things to eat is—you guessed it—human bone marrow. If Mom's stories were accurate, Uncle Kappy was planning to drag Danny underwater until he drowned, and then gnaw off his limbs, break his bones, and suck out the marrow. Why hadn't I figured this out earlier? He had barely even tried to disguise himself. I mean, *Uncle Kappy?* Come on.

"Danny, get out of there!" I shouted. "I'm free! Let's go!" But Danny paid no attention to me. He was totally focused on the kappa.

I tried again. "Danny! You won't win! He's a kappa! He's stronger than you!"

Danny's eyes flicked toward me, and in that moment, Uncle Kappy lunged and grabbed him around the waist like a little kid, and started waddling off toward the water again, cackling.

I froze. What had I done? I looked around the beach, in case a pack of MMA fighters happened to be out for an evening jog. But the beach was empty.

Niko ran down the beach and snapped at Uncle Kappy's ankles, trying to get a bite in, but Uncle Kappy gave him a good kick, and Niko tumbled across the sand with a yelp.

"Help! Help me!" Danny cried. Kicking Niko had thrown

Uncle Kappy off balance, and he was steadying himself, holding Danny firmly with one strong arm and straightening his hat with the other.

But I was still frozen with fear and indecision. How was I supposed to take out a kappa, who according to Mom was as strong as three grown men? What if I failed and Danny died? What if Uncle Kappy got me and Danny both?

"Go for the knees! Grab him around the knees!" It was Niko, who'd gotten up and was standing by my side. "I'll try for his ankle again. Ready? One, two, *three!*"

Somehow, that helped snap me out of it—the countdown, and knowing Niko was right with me. I took a running dive at Uncle Kappy's knees and wrapped my arms around them as tightly as I could. I felt wiry muscles, knobby knee bones, and cold, slimy skin against my arms as the kappa toppled over with a scream.

I scrambled up and went to help Danny squirm out from underneath Uncle Kappy, but I shouldn't have worried. Danny flipped him onto his back with ease, and stood up.

"Come on, let's get out of here!" I was practically panting with fear. All I wanted was to get as far away from Uncle Kappy as possible.

But Danny grinned at me. "Remember what your mom told us about kappa?"

The memory came flooding back. Danny and I were four years old—we'd just met each other in preschool that year, and we were having our first playdate. We were standing with Mom on a footbridge that spanned a little creek in the woods, looking at a kappa.

"I see it! I see it!" Danny was wild with excitement.

"See that little bowl at the top of its skull?" Mom pointed at a round indentation in the kappa's head. It was full of creek water. "The only way to defeat a kappa is to make it spill that water—that's where they get all their power." It had taken Mom a long time to convince Danny that he wasn't strong enough to wrestle a kappa and win.

"Water . . . please, you wouldn't deny your Uncle Kappy a bit of water, would you?" Uncle Kappy rasped. He flapped his arms and legs around weakly.

I gripped Danny's arm and edged away. "Please, Danny, let's go."

"No! Please don't leave me! I'll do anything—anything!" Uncle Kappy clutched his head with his hands and babbled pathetically, "Have mercy, have mercy, it wasn't my idea to eat you, I swear on my mother's flippers I don't even live here, oh, piteous-patteous me, I never should have left my little pond, I never should have listened to those bat-winged birdbrains. . . ."

Bat-winged birdbrains? That stopped me in my tracks. I looked at Danny and Niko.

"That's enough. We'll get you some water," Niko said. "But not before you make us a promise."

"Yes, yes, of course! I promise. I'll do anything—anything for my nice new friends . . . and some water."

"You won't hurt us. You'll go back to where you came from and never bother us again."

"Wouldn't harm a hair on your blessed heads," Uncle Kappy gasped. "I'll forget all about you."

"Momo, will you fetch a bottle of water from Uncle Kappy's cart, please?" said Niko.

"How do you know we can trust him?" I asked.

"Once a kappa makes a promise, it's physically impossible for them to break it," Niko reassured me.

Oh. Well, in that case. "You'll answer our questions truthfully and do whatever we ask," I said.

"I'll answer every quirky-quacky question. I'll help you with your mimble-mumble math homework. I can help you pass your social studies quizzes. I know all the sticky-stumpy state capitals."

"Now, go," said Niko.

"Yes, please! Hurry, scurry before I die of dehydration!"

I sprinted to the cart and brought back a bottle of water with the phrase "bat-winged birdbrains" still fluttering around in my head. Danny helped Uncle Kappy sit up, and I poured the entire bottle of water into the bowl on top of his head. He gurgled with relief.

"Ah, yes, that hits the spitty-spatty spot!" he said as his face turned a vivid leaf-green. "Thank you! Bless you!"

The sun had disappeared completely now, and with night creeping across the sky, I was feeling impatient. We needed to get answers and move on.

"Who are the bat-winged birdbrains?" I asked.

"I . . ." Uncle Kappy hesitated a moment before smiling craftily. "Who do *you* think they are?"

"Tengu," Danny said forcefully, seeing where I was going. "Am I right?"

"If you think that tengu are bat-winged birdbrains, I certainly won't disagree," Uncle Kappy said, nodding vigorously.

That was a strange way to say yes, and I didn't like the gleam in Uncle Kappy's eye. I glanced at Niko for help.

"He did promise to tell the truth," said Niko, though he looked as confused as me. "Kappa cannot go back on their promises."

So I kept going. "What did they tell you? Why did they send you to kill us?"

"What do *you* think they told me?" Uncle Kappy countered.

"Obviously they told you to kill us and eat us, but why? What else?" I said impatiently. "And can you please just answer the questions instead of turning them around?"

Uncle Kappy's eyes widened pitifully. "I'm doing my best!" he whined.

"Maybe he doesn't know the answers?" Danny suggested.

But it was obvious that Uncle Kappy knew *something*. I felt the impatience turn to anger that started bubbling through me like lava—I hated mind games like this. They were so mean and degrading. I gritted my teeth and tried for an easier question. One he had to know the answer to. "Was it Shuten-dōji?" I asked. "Does he know what we're trying to do?"

"His Royal Darkness, you say? Do *you* think—"

"I don't have time for your games!" I exploded. "Just! Answer! The! Question!"

Uncle Kappy looked genuinely distressed. *That's right*, I thought, seething. *Maybe now you'll listen.* His face took on a shifty smile. "Err . . . yes, of course. Only . . . ahem . . . What was the question, again?"

"Who. Sent. You." I was practically humming with rage

167

now. He was playing with us—laughing at us, probably—and meanwhile, precious seconds were slipping by. "Tell me *now.*"

I saw something change in Uncle Kappy's eyes, and I knew that he would answer, that my anger had done it, and I felt a vague, tingling sense of satisfaction. Good. I folded my arms and waited expectantly.

"Ah. Ahem. It, it . . . it w-w-was—" Uncle Kappy stammered. Uncle Kappy's eyes bulged, and he started shaking all over. He looked desperately at Niko, who shook his head. I looked at Niko and Danny in alarm. What was happening?

"Um, are you okay?" I asked. "What's wrong?"

"It w-w-was . . . it w- . . . i-i-i—"

The air around Uncle Kappy shimmered, then popped once, and I gasped. He'd turned to stone! No—not stone. Uncle Kappy had turned into gallons and gallons of murky, stinky, Uncle Kappy–shaped water. He wobbled in place for a second before collapsing in a giant *SPLOOSH*.

With a shout, Danny, Niko, and I leaped backward. Uncle Kappy—or whatever he had become—seeped quickly and quietly into the sand at our feet.

Team DaMoNik

"Uh . . . what just happened?" I asked. My voice was shaky. *I* was a little shaky, to be honest.

It was properly dark now, with the moon hovering just over the lake like a spotlight. Like a witness.

Niko sniffed the wet sand and looked thoughtful. "He must have made a promise to whoever sent him that he wouldn't tell. That conflicted with his promise to tell us the truth."

"That's why he was acting so weird about answering our questions!" Danny said. "Everything we asked him must have been stuff he'd already promised not to tell."

"And yet he managed to tell us what we wanted to know," I said, thinking back. *That* was why he'd looked so sneaky and proud of himself at first.

"Except for that last question about who sent him," Niko said gloomily.

Something awful dawned on me. "Because he had to answer it directly. I told him to tell me who sent him, and he had to do what I said. I made him break his promise to . . . to whoever told him not to tell."

"Technically, he ended up *not* breaking it," Danny pointed out.

"Because he died!" I shouted. "I made him have to choose between promises, and it killed him!"

"You didn't know it would kill him, my clueless cub," said Niko, speaking more gently than I'd heard him speak before. "And anyway, he did try to murder you only minutes ago."

"Still."

"You saved his life, too, though. You brought him water," Danny pointed out.

"Only because I thought he would give us information. And I didn't even get it, because I was so mad at him for jerking us around that I ordered him to answer. And he *died*." What was worse—what I was afraid to say out loud—was that a small, ugly part of me was still really mad that I hadn't found out who he was working for.

"You're going to have to get used to that sort of thing if you intend to defeat the oni on the Island of Mysteries," said a new voice.

The three of us whipped around. No one.

"Over here."

The voice came from a white rabbit who was scampering across the surface of the lake, on the glimmering white path of the moonbeam.

"The rabbit in the moon!" Danny said.

"Correct." With a couple of huge, bounding leaps, the rabbit landed at our feet and bowed gracefully. "Good evening, children."

You've heard of the man in the moon, right? Well, I grew up

hearing about the rabbit in the moon. You can see it if you look closely at the full moon—he's sitting on his hind legs, facing the right. But just then, he was sitting in front of us—someone familiar, safe, and famously kindhearted. For the first time since this whole thing had started, I felt comforted and relieved instead of bewildered, nervous, or terrified.

"I bear an urgent message from Tsukiyomi, the Moon Prince. It concerns your mission to the Land of Roots and the Island of Mysteries."

"He knows about our mission?" I asked. That seemed odd.

"He is the Moon Prince," said the rabbit simply, as if that explained everything. Then he added, "He rides his boat across the Sea of Heaven every night. Do you not think he might communicate with the Ship of Treasures every once in a while?"

"Oh." Well, of course. That made sense. I felt a little silly for asking.

"What's the message?" Danny asked.

The rabbit beckoned us closer. "You are being watched," he whispered. "Whoever sent the kappa knew you would be here, as you have correctly guessed."

My mouth went dry and my heart started racing as I remembered the final part of my dream—that awful mist, the feeling that something unspeakably evil was watching me. Maybe it had been more than a dream, after all.

"Shuten-dōji's spies must have alerted him to your intentions. He has added another hundred oni to the island, to speed its destruction—he is anticipating your attack. It is therefore more important than ever that you convince Susano'o to give you the great sword Kusanagi. You must not fail. If you go into battle without it, you cannot win."

Danny muttered, "Oh man." Even in the moonlight, I could tell his face had gone pale. I felt like I might throw up. Niko looked like he might cry.

So much for feeling comforted and happy.

The rabbit must have sensed our panic—not that it would have been difficult for even a normal person to see—because he held his paw out and said gently, "Have courage, children. Remember: Shuten-dōji has strengthened his defenses because *he* is afraid of *you.*"

Next to me, Danny nodded and whispered, *"He's* afraid of *us."*

"And you may take comfort in the fact that you are far better prepared than you were even a few days ago."

"Um." I hated to contradict the beautiful animal sitting in front of me. "Excuse me?"

"You saved your friend's life, dear girl," said the rabbit, "without any regard for your own."

"Oh, that's right. I haven't thanked you yet," Danny said. "So, um, yeah. Thanks."

"But I only managed to do it because Niko told me what to do. I was scared stiff. Like, literally, I couldn't—"

"You saved his life even though you were scared stiff." The rabbit smiled. "That deserves even greater praise. And of course, Danny, you saved Momo. For the second time."

I looked at Danny, who was digging the toe of his shoe into the sand, trying to look like it was no big deal. He'd saved my life without any prompting or help, either with the shikome or with Uncle Kappy. Maybe it was time I started trusting him. At least a little bit, anyway. "Thanks, Danny."

Danny gave me a thumbs-up. "No problem."

"And I believe that you, Momo, managed to feel remorse over a certain green yōkai's untimely demise, even though he would have killed you if he could have. And I found Danny and Niko trying to remind you how good-hearted you are—something they truly believe."

Danny and Niko nodded, and I blushed.

"You have all behaved admirably, and grown much together, as good friends should. You care for each other, and you trust and support each other. This is more than can be said about Shuten-dōji or his demons, who are incapable of trusting each other, and who cooperate only as much as it serves their own selfish desires and lust for power. I think perhaps your bond, as much as the power of Kusanagi, is what will bring you victory."

"So you're saying we're a good team," said Danny.

"Yes, I suppose that is what I am saying."

"Well, then I think we should have a team name. I was thinking about it on the taxi, actually."

Niko and I glanced at each other, and I could see that we were having the same thought: of *course* that's what Danny was thinking about.

"You wanna hear it?" He didn't even wait for us to say yes. "Demonic."

I blinked. "What?"

He drew it in the sand with his finger: DaMoNik.

"Get it? It sounds like 'demonic,' but it's spelled with the first letters of each of our names. So it's like, Team DaMoNik is gonna defeat a team of actual demons. Cool, right?"

It was surprisingly *un*cool, actually. I couldn't imagine Danny Haragan, Number Two Most Popular Boy at Oak Valley Middle School, saying this to his cool, mean friends. And that's what was so cool about it, if you know what I mean. My old friend was finally coming back.

"I love it." I smiled, and he grinned proudly.

Niko sniffed. "It's acceptable. As long as you don't turn me into one of those miserable mascots."

"Nah," said Danny. "Not if you don't want to be one."

The rabbit smiled. "You are giving me more and more confidence in the success of your mission. But let us not forget that it is crucial for you to have Kusanagi with you. The Moon Prince and I cannot help you underground, for obvious reasons, but I can arrange for you to be driven to the portal." He twitched his nose and wiggled his ears, and few seconds later, a big red muscle car came roaring out of the lake.

Okay, Now Can
I Panic?

I won't lie—I was nervous about getting into that car. In my defense, it wasn't the kind of vehicle that inspired a lot of trust. I mean, it looked like something you might see in a movie called *Cars 4: Death Wish*. The windshield was a pair of glowing red eyes, the grille was set in a hostile frown under a dented, scarred hood, and the license plate said STEAKNYF. Would *you* jump right into a car like that without a second thought?

"I take it you've never seen an oboguruma before," the rabbit said as the back door popped open.

Danny and I shook our heads.

"They are vehicles who are animated by the anger of their previous owners. This one used to belong to Wayne Steak."

"Whoa! As in Steak Knife? The rock star?" said Danny. "The one who was banned from the Ritz-Carlton for trying to have a bonfire in his hotel room?"

"The very one," said the rabbit. "He got into a fight with another celebrity over a prime parking spot during Lollapalooza, and they smashed each other until Steak's car was damaged beyond repair. Being who he is, Steak Knife had it secretly dragged into the lake when he realized he couldn't drive it anymore. His bitterness and jealousy were so strong, they brought the car to life, and now it lives here, ready to transport anyone who knows how to call it."

"But I thought the Moon Prince didn't like to sully himself with earthly things and petty emotions," said Niko.

"That is why he sends me," said the rabbit, with a slightly resigned sigh.

"Is it safe?" I asked.

"Perfectly safe," said the rabbit. "I would have summoned something a little less unsavory, but unfortunately, nighttime is more conducive to the darker kind of magic, and one cannot be picky when one is in a hurry."

Niko and Danny climbed in, but before I could follow them, the rabbit laid a paw on my arm and pulled me aside. "The Moon Prince has bidden me to give you a private message," he said in a low voice.

"Uh, okay." I nodded and lowered my head, not sure whether to feel nervous or excited.

The rabbit continued. "My master often sees and hears what happens in dark places, and he wishes to give you a warning: the demon king has become more powerful in Yomi than anyone realizes. Before, he was merely the biggest and the strongest. But he has had centuries to learn strategies that extend beyond brute force. He knows how to manipulate his enemies, how to find and exploit their weaknesses to turn them against each other. He revels in discord and betrayal. And his powers now extend beyond the physical. You would do well to be on your guard against this at all times."

Amabie's prophecy came back to me—her vacant eyes, her

eerie voice. *Betrayal,* she had said. I glanced into the car, where Niko and Danny sat waiting for me, then back at the rabbit, asking a silent question. But all he did was bow and murmur, "Be careful."

I climbed in after Danny and Niko, and soon we were cruising down the streets of downtown Chicago in the back of the limo like VIPs, sipping soda and munching on chips. We drove past glittery high-rise apartment buildings and shops and hotels, and then crossed the drawbridge over the Chicago River, and I was just starting to wonder how long this would take when the car veered off the street and onto the sidewalk.

"I thought he said this thing was safe!" I yelped as we clipped a newspaper stand. We were headed straight for an escalator that led underground. Over the entrance was a sign that read

SUBWAY
Exit Only

People dove screaming out of the way as the car bumped downward and took a hard left at the bottom. Once we got to the ticket gates, it climbed over them like a bear with wheels for legs and rumbled down yet another escalator.

"This is chaos!" I said. I clutched the armrest and braced my feet against the driver's seat. "This car is going to murder someone!"

"Are you kidding me? This is freakin' awesome!" Danny whooped. "Stop worrying, Momo. We're going too slow to hurt anyone. Remember when Niko drove us the other night? Now, *that* was scary."

"I'm an excellent driver," Niko protested.

"You're a dangerous driver, is all I'm saying," said Danny.

"I was trying to save us from a death hag!"

"Oh, right. I forgot about that. Good point." Danny raised his hand for a high five. Niko reluctantly met it with his paw.

Danny was a little less enthusiastic about the car's lack of safety protocols when we drove off the subway platform and jounced onto the track. And when we saw a tiny light in the distance, Danny changed his mind completely.

"We have to stop this thing!" he shouted.

"Oh, you *think*?"

Danny ignored me and climbed into the driver's seat. "There's no pedals," he reported from the front. "No gas, no brakes, nothing! And the steering wheel—" He spun it like a bicycle wheel, but we kept rattling straight down the tracks. He looked at me, his face white. "What do we do?"

"We have to get out!" I tried the door on my side—the handle didn't budge. Niko was muttering feverishly at the door on his side, to no avail. Danny had the presence of mind to check his backpack, but it was empty.

Rattling the door handles, kicking the windows, and hollering our lungs out did us no good. The train bore down on us, the light grew bigger and brighter, and the scream of its brakes nearly drowned out Niko, who was wailing, "We're roasted radishes! We're crunched-up coconuts! We're—"

The car swung sideways and skidded to a stop, its headlights shining on an arched opening in the wall. The doors popped open, and we tumbled out and dove through the archway just in time to avoid getting slammed into oblivion by fifty thousand tons of steel.

We found ourselves on a metal balcony with a ladder attached to it—kind of like a fire escape—and there was nowhere to go but down. So down we went. The air swirled around us, blowing through little cracks and holes in the walls and howling as it passed upward toward the surface. As the descent stretched on and on, thousands and thousands of steps down, I stopped worrying about monsters at the bottom and started wishing we'd just *reach* the bottom already. How much time had passed? I had no idea. It felt almost like time didn't exist here in this . . . whatever it was. But it was definitely ticking by *somewhere,* and the longer we climbed down, the more anxious I got. And there was something else, too—something unsettled and restless that buzzed around inside me like a bee trapped in a jar.

Finally, I put my foot down on something that wasn't an iron ladder rung—solid rock. "Watch out! We're at the bottom!" I called up.

"Woo-hoooo!" Danny's shout echoed around the tunnel as he stepped off the ladder. "Oof, I'm so sore from all that climbing," he said, rubbing his thighs. "It's gonna take forever to climb back up."

Back *up*? I hadn't thought of that.

"If we make it out of the fortress alive, that is," muttered Niko. "Let's just focus on that, shall we? In fact, let's focus on getting out of this tunnel. Where in the blistering blazes do you suppose the door is?"

But I'd already figured that out. That restless, buzzy sensation inside grew stronger as I inched my way toward one section of the wall, and weaker as I moved away. It had to be showing me the way out. Don't ask me how I knew. I just did.

"It's right around here, I think." I felt around for a crack, or a handle, or a secret button.

"How do you know?"

"I just—I have a feeling."

Danny held the flashlight up, but it had stopped working. "A feeling?" he said.

I gave the wall a shove, but it didn't budge. "Can you just help me? It's through here. I'm sure of it."

Shrugging good-naturedly, Danny came and stood next to me. That was one nice thing about Danny, I realized—he was down to try almost anything. "Okay, ready? Push on three. One, two, *three!*" We pushed. I could see Danny's face scrunched up with the effort, and my head felt like it might explode, I was pushing so hard. But it was like—well, it was like pushing a rock wall.

"Maybe it's locked," Danny said hopefully. "Niko, could you do your lock-opening thing?"

Niko muttered at the rock three different times, in three different places. Nothing happened.

"But this *has* to be the way out. I *know* it!"

"How do you know?" Danny asked.

"I just . . ." My emotions were getting all jumbled up. I was sure I was right, but I wasn't sure why. At the same time, I was worried that I was wrong. And underneath it all was a hot, prickling frustration at the way every single freaking step of this journey had to be so hard. I wanted to smack whoever—or whatever—had set me up like this. "I just have a feeling," I finished weakly.

"What kind of feeling?"

"I don't know." How could I explain it to him? I couldn't. "It's just a feeling, okay?"

Danny ran his fingers all over the place where the door should have been. "Are you sure your feeling isn't, like, indigestion or something?"

"*Yes,* I'm sure!"

"It's just that I don't see anything that looks like a door."

"I expect she is feeling her divine connection to Susano'o," said Niko.

"If it's your divine connection to Susano'o, why won't it open the door for you?"

"How should I know? Can you just stop?" I snapped. I felt bad arguing with him, since he had a very good evidence-based reason to doubt me and my so-far-nonexistent magical goddess powers. But ugh! It wasn't like I needed reminding. It made me think of all the times that kids used to tease me and say, "If there's a tiger in the sky, why can't we see it?" I felt horrible inside. And mad. Why didn't my powers manifest? What was the point of being the granddaughter of the most powerful earth god if you couldn't do anything? It wasn't fair! I kicked the wall in frustration.

And the door swung open.

We were surrounded by scrubby grassland, scattered with boulders and stretching endlessly to the horizon. The sky was covered by dark, low-hanging clouds, and the light was murky and gray. Far in the distance was something big, bulky, and black. The fortress, I guessed. Even from all the way over here, it looked scary and ominous.

"Hurry up, slowpoke!" Danny said from behind me.

"I'm just making sure it's safe, okay? Jeez."

I stepped all the way out, and as I turned to watch Danny and Niko come through, it was like watching them step out of nowhere. All I could see behind them was the same grassland that stretched in every other direction. The only clue that we'd come from anywhere was a whiff of dank, musty subway air.

"I thought we were supposed to be in the underworld. Why is there a sky?" Danny asked.

"First of all," Niko explained, "we are under*ground*, not in the under*world*. Remember, the earth and its sky are the Middle Lands—where you humans exist. The spirit dimension overlaps it, but also extends above it, into the Sky Kingdom, and below it, into Yomi, the land of the dead. Ne-no-kuni is still in the earth, in the Middle Lands. That's why we call it the Land of Roots."

"But the sky—"

"I'm getting to that! The sky and the light that you see is all Susano'o's magic. He replicates the sky and the ground to mimic the surface according to his whim."

"Okay, I've got a question." I'd reached my hand out to make sure we'd be able to find the door back to the tunnel—but it was gone. "How are we supposed to get out of here?" I swished my hands around, in case I'd missed something—a doorknob, or maybe an edge or a corner somewhere. I could feel my anxiety spiking, and I had to work hard to control my breath. "Where'd the door go?"

"Don't panic," Danny said. "We got in, right? There has to be a way out. Right?" When Niko didn't answer, Danny poked him. "Right, Niko?"

"I sincerely hope so," said Niko, not very hopefully.

"*What?*" My heart took off at full speed. "Okay, *now* can I panic?"

"We'll figure something out," said Danny. I appreciated his optimism, but his shaky voice didn't match his words.

I looked at the fortress, and all around us at the field. We didn't have a plan to get in, and our only exit was now completely unfindable. I reached into my pocket and found the spool—and a plan came to me. Maybe Hotei's gift hadn't been so silly after all. I opened my backpack, hoping for a big flag or something that I could leave as a marker, or maybe pebbles that I could use to leave a trail. Nothing. Darn that useless backpack.

"Should we wait until it gets darker?" I asked. "Would that be safer?" I knew it made zero sense and that we didn't have that kind of time to waste, but somehow deciding to wait felt like I was doing something on purpose, which made me feel like I was still in control, which was better than moving on without a single crumb of an idea of what would happen next.

Niko shook his head. "We're in too much of a hurry. And anyway, Susano'o has an army of millions who will have warned him already. There's no point in hiding. He knows we're coming."

Great.

Fake It Till You Make It

Sure enough, as we got closer to the fortress, I got the distinct sense that we were being watched. The jittery feeling inside me intensified. Now that we were closer, I could see that the fortress wasn't so much a building as a giant black plateau that stuck out of the land around it. Eight massive black torii loomed over the path that led to the center of the fortress. I imagined monster-guards peeking out from between the cracks of the boulders at its base, ready to attack us the moment we got within attacking distance.

A voice boomed out at us. Actually, it was more like a hundred voices—a thousand voices. It seemed to come not just from the fortress but from the ground itself, which practically shook from the sound.

"WHO DARES DISTURB THE PEACE OF THE MIGHTY SUSANO'O, LORD OF THE SEAS, MASTER OF STORMS, AND RULER OF NE-NO-KUNI, THE LAND OF ROOTS?"

Even if I could have caught my breath enough to speak, I couldn't think of what to say. It was like the voices had rolled through my brain and knocked out every thought, like a bunch of little dominoes, and the only thing left was terror. I hoped one of the others would say something, but Danny and Niko looked just as scared as me.

"Ahem, granddaughter of the mighty Susano'o, Lord of the Seas, Master of Storms, and Ruler of Ne-no-kuni," Niko whispered after a moment. "Perhaps you should answer the question. He might take more kindly to us if he knows you're related."

"WHO DARES DISTURB THE PEACE OF THE MIGHTY SUSANO'O, LORD OF THE SEAS, MASTER OF STORMS, AND RULER OF NE-NO-KUNI?" the voices repeated. "AND HURRY UP WITH YOUR ANSWER. WE DON'T HAVE ALL DAY."

"They literally have all day. What else are they going to do? There's nothing going on here but us," Danny muttered, and for once I was grateful for his cocky attitude. It made me feel a little less scared.

Niko growled at him, then nudged me. "Be regal. Claim your divinity. But also be humble!"

Regal, divine, *and* humble? I felt anything but regal and divine, but I took a shaky breath and tried to stand up straight.

"It is I, Momo Arashima, the um, great and mighty daughter of the—"

"No, that's too much! You have to be humble!" hissed Niko.

"But you said—"

He made a face like someone who'd resigned himself to his fate. "Just keep going."

My confidence was now completely shattered, and I tripped and stumbled my way through the rest of my introduction. "I mean, the, uh, *humble* daughter of the kami Takiri-bime, the . . .

uh . . . granddaughter—I mean, the *guardian* of the gates of Yomi—the forgotten passageway, I mean—and daughter of— I mean, *she's* the daughter and I'm the granddaughter—of the mighty Susano'o, the King of the Seas—" Niko shook his head hard, and I gulped. "I mean, *Lord* of the Seas, Master of Storms, and the, uh, Ruler of the Land of Roots." I cringed, and my heart sank to my stomach. I'd made so many mistakes!

"SORRY, *WHAT*? ARE YOU *JOKING*?"

Niko was muttering to himself, "We're done for, we're bruised bananas, we're mashed mangoes." My heart did a few laps around my stomach, then took a dive. I was pretty sure I heard it go *plop* as it landed inside my right foot. Where was that maybe-kind-of connection to Susano'o when I needed it? Probably it didn't exist, after all. Probably it had just been nerves.

"I can't do this," I whispered.

"Yes, you can," Danny whispered back. "What you *can't* do is give up on the first try."

"I've tried twice already."

"Then you can't give up on the second try. Come on. Fake it till you make it, remember?"

I swallowed. I thought about telling Danny that this was not the same thing as trying to fit in at school. On the other hand, Danny was right. If I gave up, Mom would die. And the world could end. That didn't give me courage, exactly, but it did give me the push I needed.

"No, I'm not joking!" I tried to sound more confident. "I am Momo Arashima and I, er, humbly request permission to see my grandfather Susano'o!" I paused for a moment before continuing. "It's a matter of life and death!"

The voices laughed. "HA-HA-HA! THE MIGHTY SUSANO'O IS BEYOND SUCH TRIVIAL MATTERS. HUMAN LIVES ARE BUT DROPS OF WATER IN THE VAST OCEAN OF TIME. MERE GRAINS OF SAND IN THE ENDLESS DESERT OF SPACE MATTER. BLADES OF GRASS IN THE INFINITE FIELDS OF CONSCIOUSNESS..."

Even a huge, scary chorus of voices that seem to come from everywhere can get boring after a while. While the voices droned on about how puny and insignificant my life was, a scary-looking bug crawling on a nearby rock caught my eye. It was almost a foot long, and black and squiggly with a whole bunch of body sections, lots of golden legs, and a bright red head with curlicue-horn things. And it was acting very odd.

"TINY TWIGS IN THE PRIMEVAL FOREST OF LIFE..." The centipede lifted its head and waved a few of its arms (or were they legs?) around... "LICE ON THE HAIRS OF THE MIGHTY SUSANO'O'S BEARD!"... in time to the words I was hearing.

As if it were making a point.

As if it were actually *saying the words.*

I was being intimidated by a *bug.*

Granted, it was a huge bug. And as I said before, it was scary-looking, even for a bug. But it wasn't *that* scary. It made me think of the caterpillar in *Alice in Wonderland.* I wondered if it was using some kind of voice enhancer like the dogs in that movie *Up.*

That gave me courage.

"How about bugs on a rock in front of the mighty Susano'o's fortress?"

"*Wha—?*" The voice squeaked in surprise instead of booming like it had been, and I got even braver.

"I see what you are. You're just a bug with a big, scary voice. I'm not afraid of you."

"No!" I heard Niko whispering urgently. "No, you should definitely be afraid! Don't threaten it!"

"JUST? A *BUG*?!" The deep, echoey voice came back, and the centipede drew itself up to its full height. It folded its very top arms, and stuck the next few rows of elbows out, and put its fists on its . . . well, its hips, I guess. If this were real life—earth life, that is—I would have agreed with Niko and been very afraid of a centipede that big. But it had *squeaked*. And it looked kind of cute with its arms folded and its hands on its hips.

Danny laughed. "Ha! You mean all this time we were— I mean, you were afraid of *that* thing?"

"SHHHHH!" Niko was frantic now. "Stop! Talking!"

"HOW DARE YOU! YOU DO NOT KNOW WHAT YOU ARE DEALING WITH, PUNY HUMANS!"

"Yeah, yeah, we know. We're dandruff on the scalp of the mighty Susano'o's head," I said. "But you're even smaller."

Okay. Looking back, I can see that this wasn't the smartest attitude to take. But that bug just looked so silly. And it was acting so bigheaded and bossy, I felt like I *had* to take it down a peg, even if that meant provoking it. I thought about Danny and how he'd apologized to Niko, but how he still seemed to think it was okay to go along with his mean friends. I was tired of backing down in the face of people like him, like this centipede—people who thought they were so much bigger and better than me, even though they were just . . . bugs.

"*WE ARE MUCH . . . MUCH . . . LARGER.*"

As it spoke, something dark began spreading on the ground. Something . . . not quite liquid, but not quite solid.

It seemed alive.

It *was* alive.

Hundreds of thousands of foot-long centipedes with black bodies, yellow legs, red heads, and golden horns came pouring out of holes and cracks in the ground, moving as one, oozing across the ground like oil.

"Please forgive them, O great and terrible Mukade!" Niko moaned. "They meant no disrespect! Certainly *I* meant no disrespect!" But the centipedes kept streaming toward us. We were surrounded now, on all sides. "Spare an innocent fox!" he yelped. He leaped onto my shoulders like a cat and wrapped himself around my neck—so much for protecting me with his life. "I told you not to provoke him! I told you not to poke fun!"

"Get off me!" If I could just get to my backpack—yeah, I'd said it was useless before, but it *had* to have something for me now. But Niko's fluffy tail was in my face, and every time I tried to take off the backpack, he'd scrabble around and dig his claws into my shoulders. Meanwhile, I could feel those centipedes closing in.

"Tell them who you are!" Danny shouted. "Pull rank on them!"

"I did! I did your little 'fake it till you make it' thing and they didn't care, remember?"

"They didn't care because you didn't sell it! You have to act like you mean it, or no one will believe you!"

"I tried! I—I can't mean it. Look at me, do I *look* like someone they should respect?" I tried to shove Niko off again, but he whined and clung even harder to my neck. "What if I mess up

189

again? Or what if I don't mess up and they still don't believe me? What if—"

"YOU SHALL NOT PASS!"

I stared at Danny, who was standing with his legs apart, one fist outstretched, like he was holding a magical wizard's staff.

Even in my terror, I wanted to roll my eyes. "Danny, what are you doing?" I hissed at him. "This isn't pretend! We're not in an epic fantasy movie!"

Danny bellowed again, and I could tell he was making his voice as deep as he could. "I SPEAK FOR THE GRAND-DAUGHTER OF SUSANO'O, LORD OF THE SEAS, MASTER OF STORMS, AND RULER OF NE-NO-KUNI! IF YOU HARM A HAIR ON HER HEAD, YOU WILL SUFFER HIS ALMIGHTY *WRAAATH!*"

His voice broke a little bit on "WRAAATH," but otherwise it was a pretty impressive performance. So impressive, in fact, that the tide of centipedes actually stopped in their tracks. The one on the stone in front of us—Mukade—jumped.

"No, we won't!" he said. But his all-caps voice was gone.

"YES! YOU! *WILLLL!*" This time, Danny struck a sort of pro wrestler pose, half bent over and flexing his arms under his chest like a gorilla. Beneath his breath, he muttered, "Come on, Momo, don't punk out on me. Do it! Go hard or go home!"

I'd heard Danny and his bro-bots say this exact thing to each other all the time during lunch recess, when they would dare each other to do stuff like drink a cup of mustard or do a backflip off a lunch table. It was weird hearing it now, when "go home" meant "be stung to death by a hundred thousand centipedes." I started to say, "What is this, football?" but then I realized that

Danny was just doing his best to help me, and—judging by the centipedes, who were frozen and staring at Danny's fierce expression—it was working. So maybe I should trust him.

But what Danny was doing was much bigger than school-level fake it till you make it, like pretending to think stuff was funny when it wasn't. And anyway, I really couldn't do it. I couldn't pretend to be something I didn't believe in. So, fine. I was going to have to find a way to believe my own act. I thought about Mom fighting off the shikome, how deep she must have had to dig for that strength when she was already so sick. If Mom could do it for me, I could do it for Mom. I searched inside for something— for the daughter of the kami Takiri-bime, who blew up a death hag with a wave of her arms. For the granddaughter of the Master of Storms. For that jittery, restless feeling from before.

There it was. Just the tiniest little drop. I focused on it, felt its intense, vibrating energy, and took a deep breath.

"TAKE ME TO MY GRANDFATHER IMMEDI-ATELY," I bellowed, "AND I WILL NOT MENTION THAT YOU THREATENED ME. OTHERWISE, PRE-PARE FOR *INEVITABLE DEATH!*"

I could hardly believe it when the entire centipede army retreated one step. Whoa. Had it actually worked? Or were they just surprised?

"You—you lie!" Mukade sounded less confident than before. I could only hear one voice now. The voice I'd heard before must have been the combined voices of all the centipedes. Maybe they weren't unified anymore.

I looked at the sea of centipedes around us; a *shushhh*-ing sound rose up, mingled with tiny little ticks and clicks.

They must be talking to each other, I thought. *They must be scared.* Yes!

"I DO NOT LIE," I shouted, which was technically true—I *didn't* plan to mention the threats, and they *would* all die . . . eventually. "TAKE US TO HIM NOW!"

"Keep it up," I heard Niko whisper. "But how about getting the rest of them to go home? I don't like having all that vicious venom around us. One bite from a regular mukade can send an adult human being to the hospital, you know. I don't want to find out what an enchanted mukade could do."

How could I get a hundred thousand enchanted centipedes to turn around? *Vicious venom,* Niko had said. It reminded me of Kiki and Ryleigh—ha. But then I had it. I remembered one time at school when Kiki and Ryleigh had a fight, and somehow Kiki got all the minions on her side, and for a week, Ryleigh had no friends. How much loyalty did these centipedes have to their leader? I pointed at Mukade. I raised my voice as loud as I could so that the entire field could hear me and shouted, "BE-CAUSE I AM GENEROUS AND KIND, ONLY YOU WILL COME WITH US. THAT WAY, EVEN IF YOU DIE, YOUR FRIENDS WILL BE SAFE." A hundred thousand little red heads bobbed up and down in agreement, and the million-legged army began to retreat. I could have sworn I heard a few of them saying, *Yes, good idea,* and *Better the general than all of us,* and *I never liked him anyway.*

"Hey! Get back here!" Mukade shouted, but it was too late.

It had worked! They'd all believed me! Who knew that Kiki and Ryleigh and their popularity-obsessed fake friends would help me save my own life? I smiled at Danny, and he gave me a thumbs-up.

"TAKE US TO SUSANO'O," I said again.

Mukade made a chittering, chattering sound—centipede for "Ughhhh," probably. He squiggled off the rock, mumbling, "Fine. Fine, fine, fine. Cowardly cowards. Wretched wretches. Leave me with the scary job, will they? They will."

He waved a few of his arms in the direction of the fortress. "Follow me, follow me, granddaughter of the mighty Susano'o, Lord of the Seas, Master of Storms, and Ruler of Ne-no-kuni. And we shall see what we shall see." He gave another wave, and a wasp appeared. "Tell His Mightiness that his humble servant Mukade approaches the fortress with a mortal claiming to be his granddaughter, and her lackeys."

"Hey!" Danny and Niko said together.

The wasp buzzed off, and Mukade grumbled again. "Will I regret this? I suppose I will." He seemed genuinely worried.

"I'll make sure he knows how helpful you are," I told Mukade in my normal voice, to make him feel better, and then felt weird about it; why was I trying to make him feel better?

"Ha," grumbled the centipede. "Helpful, indeed. My comrades could have been more helpful to *me*. Most likely His Mightiness will smash me for allowing a mortal to enter his fortress. Smash me to a pulpy pulp, most likely. And then someone else will have to lead that army of traitorous traitors. Which is fine with me."

That's when I knew what it was. I felt sorry for him. For having made his army betray him. For putting him in danger. Maybe I should have tried to convince them to stand down without using Kiki's mean-girl tactics. Maybe I should tell him to get a new army. Or new friends, anyway.

But why should I feel bad? a voice inside me demanded. *He was a bully, and I just pushed a button that was already there— they obviously didn't like him already. You could almost say that I got what I needed and he got what he deserved.*

But that was mean. And wrong.

"I'll ask him not to hurt you," I said.

"If only we could guarantee he won't hurt *us*," muttered Niko.

"Ha," said the centipede again. "Well said, fox, well said."

I did not appreciate the reminder that my very own grandfather might kill me just for fun. On the other hand, if I wanted to get my hands on Kusanagi, I'd have to risk it. Though now that I'd had a moment to settle down, it occurred to me that maybe a better way to get the sword would be to get Mukade to sneak into the fortress somehow—to make some kind of bargain with him and get him to help us steal it. Except he'd already sent a messenger ahead. How had I allowed this to happen? I'd finally gotten a little wiggle room, and I was wasting it by barging ahead without a plan! The little spark I'd been drawing on earlier fizzled out.

Grabbing the spool in my pocket for good luck, I said, "Um. Mukade? Sir? Maybe we don't have to go see Susano'o right away. Maybe we can work something out where no one has to risk getting hurt. Can you call the messenger back?"

"Call him back? Ha," Mukade said gloomily, and gestured toward the first stony black torii ahead of us, where a bright yellow spark flared and went out. "The wasp has just passed through the gate to announce your presence and purpose. It's too late for us now."

Eyes. Those Are Eyes.

When we passed under the first of the eight massive torii, the ground started shaking, and a bolt of lightning burst above us like a giant flashbulb. I fully expected the torii to crash down and bury us as we sprinted through the other seven.

"Welp," said Mukade. "That was the front-door alarm, that was. He knows we've arrived."

"You couldn't have disarmed it from the outside?" I asked.

"It's magic, human girl, powerful enough to make the earth trimble-tremble. And you ask me to disarm it?" Mukade chittered.

My heart was racing, and the chaotic feeling that had started swirling inside my chest again rushed outward into the rest of me, like it was in my blood; my whole body felt like it was vibrating with this weird energy. I was becoming more and more convinced that this was Susano'o—our connection. It was both reassuring and terrifying. I wondered if he felt it, too, or if this was the way he felt all the time.

We were standing in front of a giant rock wall with no windows, no doors, no steps carved into it, nothing. "What now?" Danny asked. "Do we knock?"

"Bow down," Mukade said, and his words were barely out of his mouth before we were hit by a gust of wind so strong it nearly knocked me backward. Dust devils whirled up around us and pulled at my hair, and sand stung my cheeks. I dropped to my knees and put my forehead on the ground as much for my own protection as out of respect.

"Your grandpa's not the most subtle guy, is he?" Danny shouted at me over the roar of the wind.

"Yeah, you and him should get along great!" I shouted back.

"Heads down, mouths closed, you yammering yo-yos!" Niko barked.

"Follow your own advice, foxy fox!" Mukade said, and I started to laugh, but the wind picked up the sound and spun it into nothing, and when I took a breath, I choked on the dust. That's when I decided to squeeze my eyes and mouth shut and hold my breath instead.

Before long I was barely aware of anything else: my eyes were still shut, and the roar of the dust storm filled my ears. It whipped right through my clothes and bit my skin. I couldn't even feel the ground underneath me.

Ages later, the wind died down and Mukade told us to stand. Before I even came out of my little curled-up ball, I knew something was off. The ground wasn't hard-packed dirt anymore, but knobby and cold, like stone. The air was cold, too, and still, and there was the distinct sound of water trickling somewhere in the distance. I opened my eyes and lifted my head and realized that we'd been transported inside somehow.

We were in the middle of an enormous stone chamber, lit by hundreds of tiny orange flames that flickered in the air above us.

If there was a ceiling, it was so high that I couldn't even see it—the room sort of disappeared into the darkness above the little fires. Three doorways led out of the room—one in front of us and one each on the left and right. Through the doorway ahead of us marched two creatures that made me wish we'd stayed outside.

They were easily six feet tall and stood on two legs, and their chests were protected by scary-looking armor decorated with shiny black disks, like regular human soldiers—but that was where the "human" part ended. Four beady black eyes in each face stared at us over a pair of giant fangs. Six limbs stuck out like the claws of a deadly UFO catcher game: four long, skinny ones and one pair of thick, strong pincers at the top. A golden, multijointed armored tail that ended in an evil-looking needle as long as my pointer finger lashed back and forth over each head. Scorpions.

And then one of them blinked, and I realized that what I had originally thought were a bunch of circular decorations on their armor were actually—

"Eyes," Danny breathed. "Those are *eyes.*"

"And we've each got one on the back of our head, so if you know what's good for you, you won't try nothin' stupid like running away," snarled the scorpion on the left.

"You!" The scorpion on the right pointed an arm-claw at Mukade. "Go down to security and file a report. We'll take it from here."

Mukade scuttled down the passageway to the left, mumbling about disrespectful underlings and bad manners and how much he hated paperwork.

"You three follow me." Scorpion Number One (the one on the left) jerked its head and turned down the corridor where it had come from. The eye in the back of its skull narrowed and fixed its gaze on us. "And remember, I've got my eye on you, so no funny business." We fell in line, with Scorpion Number Two looming behind us.

We trooped through a maze of intersecting tunnels for what seemed like forever, until Scorpion Number One stopped in front of a massive set of sliding doors made of iron. I felt like I was made of monkeys, or electricity, or maybe monkeys made of electricity. And if it hadn't been for those electric monkeys, my stomach would have been a painful ball of nerves and anxiety. Would Susano'o know who I was? Would he recognize our connection? Would he acknowledge it? Would he care enough to listen to me? I wanted so, so much for everything I'd heard about him to be wrong, for him to be a proper, loving but powerful grandfather who would leap at the chance to help his long-lost granddaughter. I squashed that hope down as hard as I could. It was easier and less scary not to hope, and I was wound up enough as it was.

Scorpion Number One banged on the doors three times with its pincer, then heaved one of them open.

An earsplitting whine speared through the opening, followed by metallic crashes and bangs and a "YAARGHHHH!"

"Well?" Scorpion Number One tilted its buggy head toward the opening. It didn't have a mouth that I could see, but I felt sure that it was giving us an evil grin. "Go say hello to your grandpa."

Grandpa?

My first view of the mighty Susano'o, Lord of the Seas, Master of Storms, and Ruler of Ne-no-kuni—that is to say, my grandfather—was . . . well, let's just say he was not what I expected.

What I expected was a towering, wild-eyed guy with bulging muscles, and long, matted black hair, and a beard full of centipedes. I thought he'd be dressed in samurai armor, wave a sword around, and yell a lot, maybe with the blood of his enemies dripping from his mouth or something.

What I saw was a towering, wild-eyed guy with a dad bod, and long, matted gray hair, and a beard full of crumbs and candy wrappers. He was dressed in black leather jeans and a worn leather jacket over a black T-shirt stretched across a slightly bulging belly, and he was windmilling away on an electric guitar and screaming unintelligibly into a microphone, under a big banner that said SUSANO'O AND THE SCORPIONS.

I didn't know whether to be relieved, disappointed, amused, or annoyed. *This* was the mighty Susano'o, Lord of the Seas, Master of Storms, and Ruler of Ne-no-kuni? One of the most powerful gods in existence? The guy everyone was afraid to offend, the guy I'd been terrified to meet, the guy who had banished Mom from her beloved island and who might just murder me for showing up and introducing myself? This was my *grandfather*? He looked like an aging rock star. Or like a dad who thought he was still a rebellious grunge-rock teenager.

What. The. Heck.

Still, better safe than sorry. We crept in, making ourselves as small as possible and pressing close to each other. The iron door shut behind us with a *clang* that Susano'o didn't seem to hear. He had a backup band of scorpion dudes behind him: There was a drummer who used four arms to play the loudest, fastest riffs I'd ever heard, while his two pincers acted as their own *clackety-clackety* sound-making instruments. There was another guitarist, and a bassist, too. Probably because none of them had hands or fingers at the ends of their arms, they weren't very good— just very loud.

The song came to an end with a long howl from Susano'o and a *biaaww-woww-woww . . . ba-da-bum!* from the rest of the band.

"Whooo!" Susano'o threw his head back and pumped his fist in the air with his pinky and first finger extended. "Yeah! Woo-hooo!"

After an uncertain look at each other, Danny, Niko, and I acted as one. Niko barked and yipped, and Danny and I clapped and cheered. Danny even threw in one of those really loud whistles that I'd always wished I could do. "Whooo!" we yelled. "Rock on! Yeah!"

Susano'o lowered his fist, lifted his head, and turned to face us. He stretched his arms out and did that palms-up flapping gesture with his hands that meant, *More! More!*

So we kept cheering, and he raised both of his fists this time and shook them.

"YEEEAHHH!" he bellowed, and the scorpions in his backup band banged their instruments and clacked their pincers and bellowed along with him. "YEEAAHHH! All hail the mighty Susano'o!"

"Woo-hoo!" I shouted. "Woo-woo-wooo!"

"Encore! Encore!" yelled Danny.

"All hail the mighty Susano'oooo!" Niko howled.

Every time we started to quiet down, Susano'o would do the "More!" gesture and we'd have to crank it up again. The longer we clapped, the more awkward it got. Also, oddly, my electric monkeys had dissolved or disappeared, maybe because they were disappointed, or maybe because Susano'o's chaotic energy was so huge that it extinguished them. Or maybe it was just the awkwardness of finding out that my grandfather was an obnoxious old man with a huge ego. During the fourth round of applause, I shook my head at Danny and whispered, "This is nuts. When are we going to stop?"

"When he says!" whispered Niko. "Woo-hooo! We love you, mighty Susano'o!"

"My hands are gonna fall off," Danny complained as he clapped.

As we entered round number five, I lost my patience. I was done clapping and cheering for anyone who thought they naturally deserved everyone else's adoration and obedience, even if they were my grandpa and also the Lord of the Seas, Master of Storms, etc. He was just being a jerk at this point.

So I stopped clapping and called out, "Um, hi, Grandpa," and waved.

Danny, looking relieved, also stopped clapping and cheering. Niko gave me a panicked look and almost choked mid-"whooo," but recovered and kept going even louder than before.

"YEAHHHH! SUSANO'OOO! WOO-HOOO!" he yelped—but Susano'o had silenced his scorpions, so Niko was the only one cheering. He realized this a couple of seconds too late, and with the rest of us staring at him, he gave one last half-hearted "Whoo!" before tucking his tail, coughing nervously, and smiling the kind of smile where you show all your teeth and it looks like you have parentheses around your eyes.

Now that Niko had been silenced, Susano'o turned his attention to me. And wow, was it ever different, being under his gaze. Instead of an aging wannabe rock star, I saw his true self—his true power. His electric guitar had turned into a deadly-looking sword that sparked and crackled like lightning. His eyes were dark, and when I looked into them, I heard howling hurricane winds and claps of thunder. Everything around me disappeared as I felt the uncontrollable power of the entire ocean surging and crashing around me like a tidal wave—like I'd been swept away from where I was standing, and I could get sucked under and drown in all that power, and Susano'o would watch me and not care one bit about my teeny-tiny life, even if I *was* his granddaughter.

No, I thought. *This isn't fair! I have to save Mom. Why is he being so awful?*

But my thoughts disappeared in the wind and waves, and I had to focus all my attention on breathing and finding a way out of the chaos. I tried to summon my buzzy-monkey energy from before, but it felt just out of reach, like a life buoy bobbing away from me in a violently churning sea. And just when I thought I *would* drown, the feeling of being tossed around in a stormy ocean subsided, and I was back in the fortress looking at an old guy with long, scraggly hair who was wearing a leather jacket and pants that were just a *little* too tight. Instinctively, I raised my hands to my face to brush the water off—but my face was dry.

"*Grandpa?*" He opened his mouth and roared with laughter. It made me think of boulders crashing down a hill. "Why, you impertinent little guppy! Grandpa! I don't think anyone in the history of time has ever had the nerve to call me Grandpa!" He laughed again, and added, "And I should tell you that very few have looked me in the eye and survived with their minds intact, so bonus points for you, guppy. It shows you really are one of mine."

My insides leaped when I heard that, and the sliver of hope I'd squashed earlier struggled free and went darting around inside me like a shiny little fish. Things were off to a good start—he seemed to know who I was, *and* he hadn't killed me (yet). He even seemed proud of me. Maybe he was sorry about what he'd done to Mom. Maybe he'd been too proud to apologize, but now that I was here, he'd help me save Mom's life and welcome us back. I didn't love his nickname for me, but I guessed it was better than "squid" or "flounder" or "hagfish."

Feeling more confident, I decided to introduce my friends.

"This is Niko." I gestured to Niko, who immediately flopped to the ground and began murmuring words like "Your Mightiness" and "I am your humble servant."

"And this is Danny." Danny didn't get flat on the floor and start mumbling like Niko, but he did bow very deeply. I noticed that both of them were carefully avoiding any eye contact with Susano'o.

"Ah yes. I was told about you and your little power play out there, your little 'You shall not pass!' bit. Took guts! I like a kid with guts. I do, indeed." He licked his lips and patted his belly, and I wondered nervously if he might have meant he liked to eat them.

Danny, who hadn't looked directly at Susano'o this whole time and had therefore missed the lip-licking and belly-patting, said, "Thanks!" and looked pleased with himself.

There was a long silence while Susano'o stroked his beard and tossed away whatever got caught in his fingers: a KitKat wrapper, a gummy worm, and a cockroach that squeaked as it sailed through the air.

"So. You're here to beg for Kusanagi," he said finally. It wasn't a question. "Don't deny it; I saw it in there." He tapped his head and pointed to mine, and rested his arm possessively on his guitar, which I could now see had a kind of animated painting on it of grass being blown flat by an unseen wind. I remembered that this was how Kusanagi had gotten its name, which means "grass-cutter": it mowed down soldiers in its path like grass. At least it wasn't an animation of a literal sword mowing down a field of soldiers. That would have been gross.

"Well, yes," I said. "We really, really need it because—"

I remembered that he'd just read my mind, and he probably wouldn't want me to waste his time. "I mean, yes, that's why we're here."

There was a pause while my grandfather (it was so strange to think of him that way) seemed to consider my request. Danny showed me his crossed fingers and grinned.

"Well? Because what?" Susano'o shouted, making Danny, Niko, and me jump. "Tell me, girl! I haven't got all day!"

"Oh! I thought . . . because you knew we were here for—"

"I saw Kusanagi, but I'm not interested in poking around in that little brain of yours for your *reasons* and your *feelings* and all that balderdash. So? Let's hear it! What do you want it for? Why do you need my dearest, most prized possession?"

Let's Get Down to Business

"**We—I—need it to save** my mother's life," I said. "Your daughter, Takiri-bime. And also—"

"TAKIRI-BIME?" Susano'o bellowed. He looked like he might explode. "My very first, beloved daughter, to whom I entrusted the guardianship of the hidden gate between Earth and Yomi, who betrayed me and abandoned her sacred duties for the sake of that puny . . . little . . . mortal . . . *PUNK*?"

"Um . . ." I didn't know how to react. "Yes?" I said in a tiny voice.

"Er, technically, Your Magnificent Mightiness, she didn't abandon her duties so much as . . . Ahem, that is to say, perhaps you may recall that she was forced to flee," Niko babbled, "during a typhoon that, ahem, that *you* sent after her fledgling family . . . er, after which you cursed her and banned her from returning to the island forevermore."

It was pretty weak, as far as backups go, but I could tell that it was taking Niko every ounce of courage he had to even say this much, and I felt grateful to him for his loyalty to Mom. Maybe the word "family" would help Susano'o focus on what was important.

"Ha! Good point, fox," Susano'o said. "I'd forgotten about

that curse. That was one of my better storms, if I do say so my-self. Nearly drowned the entire island, didn't I?"

My shiny little sliver of hope turned to a glop of muddy disappointment. It was becoming clear that I couldn't count on Susano'o being nice to me on account of us being family—family obviously didn't mean the same thing to him as it did to me. Maybe that was what happened when you were one of the most powerful gods in the world and had been around for thousands of years—stuff like personal relationships and human life and death just didn't mean as much anymore. It made me think Mom must have been pretty special if she could fall in love with a human and love her half-human daughter the way she did. My heart throbbed with homesickness and guilt. I *had* to get Kusanagi. I could not fail.

If I couldn't make him care about Mom, maybe I could make him care about a demon invasion of Earth. "Uh, anyway, the thing is, since you banished Mom—I mean, Takiri-bime—" I took a breath and went for it. "Shuten-dōji got some tengu to steal Dōjigiri for him, and he's got his head back, too. And a bunch of oni from Yomi have attacked the Island of Mysteries, and they're ruining it, which is killing Mom, and if she dies, her binding spell will die with her. And if I don't stop the oni from killing Mom before Kami-Con, Shuten-dōji will lead an army from Yomi through the portal to take over the earth while the kami are away. But I'm not a legendary samurai or anything, and Niko and Danny and I aren't strong enough to defeat the oni on our own, so Kusanagi is our only hope!"

Susano'o lifted a bushy eyebrow. "Take over the earth, you say? The Middle Lands?"

That's right! I thought. Mom used to say that since he'd made his home on Earth, Susano'o considered himself to be in charge of not just the seas but all the Middle Lands, and that some people even saw him as a sort of Father Nature.

"You wouldn't want Shuten-dōji to ruin all your work on Earth, would you? He'll pollute the seas, he'll cut down forests . . . ," I said. "I bet Amaterasu would make fun of you for letting that happen, and for being in charge of such a dirty, polluted place. We could prevent all of that."

Susano'o lowered his eyebrows. I held my breath. "Hmm. That does sound just like her," he growled. "She's always thought she was better than me. Just because she's older."

"Yeah, and Shuten-dōji might even try to come for Ne-no-kuni," Danny jumped in. "I bet he wants to be the next lord of storms and master of the sea. He'll probably steal your centipede army and take over your fortress while you're at Kami-Con! That would *really* be terrible!"

"I'd like to see him try!" Susano'o rumbled. His face went dark, and the ground shook so hard that one of the cymbals fell to the floor with a crash. "YARRRGHH! I'll bash him to bits! I'll smash him to smithereens! I'll mash him to mincemeat! Bring it, baby! Bring that sneaky little upstart to my fortress and WE'LL. SEE. WHO'S! *BOSS!*" Susano'o's voice rose until I thought my ears would explode, and wind and rain whipped around the chamber as he started morphing into his elemental form again.

Danny and I looked at each other in horror. Had we gone too far? I'd had no idea how much Susano'o loved a fight. But if we couldn't convince him to let us fight the oni before Kami-Con, Mom would die.

"Ah . . . ahem. If I may, Your Gloriousness!" Niko called into the storm. "The problem, as we have said, is that Shuten-dōji will have had several days during Kami-Con to wreak havoc on your kingdom before you get a chance to, er, crush him to crumbs. Wouldn't it be wiser to send a select group of warriors to stop him *before* he ruins everything?" The wind died down a little bit.

"You could undo your curse and let Mom go back to the Island of Mysteries," I suggested. "Then she could undo the binding spell and the two of you could take care of the oni and everything would be fine."

"I will do no such thing!" Susano'o's face grew red, and I heard the rumble of distant thunder. "I am the mighty Susano'o, and I stand by every action I have ever taken! I change my mind for no one! I . . . REGRET . . . *NOTHING!*"

. . . aand we were in the middle of another storm.

Knowing that he'd rejected Mom, Dad, and me once before should have prepared me for his reaction, but seeing for myself just how little Susano'o cared about us was much more painful than I'd expected. I fought to swallow the lump in my throat.

As we waited for him to calm down, I had time to think about why Susano'o had gotten kicked out of the Sky Kingdom. It wasn't just that he was basically an overgrown toddler with the destructive power of a Category 5 hurricane. He had to show it off and wreak havoc with it in order to *feel* powerful. Who wants to live with that?

But I also had a feeling that he was pretty fragile underneath all that bluster. I wondered if it had to do with the way he was born: his dad, Izanagi the Creator, blew his nose, and the snot that came out was Susano'o. That would give anyone a complex. That's why I'd always felt a little sorry for him for getting booted out of the Sky Kingdom by his beautiful, shining, snobby brothers and sisters, basically for being weird and socially awkward. Okay, so he also had huge, incredibly problematic anger management issues. But I totally got how he must have felt.

Once Susano'o was back down to a light simmer and the storm had calmed to a drizzle, I went for it. He liked plucky? I'd give him plucky. And maybe he didn't love me or even Mom, but he did seem to have *some* family pride. Maybe I could use that. "So anyway, that's why we're here! Shuten-dōji is obviously no match for you—but he'll ruin everything before you get a chance to fight him, right? So why not lend Kusanagi to me and let us have a try? I'm part of the Susano'o line, after all. I know I've got what it takes."

I tried to stand up straight and look powerful and plucky. *I am the granddaughter of Susano'o,* I reminded myself. *And the daughter of Takiri-bime. I have their power.* Inside, of course, the electric monkeys had disappeared again and I now felt like I was made of squirrels—jumpy and skittish and ready to run for cover at any moment. Why did that feeling have to be so unpredictable?

Susano'o smirked at me. "Why would I give Kusanagi to a little guppy like you, who can't fight? You've probably never even held a sword like this one." He brandished his guitar, and for a moment its true nature—a gleaming silver sword—flashed in front of us.

"Well, I uh . . ." My attempt at pluckiness sputtered out. We were doomed.

"She never said she wasn't good at fighting, sir." It was Danny. "She only said that she wasn't a legendary samurai. So she's not legendary *yet*. Who knows—she could be the next Tomoe Gozen!"

Ha! If only I could be like Tomoe Gozen, one of the greatest samurai who ever lived—and a woman. Even if it was impossible, it felt good to hear Danny say it, like he really had faith in me. I shot him a grateful smile. It felt a little like old times, when we were real friends who had each other's backs. Maybe after all of this was over, we could go back to that. Maybe that was why he was here with me.

Then Niko spoke up. "Ah yes, Your Mightiness! This granddaughter of yours—even if she has a human father—is destined to be a great warrior! Her victory over the oni will reflect back on your august name. New legends will be told about you, new songs sung—" He stopped abruptly when Susano'o held up his hand. We waited in agonized silence while Susano'o groomed his beard and grumbled darkly to himself for a very, very long time.

"All right, you've convinced me!" he said at last, and I let out a sigh of relief. "Or you've convinced me to give you a chance, anyway. It's been thousands of years since the last time anyone had the gall to visit me and ask for the kind of help you're asking for. That person was a grandchild as well, come to think of it. Had eighty brothers trying to murder him because some princess chose to marry him over them. And do you know what he did? Came down here to ask for help, fell in love with my daughter, and stole her away from me!"

"Wait . . . he fell in love with his *mom?*" Danny gasped.

"His auntie. She was young and beautiful, so I can see why the boy fell for her."

"Ew."

Susano'o gave an irritated sigh. "Not 'ew.' You humans are alive for such a short time—you're still newborns at the end of your puny little lives, with your eyes and ears sealed shut. Even the very wisest among you have only squinted at a corner of the kami-verse. Accept this, and stop mewling about what you do not understand."

"Yes, sir," said Danny. But when Susano'o wasn't looking, he wrinkled his nose at me. I shrugged. I'd heard this story since I was little, and I'd never really thought about it. Clearly, neither had Danny. And now that he pointed it out, I guessed it was weird to fall in love with your aunt. But Susano'o had a point— these were kami we were talking about, and kami did things differently.

"Now! Let's get down to business." Susano'o rubbed his hands together. "You're right, guppy. I do not want Shuten-dōji to mess with my stuff, and the pleasure of heading over right now and beating those oni back to where they came from is not worth spending the rest of eternity on the Island of Mysteries. And I'm not going to erase my spirit to break your mother's binding spell. However, I have no intention of forking over my most valuable possession to just any little pip-squeak who comes across my path, grandchild or no. You must prove yourself worthy of the Sword of the Wind before I can trust you with it."

With that, he waved Kusanagi in a circle over his head, and everything disappeared in a flash of blinding white light.

A Whole Panel of Panic Buttons

When my vision came back, we were standing at the entrance of an outdoor shopping mall, between a Japanese sushi-and-steak restaurant and a Gap store. The sign over the gateway read WESTFIELD OLD ORCHARD.

"Where are we?" I asked. "I mean, besides the mall. And why are we here? Are you going to conjure up a shikome and we have to fight her or something?" I asked nervously. There was no way we could defeat a shikome. If it hadn't been for Mom, the one from a few days ago would have eaten us alive for sure. "Do we . . . do we get to use Kusanagi?"

Susano'o burst into laughter. "Wahhh-hahahahah, you must be joking! You're no match for a shikome. She'd snap you right in half and crunch you up like a KitKat bar. Ahh, little guppy, I like your nerve. So entertaining." He laughed again, then sighed and wiped a tear from his eye. "No, no, guppy. I've just been craving a hot dog lately—a good old-fashioned Chicago-style hot dog. A nice, crisp Vienna Beef dog with mustard, pickle relish, onions, tomatoes, peppers . . . oh, and a spear of dill pickle and a dash of celery salt, all on a soft poppy-seed bun. . . ." Susano'o's eyes glazed over, and he smacked his lips loudly.

213

"One of humanity's greatest accomplishments, if you ask me."
Next to me, I heard Niko licking his own lips. Or his snout, or
whatever foxes have instead of lips.

"That does sound like quite the culinary coup, Your Mightiness," he said dreamily as a bit of drool dribbled out of his
mouth.

"So, uh . . ." I looked around. People were streaming past
us; a few of them stared at Susano'o, but that was it. I supposed
Susano'o looked like an ordinary human being to them, even
though you could feel the power practically radiating off him.
"Is this the trial? We have to get you a hot dog?" I asked. "Seriously?" There had to be a catch.

"Wahhh-hahahaha!" Susano'o threw his head back, which
sent crumbs and candy wrappers flying. "Of course not! That
was just a little joke, guppy girl! Sending you into a Westfield
shopping center to find a hot dog? That's not a challenge worthy
of Kusanagi!" He paused to brush a crumb out of his eyebrow,
still chuckling. "You know what *is* a worthy trial, though?"

Susano'o snapped his fingers, and suddenly we were standing at the edge of a large field of grass as high as my hip. "Sending you into an *actual* field to find my golden arrow!" He was
holding an arrow in his right hand, and a bow in his left hand
that was as tall as he was. He held up the arrow and moved it
slowly in front of us, like a magician, before nocking it on the
bow and drawing the string back. "Bring it to me by nightfall,
and Kusanagi is yours." I could hear the bow creak as it bent,
and just when I was sure it was going to crack right in half, there
was a *twayayayayang* as he released the string and the arrow shot
into the air.

"Where is it?" I asked, searching the sky frantically. "I can't see it!"

"There!" Danny pointed, and finally I saw a slow-moving dot way above the field. I shaded my eyes and tried to follow it.

"What are you waiting for, you flat-footed flibberty-gibbets? We haven't got all day! Run!" Niko said, and bounded off in the direction the arrow was headed.

"Hahahaaa! Yes, run! Run like the wind, little fox! Run like the wind, little guppy and your runty friend!" Susano'o bellowed, and laughed his rumbly laugh. There was a boom of thunder, even though the sky was cloudless and blue, and he was gone.

I looked out over the field. It had to be miles and miles around, and Niko had completely disappeared in the tall grass. What were we going to do? I tried to reach into myself to find that hum of power from before, but it wasn't there. As a last resort, I plunged my hand into my pocket for my spool—but my pocket was empty. I don't know why, but that one small loss pushed a whole panel of panic buttons.

"It is *on!*" Danny was saying. "We're all over this. Come on, Momo!" He squinted at the sky. "Look, it's still falling! Can you see it? Let's go!"

"No, wait!" I grabbed his arm. My spool was missing. I didn't have a plan. I thought about how big the field was, how fast and far away the arrow was flying, and how small it was, and suddenly the task seemed impossible. I felt paralyzed. My knees went weak, and my heart started pounding—just like with Uncle Kappy, just like with the mukade.

"What? Hey, let go!" Danny tugged himself away from me, still looking at the arrow.

"It's too hard," I whispered back.

"It's *not* too hard. Look, the arrow falls, we find it, end of story. The only hard part is that we have to do it before it gets dark, so come *on*, Momo, stop freaking out about it and hurry up!"

"Are you kidding?" I said. "There's no way we're going to find an arrow in all of that grass. Look!" I pointed to where the arrow had just reached the grass and disappeared. "How are we going to know when we get there? That could be a mile away, or two miles away. And what if we get dehydrated? Or—or sunburned? And what about Niko? How are we going to find him? What if he finds the arrow and then he can't find us? Or we find it and can't find him? And—" I suddenly remembered Susano'o's words. "Susano'o said to *bring the arrow back to him*. But he's gone! What are we supposed to do about that? What if this is a trick? Or a trap? How do we bring it to him if we don't—"

"Whoa, calm down! Breathe! Why are you freaking out like this? We've literally escaped an army of ghost crabs, defeated a kappa, and tricked a million giant centipedes into not attacking us, and you're worried about finding an arrow in a field? We're a team, remember? We can do this!"

"I know, I know. . . ." But my mind wouldn't stop churning out reasons why this time, we'd fail.

"What's going on, Momo? Also, can we get moving, please?"

"I don't know." I tried to focus on slowing my breath down. "Those times, it was like . . ." I thought for a second. "I didn't have a choice. I had to do something *right then* or we'd be dead. Plus, I had help, remember? Niko told me how to tackle Uncle

Kappy. You got the mukade started on the idea that I was some kind of powerful demi-kami. Which I'm not."

"Yeah, but you totally crushed it every time. Also, um, hello, you are literally Susano'o's granddaughter. You're the only one of us who can look him in the eye. If you can survive all of that, you can handle whatever he throws at us."

Danny's pep talk did make me feel a bit better. Still, there was so much I couldn't control. Like my connection with Susano'o, if that's really what it was. Where was it now that I needed it? Maybe it wasn't real. Or maybe Susano'o had disabled it somehow.

And also, "What about Niko?"

"Foxes have a good sense of smell, right? Plus, ever hear of shouting? We'll totally find each other."

"Okay, then how do we find Susano'o? If we find the arrow, that is."

"Stop worrying! I'm sure it'll be fine. He'll probably just appear, or maybe there'll be a portal or something. Or we'll go back to where we started. We'll deal with that when we find the arrow, okay?"

"I don't know. I feel like we're already lost . . ." Wait—why did I feel like we were lost? I looked around and realized we'd been walking through the field for most of our conversation. "Hey! You tricked me!"

"I didn't trick you. I just started walking and you came with me." Danny grinned. "See? Not so hard. Don't think. Just do. We're totally going to beat Susano'o. Your mom's gonna be so proud."

Now that we were on our way, I couldn't exactly back out.

Especially since I couldn't see where we'd started anymore. And because I had to save Mom. I'd been so panicked, I'd lost sight of my whole reason for being here. "Fine. But as long as we're here, can we go a little faster?"

"Um, *yeah*." He picked up the pace until we were jogging.

"You can go ahead, I guess," I said after a few minutes. "The sooner we start looking, the better."

"No, we should stick together. We're a team, right?"

I have no idea how long we were out there in that awful field. It was one of those situations where you keep wondering how long you've been slogging around in the hot sun, but you also don't really want to know because no matter what the answer is, it would probably make you cry. It must have been hours, though, because the sun was high in the sky when we started, and it was now getting dangerously close to the horizon.

"I think we've already searched this area," said Danny. "This grass looks walked on. See right here, how it's sort of flatter than the other grass?"

"We haven't searched this area," I said, probably a little more rudely than I needed to.

"I dunno, Momo. I think we have."

"We haven't! Because of the system!" I snapped.

"We haven't, because of the system!" Danny mimicked me in a high, whiny voice. "You and your 'systems.'" He put sarcastic air quotes around the word and rolled his eyes.

I mentally took back what I'd thought earlier about us maybe being friends again. He was the worst. He didn't understand me, he didn't appreciate my careful planning, and he was just plain old mean.

The first thing we'd done was try the laser pointer on Danny's phone. But it seemed like it just didn't get reception down here. By the time we had reached the part of the field where we thought the arrow had fallen, though, I'd figured out a system. Danny and I would walk a hundred steps in one direction, then move up a couple of feet and walk a hundred steps back. "That way we won't accidentally retrace our steps, and we'll know that we've covered every inch of ground," I'd said.

Danny had been skeptical at first, but after a brief argument, he'd agreed to give it a shot, and we'd started searching. But like I said, it had been hours. We might have been a *little* bit crabby and stressed.

"Just admit it, Momo. It's not working. I mean, it was a good idea, but we've definitely been on this spot before. I think we need to give up and try something new."

I looked down at the broken stems of grass where Danny was pointing. Then I looked at Danny and saw real worry on his face. If overconfident, optimistic-for-no-good-reason Danny was worried, maybe we really were in trouble, and my system had failed.

But if I accepted that my system had failed, where did that leave us? In the middle of a giant field of dry grass with nothing to rely on but pure chance. We'd covered so many rectangles in so many different directions that by this point, I was all turned around. We probably *were* retracing our steps. But I *needed* this system to work, or I would completely lose control—not just of the situation but of my actual self. I'd have to listen to the panic worm in the back of my brain, which was screeching in its wormy little voice, *What if we picked the wrong spot? What if the arrow actually landed a mile away? What if we walked by it already and missed it? We'll never find it before sundown! We're going to fail and Mom will die and Shuten-dōji will destroy the world!*

I had just opened my mouth to drown out the screeching with a long, angry rant about how I hadn't seen *Danny* come up with a plan, and if he could think of a better way—which I doubted—he should go ahead and tell me, when he held up his hand and said, "Do you smell smoke?"

We're in a Literal Ring of Fire . . . or Haven't You Noticed?

I closed my mouth and sniffed the air. It *was* a little smoky. "Where's it coming from?"

"There." I looked where Danny was pointing.

"What the—" A gray smudge sat on the horizon, so small that I could cover it with my thumb and pretend it didn't exist.

"This is not good," said Danny.

"Oh, you don't think so?" I snapped. My panic worm got louder. *Help! Hurry! We're doomed!* it shouted, and I felt like it was not only shouting but also running around in circles inside my brain and getting my other thoughts all jumbled and confused. I turned away and closed my eyes and tried to focus on breathing, which was only halfway helpful, since every smoky breath reminded me of our situation. But after I counted ten breaths, I felt a little bit better. I opened my eyes—and immediately felt even worse than before.

There, on another spot on the horizon, was another gray smudge.

I grabbed Danny's arm at the same time that he grabbed mine. "Danny."

He tightened his grip. "This is really, really bad."

"No kidding, genius."

"No, I mean *really* bad." He pointed off to the side. "Look."

Another gray smudge.

I spun around. On the opposite side of the third smudge, just as I'd feared, was a fourth one. And then a fifth. And a sixth. Everywhere we turned, we saw more smudges of smoke on the horizon. And they were growing. And was it my imagination, or had the wind picked up?

"We have to get out of here," Danny said in a tight, choked voice. But I didn't see how. With every second that passed, the gaps between the individual fires on the horizon were getting smaller and smaller. There was no way we'd be able to make it to the edge of the field before those gaps closed.

"This whole thing was a setup," I said, finally understanding the situation. "He never meant for us to find the arrow. He set those fires. He sent us out here so we'd be trapped."

Amabie's prophecy came back to me, her vacant eyes and eerie voice. *Betrayal,* she had said. I felt like I'd been shot into space—or sunk to the bottom of the ocean—somewhere cold, dark, and empty. She'd been right. Susano'o had betrayed me. He'd said he would help me, but all along he was planning to kill me, just like everyone said he would. My very own grandfather.

A glimmer of that jittery feeling pulsed through me—*oh, now I feel it, now that I'm about to die,* I thought. But it wasn't listening to me. *How dare he treat me this way?* the feeling whispered. *His very own granddaughter!* For a brief moment, I forgot about feeling sad and rejected. All I wanted was to fight back. I wanted revenge.

But Danny's voice jolted me back to the problem at hand, and the feeling evaporated.

"Where's Niko? He's gotta be out here somewhere. Why hasn't he shown up?" He sounded impatient, like we'd made an appointment to meet Niko here and he had bailed on us. But I could hear the worry underneath.

"I'm worried about him, too," I said. I looked around in despair. "There's no way we're getting out of this alive." I hated thinking about Niko dying alone out there; if we were going to die, then I wanted to die together.

"Niko!" Danny started shouting. "Niiikooo!"

I joined in, but after a minute or so of shouting without hearing an answering yip, I knew it was no use. "He's out of earshot," I said, and the slump of Danny's shoulders told me that he knew I was right.

"Hey. What if we stay here and, like, pull up the grass? I'm sure he's looking for us, so if we stay here and just call for him every once in a while, he's bound to find us. And when he does, we'll have this little safety area."

I wasn't sure how much protection a little patch of dirt would give us from a raging prairie fire coming at us from all sides, but I didn't have any better ideas. Then as I watched Danny pulling up and tossing aside random handfuls of grass, I realized I did.

"Wait! First let's make a perimeter, like a circle. Then we'll move around the circle and pull the grass up on the outside as we go—"

"Gah! Why do you always have to make things complicated? Just hurry and pull the grass!"

"—a little at a time so we have a firebreak. *Then* we can pull up the grass in the middle. We'll have way more time that way to clear a larger space."

Danny looked down at the teeny-tiny patch of ground he'd cleared. "Ugh, why do your plans always have to make sense?"

It *did* make sense. And like my arrow-searching system, it made me feel like we had a *little* bit of control over this uncontrollable situation. We moved in a circle and methodically yanked handful after handful of grass out of the ground, shouting Niko's name every so often. But there was *so* much grass, and it didn't come up easily, and after a while, my back was sore, my hands were blistered, the firebreak we'd made around our "safety circle" wasn't even a foot wide, and there was still no sign of Niko. Meanwhile, the fire roared closer and the air seemed to grow smokier with each breath. Maybe I'd made a huge mistake. I could feel panic creeping up on me again.

For the hundredth time, I scanned the field for Niko's bushy red tail, but all I could see was an ocean of dry yellow grass and a little rim of orange dancing beneath the thick gray ring around us.

"I wish Niko was with us already," I said.

"Yeah, me too. He must be so scared, all alone out there." Danny threw a handful of grass and dirt out over the field. "At least we have each other."

I watched as Danny stooped to grab another handful of grass. *At least we have each other.* He'd sounded like he'd meant it, too. Who would have guessed that Danny Haragan would ever say to me, Momo Arashima, "At least we have each other"? It didn't even matter, because we were all going to die anyway. Except it did matter. Because that's what friends—real friends—said to each other. Probably it was just the threat of death closing in on us that had made him say it. But maybe, just maybe, my best friend—the old Danny, the *real* Danny, the one I'd missed so much—was coming back to me. In spite of our dire situation, my heart suddenly felt so full of joy, I almost hugged him.

My thoughts were interrupted by a peevish growl. "Oh, I like that! Leave a poor fox to die in the field all alone so you can save your own sorry skins, will you?"

"Niko!" I ran to him, sank to my knees, and wrapped my arms around him. "I was so worried about you!"

"Oh, now stop that sentimental nonsense," he huffed. But he didn't try to wriggle out of it, and when I let go of him, I saw him blink away a tear.

"We wanted to look for you—we kept calling you!" said Danny. "We just didn't want to give up on surviving. And I didn't want to leave Momo alone."

"Excuses, excuses," sniffed Niko. "I suppose I will be able to find it in my heart to forgive you, you coldhearted cad."

"He's not coldhearted," I said when I saw Danny looking upset. "We were both worried about you."

"Hmph. Be that as it may, we don't have time for this blither-blather. What in the name of the Sky Kingdom have you been doing here?"

I started to explain my plan, but Niko cut me off. "Stop. This is futile. This is a wild waste of time. A silly strategy. What we need to do is find an exit."

"Are you nuts? We're in a literal ring of fire, Niko, or haven't you noticed? There *is* no exit!" Danny shouted.

"That's where you're wrong, my blustering boy. And that's

why I came looking for you—because I knew you'd never think to look down."

"Down?" I asked.

"For an exit."

"Oh! Like another portal in the ground? Or a trapdoor or something, like in the Taira palace?" Danny started stamping the ground with his foot, like maybe he might trigger a switch somewhere.

Niko paced around the circle we'd made, staring at the ground. "They're everywhere. You just need to know what to look for."

"Okay, so what are we looking for?" I started examining the ground around my feet. "A crack? A handle?"

"A hole, of course!"

"But—"

"Aha! Right here! What did I tell you?" Niko lifted his head and grinned. He pointed with his nose down at a hole in the ground. "This is our path to safety!"

"But that's tiny!" I blurted.

Danny held up a hand. "I couldn't even get one of my hands through there, let alone the rest of me!"

The fire was so close that waves of heat were coming at us like wind, carrying bright orange sparks that fell around us and started smoldering in the grass. My eyes had begun to water, and I could barely breathe without choking.

"Do you want to escape the fire, or do you want to turn into a strip of seared meat?"

"I—*whoa.*" I have no idea how it happened or how it worked. All I know is that one second, Niko bent his head down and stuck the tip of his nose into the hole like he really meant to squeeze his entire body through it—and the next second, he sort of drained into the hole the way water drains through a funnel.

"Okay, then. Let's do this," Danny said.

We walked up to the hole. "You go ahead." Danny swept his arm out gallantly. "Since you're the demi-kami and everything."

"Whatever." Cautiously, I stuck my toe in. For a moment, nothing happened, and the panic worm jerked its head up and I wondered if something was wrong with me. I turned to Danny and started to say, "What's going on?" when *sploop!* I slipped through.

It was like going down a slide: smooth, slick, and fast, and then *flump!* I landed on what felt like a pile of straw. A moment later, I heard Danny land next to me. I couldn't see him—it was so dark that I couldn't tell if my eyes were open or closed. It made sense. We were underground, after all. Under-underground, in fact.

"Hello, what's this?"

Someone lit a lantern, and three figures appeared in front of us. When my eyes adjusted to the light, I almost screamed. I was looking into the faces of three humongous black-eyed, twitchy-nosed mice. The most humongous mouse was frowning at us, the middle-sized (but still humongous) mouse was smiling, and the smallest (but still humongous) one was staring at us like we were a gross but fascinating new bug it had just discovered. It was holding something the size and shape of a football in its hands and nibbling intently as it stared. You know how when you see a mouse eat a seed in a video, and it holds the seed in its teeny-tiny hands, and its teeny-tiny mouth moves in fast motion and it's so cute? Well, let me tell you something. When the mouse eating the seeds is taller than you are, and its teeth are three inches long, and it could probably chew your arm off if it wanted to, it's not so cute. It's terrifying.

Niko shushed me before I could even take a breath. "Well? Where are your manners? Bow to the nice mice!"

Good manners are always a wise idea when you're facing three rodents much bigger than you, so Danny and I bowed, and the mice nodded their heads.

The serious one said, "Good evening, earthly fox and human children. I am Emi, the eldest."

"And I am Mika, the middlest," said the middle-sized-but-still-humongous one.

The least-humongous one took a big bite out of his football-seed and chewed a million miles an hour and didn't say anything.

"Hey! It's your turn!" Mika nudged him.

"Oh! Thorry." Bits of brown seed fell out of his mouth. "And I'm Kai, the cleverest."

"He is not the cleverest. He's the youngest," said Emi, rolling her eyes. Kai stuck his tongue out at her, but she ignored him. "Anyway. Ahem. I regret to inform you that you are intruders in our kingdom, and we must kick you out. Goodbye."
All three mice waved.

"Wha—" *Splooop!*

We were back up on the field, stumbling in the choking, eye-watering smoke, the hot, swirling wind, and the crackle of flames eating up dry grass. The area inside the ring of fire had gotten much smaller even in the few seconds that we'd been gone. It was maybe the size of a soccer field (that is, if soccer fields were round—but you know what I mean, right?) and closing in steadily.

"Hey! Hey, please! Let us back in!" Danny was already kneeling above the hole, calling into it. "The world is literally on fire out here! Please let us in!" He reached into the hole, but instead of sliding through, he jumped back. "Ow! I think one of them bit me!" Sure enough, a drop of blood appeared on his index finger.

A normal-sized mouse stuck her head out of the hole and squeaked furiously, "What part of 'You are intruders and we must kick you out' did you not understand?" She crawled all the way out and shook her tiny mouse-finger at us. "I've got half a mind to let you back in and feed you to Uncle Rat!"

"I beg your forgiveness a million times over, Miss Emi," Niko cut in quickly. "He's just a human boy. He hasn't been brought up properly. Please, O magnanimous, majestic, magnificent mouse." He crouched down low. "You see the danger we are in. These children are on a quest to save the world from the demons of Yomi. They must survive. And they're just children."

"Plus, Momo's half kami," said Danny.

Emi looked thoughtful. "Hmm. I am not fond of humans. But I am less fond of demons."

"We should help them. They're children, after all," said Mika, who had just popped up. "Even if they are hairless and ugly."

"Why don't they have fur yet?" asked Kai, sticking his head out of the hole. "They're not babies anymore, are they?"

"Please," I said, kneeling. "We're begging you." I turned to cover a cough. I could practically taste the smoke in my mouth.

229

"We could let *you* in, fox, but the rule is, no humans."

"Why?" Danny asked. "That's not fair."

Emi sighed impatiently. "Because humans ruin everything—no offense. But look at what you've done with the earth."

"Good point."

"But the oni will make it even worse! And we can't let that happen. Please, there must be something we can do." I looked around anxiously. Our soccer field–sized space was growing smaller. Sparks and bits of ash were flying through the air like orange and black snow.

"Let's see how much they know about mice!" suggested Kai. "If they can answer our questions right, we'll know they're friends."

"Oh yes, good idea!" Mika said. "I couldn't bear it if we left these poor hairless babies out here without giving them even a little chance."

Kai and Mika turned to Emi, who seemed to be the one in charge. She looked thoughtful. "Oh, all right," she said, and Kai, Mika, Danny, Niko, and I cheered. "I will ask you three questions. If you get even one of them right, you can come in. I think that's more than generous."

"Thank you! Oh, thank you, thank you, thank you, most merciful mice!" Niko practically sobbed. "Now, if you could please hurry . . ."

I Know This One! Pick Me!

"Question number one," said Emi. We were crouched around her with our hands cupped to our ears, listening hard. "If three mice can eat three seeds in three minutes, how many mice does it take to eat a hundred seeds in a hundred minutes?"

This wasn't a mouse question. This was a math question. I looked at Danny, my mind spinning. Three mice, three seeds, three minutes. So if you pretended that it was one seed per mouse, that meant it took each mouse three minutes to eat one seed each. So if you had four mice and four seeds . . . it would still take three minutes. Hmm. What if—

"A hundred mice!" said Danny.

"No! No, that's not our answer! We take it back!" I shrieked. "Danny, that's wrong! We take it back!"

"There are no take-backs," said Emi gravely. "The answer is—"

"Three! Three mice!" I shouted. "Because if you give them each two seeds, it will take six minutes for six seeds. If they each get three seeds, it takes nine minutes for nine seeds. And all the way up to a hundred! Three mice, a hundred seeds, a hundred minutes!"

"That is correct, but your friend has already submitted an answer," said Mika. She gave us a kind smile. "Don't worry, you've got two more chances."

Noooo!

Kai was still counting on his fingers, muttering, "Six mice, no, three mice, two seeds . . ."

"Question number two. What is a mouse's favorite winter sport?"

Danny, Niko, and I looked at each other. "Niko, you're an animal. Do you know?" I asked.

He shook his head.

"Do not yell the first thing you think of," I warned Danny.

"Okay, okay. Lesson learned. You don't have to rub it in," he groused.

What did mice like to do in the winter?

"Go sledding?" Danny whispered.

"Snowball fights?"

"Hibernate?"

"That's not a sport. And I did a report on mice in fifth grade. They don't hibernate," I said.

"Okay, smarty-pants. What do they do, then?"

"Um . . ." I thought about mice and snow. Snow and mice.

"Time's up! The answer is—"

"Mice hockey!" Kai shouted.

"*Mice* hockey?" Danny was also shouting. "But that's not a—"

"Get out those mice skates, put on those pads and helmets, and woo-hooo, we're good to go!" Kai began pretending to skate in a circle around Mika and Emi. "Last year, we *crushed* the mukade in the NHL championship final."

"Let me guess—the Ne-no-kuni Hockey League?" I said.

"Well, of course. What else would it be called?" asked Kai. "She's not very smart, is she," he whispered to Mika.

"Shhh, that's not nice!" she scolded him.

"Question three," said Emi, barreling ahead with the quiz, which was fine with me because our not-on-fire-yet area was now the size of a basketball court.

"What is a mouse's favorite dessert?"

Seeds? Berries? Cake crumbs?

"I got this," said Danny, and he whispered his answer in my ear.

"Yes," I said. "That's perfect! That has to be it!" I smiled at Danny and felt a swell of relief and hope. He'd lost us our first chance at safety, but he'd just come through.

"Mice cream!" he shouted triumphantly, and he raised his hand and I high-fived it and got ready to *sploop* back under-underground.

"Noooo!" Niko flopped onto the grass and covered his eyes with his paws.

"You monsters! What is *wrong* with you?" Emi looked horrified. "The correct answer is blackberries! There, there, Kai, it's all right. Don't be afraid." Kai had dived behind her, and she gathered him into her arms and gave him a hug while he whimpered into her shoulder.

"What a cruel, cruel answer," said Mika, shaking her head. "I—I'm sure you didn't mean it, though, right? You look like good children."

"What—what did I say wrong?" Danny asked.

"Mice cream is a *cat's* favorite dessert," explained Niko.

"They catch mice and they, er . . ." He looked nervously at Emi, who was scowling at him. He lowered his voice to a whisper. "They grind them up and mix them with cream and sugar."

Danny groaned miserably. "I didn't know! I swear I didn't know. I just thought, you know: ice hockey, mice hockey; ice cream, mice—"

"That will be quite enough," said Emi. "And that fire is becoming very uncomfortable, so thank you for playing and all that, but we'll be going now. Best of luck in the future."

Ha. All five minutes of it. The fire was so close now, and so big, I couldn't see over it. The heat was almost unbearable. This couldn't be the end! Those questions hadn't been fair! (Well, maybe except for the first one.)

"Please give us another chance," I begged her. "Danny and I couldn't know the answers to your questions. Mice in our world don't play sports or eat dessert. Come on. Kai answered that sports question for us, anyway, so it shouldn't count. We should get another one. And it should be about something we might know about in the human world, like the question about the seeds. It's only fair."

Niko chimed in, too. "They are but babbling babies. Surely you'd want the same for your own babies if they ever got into a fix like this." He gave them a pretty impressive fox version of puppy-dog eyes.

"Oh dear," said Mika. "Oh, Emi, please, let's give them just one more chance. The poor naked babies."

"If we survive, we'll make sure your names are known all around the world. In our world. And we'll tell the mice in the human dimension about mice hockey," said Danny hopefully. "Maybe you could even do an out-of-league scrimmage."

"Oooh, that sounds fun!" said Kai, perking up. "I like that!"

Emi crossed her arms and sighed. "Oh, all right. One last question. But that's it! Now, let's see . . ." She held her tail in one hand and tapped her chin with it. "Aha! I have the perfect question. Ready?"

We nodded. The fire had paused at the little circle that Danny and I had made by pulling the grass out of the ground, thank goodness, but I knew it wouldn't be long before a spark landed inside the circle, or the flames just got so big that they crossed right over.

"Question number four: What is long and thin and deadly and says, 'Sssss'?"

A snake was my first thought. But that couldn't be right. It was too easy.

"Oh! Oh, I know this one!" Kai jumped up and down and raised one paw. "Me! Pick me!"

"Shush!" Emi said. "This one isn't for you, silly boy!"

Snake? Danny mouthed at me, making a squiggly motion with his arm. But his nose was squinched up and his eyebrows were in a little V. So he was on the same page as me: totally unsure.

Niko shook his head. "What else could it be?"

Kai was dancing from one foot to the other. "Oooh, this is a good one! You'll never guess it!"

"We want them to guess it!" Mika and Emi said, and Kai immediately stopped dancing.

"Oh, right. Oh, please guess it! Can I give them a hint, Emi? Please?" And before Emi could answer, he went ahead and said, "We found one in the grass today!"

That wasn't helpful. Of course you'd find a snake in the grass.

But it couldn't be a snake. I *knew* it couldn't. But it probably wasn't a trick answer, either, like when you say, "What has hands and a face but no eyes or fingers? A clock!" because technically, none of their answers had been trick answers. Mice hockey was a real thing. The other two questions had also been about real things. Which meant that Emi wasn't asking riddles. She was asking actual questions. It was just that the answers weren't the first thing that popped into your head. So what was long and thin and dangerous and went *"sssss"* that they had found in the grass that wasn't a snake?

There was a popping sound and I saw a bright orange spark fly out of the fire around us and float toward the grass just inside the circle.

It reminded me of something I couldn't quite put my finger on—and no, it wasn't the fact that we were about to be burned to cinders. That was obvious. But what had that spark reminded me of?

Smoke began to rise from the spot where the spark had landed in the grass.

"Hurry! Just say snake! Even if it's not the actual answer, it's still not wrong, right?" Danny said.

Somehow the thing I wasn't remembering seemed important. I tried to picture the spark as it curved through the air. . . .

Tiny flames flickered under the smoke and began to grow . . .

236

. . . and landed in the grass.

"If you don't say something, I will!" Danny was frantic, and Niko had begun to howl.

What had Kai said as a clue? *We found one in the grass today!* And then I knew.

"Susano'o's arrow!"

"Yes!" Emi's face broke into a big smile. "What a relief. I was so worried you'd say something silly like 'a snake.' Hurry now, we don't have a moment to lose!"

She herded Kai and Mika into the hole, and then Niko, then Danny, then me before she *sploop*ed through right behind me and the little circle we'd been standing in was completely engulfed in flames.

I've Got a Plan in My Pocket

"Here it is," said Kai proudly, gesturing at an arrow as long as a telephone pole and as thick as a pool noodle. But I guess since we were small enough to fit inside a mouse's nest, the arrow was really the size of . . . an arrow. "See how it says 'ssssss'?" He pointed to a golden S painted near the tail end of the arrow.

We told the mice our story—how we needed Kusanagi to fight the oni and prevent Shuten-dōji and his army from invading the earth, and how Susano'o had promised to consider giving it to us if we found the arrow he'd shot into the field.

Emi nodded skeptically. "I hope he keeps his promise" was all she said, and I mean, she had a very good point.

But we didn't really have a choice, so we lined up next to the arrow the way she told us to.

"Put your hands on it—or you can bite it, I suppose," she said, nodding at Niko, "and it will take you back to Susano'o. But make sure to do it together, or one of you will fly back and the other two will still be here with us."

We bowed, and the mice bowed back, and Niko said, "Ready? On the count of three. One, two, *three!*"

I closed my hand around the arrow. Instantly I was flying

through someplace dark and cold, going so fast that my eyes watered. And then I was back in Susano'o's practice room, holding on to the arrow with Danny and Niko.

On the stage in front of us, fast asleep on his back and snoring so hard that a foul-smelling wind swept around the room every time he exhaled, was Susano'o. And right there on his belly, with one of Susano'o's hands resting on its body and the other clasped loosely around its neck, was Kusanagi in its guitar form.

"Should we wake him up?" I asked the other two, very softly because I really *didn't* want to wake him up. "Or maybe just put the arrow down next to him and wait?"

"Or we could put the arrow down and sneak out," said Niko.

"Or we could keep the arrow, take Kusanagi, and sneak out," suggested Danny. Then he put the arrow in his backpack and grinned.

Niko's jaw fell open. "Have you gone bananas?" he hissed. "No way! Never! Not on your life!"

"No, wait." I held my hand up. That buzzy feeling was back, and it was on Danny's side. *Susano'o owes you,* it said. "Susano'o just tried to burn us to death, Niko! Like, on *purpose*! If we give him his arrow back and wait around to see what happens, do you really think he's going to say, 'Great job, kids, here's my sacred sword!'?"

"Exactly!" Danny said. "He didn't care whether Momo lived or died, and she's his *granddaughter*! I know guys like him, and trust me, the only way to get what you want from Susano'o is to kick his butt." I wondered briefly which bro-bot Danny was talking about.

"But we *can't* kick his butt, which is why we have to escape," I said. "With Kusanagi." The thought of sneaking up to the giant snoring on the stage was terrifying, but Kusanagi was *right there*.

Niko's whiskers quivered. "May I remind you that we don't know the way out of the fortress? Or Ne-no-kuni, for that matter? And Danny's phone has no signal! And what about the towering temper your grandfather will be in when he discovers that we have snuck off with his sword? We will get lost, captured, and ground into mush! What will I tell your mother? Oh, no, wait—I won't be able to tell her anything because I'll be dead! In Yomi!"

"Look at it this way," I reasoned. "If we stick around, he tries to kill us. If we take Kusanagi and run, he tries to kill us. Not to make it too obvious, but which option gives us a chance to get out of here with Kusanagi?"

"Yeah! Go, Momo! Go, Team DaMoNik!" Danny put out his fist, and it took me a second to realize what he was doing, but then I figured it out and we bumped fists like real teammates. "And check this out." He reached into his pocket and pulled out the empty spool of thread. "I've got a plan in my pocket."

I stared at it. "Where did you . . ."

"I think it fell out of your pocket just outside the fortress, when we all fell down."

"Can I have it back?"

"Hold out your hand."

I did, and instead of the spool, Danny placed something across my fingers—thread! "How did you—?" I followed it inch by inch to the doorway that led out to the hall.

"It rolled in front of my face during all that wind outside the entrance to the fortress, and it had thread on it. So I tied it to a rock," Danny said with a satisfied smile. "Since my flashlight wasn't working. Uh-huh. That's right. You're not the only one who can plan ahead."

I had to admit I was impressed. "That's just what I would have done."

Danny rolled his eyes. "Oh, yay. I'm as smart as you."

"Oh. I mean . . ." I blushed. I hadn't meant to sound so condescending. "Great thinking, Danny. Thanks."

"You're welcome." He was grinning again. Whew.

Niko was still skeptical. "How do you intend to flee the fortress once we're at the exit? Have you picked up some teleportal magic since we've been inside? And even if we make it outside, how will we get out of Ne-no-kuni?"

"You can do your lock-opening thing, can't you?"

"My lock-opening magic doesn't work here. Or had you already forgotten?"

"That's okay. We'll—we'll figure it out as we go," I said— though the truth was, if I thought too carefully about the details of this plan, my reckless confidence faded. And now that I *was* thinking about it, was it even a plan? I started feeling sick.

"Momo! Did I just hear you say *'we'll figure it out as we go'*?" Danny said in fake shock. "Did the mice hit you on the head when we weren't looking?"

"Ha-ha," I said, doing my best to sound confident again. "You're not the only one who doesn't plan ahead."

"Well, what are you waiting for, then?" said Niko, who had apparently completely changed his mind. "Let's get going before this overbearing oaf wakes up and decides to throw us into a room full of vipers."

Working carefully, I eased Susano'o's hands off the guitar while Danny unclipped the strap. I don't know exactly what I'd been expecting when I actually put my hands on it—an electric jolt, maybe, or a full-body rush of that feeling that had been flickering in and out of me since we'd arrived in Ne-no-kuni. But I felt nothing—just the neck and metallic strings, and the lacquered wood body. Just a guitar. Was it even the real thing?

I'd just stood up with the disturbingly not-magical-feeling guitar in my hands when Susano'o grunted and started waving his own now-empty hands around. I stumbled backward with a squeak and nearly dropped Kusanagi. "Thunderbolts and lightning, very, very frightening," Susano'o mumbled as I tried to get my heart to stop banging around like a drum accompaniment to his terrible singing. Fake or real, I realized, it was in my hands. I was committed now.

"That was a close one," Danny whispered as he tiptoed toward the door. "Come on, let's get out of here before he wakes up!"

"Hang on." The thing was, I just *knew* Susano'o was going to wake up, and I knew that Niko was right about him crushing us into mush if he caught us. And it turned out that even though I was ready to jump in and take a risk, I also still needed to take a couple of safety precautions, because I sure as heck didn't want to make a break for it just to be turned into Momo pudding.

I knelt at Susano'o's feet and untied his boots.

"What are you doing? We haven't got time for puerile pranks!" whined Niko from the door.

"Help me!" I gestured to the electrical cords that lay all over the stage, and started tying the laces from the right boot to the laces from the left boot. "We don't want him chasing us, right?"

Danny understood immediately and began unplugging the cords from the mics and amplifiers, looping the ends around Susano'o's knees. He passed another cord around Susano'o's ankles a couple of times in a figure eight, and we knotted everything to a nearby pillar. Niko paced back and forth, moaning and growling at us to hurry.

"There!" I stood up and took a look at our work. Susano'o's boots were tied together, and the rest of him was tangled up in cords and tied to the pillars around the stage. Hopefully it would buy us more time than we'd just spent.

On the way to the door, Danny rushed to the back of the stage, then returned holding Susano'o's giant bow in his hand. "To go with my other souvenir," he said with a grin.

"Bye, Grandpa!" I called softly as I picked up Kusanagi at the door. "Thanks for the very nice presents!"

We slipped into the corridor, and Danny used the invisible spool of thread to guide us quickly through the maze of hallways that led back to the entrance hall. We couldn't move fast enough for Niko, though; he kept trotting ahead and coming back, going, "Hurry, hurry, hurry!"

"It's too dark in here to hurry!" I whispered.

"We don't have time to dawdle!" he whispered back. He circled around me, trying to herd me forward like a sheep, and either he circled too close, or I walked too fast, because all of a sudden I was falling. I felt Kusanagi slip out of my hand as I flew forward. I knocked into Danny, and we hit the ground at the same time. Danny and I went *"Oof."* Danny's bow went *snap.* Kusanagi went *KUNG-KA-KUNG-KUNGG-ka-BAOW-WAOW-WAOW-WAAAAOWWWW.*

For about three seconds, everything was completely silent as Danny, Niko, and I stared at each other, frozen with horror.

And then the ground shook, the lanterns on the walls rattled, and even the actual air seemed to vibrate as Susano'o's roar of rage thundered through the fortress like a hurricane.

"RRRAUUUGHHHHHH!!! WHERE IS KUSANAGI?!"

Man Up—I Mean, Woman Up. Or Whatever.

"At least we don't have to worry about being quiet anymore," Danny said as we took off. And the yelling seemed to prove that I had the real Kusanagi by the neck. Unfortunately, we had to leave the broken bow behind.

Moments later, another roar echoed through the halls: "SOMEONE COME HERE AT ONCE AND HELP ME WITH THESE FLIPPIN' CORDS!"

Even though I was terrified, it was kind of funny to imagine the mighty Susano'o, Lord of the Seas, Master of Storms, and Ruler of Ne-no-kuni tripping over his tied-together bootlaces, so when Danny smiled and gave me a thumbs-up, I smiled back.

But once we got to the entrance chamber, the thread disappeared into the slick gray granite wall, and there was nothing left to smile about.

Danny was fishing around in his backpack and muttering to himself with growing intensity, "I need a weapon, backpack! Like, now! Please!" Grateful that at least I hadn't put Kusanagi in my backpack, I held it out in front of me and wondered how the heck I was going to turn it into a sword.

"You'd better get ready to use your ninjutsu and karate

skills," I said to Danny. "If you haven't found anything by now, it's pointless to keep looking."

"Yeah, um. About those skills," Danny said, looking up from his backpack. The way he said it made me very worried about what he would say next. "I mean, I'll do my best. But I only got to blue belt before I quit, and I haven't really done the ninjutsu stuff—I've just read about it online—so we might need to focus on getting that guitar to turn into a sword."

For a second, I wavered between petrified and furious. I landed on furious. "A *blue belt*? Before you *quit*? *Stuff you've read online*? Are you *kidding* me? You had me thinking you were some kind of martial-arts ninja master!"

"Hey, I didn't actually say I was a black belt or anything. I said I studied martial arts and ninjutsu, and that's true."

"You *did* say you were a black belt! You lied to me!"

Danny looked mortified, but I didn't care. I needed to figure out how to make Kusanagi transform, or we were doomed. I looked at it carefully. Maybe by playing it?

I gave it a good strum. The room filled with sound, but nothing else happened. As the sound faded, I could hear the distant *clomp, clomp, clomp* of scorpion soldier boots on the floor, and a slower *thud . . . thud . . . thud*—Susano'o, I guessed.

I tried holding Kusanagi out in front of me like a real sword, but it stayed guitar-shaped, and when I tried swinging it, the momentum knocked me off center and I almost fell.

I wanted to cry, scream, and throw the guitar across the room all at once. "Why won't it work for me? What's wrong with me?"

Clomp, clomp, clomp.

Thud . . . thud . . . thud.

"Here, give it to me," said Danny, holding out his hands. "Hurry."

"Why?" Suddenly I felt really possessive.

"There's no point in you having it, Momo. You can't make it transform, and you can't swing it without falling over. Even if I can't make it turn into a sword, at least I won't hurt myself trying to use it."

To be honest, what he was saying made sense. But it made me mad. Kusanagi was *my* sword, and it wasn't fair of Danny to say things like that to me. And if my grandfather was going to kill his own granddaughter for taking his sword so that I could save my mother's—his daughter's—life, then I wanted to fight and die holding that sword. Even if it was still a guitar.

"Just give it to me! We don't have time to argue!"

"No!"

CLOMP, CLOMP, CLOMP!

THUD! THUD! THUD!

Danny stepped forward and tried to grab Kusanagi away from me.

"Hey! I said no! Kusanagi is *mine!*" I tightened my grip on the neck as Danny's fingers closed around it, and a tidal wave of chaotic, earthshaking energy surged through me.

There was a *BANG!* and a flash of red light, and I thought maybe Susano'o had entered the hall, but when I blinked and looked around, Danny was sitting on his butt on the floor a few feet away, looking dazed. And I was holding a shimmering sword in my hands. Finally. The weird electric energy I'd felt earlier was here, in the sword, and it was flowing through me, too.

"YAAAAGHHH! Hello, guppy girl! Going somewhere?"
Susano'o boomed as he entered the hall.

Shaking, I turned toward his voice. Yeah, I had this amazing sword, and yeah, it felt pretty great, but even without Kusanagi in his hands, power rolled off Susano'o in huge waves. I was pretty sure that he could have bowled us all over in a second if he'd wanted to. Then there was the squadron of six-foot-tall scorpions behind him, each one holding every sharp, pointy weapon you can imagine, all aimed at us. And of course, Kusanagi chose that moment to start glitching and sputtering back and forth between its guitar form and its sword form, like it was changing its mind about me. I felt my own power—and my connection to Kusanagi—draining away.

"Oh-ho! What's this I see? A bit nervous, are we? Looks like Kusanagi remembers who the true master is around here. Looks like maybe you aren't as worthy as you thought you were. Didn't realize that Kusanagi only works for those who can handle its power, did you? So how 'bout you give it back to your dear old Pop-Pop like a good little guppy?"

"Don't let him scare you, Momo!" It was Niko. "Did you see what just happened? Danny couldn't touch Kusanagi—it *chose* you. It belongs with you just as much as it belongs with His Mightiness! Own it! Become one with it!"

Okay. Okay. True.

"You got this, Momo. Come on. Man up—I mean, woman up. Or whatever," Danny said. He got to his feet and winced. "Niko's right. If you can hold it and I can't, that *has* to mean something."

If I hadn't been so focused on becoming one with Kusanagi,

I might have told Danny to get over himself. But I was also glad to hear him backing me up.

I can do this, I told myself as I tried desperately to reach inside for what I was now starting to think of as "my powers." I had to. Mom was counting on me. Her life depended on me. In reality, of course, the *whole world* depended on me, I knew, but saving the whole world was too much pressure. It was easier to focus on Mom.

Slowly, Kusanagi began to stabilize in its sword form, and I felt a faint pulse of electricity as its power flowed through my hands and into the rest of my body, searching for a connection. I realized my eyes were closed. When I opened them, I saw Susano'o watching me with one bushy eyebrow raised.

"So you think you're ready to play with the big kids, eh?"

I had no idea if I was ready to "play with the big kids." But I had a feeling I was about to find out.

Not Bad for a Sneaky, Thieving Guppy Girl

"No." Niko stepped in front of me. "She has to save Takiri-bime and she has to fight the oni. If you want a fight, then fight me instead."

"And—and me." Danny stepped up as well.

"What are you doing?" I muttered at them. "He'll kill you!"

"You're the most important part of this team," Danny said under his breath. "Plus, I'm better at fighting than you." I didn't know whether to be grateful or incredibly annoyed.

Susano'o grinned. "What valiant friends you have, Momo. But I want to see what *you've* got inside, not them." He waved his hand, and both Niko and Danny fell to the floor. Then he nodded at one of his scorpions. "You. Go out there and see what this guppy girl can do."

Panic washed over me like a waterfall. Kusanagi flickered dangerously in my hands. But through the roar of fear in my head, I heard Danny shouting, "Kusanagi chose you, Momo! It thinks you're worthy!"

"Kusanagi chose me," I repeated under my breath. "It thinks I'm worthy." Susano'o was the reason all of this was happening. He was the one who'd banished Mom, who'd made her give up everything so that she could stay with me and Dad. He was the reason I had to spend my life worried about Mom and miserable at school instead of living with both of my parents on an island paradise. I felt the rush of anger and prickly energy, stronger than ever before. Susano'o had ruined my life. He'd ruined Mom's life. And now he was just toying with me. I hated him for it.

The scorpion came bounding across the space that separated us, hissing and brandishing evil-looking knives in four of its hands. Without quite knowing how I was doing it, I focused all my anger into a single stream and directed it into Kusanagi. That scorpion was dead meat.

I found myself stepping into the fight with a power and skill that wasn't my own. The scorpion lunged forward. I jumped aside just in time, using Kusanagi to cut a deep slice into its shiny black armor. With a scream of pain, the scorpion wheeled around and hurled one, two, three knives at me, but I batted them all away like tennis balls: *ping, ping, ping!* I'd barely finished swinging Kusanagi the third time when the scorpion attacked again—the knives had been a distraction, so I wasn't ready when his tail whipped around from the other direction and knocked my feet out from under me. Kusanagi clattered to the floor, just out of reach.

As if in slow motion, I saw the glittering stinger on the end of the scorpion's tail diving toward me as I rolled sideways and reached desperately for my sword. I swear it jumped into my hands and slashed the scorpion in half by itself. There was a squealing, metallic sound like train brakes, and a smell like burning tar. Panting, I staggered to my feet and stared as black goo oozed from both halves of the scorpion's body, which then collapsed in on itself until it disappeared, just like the shikome had.

I had just killed a giant magical scorpion. Me, Momo Arashima. A golden rush of triumph swept through my veins as the black goo sizzled and smoked on the ground in front of me. Kusanagi morphed back into a guitar, and all the energy we'd been sharing evaporated along with the dead scorpion. I felt exhausted but exhilarated.

"YESSS! Way to go, Momo! You did it!" Danny threw an arm around my shoulders for a side-hug. "You were a *monster* out there!"

"Not bad for a sneaky, thieving guppy girl," Susano'o added. I looked up at him, and he smiled. "I'm impressed." The scorpions must have been impressed, too, because they'd all retreated about ten steps.

"Kusanagi chose me," I said. "It thinks I'm worthy. You and your soldiers have tried to kill me three times now, and I survived. You owe it to me and to my mom to let me take Kusanagi to fight the oni." *YES.* What a mic-drop moment!

Susano'o looked at me long and hard. *Oh yeah?* I thought, still feeling cocky. I took a deep breath, gathered my strength, and stared back. Once again, his power buffeted me like a rowboat in a raging sea. I struggled to keep breathing and stay afloat as wave after wave crashed over me. Then time and space strrreetchhed and twisted, and suddenly it was only me and Susano'o face to face in the middle of nothing—just cold wind whipping through a deep black void above, below, and all around us. Our eyes were still locked. I gritted my teeth and kept staring—and realized that I couldn't have looked away if I'd wanted to. It felt like he was looking *into* me, like he was really *seeing* me. In his eyes, I saw surprise, then confusion, then a flash of shocked recognition. And something else . . . just the faintest hint . . . It didn't make sense. It didn't match Susano'o's energy. . . . Was it . . . ? Could it be . . . ?

Fear.

A boom of thunderous laughter shook me like a leaf in the wind, and we were back in the present. "HAHAHAAA! You are full of surprises, I'll say that much. But so am I!"

He snapped his fingers, and Kusanagi leaped from my hands to his.

"Hey!" I shouted indignantly. "I earned that! Kusanagi *chose* me—you saw it happen!"

"True and true. I like your spirit, guppy girl! Talking back to me like I couldn't crush you between my thumb and forefinger right now. Kusanagi may have chosen you, but I am still its master, and I get the final say." He threw back his head and laughed again, but I noticed that he kept a wary eye on me. He was only pretending to be amused.

"Why won't you let me have it, then?"

"Ha! Wouldn't *you* like to know?"

"Yes, as a matter of fact, I would!"

Susano'o leaned back and studied me, looking more thoughtful than I would have guessed was possible for him. I tried to stare him down, but he chose not to manifest himself in his elemental form, so it was just a standard, uncomfortable stare-off, except Susano'o wasn't really playing, so it was really just me feeling awkward and silly and furious.

"Uh, what's going on? What are you talking about?" Danny whispered.

I ignored him and kept my eyes on Susano'o. "You saw something, didn't you." I remembered the surprise and the fear I'd seen in his eyes. "That's why you won't let me have the sword."

"Momo! What's going *on*?" said Danny again.

"I think he looked into her mind," Niko said in a hushed, awed voice.

At last, Susano'o harrumphed and nodded to himself. Apparently, he was done thinking.

"So?" I asked. I raised my chin and tried to look fierce.

"I have made a decision." He snapped his fingers, and Kusanagi was back in my hands again. "You may keep Kusanagi and continue on your quest to banish the oni from the Island of Mysteries."

"What did you see?" I demanded.

"Not telling. Better if you don't know."

"*What?* Why?"

"You're in a fragile state. Couldn't handle it."

"Is it bad?" asked Danny.

"Is she dying?" asked Niko.

"Niko!" Danny and I both stared at him, horrified.

He looked embarrassed. "I thought it best to start with the most painful possibility."

"She is not dying, you foolish little beastie."

Well, that was a relief, at least.

"Is she in danger?" It was Danny this time.

"Of course she's in danger!" Susano'o snorted. "You're all in danger! You're going to battle against an island full of demons, aren't you?"

"You have to tell me something. Just give me a hint," I pleaded.

"*I said NO!*" Susano'o roared. His voice shook the walls, and everyone cowered, including me. He lowered his voice to a growl and said, "What I saw, guppy girl, could change everything. *I* am still in shock. I, the mighty Susano'o, Lord of the Seas, Master of Storms, and Ruler of Ne-no-kuni! You? Ha! If you knew what I know, you'd run away screaming, and we can't have that now, can we? The way I see it, we're all better off with you not knowing."

I swallowed.

"Well, okay, then. Glad that's settled." Susano'o slapped his palm on his thigh. "Now, where were we? Ah, yes. I had just bestowed Kusanagi upon you for having proven against all odds to be a fighter worthy of the honor. You're welcome."

"Er, thank you," I said. "But—"

Susano'o ignored me and pointed at Danny. "And you, worm boy! To reward you for your misguided but well-intentioned bravery, and seeing as you've already stolen one of my arrows"— Danny gulped, but Susano'o just grinned—"you may as well have the set, and the bow that goes with it. I admire your spirit." He whistled and held out his hand, and his bow appeared just like it had in the field, whole and unbroken and resized to fit Danny. He tossed it to Danny, who caught it easily. Then Susano'o snapped his fingers, and a scorpion soldier presented Danny with a bundle of eight arrows. "The arrow you stole is charmed so that it will never fail to hit its target. The other arrows are not so charmed, but they *will* split into eight once you let them fly."

"Seriously? No way! These are *dope!*" Danny looked at the arrows with an awestruck smile on his face until Niko nudged him and he remembered his manners. "Uh, thank you, O mighty Susano'o," he said, and bowed until he was practically folded in half.

"Speaking of thanking me," said Susano'o, "I will also grant you safe passage to wherever you wish to go next. If you have any time to spare, I advise you to use it to learn to tap into Kusanagi's full power. You did reasonably well against my poor soldier, guppy girl, but Shuten-dōji is an immeasurably bigger threat than a scorpion. Unless you can do better, it'll be *your* blood that soaks the ground in the end, and that won't be any fun, will it? Not for you, anyway."

I shook my head. "No, sir."

"Ahh, what a fight this will be! You'll have to tell me all about it—assuming you survive." Susano'o brayed with laughter and slapped his thigh again.

Meanwhile, Danny had put away his bow and arrows and pulled out his phone. He looked at it. "Two days left until Kami-Con starts."

Susano'o raised a hairy eyebrow. "Better work quickly, then. Well, fox, despite your groveling and whining, you seem to be the one in charge of this outfit. Where will you go on the last day before the beginning of the end of the world as you know it?"

"Oh, thank you, for your generosity and protection, Your Most Gracious Might—"

"Yeah, yeah. Yada, yada, yada. Just tell me where you're going!"

"Yes sir, thank you, sir. I was hoping to take them to Mikado-bashira. The Sacred Gateway Pillars."

"Good choice, fox. So be it."

Susano'o clapped his hands three times. Each time his hands came together, the air around us exploded with the sound of thunder. Just before the final clap, I saw his eyes gleaming at me. Then the light blinked out and the wind blew us through the portal to Mikado-bashira like a cloud of atoms.

I'm Not Afraid.
I'm Just Not . . . Not Afraid.

When the wind died down and the darkness lifted, we were standing on a rocky beach at the base of a craggy gray cliff. Massive boulders lined the shore on either side of us, and wave after wave bashed into them and burst into sparkling white spray that the wind carried and scattered over us. The sea stretched around the island under a cloudless sky. Not too far away, the sea and sky met in a soft line of puffy white fog that was broken only by a smear of grayish-greenish sludge.

"Is that . . ." I nodded at the darkened area.

"The Island of Mysteries," said Niko, nodding.

"Oh," said Danny softly. "So all that gray stuff—is that because of the oni?"

Niko nodded again.

I still had questions about what Susano'o had seen and what he'd just said to me, but the visible evidence of the oni on the island demanded my attention. I took another look around. "Is this where we're supposed to get ready to fight the oni? Are we supposed to stay here on the beach?" It didn't look very comfortable. Actually, when I thought about it, it had been ages since the last time we'd slept. I could probably have fallen asleep right then and there.

"Open your eyes, girl. Look around. You'll need to assess your environment faster than that if you want to defeat those dim-witted demons."

If they really were dim-witted, I didn't see why I needed to learn to think faster, but I let that go and looked at the cliff behind us. A network of fraying rope ladders, narrow ledges, and steps cut into the stone led up to the top, where a few scraggly shrubs waved in the wind.

I gasped. "We have to climb up there? That must be a hundred feet!"

"At least," agreed Niko.

"You'd think he could have dropped us off at the top," Danny grumbled. "I don't suppose there's one of those portals around here somewhere? Or a secret elevator?"

"The only portal available to us is the one at the top that connects to the Island of Mysteries."

"How about helmets, then? Or, like, safety ropes or anything?" Danny asked.

Niko just snorted.

I stared at Danny in surprise, because climbing up a cliff seemed like just the kind of thing he'd be great at. And since when did he worry about helmets and safety ropes? That was what *I* was supposed to do. Maybe he was making fun of me?

But Danny was rooting frantically around in his backpack, and when he came up empty-handed, he looked like he might be sick all over the beach.

"Do we have to go up there? What's wrong with staying down here?"

"You may stay down here if you wish. But there is more room at the top, and when the tide comes in, you're going to have to hope there's a raft in that backpack, or you'll be treading water all night."

Danny looked even sicker. "Treading water?"

"Even if you could swim, we can't stay down here, Danny. We need to climb that cliff," I said.

"I *know*," he snapped. Which was when I finally got it. He was afraid of heights! I thought of how scared he'd been when we jumped into the boat on the Sea of Heaven. Then other, older memories came flooding back to me. He never wanted to ride the Ferris wheel at the county fair. He'd refused to do the climbing wall at the school carnival, claiming it was for losers. He'd behaved so badly on our class field trip to San Francisco that he'd had to stay with the bus driver while the rest of us went to the top of Coit Tower. It all made sense now.

"It's okay to be afraid, Danny. That cliff is really tall. *I'm* afraid."

"I'm not afraid. I'm just not . . . *not* afraid. Of heights. I'm . . . I'm not great with heights. That's all. So just leave me alone."

I lost my patience. "Why do you always have to be such a show-off? There's nothing wrong with needing a little help getting through something. Why can't you just admit that you're afraid of this one thing?"

Danny's answer came bursting out in an angry rush. "Because boys are supposed to be brave, okay? Leaders are supposed to be brave. *I'm* supposed to be brave. If the guys at school ever knew that I was scared of heights, they'd laugh at me. They'd never let me forget what a wuss I am for being afraid of heights, or not being able to swim, or . . . And my dad—" He stopped suddenly. His face was all red and he was breathing hard. "Anyway, you're a girl, *and* you're not . . . I mean . . . whatever. The point is, you wouldn't understand."

"I'm a girl and I'm not what?" I demanded. "I'm not cool? I'm not popular? Is that why I wouldn't understand? Because girls aren't supposed to be brave? And losers like me don't have a cool reputation to uphold, so I can be as cowardly as I want and no one will care?"

"That's not what I meant!"

"Yes, it was."

"Anyway, girls *aren't* supposed to be brave!" he said. "It's true! I know it's sexist. I'm not saying it's right. I'm not saying that girls aren't *actually* brave. But, like, girls aren't under the same kind of pressure. People don't make fun of girls who get scared. But they do make fun of boys."

"Well, they shouldn't," I said.

"Well, they do. That's why if you want to succeed as a guy, you can never show fear. People will think you're weak."

"What a pile of festering fish! Whoever taught you that nonsense?" Niko cut in, his fur bristling.

"Um, like, every successful male athlete and businessperson ever, practically? And didn't some world leader say that the only thing we have to fear is fear itself? It's stuff everyone just . . . knows!" Then he said, "And look at my dad. He never shows fear, and he's super successful. He makes a ton of money."

"People like that are jerks, and you should stop listening to their advice because it's made *you* into a jerk, too," I blurted out, thinking of how Danny's dad had taught him how to "get along with people" by abandoning me and turning into a bro-bot.

Danny's face went red again.

"I—I mean . . ." I stammered. I hadn't meant to say Danny's dad was a jerk. Not exactly, anyway. Ugh. I tried again. "You're not really a jerk. But I think that stuff about not showing fear is bad advice. You shouldn't be afraid to tell people you're afraid."

"I know, but . . ." Danny heaved a sigh and shrugged, like there was nothing he could do about it. "I don't make the rules."

"For what? Being popular?"

"For succeeding. For *surviving*. And you have to follow the rules if you want to survive."

I hated to admit it, but he wasn't totally wrong. I definitely wasn't the seventy-first most popular kid at Oak Valley Middle School because I was great at following the rules of middle-school survival. It was so unfair. Why did the rules have to be so awful? And why did the popular kids insist on following them and enforcing them? They had the power to change them and make everyone be nice to each other, if they wanted. Why didn't they?

I thought of Mom, who also didn't understand the rules for how to fit in. I'd always blamed her for making me this way, too, but now I understood how cool she really was. Mom never made me feel bad for not fitting in—she'd tried to make me feel like it was okay not to understand or even follow the rules, but to be my own weird self, like her. She'd never tell me to hide my feelings in order to succeed or survive. For a moment, I missed her so much, my chest got tight and my throat hurt and I had to blink back a few tears.

"You can be scared of things when you're with us," I said. "Niko and I won't make fun of you. Because we know how it feels to be scared, and being scared isn't funny."

Danny nodded. "Okay. Um. That's cool." He paused and cleared his throat a few times, then added a little stiffly, "Thanks." And then he smiled. Not the charming smile he used at school, but a smaller one. A real one. The kind we used to share before he turned into Danny Haragan, Popular Kid™.

That reminded me of what he'd just said about me not understanding his feelings because I wasn't popular like him. Which hurt. I was about to tell him that maybe he shouldn't care so much about being popular, and by the way, maybe he shouldn't have abandoned me for those kids in the first place, when Niko cut me off.

"I hate to interrupt this endearing emotional moment, but the tide is still coming in and the wind is still coming up, and I, for one, would like to be at the top before this beach is submerged in salt water." He turned and scampered up the rocks to the first ledge, and with his jaws he grabbed the rope ladder that hung above it. He gave it a couple of good tugs and turned to us. "It's perfectly safe," he said, and began climbing.

Niko was right. The tide was coming in like it meant business, and we'd be knee-deep in the ocean before we finished hashing out whether Danny should bother trying to be popular and why he owed me an apology. So I said, "I guess we should start climbing, then."

Danny swallowed and looked up at the ledges, ladders, and narrow stairs. "I don't know if I can do this. How about if you go up on your own? I—I'm sure I can figure out something down here."

"I'm not going up there without you," I said. "We're Team DaMoNik, remember? Teammates don't leave each other behind. Plus, I know how brave you really are. You were the one who stood up to Mukade and his army first. You got me into the field to find the arrow. And when we had to face Susano'o and the guards . . . I mean, okay, it was kind of obnoxious of you to try to take Kusanagi from me, but you were ready to die defending me. That was super brave."

"Yeah, I guess."

"Just don't look up too high. Or look down. Take it one step at a time." I scrambled up the first boulder and gestured toward the ledge. "Pretend it's a play structure or something. Come on, you can do this. I know you can."

Danny snorted. "You're starting to sound like me, with all your team spirit and your 'you can do this.'"

I blinked in surprise. He was right—I did sound just like him. I grinned and said, "I guess that's not *entirely* a bad thing."

Danny smiled back at me and turned to face the cliff. "Okay. One step at a time," he said to himself. "Play structure. I can do this."

"You can totally do this."

Danny grabbed the rope ladder and, with trembling legs, started to climb.

There were moments when I was sure the wind would blow us right off the cliff and into the rocky sea below. Once, I accidentally looked down and got so freaked out that I thought I'd never be able to take another step, and one time, Danny's foot slipped on some loose gravel and he nearly fell off a ledge. But after hours of climbing—or maybe it was only a few minutes (What is time, anyway?)—we finally reached the top. Danny army-crawled a few feet away from the cliff edge and groaned.

"Thank the gods. I never want to do that again."

I crawled over to him and held my fist out. "Way to go, Danny. You totally rocked that climb."

Danny bumped fists with me and smiled weakly. " 'Rocked that climb.' That's funny. Like rock climbing, get it?" When I rolled my eyes, he added, "Hey, thanks for having my back. I wouldn't have made it without you." And he smiled his old smile again.

Once we'd recovered, Niko looked at the setting sun and announced that the best thing to do would be to eat and get a good night's sleep. Danny agreed, and so did my growling stomach and aching muscles.

"Please let there be a hamburger and a milkshake in here," Danny said as he reached into his backpack. "Yes! Finally! Thank you, Hotei!" He put the hamburger and plate of fries on his knees and the milkshake on the ground in front of him.

"What about me?" Niko said. "Those bountiful backpacks are meant to feed me, too, I believe."

"Here." I reached into my backpack and pulled out a whole pepperoni pizza. It was a bit tough to get it out of the opening without getting cheese and tomato sauce everywhere.

"Galloping grasshoppers," murmured Niko. He licked his lips. "Thank the heavens for Hotei."

My backpack gave me a platter of two of my favorite foods: tonkatsu—pork cutlets breaded and deep-fried to a golden brown—and a pile of rectangular mochi cakes toasted just the way I like . . . crispy, crunchy, and the tiniest bit burnt on the outside, and gooey and chewy on the inside.

"For victory and strength," Niko observed.

"Hm?" Danny said as he crammed his hamburger into his mouth.

"Tonkatsu: 'katsu' sounds like 'victory' in Japanese," he explained. "And mochi is made of rice, the holy food of Inari— the kami of the harvest, and my mother-father."

"Your what?" Danny wrinkled his nose in confusion.

"Mother-father. Sometimes she is female, sometimes he is male." Niko sighed impatiently and rolled his eyes. "You mortals and your limited perceptions."

"*Anyway . . . ,*" I prompted him.

"Anyway, rice is the source of life and strength; it feeds the living, the dead, and everything in between and beyond."

It got quiet for a few minutes while we ate. Once I'd had enough not to feel like I was going to be eaten up by my own hunger, my mind went back to that moment I'd had with Susano'o. I put down my chopsticks and said, "Hey, so I've been kind of freaking out about what Susano'o saw in my head back at his fortress. Niko, do you have any idea what it could have been?"

Niko shook his head. "I don't think we should worry ourselves with it. Susano'o told us that you're not ready."

"Oh, okay, sure! No problem!" I sniped. "I'll just 'not worry' about something that scared *Susano'o,* one of the MOST

POWERFUL KAMI IN THE WORLD, because he says I'm 'not ready'! Because if there's anything I'm *excellent* at, it's not worrying about stuff I'm not ready for!"

Niko just shrugged. Arghh!

"I have a theory," said Danny around a mouthful of hamburger. "Wanna hear it?"

"No," said Niko. His voice was firm, but his ears and whiskers twitched the way they sometimes did when he was nervous. Why would he be nervous?

Danny ignored him and looked at me. "Go ahead," I said.

"I think that you've inherited Susano'o's superpowers. But, like, maybe even stronger. Like maybe your dad wasn't a mortal. Maybe he was some other kami, like a really powerful one, and that's why Susano'o's nervous. That's why he doesn't want you to know about it. Because if you're a full kami and you figure it out and learn to use your Susano'o-powers, you might decide to challenge him for the throne or something. Right? What do you think?"

He was wrong. At least, he was partly wrong—I didn't want to think about what he might have gotten right. "My dad was a mortal," I said.

"That's what your mom told you. But she lied about herself, didn't she? Who knows what else she didn't tell you?"

That made me uncomfortable: What if Mom did have other secrets? But I was sure about Dad, anyway. "My dad could never see what my mom and I saw, and there was no reason for him to fake that. Plus, him being a mortal was the reason Susano'o got mad at my mom in the first place, remember?"

"Oh. Right." Danny stuffed a few French fries into his mouth and chewed thoughtfully.

"I demand that you stop this silly speculation at once," said Niko. "It can only lead to trouble."

I gave him a hard look. "Are you hiding something? 'Cause it seems like this topic is stressing you out."

"No, of course not!" Niko huffed indignantly—though his ears and whiskers were still twitching. "I just think that if Susano'o says don't ask, then we shouldn't ask!"

Every time I brought up the topic after that, Niko yipped and howled and whined until finally I gave up. He seemed afraid to even think about it. I couldn't blame him. It scared me, too.

Danny's backpack provided sleeping mats and blankets, which we laid on the ground once we'd brushed our teeth (thanks to my backpack). Every time I reached in, I'd feel around for Kusanagi; it was always there. It was like its kami knew that as great as I felt about having unlocked its power, I'd lose my confidence if I couldn't find it. I did worry that I only felt a guitar and not a sword, but I told myself that it probably had safety protocols or something, so I wouldn't accidentally cut myself on the blade.

I told myself a lot of things as we lay under the stars and the bright silver moon that first night at the top of Mikado-bashira. I'd defeated Susano'o's scorpion soldier! I was awesome! Kusanagi had chosen me and now we had a real, fighting chance to accomplish our mission!

But I was only able to hang on to these thoughts for a few minutes before my mind went back to Susano'o. What had he seen that had surprised—and scared—him so much? Why did he think I'd run away screaming if I knew what it was? And why was Niko being so weird about it?

Every time I asked myself these questions, something small and dark squirmed inside my heart. Because I was beginning to think that I knew the answer. I thought of the rage that had made me try to tackle Brad Bowman at the seventh-grade dance. The sense of satisfaction I'd felt when I'd been shouting at Uncle Kappy to tell us who he'd been working for—until he died. The thrill that had shot through me when I'd first connected with Kusanagi, and the hot fury that had guided me in the battle against the scorpion. The golden glow I'd felt after killing it. What if Danny was right, and deep down, Susano'o and I were the same? What if he'd recognized his own violent, cruel, chaotic nature in mine? What if it was worse than his— was that why he looked scared?

I didn't want to become someone who was always on the verge of flying into a violent rage, who loved to fight and didn't care who they hurt or even killed. The kind of power he had, and the way he threw it around—it scared me. I wasn't sure I could handle being more violent, more angry, and more out of control. If this was the only way to survive a fight with Shuten-dōji and his army, I didn't know if I could do it. Was this what Susano'o had meant by me not being ready? Because I *wasn't* ready. I *did* want to run away screaming.

I thought I would stay up all night worrying about this, but I must have fallen asleep, because I woke up to Niko shoving his wet nose in my face just before dawn the next morning.

"Ughhh, can't we at least wait until it's light out?" I groaned, and pulled the blankets over my head.

269

"Yeah, I mean, how much do we really need to practice? Susano'o wouldn't have trusted us with his sacred weapons if he thought we'd lose," Danny added.

"Have you broken your brains? Have you taken leave of your little-used senses?" Niko spluttered. "Susano'o doesn't care if we lose. There is nothing he likes better than a fight, and if Shuten-dōji takes over Ne-no-kuni while Susano'o's at Kami-Con, that only gives him a fight to look forward to when he returns home. Susano'o will protect the earth because it is his domain, but he stopped caring about its inhabitants long ago. And why would he, what with the way people treat the place?"

"But his weapons! If we lose, he'll lose his weapons!" I protested.

"Whether we win or lose, the weapons will still belong to him. Kusanagi chooses who it wants to work with, so it's useless to a demon. And once the battle is over, the arrows will return to their true master, and their true master is Susano'o. He has trusted you with nothing."

"So he's just *playing* with us?" Danny said. "He doesn't actually think we're going to win?"

Niko rolled his eyes. "Two children and a novice fox against a demon horde? Who would you bet on?"

Training Montage!

Once it finally sank in that Susano'o didn't necessarily think we'd beat the oni, Danny protested, "But Daikoku said that Kusanagi was our secret weapon! And I have the magic bow and arrows!"

"Yes, but did you hear what His Mightiness said to Momo before we left? Secret weapons don't mean a thing if you don't know how to use them. Which is why you lollygagging lazybones need to get up and begin training with them." Niko dug his nose under my shoulder and nudged. "Come on, girl! Up and at 'em, as they say! Your future waits for you to step toward it!"

I wasn't quite sure that getting up would lead me to the future I wanted—especially since that future looked like it might be me "stepping toward" becoming a monster who played with people's lives. But like so many choices I'd had to consider so far, it felt like the only one.

The next few hours were like a training montage in the movies. We had eggs, a green smoothie, and a couple of squares of mochi for breakfast. Niko chased Danny and me around the island a couple of times ("as a warm-up," he said), making us sprint across a little meadow, scramble over boulders, and dodge around trees and bushes. I ended up walking at one point while Niko and Danny ran ahead. But whatever, it wasn't like we were planning to race the oni to death.

Then it was weapons practice time. Danny reached into his backpack and pulled out his bow, his arrows, and a red disc painted with the face of an oni that snarled and blew foul-smelling smoke out of its nose. "What do I do with this?" he asked. He put it down, and it flew across the grass like a Frisbee, stopped in midair, and turned itself upright. It bobbed up and down for a little while, and then started advancing toward us.

"Oh, I get it!" he said. He nocked an arrow, drew back the bowstring, and let go. The arrow flew straight at the growling target and hit it with a loud *PING!* The target burst into orange flames and became eight targets. "Sweet!" Danny said, and pulled out another arrow. This one split into eight arrows the moment it left his fingers, but all eight of them went straight into the ground. The targets doubled. And kept coming.

"Only that first arrow is guaranteed to hit its target," Niko reminded him. "You need to have actual skill for the others."

"Aim a little higher next time!" the targets shouted, and they stuck their tongues out at Danny and made rude noises.

Danny shot his next six arrows, which each split into eight, but out of forty-eight arrows, he only hit four targets. My heart sank and I felt terrible for Danny as the other oni-faced targets jeered and shouted, "Game over, you're dead! Square your shoulders and line your toes up with your target!" before they melded into one and flew back across the field. All fifty-seven of Danny's arrows flew toward us, became eight arrows, and dropped into his backpack.

I was about to tell Danny it was okay, no one expected him to be perfect, but he was already giving himself a pep talk. "Okay, Haragan," Danny muttered to himself. "Let's do this. Shoulders. Toes. Aim high." His face took on a determined scowl and he shook out his arms and took aim at the target, which was already bobbing toward us.

He was a totally different Danny from the one at the bottom of the cliff yesterday. I wished I was more like that. Shaking it off when people laughed at you was probably much easier when you had his confidence. Instead, I couldn't stop worrying. Susano'o seemed pretty sure I wouldn't be able to defeat Shuten-dōji unless I really leaned into whatever dark powers he'd seen inside me. But I didn't want to be someone who *enjoyed* slaughtering two hundred demons, even if they were from Yomi. I had to learn to use Kusanagi like a regular sword, without going full evil murder-monster. But I wasn't a star athlete like Danny. How could one day of training be enough for someone like me?

On the other hand—again—what choice did I have?

Danny was already improving his shooting skills; Niko had trotted off to the other side of the island to practice throwing rocks with his mind or something. The only thing I could do was try.

I reached into my backpack for a target, but it seemed to think that Kusanagi was enough on its own. So I grasped the neck of the guitar and held it out in front of me, hoping I could make this work without calling up whatever demon nature was buried inside me. I tried to channel Danny's confidence. "Come on, Kusanagi, let's do this. Teach me how to fight," I said.

It glimmered into its sword form, and I breathed a sigh of

relief. Now what? I looked around. Was I holding it right? Was there some kind of stance I should be standing in, like how Danny had to line his feet up? How had I been holding it when I fought the scorpion? How had I been standing? Should I slice with it, or stab, or swing? I'd probably be facing six or seven oni at a time. Was there a different kind of technique for fighting multiple enemies at once?

The more I thought about it, the heavier Kusanagi felt in my hands, and the glitchier it became until finally I was back to holding a guitar upside down by its neck again.

I tried to do what Danny had done: stay positive and keep trying. I tried different stances. I tried holding Kusanagi like a baseball bat. I tried to copy what I'd done against the scorpion. I tried and tried and tried. But I could not get Kusanagi to cooperate.

But don't worry. It wasn't demoralizing at all.

I'm kidding. It was incredibly demoralizing.

Why couldn't I do this? "You chose me!" I said to Kusanagi. "What's wrong? Why aren't you helping me?"

Kusanagi glowed, as if it had heard me. Then I swear I heard Susano'o laughing at me—it was like he was inside my head somehow. *You know why. Kusanagi only works for fighters who aren't afraid of their feelings. Not for scared little guppy girls like you.*

I knew what he was doing and I tried to fight it, but the heat and energy began building inside anyway. "Hey!" I shouted back, as if he could hear me. "I *am* a fighter. I have to fight every single day. Maybe I'm not beating anyone up or smiting them with swords, but I've survived in a place where everyone thinks that I'm not good enough or cool enough, and that's *hard!*" I could practically feel Susano'o lifting an amused eyebrow, and that made me even madder. "And another thing. You have no *idea* how hard I've had to work to make sure that Mom is okay. I'm scared and I'm worried and yeah, maybe I'm insecure at school, too, but that doesn't make me weak. It makes me strong! So you just shut your mouth and help me learn to fight with this sword, because I *deserve* it!"

Kusanagi flashed to life again, and I felt the exhilarating buzz of anger-fueled energy coursing through me and connecting us. *Okay, fine,* I thought. *But this is it. No deeper.* I didn't want this battle to become my supervillain origin story.

By the time the sun had begun to go down, I could make Kusanagi change from guitar to sword and back with ease, and I had learned to allow it to lead me through whatever motions it seemed to think were necessary: lunging, feinting, slicing, stabbing. Sometimes I could almost see my opponents as I practiced: big, ugly monsters with bulging eyes, sharp yellow teeth, and breath that smelled like gasoline. They charged and roared and swung at me, but every fight ended with Kusanagi slicing their heads off, or plunging through their chests, and the oni exploding and then imploding in a cloud of thick black smoke. It felt so real—and so easy and natural.

But the more I practiced, the more Kusanagi seemed to sense the untapped energy inside me. I would feel Kusanagi calling it, and I would have to work to suppress the cold, vengeful rage that surged up in response. Whenever that happened, Kusanagi would fight me—like, literally physically jerk in the wrong direction or wrench itself out of my hands. It was like trying to walk a disobedient dog. Or a disobedient dragon. I could hear Susano'o laughing.

A gong sounded, and I knew that Niko was summoning us back to the campsite. I looked across the sea toward the Island of Mysteries; the grayish-green sludge had deepened to blackish-green. Mom would die and the whole world would follow if I failed tomorrow. I had to try opening up and unbottling whatever horrible thing was inside me if I wanted to save them. Maybe I could rebottle it and forget about it when I was done—though I doubted that.

So I stood up one last time. My heart was pounding hard enough to feel in my throat, and my stomach clenched painfully. I *really* didn't want to do this. But when Kusanagi called, I closed my eyes and looked for whatever it was that Susano'o had seen. . . .

There it was. A rage more savage and intense than anything I'd ever felt surged into my veins. As I struggled to stay in control against the rising tide of fury, I could feel Kusanagi straining toward it, eager to merge with it and amplify it so we could *really* let loose. I felt myself being swallowed whole—not only was the storm inside me becoming one with Kusanagi, it was becoming one with *me*. Like if I let go, I would lose myself entirely.

With a huge effort, I wrenched myself free and shut down the connection. Kusanagi fell out of my hands, and I dropped to the ground, panting as the monstrous energy drained away.

There was no way I could do this and survive. I had failed.

I met Danny on my way back to the campsite. He greeted me with an energetic wave of his arm. "Hey, how'd your training go? Bruh, I'm so tired, but I'm so much better at shooting now.

Watch!" He pulled a target out of his backpack and let it fly. He then proceeded to shoot down every new target that appeared as they multiplied and advanced toward us. By the time he'd shot down all but one of the magic targets, he still had three arrows sticking out of his backpack. The remaining target cackled, "Not bad, not bad! Off to bed to get some rest!" before rushing into Danny's backpack with the rest of the equipment.

"Cool, right?" he said. "How about you?"

"Oh, um. It went . . . it went really well! I've got it all under control. Kusanagi and I totally understand each other now." I smiled weakly. How could I tell him the truth—that Kusanagi and I only understood each other because *I* understood that I would die if I allowed it to connect with the evil rage monster inside me? And that I hadn't been able to master the sword or the monster and we were therefore doomed to failure?

Fortunately, Danny was too pumped up about his mad archery skills to catch my lie. He talked all the way back to the campsite about everything he'd mastered, and only stopped when we'd just arrived and Niko called out to us from across the clearing: "Watch this!"

Niko squeezed his eyes shut, and I barely had time to wonder what I was supposed to be watching when an eight-foot-tall oni stood in his place, drooling and snarling. I screamed and grabbed for Kusanagi, and Danny scrambled to get his bow and arrows, and the oni yelped and cried, "It's me, it's me! It's Niko!" He reverted back to fox form and grinned. "Pretty convincing, eh? That's the first time since my accident that I've managed to shape-shift!"

Then he glared at a pile of stones he'd made. One by one,

they rose up, whizzed through the air, and hit a tree about twenty feet away: *tunk-tunk-tunk-tunk-tunk*. "Duck, little ducklings!" he shouted, and we ducked just in time to avoid being knocked out as all the rocks came whizzing back, and flew past us over the cliff.

"Impressive," said Danny, as I clapped and cheered.

"How did you get so good all of a sudden?" I asked him.

"I expect I've been earning it back," he said. "Heroic deeds can sometimes balance out mistakes—I mean, accidents."

"Fair enough," Danny said.

"What happened in that accident, anyway?" I asked. "How did you lose that jewel, exactly?" Now that he seemed to be recovering from said accident, it felt like a good time to ask about it again.

For a few seconds Niko didn't say anything. His fur bristled, then lay flat, and his tail curled tightly around him where he sat across from me and Danny. "Nothing you need to hear," he said finally. "All you need to know is that it wasn't on purpose, and I have been doing my best to . . . to do better ever since."

"Come on, tell us," I said.

"Yeah, we can take it," said Danny. "And we're here for you. Unless you've been a secret agent this whole time, or something." He chuckled, and then looked nervous. "You're not a secret agent for Shuten-dōji, are you?"

"Of course not!" Niko huffed. "If I were, would I have bothered fetching you in the first place? Or taken you to see the Seven Lucky Gods? Or risked my life traveling to Susano'o's fortress?"

"No, I guess not," Danny admitted, and I let out a sigh of

relief. It would have ended me if Niko had been double-crossing us this whole time.

"Hmph," Niko said. And then maybe because he felt bad about snapping at us, he added, "It's just a very sensitive subject, and we all have moments in our past that we'd rather not revisit. I think it's best for us to remain as focused as possible on our mission right now. Unless you'd like to reveal something from *your* past that *you're* not proud of. Something you'd be ashamed to talk about in present company." Niko gave Danny a hard look, and Danny squirmed and looked off to the side. I wondered what Danny could possibly have done that he'd be ashamed of. Probably a lot.

"Okay, okay," he said. "Calm down. Sorry we asked."

"Thank you. Now, let's start planning, shall we?"

Being a Hero Is Noble and All, But . . .

After dinner, Niko took out the mirror that the Luckies had given him. He murmured a rhyme over it:

Mirror, dear, I ask of you
Show me everything that's true.
Secrets hidden, cloaked in lies;
Lay them bare before my eyes.

Immediately, it projected a 3D model of the Island of Mysteries, which looked like a tiny mountain sticking up out of the sea. It was all gray and brown, rock and sand and bare trees that cast stark shadows in the setting sun. Nothing like the photo of the lush green island that Mom kept on the mantel at home. My heart contracted as I thought about what this meant: the island was nearly dead, and the oni's mission to undo the binding spell and open the gates for Shuten-dōji was almost complete. And of course, it meant that Mom was also nearly dead.

"Is that a real-time image?" I asked. I almost didn't want to hear the answer.

Niko nodded. "I'm sorry, Momo."

I pictured Mom at home in bed, pale, feverish, worried about me . . . if she was even conscious anymore. Why hadn't I at least called someone to come and check on her while I was gone? I was a terrible daughter.

As if he'd read my mind, Niko laid his paw gently on my knee. "Your mother is a fighter, Momo. She has held out longer than anyone could have expected, and it's because she believes in you."

"I didn't even leave her any water" was all I could say through the lump that had formed in my throat. "She must be so thirsty, and it would have taken me two minutes to put some water bottles near her bed. I didn't even think of it." I pressed the heels of my hands into my eyes, like I could push the tears back in. I couldn't start crying now, not when I was supposed to be strong and brave.

"You're here trying to save her life, aren't you?" Danny pointed out. "That's much bigger than remembering a bottle of water. I'm sure she's grateful."

"I guess."

"You're a child, Momo," said Niko. "It's not your responsibility to take care of your mother."

"But I have to. There's no one else," I said.

Suddenly I felt exhausted. It was like the weight of all those years of worrying about Mom—being tough, being strong, pretending to look for Dad out on the ocean, pretending school was fine even when it wasn't, trying to cheer her up even when I was sad myself—had woven itself into my body and I was only just realizing how much I'd been carrying. And now, of course, there was her actual life to worry about, not to mention the fate of the world—it had been motivating me, but all of a sudden it felt like a huge burden, way too big for me.

I felt another weight on my shoulders—Danny's arm. "Hey. It's gonna be okay," he said. "We're here with you and we'll fight with you, and we're gonna kick some serious oni butt." He gave me an encouraging squeeze. "They'll never know what hit 'em. I've got a magic bow and arrow, Niko can throw rocks with his mind, and you've got superpowers and a legendary magic sword now, remember? You'll be unstoppable! Momo the Magnificent and Kusanagi, whaaat! Yeeeah, boy!" He pumped his fist and woofed a few times, like I used to see him do with his friends at school when one of them did something particularly, uh, cool (ahem—*not*), like gulp down an entire carton of chocolate milk in one go.

Danny was obviously trying to cheer me up, but it only made me feel worse; he was counting on Kusanagi and my so-called superpower connection to Susano'o to save the day tomorrow, and we so, *so* weren't going to do anything of the sort. Not only was I letting Mom die *and* letting demons take over the world, I was leading Danny and Niko into a battle I knew we would lose. It was practically the same as killing them myself.

"I can't do this," I said. I shook Danny's arm off and stood up.

"What—what do you mean?" Danny asked, looking confused.

"I mean I can't do this. I mean we should give up. I mean we're just kids and we can't win and Niko should take us home so we can at least see our parents once before the oni destroy the island and Shuten-dōji destroys the world."

Niko and Danny looked at each other, and then at me. Danny

282

spoke again. "What the heck has gotten into you, Momo? Why are you being such a—"

"We can't win tomorrow!" I shouted. "There's no way. Susano'o said the only way we can possibly win is if I master Kusanagi, and I haven't!"

"But—but I thought you said—"

"I lied! I lied, okay?" I spat the words out like I was angry at Niko and Danny, but of course, it was myself I was angry at.

They stared at me, goggle-eyed.

"You mean . . . ," Niko started.

"I mean we can only win if I can connect fully to Kusanagi's power. Susano'o *said* so. But I can't do it. I tried, and I failed. There, I said it: I failed. You're going to die, my mom's going to die, and the world is going to end, and it's all my fault." I wiped away the tears that had spilled over as I realized the truth of my words. I'd failed at the one thing I had come here to do, and there was no one who could do it for me. Everyone was counting on me, and I'd let them all down. "I'm sorry."

I turned and walked away before I fell apart completely. Once I was out of earshot, I sat down and cried my eyes out. When I'd pulled myself together, I figured, we could all go home and say goodbye. I didn't know how I could look Mom in the eye, but if she was going to die, I wanted to see her and apologize before it happened. It seemed like the least I could do.

I didn't mean to sit there for as long as I did, but by the time I heard Danny and Niko approaching, my shadow had disappeared and dusk had turned to dark. They sat down next to me, one on each side, without saying anything. But Niko leaned his foxy little head on one arm, and Danny nudged the other with his elbow.

"So, Niko and I had a talk," Danny began, "and we've decided not to give up." I didn't say anything, so he continued.

"We're a team, Momo, remember? That means if one of us is having a tough time, the rest of us don't blame them or bail on them. We stick together and figure out a way to keep going. Like in sports. When your star player is injured or isn't playing well, you don't bail. You keep playing anyway and do the best you can."

Of course he'd compare this to sports, I thought. "Am I supposed to be the star player in this scenario?"

"Well, duh. You're a superstar," Danny said, and there was just enough moonlight for me to see the grin on his face.

"Yeah, well, I don't know how to break this to you, but most people don't consider fighting an army of oni to the death to be a sport."

"Huh. Sucks to be them."

I giggled in spite of myself.

"It is our sacred duty to finish what we started," Niko said. "Your mother wanted to keep you safe, of course, but she will understand. She would be proud of you for fighting to the end. That is not failure. That is a gift."

The thing is, being a hero is noble and all, but I've sometimes wondered if it's overrated. And I was pretty sure that Danny's parents and my mom would have preferred for us to be home for the last moments of our lives than for us to give them this particular "gift." Still, I found myself wavering. Something inside me didn't want to give up—though I didn't want to think too hard about exactly what that something was.

Niko spoke again. "I've made a prayer to Ebisu, who will be

on duty tomorrow while the others are at Kami-Con. He's very hard of hearing and quite absentminded—terrible qualities for the god of luck, if you ask me—but if he gets the message, he might send us the luck we need to win."

"And who knows? You might be able to figure things out tomorrow," Danny added. "Maybe you're a clutch player—you know, the kind who does best under pressure." *That* was a stretch, but I was enjoying how kind Danny was being, so I didn't argue.

"To sum up, there is still a possibility that we will prevail," said Niko. "And therefore, we must persevere."

I looked first at Danny, then at Niko. It made no sense, but they hadn't given up on me. I couldn't give up on them—on us. And if Niko was right, if there was still a chance that we could win . . . I sighed. "Fine. I'm in."

"Yesss!" Danny high-fived me, and then put his fist out for a fist bump. "I knew you'd come through. Team DaMoNik, baby! Woot!"

Niko looked relieved more than anything else, but he grinned widely at me as he said, "Welcome back. Now let me show you the plan."

"I'll wake you up shortly before dawn," Niko said as we crouched over the projection of the Island of Mysteries. "We'll pass through a portal to this spot here"—he pointed to a little cove on the far side of the island—"and launch our attack at daybreak, when the oni are tired from carousing all night."

"Carousing?" Danny said.

"Partying. Drinking, fighting, bashing their heads into tree trunks to show how strong they are, that sort of thing."

Niko pointed out a ravine at the bottom of the mountain, where most of the oni seemed to have set up camp. We would skirt around it, fighting any oni we encountered, and make our way up to the cave where the portal to Yomi was hidden. "Obviously we want to get rid of as many oni as possible," he said, "but our main objective is to reach the cave and seal it off, just in case . . . ahem. Just in case . . ." He trailed off and cleared his throat, avoiding my eyes.

Just in case we fail to save the island itself. Just in case Mom dies and the binding spell dies with her. A few dozen escaped oni is nothing compared to an invading army led by the demon king.

"It's gonna be okay," said Danny. "We got this."

I took a deep breath and swallowed hard. "Right. I'm good."

Niko outlined the rest of the battle plan and ordered us to bed. As we each snuggled under our blankets, Danny said, "Isn't this wild? If you'd told me a week ago that you and me and a talking fox were going to use magical weapons to fight a band of demons, I would have thought you were nuts."

"Same," I said. We were quiet for a moment, gazing at the sky, where it looked like someone had tossed a giant bag of glittering white confetti. The full moon was low on the horizon. I don't know why I said what I said next—maybe it was all that we'd been through so far, or maybe it was because there was a good chance we'd both die the next day, or maybe it was just the moon. But I added, "Thanks for coming with me. I know I didn't want you in the beginning, and I wasn't very nice about it. But I'm glad you're here. You're . . ." I tried to think of what I wanted to say. "I used to think you'd become just like Brad and Kiki and them—all those kids who think they're so cool—who think it's okay to be mean to kids like me. But you're *not* like them—not really, not deep down. So I guess I misjudged you. I'm glad I figured out how great you are."

"I mean, I'm pretty great, but I'm not *that* great," Danny said, and he looked so uncomfortable that I worried I'd made things weird. But then he smiled and said, "Just so you know, I think *you're* cool. You've always been cool—I just got caught up in all that popularity stuff, and . . . I don't know. I guess I forgot who I was, a little. It's been fun getting to be friends again."

Friends. I sighed a happy sigh. We were real, actual friends again. I almost wished we didn't have to go back to our old life—assuming there was an old life to go back to after tomorrow. But if we survived, it was bound to be better, now that Danny was back. We'd still have our disagreements and our squabbles, but now I had someone who understood me, who didn't think there was something wrong with me. Someone who I could trust to have my back no matter what, whether in battle or just sitting on a rock worrying about my mom. I was still pretty sure we'd all be dead tomorrow, and I was still sad that I couldn't tell Mom that I loved her. But at least I had this. One more thing worth fighting for.

Help, I'm on Fire!

Mom was dying. I was in her room, standing at the door. The moonlight was streaming through her window, and her hair lay loose around her face. Her eyes were sunken, her cheeks were hollow, and her skin was so pale that it was almost white. She already looked like a ghost.

But I knew she was alive because her eyes were open and bright with fever, and her cracked lips were moving slightly. She took a painful, wheezing breath, and whispered hoarsely, over and over, *Momo. Momo. Where are you?*

I woke up with my heart pounding. I was gripped by an over-powering need to see her and let her know that I was okay, and that everything would be all right—or at least that I was going to try to make everything all right. I felt like I might jump into the ocean and try to swim home if I couldn't take one last look at her face before I went into battle, and have one last conversation to let her know I loved her.

I thought of Niko's mirror, and I knew—I *knew* that if I could look into it, if I could get just a tiny peek—I'd be able to see Mom and let her know that I was here for her.

I looked at Niko where he was curled into a little orange ball of fur, his tail tucked tightly around him. His pouch lay next to him, drawn shut.

One little peek. I'd ask to see Mom, and when she appeared, I could smile at her and tell her that I was alive and well. That I loved her, and that everything was going to be okay. And who knew? Maybe she'd get the message somehow. Maybe it would come true.

I got up and crept across the campsite. The moon was high in the sky. Its cool, silver light washed over me and cast long shadows on the ground. I could hear the rhythmic rush and shush of the waves at the base of the island, and far off in the distance, I thought I could hear the drums of the oni on the Island of Mysteries.

Almost there. I crouched down, took the pouch, and undid the tie. I reached inside, and just as I'd closed my hand around the mirror, Niko snorted. I froze. But then he sighed and mumbled something that sounded like *One large pepperoni pizza, please.*

Silently I slid the mirror out, turning it so that I could see its face. It glinted in the moonlight. What was it that Niko had said to make the magic work?

Mirror, dear, I ask of you
Show me everything that's true.
Secrets hidden, cloaked in lies;
Lay them bare before my eyes.

For a moment, I hesitated. I'd promised Daikoku not to mess with the mirror, after all, and I didn't even want to imagine how she might react if she knew I was disobeying orders.

But Mom . . . I still can't explain how much I *needed* to see her right then. I felt like I would have done anything—fought Niko, fought Danny, maybe even hurt them if I had to—for a chance to see her. I looked at Niko. He barely had any magic, and he managed just fine. Say the rhyme, focus on the thing you want to see. How hard could it be? There was no harm in taking one quick look.

I whispered the spell, and immediately the moonlight in the mirror began swirling like mist. My reflection distorted and swirled along with it. I stared into the glass and tried to focus on Mom.

But it was strange. Every time I thought, *Mom,* and tried to picture her face, or tried to imagine her lying on her bed, I felt the mirror tugging my thoughts away, like there was something else it wanted me to see. It was hard work, staying focused. Twice I thought I saw her room faintly through the swirling mist, and both times, just before things got clear, the fog closed in again and I was pulled in a different direction.

Finally, I gave up and let the mirror lead me where it wanted to go. Maybe it wanted to give me a clue about the oni. Maybe it would show me how to commune with Kusanagi and not lose myself to the rage monster. Okay. I'd do what it wanted and take a look, and then I'd try to see Mom again.

As soon as I made that decision, the mist cleared, and I was hovering over Oak Valley Middle School, like I was looking at drone footage. The view dipped down and into the quad. It was dusk. The quad was crawling with kids from my grade, and there was a big butcher-paper banner proclaiming WELCOME BACK, SEVVIES! My skin went cold. It was the seventh-grade back-to-school dance—the scene of that awful viral video.

I scanned the crowd. There were Ryleigh and Kiki and their minions, clustered together near the DJ table. There were Danny, Brad, and the bro-bots next to the snack table. There I was, alone and miserable, on the edge of the quad—and here came Ms. Pérez to talk to me, with a look of pity on her face. I hadn't seen that look because she'd come up from behind me. Seeing it made me cringe. Was I that pathetic?

Then came the moment of my humiliation. I didn't want to watch, but the mirror wouldn't let me look away. Kiki called me over to her little hive. You could tell I wasn't sure if I should go, but Ms. Pérez gave me an encouraging smile and a gentle push in their direction. Once I arrived, Kiki put out her hand and stuck the *Help, I'm on fire!* sign on my back. I saw Ms. Pérez frown, wave her hand, and stalk angrily across the quad. I saw myself turn to see what she was yelling about, saw Brad come running toward me with a grin on his face and a cup full of punch in his hand. I watched as he tossed the contents of the cup in my direction, flinched as the red punch splashed all over my dress, as my eyes and mouth opened wide in shock. I saw myself flying at Brad, tripping over my feet, and splatting on the ground, and then fighting not to cry as Ms. Pérez tore the sign off my back and hurried me into the bathroom while three other teachers descended on Brad and Kiki. And then I saw Danny off to the side, getting the entire thing on video. *The* video. The one that went viral and made me the butt of "Hey, Momo, you want some punch?" jokes for weeks. And he was laughing.

No, I thought. I couldn't bear to watch any more. I squeezed my eyes shut and forced myself out of the vision. The mirror fell from my hand and onto the dirt with a soft *thonk* as I shook my head, opened my eyes. The humiliation had come back hard and fast, as if someone had thrown a bucket of cold water— cold punch, haha—at me through the mirror. It clung to my skin and dripped down my back and left me breathless with shock.

I looked at Danny, fast asleep and snoring next to Niko. He'd *laughed* at me. And then he'd made it even worse by sharing the video. How could he have treated me that way?

That's not who he is anymore, I told myself firmly. *He's changed. He'd never do that to me now. He's my friend. Just like he used to be.*

Is he, though? said a voice. It spoke softly, but it was cold and clear as ice, and it sent a chill down my spine. A fine mist swirled around me, blocking out everything but the moon, the mirror, and Danny. *How can you be sure he means what he says? He used to say he was your friend, and what happened? He left you. He betrayed you. He made you feel small and stupid and alone. How do you know he won't betray you again?*

I just do. It's different this time, I argued.

It's not different at all, the voice hissed. *Just more danger- ous. He KNEW how awful that video would make you feel, and he shared it anyway. How are you not furious with him? Has he apologized for it?*

I didn't answer.

You see? You cannot trust him. Hold on to your anger. Keep your guard up. Stay alert so that he cannot betray you and hurt you again.

The mist cleared, and somehow I had the mirror in my hand again.

Danny lay asleep, just like before. But I saw him differently now. We'd been best friends as little kids, but that hadn't stopped him from leaving me behind and deliberately humiliating me, had it? Resentment began bubbling up and down my spine, and an icy seed of doubt lodged itself in my heart. I could feel the monster inside me stirring fretfully.

The moonlight glinted in the mirror and caught my eye. *Do you want to take another look?* it seemed to be saying. *What about your mom? Don't you want to see how she's doing?* Oh, right—Mom. The reason I'd looked into the mirror in the first place. I'd wanted so desperately to make sure she was okay— I still did. But now I was afraid of what I'd see. What if I found out something bad about Mom? Or something really, really terrible about me?

I turned the mirror over, slid it back into its pouch, and crept back to my blanket.

Miraculously, I fell asleep almost immediately. I didn't sleep well, though. I kept having nightmares about mirrors that played viral videos of me getting splashed with fruit punch that turned into tidal waves of blood; Danny, Brad, Kiki, and Ryleigh laughing at me and then morphing into an army of demons and death hags. At the very end, I had a nightmare about Mom. It was like the one that had woken me up earlier, but instead of seeing her from the door of her bedroom, I could only hear her. I was all alone, shivering as I stood somewhere cold and dark, with a bitter wind whipping my hair around my face. But even the wind couldn't blow away the stench of sulfur and rotting meat that hung in the air. The scent of death. I heard the whisper of a woman's voice beyond the howl of the wind. "Mom?" I called— only no sound came out of my mouth. I struggled to understand what she was saying, but I could only catch a few words: *"help . . . dying . . . hurry . . ."* Her breathing was wet and ragged, like before, as if every inhalation was a terrible, painful effort. I was so cold. I was freezing. "Mom!" I shouted. "Mom, I'm here!" But my voice was drowned out by a hideous scream of laughter that turned my blood to ice. Faintly, as if from far away, I heard her again: *"Momo . . . Momo . . ."* I tried to run toward the sound of her voice, but I discovered that I couldn't move—something had wrapped iron bands around my body and trapped me. I was drowning. I couldn't breathe. *"Momo . . . Momo . . ."*

"Momo! It's time to get up." It was Niko, nudging me on the shoulder.

My eyes snapped open. My heart was racing, and I was tangled up in my blankets. The sky was still a dark blue, but the eastern horizon was growing lighter.

"You okay? You looked like you might be having a nightmare," said Danny.

"It was about my mom," I said. "She was . . ." I heard the sound of her labored breathing in my head, and cold terror washed over me, as if the nightmare was alive and trying to pull me back in.

"Hey," Danny said, and put a hand on my shoulder. "It was just a dream. She's still okay. If she wasn't, there'd be demons everywhere, right?"

The pressure of his hand reminded me of what I'd seen last night in the mirror. "Right," I said, making my voice hard and flat. "Can you just . . . ?" I shrugged myself loose and moved away. Danny backed off, looking confused and a little hurt, but he said nothing.

"Nightmare or not, it's a sign that we don't have a moment to spare," Niko said briskly. "So leave it behind and let's gear up and get going."

But as I packed my bag and ate a quick breakfast of onigiri (rice balls stuffed with my two favorite fillings: salmon and sour plum), I couldn't shake the feeling that I'd witnessed something real. I felt the sting of the cold wind against my cheeks again, and the raspy breathing filled my ears. Mom, begging. And that evil, bloodcurdling laughter. Who had been laughing? Why?

A few minutes later, we gathered under a pair of large cedar trees at the edge of the cliff. Our backpacks gave us armor, which we helped each other put on. Danny tied my gauntlets to my wrists and forearms, put both of his gloved hands on my shoulders, and looked me in the eye. "Hey. I know you're nervous, but you're a freakin' beast with that sword, Momo. You've totally got this."

He looked so sincere. He sounded just like a real friend. I found myself wanting to believe that we *were* friends, and that he really had changed. Maybe I'd been wrong. Maybe that voice in my head was just the leftover bits of my rage monster talking, and I shouldn't listen to it.

On an impulse, I said, "It sure will be weird at home after this, huh? Like, going back to the old routines, sitting with your same friends on the bus . . ." I looked at him. "Do you think you'll live your life the same way as before?"

Danny looked confused. "I mean, yeah, probably. I guess so."

I pressed him further. "I wonder what everyone would say, for example, if I sat with you and your other friends on the bus. Since we're friends now." I nearly put air quotes up, but managed to keep my hands at my sides. I held my breath.

"Oh. Right." There was a long pause, and my blood started pounding in my head as I waited. "The thing is . . . it's not like we can tell them what happened, right? They'd never believe us."

See? the cold voice from the night before hissed in my ear. *He's already changing his mind. I told you.*

My face must have given something away, because Danny immediately backtracked. "I mean, we can totally all hang together. If you want to. Obviously. It's just . . . you probably wouldn't have that much fun. 'Cause, you know. You're different from them."

"Right. Yeah. Of course. That makes total sense." My heart squeezed itself into a hard black stone. *Stupid girl,* said the voice. *Now do you trust me?*

"Here we go," Niko said. "As one."

We passed through the portal and emerged in a tiny cove, even smaller than the one on Mikado-bashira, which poked up from across the water to the east like a tiny saltshaker on a big blue table. And then the first ray of sunlight pierced the sky behind Mikado-bashira. It was dawn.

Hey, You Smelly, Disgusting Trash Monsters!

The smell of smoke and sulfur stung my nose. I looked up to see a barren gray hillside dotted with the black skeletons of burned-up trees. Ashes floated on the wind. The sky over the island waved and shimmered once, like air over hot pavement, then seemed to steady itself. Niko noticed me looking, and said in a low voice, "The binding spell. We don't have much time."

Another vision of Mom flashed in my head: lying on her bed, struggling to breathe through parched, dry lips, the outlines of her face and her emaciated body blurring—she was literally fading away. *Please don't die, Mom,* I begged her silently. *Don't leave me all alone in the world.*

No. Stop. I had to be strong. I had to be brave. I sank to my knees and dug my fingers into the sand and tried with all my might to send her a message that would help her be strong, too: *Hang on, Mom. I'm here. See? I have Kusanagi, and we're going to save you.* I pulled Kusanagi out of my backpack and I wished I could believe myself.

I couldn't tell if she'd heard me. All I could do was hope. As for Kusanagi, I could feel it sensing the oni and their destruction in the air, the way a shark can smell blood in the water. *We're here to defend the island against those monsters,* I told it silently, and it pulsed and glowed in response. *Give me your anger,* it seemed to be saying. *Let us smite our enemies together.*

I took a deep breath and turned to Niko and Danny. "Ready when you are."

"Yes! Let's do this!" Danny raised a gloved hand and high-fived me and Niko. "Team DaMoNik to the rescue!" A question rose up and prodded the base of my skull: Would Danny make up a silly team name and high-five me in front of his friends? I brushed it away angrily. I couldn't go into battle like this, all worried about whether Danny was really my friend, or if he'd hang out with me once we got home—I needed to worry about getting home at all. The question sank back down, but the fog of mistrust it had risen from kept swirling in my head.

Niko's image of the island last night had shown that the ravine where the oni were staying was on the other side of the hill in front of us. The plan was to climb up and across the slope, staying out of sight below the ridgeline, and then cut to the left and climb to the top of the island. I hated waiting to take care of Mom till after we'd sealed the portal, but it was the right thing to do.

As we climbed, we passed piles of bones and rotting carcasses of dead birds and rats. The higher we climbed—and the closer we got to the oni encampment—the more energy I could feel building up in Kusanagi. It started flowing into me even without the spark of my anger. Once, it gave a particularly strong jolt, and I saw the severed arm of an oni, covered in flies and lying in a sticky black pool of dried blood.

"Ugh, gross." Danny had noticed it, too.

"I thought spirit-dimension creatures imploded and disappeared," I croaked.

"Not all oni are spirits," Niko explained. "Some are humans who are so wicked that they become oni while they're still on Earth. Some of them stay here until they die, but others find their way down to Yomi, where they can be with others who share their nasty natures."

"Like Shuten-dōji," I said, remembering. "That's why they were able to cut off his head and bury it after they killed him."

"Precisely."

We were about halfway across the hillside when a guttural roar came down from the ridge, and two oni charged into view. One was blue and carrying a hunk of rotting meat; the other one was green and waving an evil-looking spiked wooden club.

We froze.

"Gimme!" bawled the green oni, and he whacked the blue oni with his club.

The blue oni grunted, but didn't give up. "Mine!" he snarled back. He dropped the meat and uprooted a nearby tree trunk, and the two began circling each other.

Niko gestured for us to get low and stay still, but Kusanagi had other ideas. I found myself holding it out in front of me and moving up the hill. *These guys are slowing us down,* Kusanagi seemed to whisper to me. *The longer we wait here for them to finish each other off, the weaker Mom gets and the less time we have to save the world. Let's just get them out of the way. It will only take a second.*

"Momo! Come back!" Niko hissed, but it was like the words were coming at me through a magic filter that made them lose their meaning.

I was close enough to smell the oni now: it was like opening up a garbage can that had been sitting in the hot sun for days on end. Kusanagi absorbed and amplified my feelings, and I felt its power rush into my limbs. "Hey!" I shouted. "Hey, you smelly, disgusting trash monsters, look over here!"

They turned to look at me. Their eyes were blazing yellow, with big black pupils; their mouths were twisted with rage, all snarling lips and sharp, triangular teeth. I saw their rage turn to bottomless, violent hunger, and as they charged at me, I felt a jolt of fear. But it was combined with a weird thrill of anticipation. We wanted this fight, Kusanagi and me. I raised Kusanagi, and a strategy flowed into my head: the blue one, on my left, was slightly ahead of the green one; I'd leap toward him and stab him, while the green one went barreling past us downhill, and by the time he'd stopped himself and turned around, I'd already be rushing toward him—

But before any of this could happen, the blue one stumbled, and I had just enough time to see the arrow through his chest and the surprised expression on his face before he collapsed and toppled forward like a stack of boulders.

The green one only had time to run a few more paces before he fell, too—struck in the head by a rock that Niko had teleki-netically hurled at him. Both oni crumbled into heaps of ash that imploded and disappeared.

I should have felt grateful, but instead I was furious. The energy that I should have used to fight the two dead oni boiled over. "Those two were mine!" I heard myself yelling. "I had them!"

"They were attacking you!" Danny protested. "We were just trying to keep you safe."

"Oh, because can't you trust me? Did you think Kusanagi and I weren't good enough to handle them on our own?" Kusanagi flashed its outrage with me.

"Shh! Calm yourself!" Niko warned. "Save the bickering and bantering for later. We don't want to draw any attention to ourselves before we seal the portal!"

Kusanagi fed on my anger and started whispering urgently to me. *What does he know? Why NOT draw attention? The other two can go ahead and seal the portal. WE came here to fight.*

Those living, breathing garbage heaps had caused my mother so much pain. They had trashed the island—destroyed its trees, killed its wildlife, polluted its streams and ponds, fouled the air. Because of them, my mother was dying. Kusanagi was right—if I fought them now, I could save Mom's life while Niko and Danny took care of the portal.

"Change of plans. I'm going to take care of these oni down here. You two go on ahead," I said.

Danny looked at Niko, and then at me. "But there's, like, two hundred of them down there."

"Possibly three hundred," Niko reminded him.

"Kusanagi and I can take them," I insisted.

"But I thought we agreed that we need to seal the portal first. It doesn't matter how many of these guys we get rid of, because there's more where they came from."

"It'll only take a second," I said impatiently. I could feel

Kusanagi's pent-up energy and all of my untapped anger rocketing around inside me, demanding an outlet.

Niko opened his mouth to protest, but I cut him off. "GO!" A thread of lightning crackled across the sky, as if to add its voice to mine.

Danny and Niko both flinched. For a moment, I wondered if maybe I was going too far. But that lightning bolt must have convinced them, because before I could change my mind, Niko nodded and said, "We'll meet you at the top." He and Danny began jogging back across the slope.

I climbed the rest of the way to the ridge overlooking the ravine. It was crowded with oni and carpeted with trash— apparently there was a McDonald's in Yomi, and a liquor store— and I thought I would suffocate from the scent of garbage. There were a couple of individual skirmishes going on here and there, but most of the oni were passed out and snoring, as Niko had predicted. And they weren't just oni. Other yōkai from Yomi and from Earth had gathered here as well. They must have been able to smell me, or maybe they sensed Kusanagi, because a few of the brawling oni abruptly stopped pounding each other and looked directly up at me. They shouted, and within seconds, the first wave was clambering up the hill while the others ran to grab whatever weapons they could find lying around: swords, clubs, axes, rocks.

A demon with a giant, bloodred face, hair that stuck straight out like needles, and one staring eye under a single horn in the middle of its forehead reached me first. Then an old woman with stringy hair, gray-white skin, and a tongue as long as a snake, hobbling with terrifying speed. Shikome like the one that had attacked me at the mall; gaki, skeletal ghosts whose hunger and thirst can never be satisfied; a monster with the head of a monkey, the body of a badger, the legs of a tiger, and the tail of a snake.

Kusanagi guided me as we fought them off one by one, two by two, even three, four, and five at a time, and turned them into ashes and smoke. It felt great; it felt like I'd been born to do this. The trouble was, I realized as I looked down the hill, the rest of the monsters were now swarming toward me in one ugly, smelly mass. Five at a time, sure. But ten, fifteen, or twenty at a time? I'd been wrong. I couldn't handle them by myself, not even with Kusanagi.

You can't do it? Or you won't do it? said Kusanagi. *The power is there, if you choose to use it.*

I could feel the rage monster rumbling and roaring, practically throwing itself against the mental walls I'd put around it. With it, I knew I could get rid of all these oni and yōkai at once. But at what cost? What if I killed Danny and Niko along with the them? What if I disappeared into the chaos and became just like Susano'o?

I spun and ran up the hill. If I could get Danny and Niko to help, we just might be able to defeat this horde together and I could make it out of here without losing myself and killing the two of them. I'd have to apologize like crazy and make it up to them later. But I could do that.

As I approached the top of the island, the stench of death and decay became so strong, it made my eyes water. Sulfur and smoke caught in my nose and throat. There hadn't been many oni at the top of the island when we'd looked in the mirror last night—just a few guards around the cave entrance. Niko and Danny should have had no problem defeating them and securing the area. So why did it smell so awful?

Something wasn't right. I hurried the rest of the way up the hill, and when I reached the clearing at the top, I gasped. The consequences of my decision to stay behind and fight the oni were much worse than I'd thought. I had made a terrible mistake.

Not on Your Side

My friends were tied up and trapped in two separate cages that dangled at the ends of heavy chains from the top of the cave's entrance. One of Niko's eyes was swollen shut; the fur on the back of his neck was singed. Danny's eyes were closed, and blood dripped from his nose. My heart seemed to stop beating— was he dead because of me? But then he groaned. He was alive. At least he was alive.

Between them was a single demon the size of a regular human man. He had bright red skin and black eyes that glowed red in the center, under thick black eyebrows. A mane of wild black hair grew around two golden horns, and he pulled his thin lips back in a sneer to reveal a mouthful of yellow fangs. He was carrying a sword that glowed and sparked like mine.

"Well, well, well. Look who's finally come to fight me. Do you know who I am, little girl?"

"Shuten-dōji," I whispered.

Shuten-dōji raised Dōjigiri high in the air and disappeared in a whirlwind of black smoke, which billowed out and engulfed me. It stirred up dust and ashes that got in my eyes and made me cough. Something sank its claws into my brain and knifed its way down my throat, into my heart, my stomach, and all the way through my feet, nailing me to the spot where I stood.

"Very good."

The black cloud was still swirling. I couldn't see anything. Shuten-dōji's voice was a low, menacing snarl, cold and dark and thick with the threat of blood and violence. It came from somewhere both high above me and all around me, echoing and reverberating before finally reaching into my brain and probing for my deepest, darkest fears. It wrapped itself around my lungs and clamped itself around my neck. It was pure evil, and I felt like I might suffocate. For the first time since I'd stepped onto the island, I was truly afraid.

"Let my friends go," I said. My voice sounded small and shaky, and my arms felt puny and weak as I held Kusanagi out in front of me. I still couldn't see. All around me I heard the sounds of the oni and the yōkai that had chased me up here. They shrieked and hissed and yowled as they formed a circle with me in the center.

I have Kusanagi, I reminded myself. *Together, we're unbeatable.* I willed myself to speak again. "Let my friends go. I've got Kusanagi, and I know how to use it." I searched for the wild energy that had carried me through my battle with the oni, but it seemed to have evaporated in Shuten-dōji's presence. Cold fingers of fear and self-doubt snaked through me. What was wrong?

The vortex of darkness widened and revealed the circle of monsters and the mouth of the cave, where Danny and Niko hung in their cages. Just above them, the smoke writhed and twisted until it had re-formed itself into the awful head that I'd seen the kasha dig up behind the shrine. Its eyes flickered to life, and I stood trembling under their sickly yellow glare.

Shuten-dōji chuckled: a grating, rasping sound that made my skin crawl. "Foolish girl. You thought you had control of that sword, and you'd send me back to Yomi, didn't you? You thought you'd save your mother's life, save the world from descending into chaos, and live happily ever after. Ha! *Wrong.*"

His mouth split into a malicious smile. "And let me ask you this: Has it occurred to you that even if by some miracle you should succeed, you'll be no better off than you were before? That boy, for example." He looked down at Danny. "He has never been on your side, and he never will be."

Danny raised his head and called out weakly. "That's not true! Of course I'm on your side! Momo—" He coughed painfully, spitting blood. "Don't believe him!"

Shuten-dōji puffed up his cheeks and blew gently on the dust at my feet. It spun itself into a scene: a suburban street with trees, lawns . . . it was the corner where I caught my bus to school every morning. It was wintertime. The bus stopped, and I stepped inside to see Danny in the back with all of his old friends, shouting and laughing over a video on a phone. They were bigger, taller—I was looking into the future. Danny looked up, and I waved and smiled—and he went back to the video as if he hadn't even seen me. The scene shifted to the lunch tables in the quad and repeated itself there. And again in the bus line after school. One look at Danny's shamefaced expression told me all I needed to know. It hadn't happened yet, but it would.

"Sad, isn't it? But it's true: once an outcast, always an outcast." Shuten-dōji gave an exaggerated sigh, which blew the scene away.

I gritted my teeth against my hurt feelings and the hot

resentment that seethed in my stomach. I would *not* let this get to me. Who cared if Danny went back to his old friends after we went home? Not me. "It doesn't matter. I already knew that would happen," I said, and I felt an odd sense of satisfaction when I saw Danny's face fall. "By the way, Danny, I know you were the one who posted that video," I said. Why was I going there? This was so petty. It wasn't important right now—and yet I couldn't stop myself.

Danny looked sick. "How—how did you know it was me?"

"Really? That's what you're going to ask me?"

"I mean—I'm so, sorry, Momo, I—I—"

"Shhh," Shuten-dōji said, and a stream of smoke appeared and wound around Danny's mouth like a gag. "No excuses." I felt another warm bubble of vengeful satisfaction, and I didn't question it this time. "While we're on the subject of your friends, Momo, what about your fox friend? Or should I say, your false friend?"

Niko's mirror floated out of his little pouch and bobbed in front of my face. He yelped, "No! Momo, don't look, it's—"

"Shhh," Shuten-dōji said again, and Niko's mouth was bound shut as well.

I watched in horrified fascination as my arm lifted on its own, like it was on a string, and my fingers closed around the mirror and turned it toward my face.

"Take a look. I think you'll find it most interesting."

I couldn't tear my gaze away. The mirror showed me a lush green island in sparkling turquoise water. It was the Island of Mysteries, the way it had looked before the oni had invaded. There was a rush of wind, and I zoomed down through the leaves and into the very same clearing where I was standing now. A slightly sparklier, brighter version of Niko was sitting on a rock in front of the cave like a human, his legs crossed, looking bored and grumpy. He was muttering to himself and tossing a ball up and down. No—it was a giant, silvery-pink shimmery pearl. Niko's wishing jewel. The one he wouldn't talk to us about. I understood what I was seeing: the truth about Niko's past.

Something came crawling up from the depths of the cave: a vaguely humanoid creature about a foot tall with a pinched mouth, a big, beaky nose, and horns that looked like a pair of scissors sticking out of his head—a hasami-dachi. It stopped at the threshold of the cave because of the shimenawa that Mom had strung across when we left the island. The hasami-dachi opened its mouth and seemed to call to Niko.

Niko's face brightened and he went right over. You could tell by the way he and the creature smiled and laughed with each other that they were friends. *What are you doing?* I wanted to shout. *Why are you hanging out with a creature from Yomi?* But of course, this was in the past, so there was nothing I could say or do to change it.

They seemed to get into a friendly argument, with a lot of head-shaking and eye-rolling. And then Niko started dancing around with the jewel, tossing it up in the air and spinning and catching it just before it hit the ground. He balanced it on the tip of his nose. He kicked it with his hind legs, did a flip, and caught it in his mouth. It was like watching a combination of rhythmic gymnastics and Hacky Sack. The hasami-dachi clapped and cheered him on from the cave.

The tricks got harder and harder, and the hasami-dachi kept cheering. Finally, there was a trick that involved Niko walking on the shimenawa like a tightrope, juggling the jewel, three rocks, and an apple, and taking a bite out of the apple every time it landed in his hand. He was halfway across when something glinted in the hasami-dachi's eye, and it reached out a clawed hand and shook the rope. Its hand immediately disintegrated in a puff of smoke, and its face contorted in pain. But then it smiled in triumph as Niko teetered dangerously, leaped off the rope to safety outside the cave—and dropped everything he'd been juggling, including the jewel, which rolled into the hasami-dachi's other, unharmed hand.

Niko's eyes widened in dismay as the creature laughed and danced. The shimmery light that I'd noticed around Niko's body earlier began to fade—*his magic,* I thought. *This is how he lost it.* A moment later, the shimenawa melted away—a result of the creature's wish, no doubt—and a mob of oni poured out of the cave. A few of them chased Niko down the mountain, while the rest began tearing the forest apart, throwing fireballs every which way. Niko leaped off a boulder at the shore and disappeared into nothing—he must have opened a portal—but not before a shikome followed and was pulled through after him.

The scene faded and I lifted my eyes to face Niko, whose eyes were squeezed shut. "Is that true, what I just saw?" I asked. "In front of the cave with . . . Mr. Scissor-Head?"

"I didn't mean for it to happen," he whispered miserably, finally able to talk. "He tricked me."

This was why he'd been so cagey about what had happened to his wishing jewel. This must have been the "accident" that caused him to lose his magic. The one where "no one was responsible." Except someone *was* responsible.

"How could you have been so clueless? How could you have . . . I mean, you might as well have tied a bow around it! And what happened to it? Has he been using it against us ever since?" The anger I couldn't find before was back again, and building.

"No!" said Niko eagerly. "One use per person, and then I have to recharge it, so to speak. But I didn't have enough magic left."

That was a relief. But it wasn't enough. "You betrayed my mom! You started this entire mess!"

Niko looked like he might cry. "I'm sorry, Momo. Please forgive me. I should never have trusted that creature."

"Of *course* you shouldn't have trusted it, Niko! It was from *Yomi*! It was a *demon*! You're always complaining about me and Danny being foolish and bumbling and empty-headed, and the whole time, you made the biggest mistake of all!"

I stared at Niko, the blood pounding in my head. It was Niko's fault that the portal to Yomi opened up. His fault that Mom was dying. His fault that the fate of the entire world was at risk.

"Oh—and don't forget that foxes can earn their magic back by doing heroic deeds," Shuten-dōji inserted. His voice coiled nastily around the edges of his words like a snake getting ready to strike.

"Is that true?" I asked Niko. Something cold and spiky shivered through me. "Have you been helping us just so you could get your magic back?"

311

I almost didn't want to hear the answer. I was afraid of what it would do to me. First Danny, now Niko . . . My entire body was quivering with the need to hurt someone, to bundle up all this pain and powerlessness I was feeling and make someone else feel it. To be the one who caused pain instead of the one who had to experience it. To be the one who had power instead of the one who didn't.

"No! That's not true at all! I mean, it's true that I have been earning back my magic—" Niko spluttered.

"And just how have you earned it back?" Shuten-dōji's voice was as smooth and slippery as oil, and streaked with venom.

"No," Niko moaned. "Please."

"Who posed as a service dog and dropped off an envelope of gift cards at school to draw Momo to the mall? Who snuck into the dressing rooms and cast the spell to loosen the knot in her necklace so the shikome would attack?"

I stared at Niko, dumbfounded. "Why would you do that?"

"So he could rescue you, you fool. He summoned the kappa for the same reason. From the taxi station." So that's who he'd contacted—not the Luckies at all.

"But I meant no harm! Please believe me, Momo! The thing I wanted most was to fix my mistake—to save your mother! And I guess . . . I thought I would give myself a little boost along the way. It was foolish and selfish and reckless, I see that now, and I'm sorry. I—I just missed my magic so much. . . ." Niko collapsed in tears.

"Like I said," came Shuten-dōji's voice. He sounded positively gleeful. "Not on your side."

All, All, All Alone

The pain and anger that had been building inside me roared to be let out. I shook with the effort of keeping it down and away from Kusanagi, which was also shaking and practically pouring electricity into my arms.

Give me everything. Kusanagi was beyond demanding now; it was commanding me.

I couldn't do it. If I released the storm inside me, I would lose control. It would swallow me whole, and then who would take care of Mom? It would kill Danny and Niko, and no matter how angry I was at them, I couldn't let that happen. "That's not who I am. That's not who I am," I repeated to myself. My teeth were clenched so hard, my head hurt.

Shuten-dōji's malevolent yellow eyes searched mine, and he laughed. "Ha-ha-haaa! I knew it! You humans are all alike: weak and sentimental. And with a few glorious exceptions, you are afraid to embrace your capacity for violence, for death and destruction. Even now, you refuse to do what it takes to unlock the full power of your weapon. A pity, really. You have an enormous talent for destructive rage if only you would allow yourself to use it. Lucky for me, you never will, because you want to be

313

good." He spat the word "good" from his mouth like he hated the way it tasted.

He stepped out of the smoke and sneered down at me. "Every sword, no matter how great, is limited by the individual who wields it. Kusanagi is more powerful than Dōjigiri, quite honestly, but you are only a sad, scared little human girl who values people over power. Well, it's been an absolute pleasure watching you suffer. And now I'm afraid you'll have to go."

Shuten-dōji drew his sword back to strike. It seemed to move in slow motion as it swung toward me, trailing a cloud of dark red sparks. I could see the air parting for it and whooshing back after it passed, and I closed my eyes and waited for the searing heat of the blade as it sliced through my neck.

But it never came. Instead, my body shook from the *CLANG* of steel on steel: Kusanagi had raised itself up and blocked the blow—but just barely. As I staggered backward, I felt it say, *We are NOT going out like this. Fight!*

In a fog, I obeyed. I planted my feet under me and raised Kusanagi, and saw Shuten-dōji's mouth fall open in amazement before he clenched it shut and drew his eyebrows down. He hadn't expected this any more than I had. Maybe I *could* do this my way, after all. I reached for the energy that had helped me fight against the oni, and it sprang up and flowed eagerly into Kusanagi as I charged.

But Shuten-dōji was right—it wasn't enough. Not only was it not enough, I realized, but I also had to focus on keeping my rage monster from bursting out and taking over. And now that Shuten-dōji was playing for real, he deflected my attack with such force that I went skidding into the jeering throng of oni and yōkai like a plastic Lego figure kicked across the floor. I lurched to my feet with barely enough time to dodge Shuten-dōji's next attack. He spun around and came at me snarling, swiping Dōjigiri from side to side. I didn't dare try to parry; I knew I wasn't strong enough. The crowd parted as I stumbled backward, and in between each of Shuten-dōji's lunging steps I caught glimpses of Danny and Niko still hanging in their cages in front of the cave, shouting.

Shut up. You got us into this, my rage monster seethed at Niko. And to Danny, *You were planning to abandon me after it was over.*

A bright flash jolted everyone out of the moment. We looked up: the sky over the island was spitting and sputtering. It was webbed with glowing cracks, some of which had torn open and were burning at the edges. As I watched, another crack burst with an explosion like a giant firework and rained down sparks and ashes.

"Well, would you look at that!" said Shuten-dōji, opening his eyes wide in mock wonder. "Your mother's spell is cracking! Which means your mother herself has moments left to live." I heard his dark, empty, rasping laugh again. "Ah, how I love to see your pain," he said, and sighed. "I think I'll wait to kill you until after she's dead. That should be fun to watch." He waved a hand, and I saw Mom in bed looking small and frail, gasping and panting for breath.

"Poor child. Your friends have betrayed you. Your mother is dying. And you're still too interested in being *good* to fight back." He leaned down and whispered, "How does it feel to be all alone in the world, little girl?" Shuten-dōji bared his fangs at me as the oni and yōkai shouted and laughed.

I don't know what happened next, exactly. Maybe it was Shuten-dōji mocking me for my pain and anger, or maybe it was Kusanagi calling to me, or maybe my rage monster finally got tired of being cooped up and decided to break out. But when I heard the word "alone," I lost it.

Big-time.

Everything came rushing up: the deep ache of losing Dad; the crushing responsibility I felt when Mom was sad or confused; and the bitter sting of the humiliations I'd had to face at school. How helpless I'd felt, and all the anger I'd swallowed over those things because there was nowhere for my anger to go. Then there was everything I'd been feeling lately: wrath at Susano'o for banishing Mom and not caring one bit about her, Dad, or me; burning resentment at Danny for not having the courage to be my friend; fury at Niko for being so incredibly careless and selfish; and one last time, a horrible, mean, grating anger at Mom for needing me to save her life, not just now, but all the time. I thought of how guilty I would feel about this anger, how lost and sad and scared I would be if she died. More than anything in the world, that's what I feared most. I would be alone. Angry, scared, sad, helpless, and all, all, all alone.

I never had a chance. All that pain and anger and fear whirled inside me faster and faster until I was a hurricane of raw emotions. I was drowning in them, and powerless to do anything. I barely knew who I was anymore. I was howling winds and crashing waves and booming thunder. I was ravenous for destruction; I didn't care who or what got in my way.

The darkness took over, and I stopped thinking, just rode

the force of my anger, fear, and resentment until finally I opened my eyes and saw Kusanagi glowing and crackling just the way it had in Susano'o's hands. I felt like I had left my body—the old me had, anyway. I watched myself raise the sword and swing it over my head as gale-force winds tore trees from their roots, and a monstrous tsunami gathered itself off the coast. I brought the sword down and stabbed it into the earth. A flash of lightning. A crash of thunder. The ground shook beneath my feet, the wind whipped my hair, and a massive wave roared forward and smashed itself over the island.

The ocean took the form of a giant sea dragon and wound itself through the thrashing, wailing crowd of demons and monsters, sweeping them up like the trash they were and washing them into the cave. But Shuten-dōji was still hanging on; every time the dragon came at him, he swiped at it with Dōjigiri and managed to keep himself alive.

"Okay, okay, I get it! I made a mistake—you're not afraid to get mad! Tell you what—calm down, call off the storm, and let's make a deal!" he shouted at me, his voice a little shrill. But at that point, I couldn't have called off the storm even if I'd wanted to—I was hanging on for dear life. In fact, I could barely hear him over the wind and the driving rain, and the hiss and roar of the dragon made of waves.

But Kusanagi and my rage monster heard him loud and clear. *Sorry, not sorry*, they thought. *Too bad not even the demon king can fight off the power of an ocean storm.*

I watched myself wave my hand. A tornado dropped down, lifted Shuten-dōji off the ground, and spun him until he was nothing but a red-and-black blur. As it spat him shrieking into the cave and through the portal, I merged back with my body, and a dark, glimmering, electric thrum of vengeful triumph surged through me and lifted me up. I felt like I was floating in it—flying, even. I felt as tall as the sky. I felt like I could breathe fire.

But at the very edge of my mind, through the roar of my storm, I heard a voice—two voices. "Momo!" They were thin and weak. They sounded familiar.

Danny. Niko. I'd forgotten all about them.

They were still trapped in their cages, which were still attached to the cave roof, but just barely. Wind and water crashed and churned at the entrance, and the spikes that had been driven into the rock to secure the chains were coming loose. In a minute, my friends would be swept down the tunnel to Yomi along with everyone else.

This wasn't what I'd wanted. This was never what I'd wanted. The oni, yes. Shuten-dōji, yes. They *belonged* in Yomi. But not Danny and Niko. *Stop*, I begged Kusanagi. *I don't want to do this anymore.* But it wouldn't—or couldn't—listen. Every letter of every word whirled away like leaves in the wind, until there was nothing left.

"Momo!"

I couldn't shut down the storm. I couldn't unlock their cages. I wasn't strong enough to keep them from being swept down to Yomi.

I needed help. But who could help me? I didn't even know if Mom was alive—and she couldn't come here anyway, even if she had the strength. All the other gods were at Kami-Con.

Except Ebisu. Hadn't Daikoku said that he was on duty?

"HELP ME! HELP! EBISU! SOMEONE!"

The wind kept howling and the sea kept roaring. The thunder and lightning continued to rip the sky open. There was no way anyone could hear me, let alone a kami who was already partially deaf.

And then it was silent. Like someone—or something—had just sucked the life out of the storm and hit pause. Like time had literally stopped.

I walked down a trough that had carved itself through the water, until I was standing between the cages that contained Danny and Niko. I felt like I was in a photograph: Drops of water floated in the air. Danny's face was a mask of fear. A wave hung over Niko's head, the white foam crest just about to break.

Someone had heard me. But who?

"Hello?" My voice shook a little. After the chaos of the storm, the silence was huge and scary in its own way. "Anybody there?"

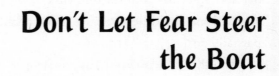

Don't Let Fear Steer
the Boat

As if in response, something shadowy snaked up from the depths of the cave—like mist, but made of darkness so intense that it seemed to give off more darkness. It split into strands that reached up like fingers that tangled themselves in my hair and dragged themselves across my cheek. I had the strangest sense that something like this had happened before. . . . When was it?

"Hello, child." It was the voice from the mirror. The one that had laughed in my dream last night. It curled around me, splitting and folding over itself and making the air around me shiver.

"Wh-who are you?"

"You mean to say you don't recognize me? Not even here? Ah, well. I suppose that's to be expected. It's been nearly twelve years, after all."

Who *was* this? And what were they doing in the cave? I tried to stay polite. "Um, I'm sorry if I should know you, but I didn't even know my mom's real identity until a few days ago. Sorry."

"Don't apologize. It's your mother who's at fault."

"Um. Okay." Something felt very, very wrong about this conversation. I wanted desperately to run away, but Niko and

Danny still needed me. "So, um. Not to be pushy, but are you here to help me save my friends, or . . . ?"

The voice laughed, and my skin prickled. "Don't worry. We'll get to them in a moment. But first, don't you want to know who I am and why I'm here?"

What I wanted to say was, *I've changed my mind about that. I just want to rescue my friends and get the heck out of here, thanks,* but all I could get out of my mouth was, "Um."

The shadow formed itself into the shape of a queen dressed in long robes and a spiky crown. Her face was skeletal—maybe it was an actual skull. I knew it had to be an illusion, but I could feel her presence as strongly as if she were actually here—she seemed to emanate damp, freezing air that clung to my skin and sank its teeth into my bones. "I am the Great and Holy Goddess Izanami the Destroyer, Queen of Death, Empress of Yomi, and Mother of the Middle Lands. It has a nice ring to it, but it is *such* a mouthful, don't you think? You may call me Auntie Izanami, if you like. Ooh, or Auntie Iz! That's fun."

Izanami the Destroyer was *not* my idea of a fun auntie, but I was too terrified to say so.

"As for my purpose here—you're sure you don't know? Not a clue?"

"B-b-because I called for help?"

She laughed softly. "That did provide a convenient excuse for a dramatic entrance. But you're wrong. Any other guesses?"

I shook my head.

"You *really* need to have a long chat with your mother. Congratulations on saving her life, by the way. Poor Shuten-dōji—his self-esteem is in absolute tatters. I warned him that you had access to powers beyond his, but he refused to believe he might be bested by a girl. Men so often underestimate women, don't you agree? Such a shame."

"So—she's okay?" Izanami made a good point about men underestimating women, but I was way more interested in the part about Mom. I needed to hear it again, just to be sure.

"Yes."

I almost collapsed with relief. Mom was going to live! I'd done it. I'd saved her.

But Izanami didn't let me enjoy the feeling for long. "As I was saying. My original plan was to kill your mother, capture you, and bring you back to Yomi. Obviously that failed, no thanks to our demon friend. Luckily for me, you lost control of your power, and . . ." She gestured grandly at me with a dark, wispy hand, like, *Ta-daaa!* "Here you are. The grand prize."

I stared her. What the heck was she talking about?

"I see you are confused," Izanami said. The shadow let out a sigh that left acid scars on the walls of the cave. "I don't want to bore you with the details, so I'll give you the short version: your mother promised me that on your twelfth birthday, she would bring you to live with me. Unfortunately, she did not honor her promise, and much of what has happened since then has been my attempt to, shall we say, *remind* her."

I stared at Izanami, horrified. "My mother would never make a promise like that."

"And yet she did." Shadow Izanami crossed her arms and cocked her head.

"But—"

"As I said, she broke that promise. But I anticipated that, so

I had a plan in place. Let's see . . ." Izanami began counting off on her fingers as she listed the events from the past few days: "I arranged for Dōjigiri's tour to coincide with Kami-Con. I sent the scissor demon to befriend your silly, selfish fox friend— I'm told it was child's play, by the way, tricking him out of his wishing jewel. I sent the oni to the surface to destroy the island. And I let Niko escape, knowing that he would eventually bring you back here to try to save your mother and make up for his mistake."

I began to feel light-headed. This wasn't about Shuten-dōji taking over the world. This wasn't about Mom and the island. This was about me. *I* was the target. But why?

Izanami was still talking. "The theft of Dōjigiri didn't go as planned, I admit—I meant for you to bring it here to the island so that Shuten-dōji could fight you for it and I could see what you were made of. But that arrogant fool couldn't wait, and he sent his own thieves and got it first. I considered sending the tengu to fetch you, but then you went after Kusanagi, and I was *very* curious to see how that would turn out. And I'm pleased to tell you that you've proven yourself more than worthy of our connection."

"Connection?" I took an involuntary step back. "We don't have a connection."

"Oh, but we do." Izanami drifted forward. "Why do you think your anger has such enormous power?"

"It's from Susano'o. I'm his granddaughter." For once, I was glad about this.

Izanami shook her head and smiled. "Oh, no, my darling. Susano'o is powerful, certainly. And you have manifested evidence

323

of his spirit, especially in your affinity for the ocean and for stormy weather. But the power behind that spirit—the only reason that you can cause tsunamis rather than tip over water glasses—that comes from me. I gave you just a drop when I found you in my realm. You're not ready to control it, of course, but you've gained access to it with remarkable speed. I've been very impressed."

It couldn't possibly be true. But Shadow Izanami bowed her head slightly, and the darkness inside me seemed to shape itself into a miniature version of the Queen of Death, and as it bowed back to her, my body went with it.

"You see? We are the same inside, you and I, though you have only the faintest whisper of what I have. And if you stay with me, I will teach you to bend it to your will."

A wave of panic and revulsion swept through me, and I felt an absurd urge to run away from myself. I *couldn't* be the same as Izanami. I could never give myself over to her. Never. I had to get back to Mom. I had to go home.

"Are you sure about that?" Izanami said, apparently having read my mind. "You don't *really* want to go back to that miserable existence, do you?"

The shadow streamed to the ground and then swirled up to form itself into an image of Mom at the beach. She was staring out to sea with a wild, desperate yearning in her face, just like she always did. The image melted and re-formed: Mom at the kitchen table, poking at a plate of scrambled eggs, her eyes empty and sad.

"Your mother should have protected you and taken care of you, should have taught you to be proud of who you are.

Instead, *you* ended up protecting and taking care of *her*. You ended up ashamed and alone." Izanami's thin, icy voice hissed as I watched Mom wander aimlessly around the house. "With me, you will learn to embrace and harness your power. I will protect you. I will take care of you. And if you like, I can protect her, as well. You would never have to worry about her again. Imagine that, Momo. Imagine how good that would feel."

It would *feel good*, said a tiny voice in the back of my mind, and I knew it was my voice and not Izanami's. It was low and cowardly. It was the worst kind of betrayal. But it was also the truth. It would be so freeing to only have to worry about myself. . . .

"I understand her better than I used to," I said frantically. "I know who she is. I know how strong she can be. We're going to be much happier from now on."

Shadow Izanami appeared in front of me again and shook her head. "No, child. She will never stop missing the things she loves most: her island and her weak little worm of a mortal husband. You've saved her life, Momo, but you have not changed it. You cannot restore what she has lost. You will never be enough."

Her words hit me so hard, I almost couldn't breathe. Because she was right. No matter what I did here, no matter how strong or heroic I was, none of the problems from my other life would go away. Niko would stay on the island, content to have his magic back. Danny would abandon me for his other friends. And Mom would still be banished. She'd still be a widow. She'd still be missing a piece of herself, and I'd still have to try to make up for that howling emptiness in her soul.

"What a tragic life—to know you're not enough for the very

person who has never been enough for you." A cruel smile crept across Izanami's shadowy face.

She was *enjoying* this, I realized. She'd dug up my worst thoughts and feelings—the ones that hurt me the most, the ones I was most ashamed of—and she was *laughing* at them. Anger flashed through me, white-hot. I hated how helpless I felt, and I hated Izanami for making me feel this way. I wanted to burn her to ashes. The familiar torrent of rage began to stream through my body, and Kusanagi sent a buzz of electricity up my arm in response—I'd forgotten that I was holding it.

"Ah, there we go. That's my girl. There's that power. What will you do now? How will you use it?"

That was the trouble. What *could* I do? Kusanagi and my rage monster, predictably, were begging to fight, but I was paralyzed with fear—or maybe Izanami was holding me there, reminding me that she could control what I couldn't.

"I would start by putting that sword away," Izanami suggested. "I know you'd never forgive yourself if you accidentally reanimated the wave and swept your friends down to Yomi with you." She glanced over my shoulder toward the mouth of the cave, where Niko and Danny and everything else were frozen in time.

I looked at Kusanagi. It pulsed and flared at me. *We can do this*, it said. *We can take her.* I gripped it tighter and looked up; Izanami shrugged as if to say, *Whatever. It's your funeral.*

I almost did it. Every scrap of common sense I had screamed at me not to give up my weapon. Kusanagi demanded that we fight. But in the end I wrestled it into my backpack, thrashing and twisting, because the only thing more powerful than

Kusanagi's rage-fueled spirit was my wild, terrible fear of what would happen if I lost control again—and couldn't get it back.

"Good girl," said Izanami. She sighed and examined her fingernails, like she was over this mess and ready to move on. "It's a shame Takiri-bime didn't just bring you here like she was supposed to. We could have saved ourselves a lot of fuss and bother."

At the sound of my mother's name, I felt like my heart might break. For all her weaknesses, she'd done her best. Maybe I couldn't replace Dad or her island, but at least she hadn't obediently surrendered me to the Queen of Death. In fact, she'd actively tried to keep me away from Izanami. I wished I'd known that so I could have said thank you instead of pushing her away. I wished I'd realized that—

Wait a minute.

I turned away from Izanami and plunged my hand into my backpack. It had been unpredictable so far about what it thought I needed, but if ever I needed Mom's protection, it was now. *Please*, I thought. *Please be there for me.*

My fingers closed around a rope—thin on the ends and thicker in the middle. Thank the gods.

I spun back around to face Izanami, holding one end of the shimenawa in each hand out in front of me like a shield. Niko had said it was useless unless Mom knotted it around my neck, but maybe, since we were here on the island . . .

Izanami's shadowy form started in surprise and seemed to fade a little as the shimenawa began to glow with the same silvery light that had radiated from Mom when she fought the shikome—it felt like ages ago. But after a beat, Izanami gathered the darkness around her and smiled again. "You cannot defeat me with that, you know." Her voice was cool and even.

"I don't want to defeat you," I said. I'd been through a lot, but I hadn't lost my freaking *mind*. Who thinks they can defeat Death, for crying out loud?

I looked at Shadow Izanami through the bright haze that surrounded me. She was still smiling, but had started to fade again. Ha. I breathed a sigh of relief—and then I realized that she hadn't been fading. She was pouring herself into misty black vines that were wrapping themselves around my little bubble of light. The edge of the bubble squished toward me on one side, forcing me to take a step farther into the cave. The darkness pushed in again, and I took another step. And another. Izanami was trying to pull me into Yomi.

You see, Momo? Your mother can't protect you, even here. Her voice came from all around me, and the cold seeped in even through my shield of light.

Darker, darker. I couldn't tell anymore if it was the cave or my own panic-induced tunnel vision. My legs went wobbly, and my head felt like it might detach itself from my neck and float right off. Every breath I took seemed to fill my lungs with fear instead of air, until I felt like I was made of it, like there was no room for anything else.

Don't let fear steer the boat.

The sentence floated up like a balloon from the last, tiny corner of my mind that hadn't quite surrendered. I clung to it and took one breath of real air and shook the darkness out of my eyes. But what else could I steer with? What was left? And just before the darkness closed in again, I saw the shimenawa, glimmering weakly and still pulled taut between my fists.

You can't defeat me, Izanami had said when she'd seen it. And I'd said that I didn't want to defeat her. What *did* I want, then?

I wanted to get out of here. I wanted to be safe. I wanted Mom and my friends and the world to be safe.

The shimenawa pulsed once, and finally I understood. *That* was why it had been there for me in my backpack. It wasn't meant to protect me—or not just me, anyway. It was meant to protect the world. Which meant I only had to do one thing: seal the portal.

The energy in the shimenawa was clearly not enough. But if I contained Susano'o's anger and Izanami's power, then some of Mom's energy had to be in me, too. Plus, she was literally here, all around me. She had to be. So I closed my eyes, dug inside myself, and searched for Mom's presence.

Then, slowly, I felt it. I felt her warmth make its way through me, from my heart all the way out to my fingers and toes. It connected with the shimenawa, amplified its light, and flowed back into my body. Now I was glowing, too. Mom was here. She was with me.

The black vines recoiled as the light grew stronger, and a few of them fell off altogether. I took one step backward, then another, focusing all the time on my mission: Seal the portal. Keep everyone safe.

I fought my way step by step up the tunnel, toward the entrance, past Niko and Danny. As I reached the threshold, the darkness loosened its grip and streamed away. On either side of the opening were iron rings that had secured the original shime-nawa to the cave. I placed one end on the ring on the right, and it tied itself obligingly into a tight little knot. The rope stretched as I walked it to the other ring, where it practically leaped out of my hand and began looping around itself to tie the second knot.

The moment it was finished, time lurched forward: The waves that had been hovering over Niko and looming around the mouth of the cave came crashing down, and Niko's and Danny's cages swung violently outward. A bolt of lightning that had stopped in midair streaked to the ground and split a tree in half. Thunder boomed so loudly, the air seemed to shiver.

And then nothing. Well, not *nothing*. The ocean drained away. The clouds dissipated. And in the silence, I heard the *click* of Niko's and Danny's cage doors unlocking.

Hi, Mom. . . . We Did It

"Niko! Danny!"

"Momo!"

In an instant, I was in the middle of a joyful three-way hug, squeezing the heck out of Niko and Danny. It is wild how exhilarating it feels to be alive when you've come *this close* to being dead—it's like every breath is a celebration.

But once the initial relief and excitement had passed, I looked from one to the other and realized I still had some pretty non-excited feelings about each of them.

"How could you have used us like that?" I asked Niko. I mean, no point in wasting time, right? "I could kind of sympathize with you getting tricked by the hasami-dachi, but you did everything else *on purpose!* What the heck, Niko?"

Niko hung his head. "I know. I'm a pathetic excuse for a fox, and I acted awfully, and if you don't like me or trust me anymore, I wouldn't blame you. But I am sorry." Two fat tears rolled down his cheeks, "I'm so very, very sorry. I promised to protect you, and I threw you directly in harm's way. It was selfish and shortsighted and, and . . . s-s-s . . ." I never found out what the last S word was because he fell apart completely.

He lifted his nose and howled as more tears dripped down and soaked his fur. Danny and I looked at each other. Niko did seem truly sorry, but I was still a little too mad to pat him on the head and tell him not to worry about it, that I forgave him, etc., etc. Danny seemed to feel the same way.

Eventually the howling sobs gave way to whimpers and sniffles, and Niko looked pitifully up at us. "Would you like me to disappear and never come back?"

Danny sighed. "No. But I'm not gonna lie, Niko. It's gonna be a minute before I can stop being mad at you."

"A lot of minutes," I said.

"A lot of minutes," Danny agreed.

"But you might eventually not be angry with me anymore?"

Danny and I looked at each other again.

"Possibly," said Danny.

"You'll have to work for it, though," I said. "For one thing, you better not lie to us ever again."

It was a while before we could unwrap Niko from around our ankles, where he sobbed and apologized and promised over and over that he'd make it up to us, that he'd never hide anything from us, ever, and that he would become the truest, most trustworthy member of our trio.

A quick look around the clearing once Niko had calmed down showed that the Island of Mysteries was already starting to recover from the oni attack. Tiny golden-green spears of grass had begun to sprout, and a freshwater spring bubbled up near the mouth of the cave.

"They ambushed us," Danny explained as we washed our

faces at the spring. "A whole mob of Yomi soldiers and monsters. My arrows didn't even work on some of them."

"I shouldn't have told you to go ahead without me," I said.
"I could have helped you."

"You wanted to help your mom," Danny said simply. "I
get it."

"Yeah," I said. I was grateful to him for understanding. "But
trying to help my mom almost got you and Niko killed." And
it had almost killed Mom, anyway. Not to mention nearly destroyed the world. It was odd that the impulse to protect someone could be a bad thing. How was I going to figure that out?

I looked at the shimenawa, now fastened securely across the
mouth of the cave. I told Danny and Niko how Izanami had
stopped me, and what she'd said about Mom promising to hand
me over to her on my birthday.

Danny listened with his mouth hanging open. "Why would
your mom promise to do something like that? Are you sure
Izanami's not lying?" he asked when I'd finished.

I looked at Niko for an answer—I couldn't help noticing
while I'd been talking that he'd gotten fidgetier and fidgetier.
His nose twitched, his whiskers quivered, and he kept getting
up, turning in a circle, and sitting back down again, like he
couldn't get comfortable. "Well?" I said.

"Well, what?"

"You know something, Niko." I stared him down. "Tell me.
Remember your promise."

He was quiet and fidgety for a few more seconds before he
cracked. "She's telling the truth!" he wailed. "When you were a

baby, Momo, you fell through the portal. Your mother ran down after you and begged Izanami to let her bring you back. Eventually, Izanami agreed to let you go, but only if you returned on your twelfth birthday, and your mother had no choice but to agree."

I hadn't realized until just now that I'd been holding on to the hope that Izanami had lied, and the loss of that hope made me explode. "You mean you knew that this *whole time*? And you weren't going to tell me? After you literally *just* promised to tell me everything? Are you kidding me? *This* is why I can't trust you!" I shouted, even though I knew it wasn't *totally* fair to be mad at him. But as always, mad felt better than scared or sad.

He looked at me sorrowfully, as if he understood. "I know it's terrible news. But please don't be angry at me. Your mother made me promise not to tell you."

"She also made you promise not to bring me here," I said, still irritated.

"What good would it have done to tell you?" Niko argued. "What would you have done—come straight here and offered yourself up to Izanami? I wouldn't have let you. There's no guarantee that she wouldn't have let your mother die anyway."

I sighed. He was right. "You better not keep any more secrets from me," I muttered.

"No more secrets, I swear!"

I gave him a healthy dose of side-eye. "Are you sure?"

"I *swear!*" he repeated. "On my magic!"

"What about—" I hesitated. What if he *didn't* know that Izanami had given me some of her power? I couldn't bear to see the fear in his and Danny's eyes when they learned that part of

Izanami was inside me. Would they stick with me, or would they run away? Or would they *say* they were on my side but meanwhile plot and scheme behind my back? I'd be all alone again.

On the other hand, I'd just made a very big deal about not keeping secrets. And maybe, if they were going to leave me, it would be best to find out right away. I took a breath and told them, fast, like ripping off a Band-Aid. Danny looked more impressed than scared, thank goodness. And Niko's bug-eyes told me that he had *not* known about it.

His jaw dropped. "She did *what*? Is that where the water dragon came from? And the storm? And the earthquake?"

"Apparently."

"Dang," Danny said in a hushed voice.

"I didn't know about it, so perhaps your mother doesn't either," Niko said. "I suppose you can ask her when you see her."

"Aren't you—are you scared of me?"

"Jealous, more like. So can you kill people at will?" said Danny.

"No! Danny, that's awful!"

"Just kidding. But I guess I better not make you mad, huh." He grinned.

"Seriously."

"Come on," he said. "I'm not worried." And we both laughed. But I thought I did see just the tiniest bit of worry flit around the corners of his smile. I knew it was flitting around mine.

I imagined Mom confronting the Queen of Death and bargaining for my life even as Izanami bound me to herself, and then later making the decision to try to hide me. I imagined her realizing that Izanami was trying to kill her, and having Niko show up and ask to bring me straight into the jaws of death, so to speak. I thought about how she'd hung on for so long, fighting to keep her spell together so that *I* would have a chance to fight.

I'd spent so much time wishing that she was more like other moms. I'd wished she'd raised me differently, that she wasn't so weird, that she was better at taking care of me. But even though she didn't know how to be a human being like everyone else, I'd felt the fierce power of her love down in the cave. I could finally see how much she'd done for me, and how hard she'd fought to keep me safe, to keep the world safe.

Suddenly I *really* needed to see her, even if we couldn't communicate. I let Niko drive the mirror, and we saw her lying in bed, pale but peaceful—resting, this time, instead of dying. Her chest rose and fell softly and easily. "Hi, Mom," I whispered. "We did it. I'm glad you're okay." A knot that I hadn't noticed before loosened itself in my chest.

"So," Danny said after a minute. "Now what? Do we just go home?"

But actually, I was in no hurry to go home. It was weird. I mean, of course I wanted see Mom and feel her arms around me as she hugged me and welcomed me back. Of course I wanted to tell her everything and ask her all the questions. *All* the questions. But there also was this tiny matter of whether Danny and I would still be friends when we went home. It felt silly to care—compared to the fate of the world, and to my awful connection to the goddess of death, it felt like nothing. But it mattered, somehow. And I was afraid to ask Danny about it. I was afraid that his answer would still be the same—and afraid that if it was different, he would be lying. So I wanted to stay here just a little longer, in a world where Danny, Niko, and I could be best friends, and Oak Valley Middle School was just a bad dream.

But Danny probably missed his parents. Even though he claimed they wouldn't have even realized he was gone, well . . . we'd been gone a long time. Maybe they were frantic with worry about him. And he was probably looking forward to seeing his real—his other friends.

"I don't think you'll be going home just yet," said Niko. He was gazing dreamily out at the sea. I looked where he was looking and saw a whale. It surfaced and blew a puff of spray, then flipped its tail as it dove again, making the water splash and churn.

"That's cool," I said with relief. "I wouldn't mind hanging out here and relaxing, after everything we've been through. We could go swimming, or whale watch, or maybe even clean up the island a little."

"That sounds good to me," said Danny, lying back and stretching.

"No, that's not what I mean. You won't be going home, but you won't be staying here, either."

"Why not?" I asked, frowning. "What's wrong with here?"

"Nothing's wrong with here," Niko said. "But I think we're expected elsewhere."

"What? How do you know?"

"They've sent a taxi."

"Huh?" Danny sat up. "Where?"

Niko lifted his paw and pointed. "There."

Part of the Family
of Kami

Niko hadn't been looking at the whale. He'd been looking at the water boiling and bubbling around it. As we watched, a rowboat popped out of the froth, followed by the lazily undulating bodies of the dragons from the Ship of Treasures.

We hurried down to the beach and found our old rowboat washed up on the shore and waiting for us. We climbed in and rowed back out to the spot where it had appeared. The whale was still there, surfacing and diving around the slowly circling dragons like a curious dog.

As we got closer, the whale came over and nosed right up against us.

"Good whale, good boy," I quavered. "Please don't flip us."

It *pfffffff*ed air and spray and lifted its creased gray head out of the water just high enough for an eye to appear above the surface. It bobbed there for a long moment while Danny, Niko, and I stared into that eye, spellbound.

You know that old saying about how eyes are the windows to the soul? That's what it was like, looking into that whale's eye. I felt like he *understood* me, like he knew me better than I knew myself. And I sensed a deep, mournful ache in his soul, like he'd lost something, or like he himself was lost. I was certain—suddenly and absolutely—that this was the lonely whale. Without thinking, I reached out and patted his cold, rubbery skin.

"Hey, big guy," I heard myself whispering. "You all alone? I know how you feel."

Danny's hand was on the whale now, too. "Go find your family. Or your friends, or whatever. Do you know where they are?"

The whale stared at us a little longer, and then slowly, silently sank under the surface. We leaned over the edge of the boat and watched him disappear into the depths below. I heard a sniff, and I turned just in time to see Danny swallow and wipe his forearm across his eyes. "Got some seawater in my eyes," he muttered when he saw me looking.

The dragons curled around us and swam in circles until the whirlpool sucked us through the portal to the Sea of Heaven.

It was nighttime when we reached the Ship of Treasures, and the sky was thick with stars. They twinkled so brightly and hung so low that I felt like I could touch them—and then I realized that I could. They were everywhere: the sky, the air, the water. I felt like I was floating in them.

"Why are we here?" Danny asked. "Like, I get it if we were supposed to, like, report back, or turn in our weapons or something. But there's no one here." It was true. With everyone away at Kami-Con, the ship was deserted. But then I heard footsteps approaching from the stern: tha-*thup*, tha-*thup*, tha-*thup*.

I turned to see what looked like the world's happiest middle-aged fisherman limping toward us, and I knew it had to be Ebisu, the god of luck and protector of fisherfolk—and the only kami who didn't go to Kami-Con. He was barefoot and wearing one of those bucket hats, a vest with, like, eighteen pockets, and rubber fishing overalls. In his left hand, he held a fishing pole that he was using as a walking stick; his right arm grasped a red fish the size of a Labrador retriever. (I know. Gi-freaking-gantic—and it seemed to be *alive*.) His eyes were crinkled and his face was wreathed in a big, bright smile, like being here and seeing us was the highlight of his entire life.

Niko dropped into a bow, and Danny and I did the same. Ebisu was my favorite of the Seven Lucky Gods, and Mom's, too. He and Daikoku were supposed to be good friends. I imagined them posing for a selfie, with him in this fishing outfit and Daikoku in her sharp business suit and heels, and smiled.

"Hello, friends, and welcome! I had one of my top scouts monitoring the situation, and he let me know the moment you triumphed—I am so proud of you." He beamed at all three of us. "Did you happen to meet him? Big guy, sad eyes?"

"The whale?" I asked.

"Yes, that one. I found him wandering the ocean, as lost as lost can be, so I invited him to join the team. Seems to have done him good to have a job, but he is still so very sad." Ebisu's smile faltered slightly, but then brightened again. "But with any luck, I'm sure we'll figure out a way to help him. Whales live a long time."

Ebisu went on to tell us that he'd brought us back to the Ship of Treasures so that we could file a report for the other kami to read once Kami-Con was over.

"Everyone there is talking about your battle with Shuten-dōji and the way you used Kusanagi to summon the elements. They even took a break from their general session to watch you.

Look, Daikoku sent me a video." Ebisu pulled out a phone (!) and showed us a video that Daikoku, evidently, had taken.

It looked like she was recording in a crowded sports bar, with a big television—or maybe it was a mirror—hung up in the corner. Bishamon was there with his spear, and Hotei was there, too, still wearing his bathrobe. Susano'o stood in the back—the other kami gave him lots of room. Everyone was shouting at the figures on the screen: Danny and Niko, confronting a mass of monsters. Danny was shooting arrow after arrow at the monsters and doing all right, but there were so many that he couldn't keep up. And as he'd said, a lot of them seemed unharmed— maybe because they were already dead. Niko was hurling stones and slamming bodies in his oni form. But then he changed tactics and instead began throwing his body in front of Danny's. Some of the Yomi soldiers had begun throwing spears at Danny, but instead of hitting him, they all lodged in Oni-Niko's chest, back, and legs. "Niko!" I shouted. "What are you doing!" I knew he'd survived, but I still found myself wanting to scream at him to stop. Though if he'd stopped, then Danny would be dead for sure.

"I had enough magic to take a few hits," said Niko. "Danny didn't."

Danny watched the screen, totally transfixed. "I didn't know this was happening."

As he took spear after spear, Niko began to shrink, and finally he turned back into a fox.

"What just happened?"

"His magic is leaving him," Ebisu said softly.

This was when Shuten-dōji appeared and ordered his soldiers

to put Niko and Danny in their cages. I heard Daikoku gasp, and watched several kami clutch each other's arms. Hotei covered his eyes, and Bishamon looked like he might burst into flames.

"You didn't even have enough magic left to undo the lock," I said, as it dawned on me. "You gave up all your magic to try to save Danny's life."

Niko barely managed a modest shrug before he was smushed in three giant hugs, first from Danny, then from Ebisu, then from me. "Maybe I can trust you after all," I whispered. "A little bit, anyway."

"Want to see the rest?" asked Ebisu, and of course the answer was yes. We watched as I rushed into the clearing, and as I stood and stared at the visions Shuten-dōji had conjured up. Then came the face-off: I held Kusanagi out and—there's no other way to say this—I exploded. I sort of started glowing, and growing, and suddenly there was a flash and there was nothing left but a ball of bright red lightning. The crowd in the bar went wild. Susano'o was standing on a table, thumping his chest and hollering, "That's my granddaughter!" Now *he claims me,* I thought. The kami jumped and cheered and hugged each other as the water dragon reared up from the ocean and swept all the oni and the yōkai into the cave, and then the tornado came down and took care of Shuten-dōji. They clearly had no idea how little control I'd had over what was happening.

I saw myself run toward Danny and Niko, stop, and step into the cave—and then the image glitched and disappeared. The kami gasped as one. They stared at the monitor, shocked. A couple of them began crying, including Hotei—even Bishamon looked pale. Susano'o started chewing on a fingernail. Several kami took out their cell phones and began shouting things like, "Ebisu! Where are you? Pick up!" and "Ebisu! Go to the Island of Mysteries, NOW!" Then the video we'd been watching on Ebisu's phone went black.

"That's when Daikoku called me," Ebisu said. "But I was already on my way."

"So . . . did any of the rest get recorded?" I asked.

"Unfortunately, no. Our tech doesn't transmit anything in between realms or in Yomi," Ebisu said. "And that's why we need you to put everything in writing."

He pulled a scroll of paper from one of his pockets. With a flick of his hand, he unrolled it and left it hanging in the air in front of us, and as we told our story, Japanese calligraphy appeared on the paper in vertical rows from right to left. Once we'd finished, he waved his hand again, the scroll rolled itself up, and he put it back into his pocket.

"I'm glad that Izanami decided to let the three of you go," he said soberly. "We will have to make sure you're extra-well-protected from now on, Momo."

"Uh, what do you mean, 'let us go'?" I asked. My heart tripped over itself. I'd fought my way to freedom—I'd *escaped*. Hadn't I?

Ebisu's eyes widened. "Oh! You mean you thought—oh dear, this is awkward." He took off his bucket hat, turned it around in his hands, put it back on his head, and cleared his throat several times before saying haltingly, "Izanami couldn't touch you when you were connected to the shimenawa, but she could easily have used her bond with you to pull you with her if she'd really wanted to. Or she could have allowed your anger to consume you and to kill Niko and Danny while you were fighting Shuten-dōji."

"Are you sure about that? Why would she let us go will-ingly?" Danny asked.

"I can't imagine. That's why we must be vigilant."

Suddenly I was seized with the conviction that Izanami was reaching up through the Sea of Heaven to drag me back down into Yomi. I felt her cold, shadowy fingers on my face and neck; I couldn't seem to get enough air. The deck tilted as she pulled me toward the railing.

"Momo!" Niko yelped.

"Oh dear." Ebisu leaped forward and caught me before I fell. "Breathe, child, breathe. You're all right, there's a good girl." I breathed and concentrated on Ebisu's warm hands on my shoulders, and the world came slowly back to itself.

"I bet Momo's stronger than we think," Danny insisted stoutly. "I bet she legit escaped with the shimenawa."

"But I almost killed you and Niko," I blurted. "Because of her. Because of our connection." The more I thought about it, the more convinced I was that Ebisu was right. The goddess I'd seen in the cave had forced me to bow to her, and she'd only been a shadow of the real Izanami. Her power had made me stop car-ing about everything I loved.

"There was that, yes. It makes sense that your bonds with Susano'o and Izanami would manifest themselves as violent, de-structive anger." Ebisu's expression grew serious. "Such power often feeds on fear and pain. You must find a new way to wield it, or it will destroy you and everything you love."

I nodded and suppressed a shudder. I wasn't sure I wanted to "wield" it ever again.

"Don't be afraid. I trust that you'll find a way. In any case, you did wonderfully. And I am so proud of you, Niko, for your selflessness in the final battle." Niko bowed. Then Ebisu turned to Danny and said gently, "And you, Danny. Well done, my boy, well done."

Danny smiled and blushed. "Thanks."

"I'm so glad that you were able to join Momo when she needed you. I knew I made the right decision about you all those years ago."

"Huh?" Danny was the one who said it, but I was definitely thinking it. And I could tell that Niko was, too.

Ebisu's eyes twinkled. "Haven't you been wondering how you could see and do all the things you've seen and done? Why you were able to see and speak to Niko that first day, and how you've been able to use a divine bow and arrow despite not having a drop of divine blood?"

Danny nodded. A spark of hope lit up his face. "Was Daikoku wrong about that? Do I have a kami for a parent after all? Are you my dad?"

"She was not wrong." I watched disappointment—even sadness—cross Danny's face at hearing this news again.

Ebisu spoke again. "But you're part of the family of kami anyway, dear boy, because I chose you to be my spirit child."

"You . . . what?"

"Susano'o is my younger brother, you know, which makes Takiri-bime my niece. I was heartbroken when he banished her from her island, but the kami do not interfere directly in each other's affairs. So instead I put a few things in place to provide Takiri-bime and her daughter"—he nodded at me—"with companions and help, should they need it. It wasn't easy, believe me—I had to look far and wide for just the right people. But after much searching, I found you! And I made sure that your family went to live near Momo."

"But—but where did you find me? Did you know my parents? I mean my birth parents? Are they alive? And um, what does 'spirit child' mean? Do I get any of your powers?"

Ebisu chuckled. "Well, you have had a very lucky life so far, don't you think? A handsome face, a strong body, a good brain, parents who love you and have plenty of money . . . and of course, I enhanced your connection to the kami-verse so you could travel with Momo if the situation demanded." He scratched his head thoughtfully. "I must say, I didn't expect it to backfire in the way that it did."

"Backfire?"

"Errr, yes. Ahem. That is, I thought it would bring you closer to us—to our stories. But instead . . . well. You pushed it all away and pretended to be something else entirely."

"Something else entire—are you saying I pretended to be white?" Danny said, his chin jutting out defensively—which made me think that when I'd challenged him back on the beach in Chicago about his dad teaching him how to "get along with people," he'd known exactly what I'd meant. "It's called *adapting*." Danny's chin was still sticking out—but it dropped a little as Ebisu gazed steadily at him.

"Well, because . . . it's just, kids started making fun of me at school a few years ago. And running around looking for yōkai was—I mean, it was fun, but . . ."

If it was fun, why didn't you stay friends with me? I wanted to shout. But I knew why. Danny had said it himself on the beach in Chicago: he wanted to belong to a group—preferably a cool group. *Things are different now,* I reminded myself. But I couldn't help feeling the old prickles of jealousy and betrayal.

Meanwhile, Ebisu looked confused. "But . . . ?"

"So my parents . . . It wasn't like they didn't *want* me to keep learning about the kami-verse with Momo. Just . . . I didn't have time anymore because they signed me up for all these activities. So I'd fit in with the other kids." He glanced at me, then looked down at his feet, his cheeks red.

That helped, oddly enough. Kind of.

"I'm sure your parents hated seeing you suffer, Danny. They love you, and they want you to succeed and be happy, so they've steered you toward things that made them happy as kids, toward activities and people that feel familiar to them. And there's no denying the power of the cloak they've taught you to wear in your world," said Ebisu. "But that cloak won't always fit, and it won't always protect you. If you search for the power in the identities you have held at bay, one day you will find a way to hold them all."

"Maybe." Danny sounded doubtful.

"You'll figure it out. I did. I was adopted myself—did you know that?"

"What?"

"I was the firstborn child of Izanagi and Izanami—yes, dear, that's right," he said, seeing me flinch at the sound of her name. "She was the Great Mother back then, remember? She gave birth to many, many good kami, and I was the first." He winked, but then turned serious. "My body was not fully formed, and I was often ill. When I was three, my parents tucked me into a basket and put me out to sea."

Danny gasped. "How could they do that to you? You could have died!"

"I know. But I've had thousands of years to think about it, my dear, and I've concluded that they tried their best and didn't know what else to do; perhaps they hoped that someone else might find me and do better."

"I wouldn't forgive them in a *million* years," muttered Danny. I kind of agreed.

"I understand. It's a lot to forgive," said Ebisu. "But the good thing is, I floated north to the land of the Ainu, who did know how to care for me. They took me in and raised me, and now—ta-da!" He bowed. "Here I am."

"Wow." Danny cleared his throat and hesitated. "So, if you're, like, the god of adoptees—"

"I am not, my dear. I am the god of luck. I just happen to have a soft spot for adopted children."

"Okay. But I mean—well, if you chose me and everything . . . because I was adopted . . ."

Ebisu shook his head in answer to Danny's unspoken question. "I cannot tell you anything about your birth parents."

"Oh. Um. Okay, that's fine. I was just, you know. Just curious."

As I watched Danny trying to be brave, I wondered if maybe the reason he always seemed so disappointed that he didn't have a kami for a parent wasn't just because he wanted to be part divine. Maybe what he really wanted was a clue about the family he'd belonged to before the Haragans. I wondered what it was like to know that there were people out there whose names and faces and stories had been linked to yours since before you were born—and not to know a single one of them.

"Maybe we can figure out a way to find them," I said. "Maybe we can look in Niko's mirror—"

"I already did," Danny said. He looked embarrassed. "I snuck a look on our first night on Mikado-bashira. It wouldn't even, like, turn on. All I saw was my own face."

Niko looked shocked. "You stole my mirror? Of course it didn't work for you! It's mine!"

"I only took one look! And I didn't steal it. It was really more like I borrowed it."

I decided that now might not be the best time to confess that I'd also borrowed the mirror, and it *had* worked for me, sort of.

After much apologizing and cajoling, Niko agreed to use his mirror to search for Danny's birth parents. But either he wasn't trying for real or the mirror didn't want to cooperate, because all we saw was what Danny had seen already: his face.

"I wish I could help," said Ebisu. "But you should know that your parents—the ones who are raising you now—love you and will be expecting you to walk in the door very soon."

"What? But—how long have we been gone?" He pulled out his phone and looked like he might faint. "*Eight days?* But we've only been gone for—"

"The time conundrum," Ebisu reminded him.

"But my parents are coming home today! They might already be there!"

"And that is why now is the perfect time for you to return."

A Manly Clap on the Back

"**Hotei sent a gift to help** you stay in touch with each other. It will make parting easier, I think." Ebisu reached into one of his many pockets and handed each of us a pad of paper and a calligraphy brush. "You can communicate with these once you return to the Middle Lands," he explained. To demonstrate, he made a few strokes with the brush across the top sheet of Niko's pad, and Danny's and my names appeared in glistening black ink. The ink sank into the whiteness and disappeared, only to appear a moment later on Danny's paper and mine. Underneath our names was Niko's, in smaller letters.

"The image will stay there until you reply," Ebisu said. "And if you want to communicate with anyone else, you can write their name, add your message, and send it like this." He swirled the brush on my paper; several Japanese characters and letters appeared and disappeared. Then he tore off the sheet, folded it into an airplane, and launched it into the air, where it promptly vanished from sight. "Now, Momo, your mother knows to expect you home soon," he said with a satisfied smile. He instructed Danny and me to stow the brushes and the paper in our backpacks, noting, "They are enchanted and will be available whenever you want them, so you can use them as much as you like."

After a lot of furry hugs and possibly a few tears, Niko hopped into the rowboat, and the dragons whirled him back to the Island of Mysteries. Then it was Danny's and my turn. Ebisu led us to the cabin in the middle of the deck that Daikoku had come out of when we'd first met her. He took us each by the hand as we stepped through the door, and one atom-expanding-and-squishing, colors-that-don't-exist-flashing, head-spinning second later, the three of us were back in California.

We dropped Danny off first. The Haragans had moved since I'd last been invited over, and instead of the smallish three-bedroom bungalow that I remembered, they now lived in a sleek, shiny modern house with huge windows and a three-car garage. It was dark out, so I could see straight through the combination living room–dining room in front, all the way into the gleaming kitchen in the back, and I understood why Danny would trust his dad's advice on how to succeed in the world.

Danny stood in the rectangle of light that poured out of the open front door, and gave us one last wave before closing it behind him. Ebisu and I watched him head to the kitchen, where his mom was leaning against a counter and tapping at her phone. As he walked through the door, she looked up absently, then started in surprise when Danny threw his arms around her. She recovered quickly and hugged him back, still looking surprised but smiling like it was a *nice* surprise.

He wasn't wearing his backpack, I noticed suddenly. "He'd have to explain where he got it," said Ebisu, reading my mind.

Danny's father appeared, gave him a big hug and a manly

clap on the back, and turned and disappeared behind a wall. After enduring a kiss on the cheek from his mom, Danny disappeared, too, and a few seconds later, a window on the second floor lit up.

"He can't tell them *anything*, can he," I said. I couldn't imagine coming home after what had just happened and having to keep it all to myself—not just because it was a huge secret, but also because everyone would think I was making it up. "I bet that's pretty lonely."

"He has been lonely already."

"How? He has tons of friends."

"His parents believe that love means looking past outer differences and focusing only on our shared humanity. But Danny knows that he is different from his white parents in one important way—how can he not? And he's had no one to share it with because his parents believe they should act as if that difference does not exist. That is why he has been lonely."

"He had me."

"Yes. And your mother. She was teaching him to love that part of himself—and to embrace everything else that made him unique. Perhaps that scared them—perhaps they saw that being different was causing him to suffer. So they encouraged him to focus on the things that made him most like themselves and everyone else."

"Oh." Maybe Ebisu was right. It sure would explain a lot.

"How lucky you both are to be friends again!" Ebisu winked. "Get it? Because I'm the god of luck. You'll be there for him when he needs you, won't you?"

Hmm. The real question was, would he be there for me? I

wondered if, now that he was back in his room, back in his old life, he was already texting his bro-bots and pretending to be the old Danny again. The thought of facing them on the bus and Danny pretending not to see me made my heart thud and brought a familiar ache to my belly. Ugh—you'd think all my adventures would have made me tougher.

"I suppose we'll see what happens when it happens," said Ebisu. Darn the kami and their mind-reading abilities.

Someone Who Knows
Who You Are

Mom was in bed when I got home, but she was awake and had color in her cheeks, and when she hugged me, I felt like I was a little girl again. I could have stayed cuddled up in her arms forever.

I told her everything that had happened since I'd left the note on her bedside table, and she listened raptly, gasping and clapping her hands at all the right times. "Takamori! How is he?" she asked when I got to the Taira crab army. And, "Mukade, ugh. Such a windbag." When I got to the part where I entered the cave, I watched Mom closely. My questions were boiling inside me like water in a lidded pot, but I really, really wanted her to tell me everything without me having to ask—didn't she owe me that, at least? She bunched and twisted the bedcovers in her hands as I talked, pressing her lips like she was working to hold something back. Finally, at the mention of Izanami's name, she dropped the covers and threw her arms around me.

"Forgive me!" she sobbed into my neck. "I offered to trade my life for yours—I begged her—but she refused. I was in such a panic, I didn't know what else to do. Twelve years . . . I thought I could find a way to hide you from her."

"She said we're connected. Me and Izanami, I mean," I said. "She said she gave me some of her power to bind me to her."

Mom squeezed me tighter and said nothing. After a while, she said bleakly, "Yes. I saw her do it."

She told me how Susano'o had heard me laughing on the beach one day and had called up a tsunami to kill me and Dad. Dad had been swept out to sea, and I got washed down through the cave and into Yomi. Mom had rushed through the portal and found Izanami standing over a huge stone basin full of black water, holding me in her arms.

The nightmare sensation of icy fingers trailing themselves across my cheeks, tangling themselves in my hair . . . of something cold and dark clinging to my skin, filling my lungs, sinking into my bones. . . . It hadn't been Shuten-dōji, or Izanami's mere presence. It was the memory of Izanami holding me in her arms, establishing our connection.

"I was so afraid that she was going to drop you into that basin. She said that she'd always wanted a daughter, that fate had brought you to her, and all the while she was passing her hand over you—I remember seeing the energy coming off it. But I just wanted to get you out of her clutches, and your father was still out in the storm. . . ."

So Mom had accepted Izanami's terms and rushed back up to the surface with me to save Dad. Then she did what she could to secure the island, and we left.

Mom buried her face in her hands. "I should have realized what was happening. I should have done more to protect you."

"How come you never told me about any of this?"

"Oh, Momo. Can you imagine living with the knowledge

that you only had twelve years to live on the earth before you were sacrificed to the land of the dead? How could I do that to you?"

She definitely had a point there.

"You could have just told me the rescue part. I would have thought you were so cool."

She smiled. "Perhaps. But your father worried that you might tell someone what I was telling you, and I would get in trouble, or someone might try to take you from me, thinking they were protecting you. I didn't want to tell you that story anyway. It scared me too much. And now that I know about her bond with you . . ." She hugged me tightly to her, as if Izanami were in the room with us, threatening to snatch me away again.

"It scares me, too."

Mom nodded against my head. "I had hoped to trick her and keep you safe with the shimenawa. I should have known better. Perhaps I should have done more. But being away from the island weakened me and made me forget the extent of my power. Your father was the only one who knew who I really was, and I depended on him and on my stories of the kami to remind me. And when he was gone, I became more and more lost. I kept looking for him because I knew he would help me remember."

All those long days staring desperately out at the ocean came back to me. "But you couldn't find him, so all you had were the stories."

She nodded.

"And I made you stop telling them."

Mom sighed and gave me a squeeze. "It's not your fault. It's natural for children to want to face a different direction from their parents sometimes—your father warned me that it might happen. It was so difficult for me to know who I was in this world; I understood why you wanted to be like everyone else. So I decided that I should let you try if you wanted to."

Just like Danny and his parents. Only *I* was the one who pushed Mom away because I was afraid that she made me weird. And, of course, Mom didn't know how to be like everyone else, much less teach me how to do it. I used to be mad at her for that. But now I was glad that she was different and only knew how to be herself. Even if it was a lot harder.

We were silent for a moment. Then I said, "I'm sorry I told you to stop telling me about the kami. I'm sorry I stopped believing in them."

"I already told you, Momo—I knew that would happen. And I was ready. I just wish I had been stronger for you. I wish I had been able to protect you from Izanami."

"You did your best," I said, remembering how easily Izanami had made me bend to her will.

"I can do better. I remember fully who I am now, which makes me stronger."

"And you have someone who knows who you are," I added. "Who wants you to tell all the stories. Plus, I still have Kusanagi." I pulled it out of my bag, and it became a sword instantly. The dark, restless, angry energy in me vibrated in response, and I hurriedly shoved Kusanagi back inside the backpack. Maybe I wouldn't use it again.

Mom smiled, then turned serious. "I will protect you with all of my strength, Momo. Maybe you will figure out how to use Izanami's power in a way that won't harm you."

"Maybe." I really, really hoped I'd never have to try. "Hey, I'm starving." I opened my backpack, silently begging Hotei to give me something to eat. He didn't disappoint. I found a harvest moon feast, complete with two tray tables so Mom and I could eat it all on her bed: a bowl of soba noodles in broth with a poached egg on top; pumpkin boiled in soy-sugar broth; roasted sweet potatoes; grilled eggplant with miso sauce; and fresh apples and persimmons for dessert. Izanami and my super-evil superpowers would have to wait. Right now, I was going to enjoy being home and sharing a meal with my strange, strong mother.

The next day, Mom wanted to drive to the coast, and I figured, why not? I owed her that much after all that time I'd spent rejecting her stories. Our stories. And she wasn't completely better yet, but she'd been getting stronger practically by the minute since I'd arrived home. When I asked her about it, she smiled and said, "Being a kami has its benefits."

No kidding.

We stood together on a high bluff overlooking the ocean, watching the sun go down; she'd always liked the bluffs because she could see more of the water that way. She told me about the time that Gozuryū the dragon fell in love with Benzaiten, the goddess of music, who agreed to marry him but only if he promised to stop eating people. And the time when Tsukiyomi, the Moon Prince, had made Amaterasu so angry that she refused to ever look at him again, which is why nighttime is separate from daytime. And the time that Susano'o trashed Amaterasu's palace, and she had been so upset that she'd hidden in a cave and plunged the world into darkness until Uzume, the goddess of laughter, had lured her out.

"You should have seen it, Momo. She was on top of this enormous upside-down washtub, stomping around and shaking her bottom. That was the world's first drum and the world's first dance, did you know that? And then—" Mom stopped speaking and gasped. Her eyes were fixed on a spot far out on the ocean.

"What?" I squinted at the horizon, where the sun was just about to dip under the water.

"Oh. Nothing. I thought for a second that I saw your father."

I looked again. I saw a pod of whales, which was very exciting, but definitely not Dad. "Look, Mom." I pointed them out to her.

Mom nodded. "Mm-hmm. Not Dad."

At least she didn't think he was a whale.

"One day he'll come back," she said firmly. "One day, we'll see him."

I didn't believe her, but I didn't argue, either. I just smiled at her and said, "One day."

Epilogue

Izanami withdrew her pale fingertips from the basin and gazed through the rippled surface of the water as Momo secured the shimenawa across the entrance to the cave. The locks on the cages clicked open and Danny and Niko tumbled out; now that Shuten-dōji was back in Yomi and the entrance was sealed, his magic could no longer hold them captive. Izanami passed her hand over the water, which went still and dark.

She turned her icy glare on the demon king, who knelt at her feet with his forehead pressed to the floor. "Your only job was to capture the child and prepare the way for me," she said. The quiet menace in her voice filled the room. "I told you to be careful. I told you not to provoke her. But you didn't listen."

"You—you could have come with me through the portal, Your Highness." He didn't dare look up. "And I thought you told me that she was of greater use in the World Above than down he—" Tendrils of black mist wrapped around his neck and squeezed.

"I am THE QUEEN OF DEATH!" Her rage was incandescent. "I do not sneak through the back entrance like a coward, you disgusting worm. When I arrive in the World Above, it will be on the Great Return Road with the full power of Yomi at my back and the Infinite Family of Immortals cowering at my feet!"

Shuten-dōji scrabbled at his throat and did his best to nod his agreement. The mist released him. He drew a long, ragged breath.

"But yes. With the Prince of Darkness on our side, Momo will be far more useful in the World Above than here with me. It's a pity that I won't be able to teach her directly—I did so enjoy watching her defeat you—but there will be time for that later. I have waited centuries. I can wait a little longer."

She leaned over the basin once more and blew gently on the water. Momo was back at home, nestled in Takiri-bime's arms. Izanami's eyes glittered. "Don't forget about me, Momo," she whispered. "I have big plans for you."

Acknowledgments

Momo Arashima Steals the Sword of the Wind is my fourth book. You'd think I'd be an expert at book-writing by now, but no, I needed just as much support with *Momo* as I did with my very first novel. Possibly even more. Luckily for me, I was—and continue to be—surrounded by a deeply talented and caring community of friends, fellow writers, and family. And of course, I won the publishing lottery in terms of my agent, my editor, and the many incredible professionals who brought this book from idea to reality. Thank you, thank you, thank you to the following people:

Leigh Feldman, my agent, for encouraging me to write Momo's story even though middle-grade fantasy was new territory for both of us. I was nervous until Leigh said she loved it and wanted to find an editor for it—and then I relaxed. Other authors talk about the anxiety of being "on sub" with a manuscript, but I have never felt that anxiety, because Leigh is so amazing at her job.

Liesa Abrams, who is the perfect editor for this book and this series in so many ways; I can still hardly believe my good luck. Liesa is an expert among experts and a wise, compassionate editor. Her passion for stories that offer kids a safe place to

362

be whoever and whatever they need to be is contagious and inspiring, and I am so happy that *Momo* found a home with Liesa and Labyrinth Road.

Emily Harburg, Rebecca Vitkus, Barbara Bakowski, Brenna Franzitta, Abby Fritz, and the many, many other talented and dedicated individuals at Penguin Random House who brought this book into the world. Because of the way the publishing schedule works, I haven't even met some of these people yet, but I am so grateful to each and every one of them.

Designers Michelle Cunningham and Jen Valero, and artist Vivienne To for an absolutely breathtaking cover—I still get chills every time I look at it. And did you know that someone has to design the interior of the book as well? I've never had illustrated chapter headings before, and I am in love with them.

Beth McMullen, middle-grade adventure author extraordinaire, for reading my very first draft and giving me the advice and encouragement I needed to reshape it into something that actually made sense.

My wildly talented Bay Area kidlit author crew for their friendship and support. I got invaluable fantasy-writing advice from Traci Chee, Andrew Shvartz, Tara Sim, and Evelyn Skye (particularly how to write a synopsis for the sequel to a book you haven't finished writing). I treasure the Zoom craft discussions, problem-solving lunches, book launch brunches, and mutual moral-support chats with those authors, as well as authors Kelly Loy Gilbert, Joanna Ho, Gordon Jack, Stacey Lee, Lisa Moore Ramée, Sonya Mukherjee, Keely Parrack, Parker Peevyhouse, Randy Ribay, Darcy Rosenblatt, Abigail Hing Wen, and former crew member Sabaa Tahir.

My writing-group colleagues Sandra Feder, Rebecca Siler, Alicia Hoey, Louise Hendricksen, and Viji Chary for helping me bring the tengu scene and the centipede scene to life.

Author Ilana Masad for the insightful comments on another early draft that pointed me toward the emotional core of the book, and for her support of my writing from the very, very beginning.

Roseann Rasul, who understands kids and books better than almost anyone else I know, for her spot-on comments on voice, character, and pacing. She also gives compassionate, honest, loving life advice, and I consider myself lucky to be able to count her as a friend.

Middle-grade author Jen Petro Roy and middle-grade student (and fantasy novel expert) Sonya Kapasi for helping me fine-tune the opening pages.

The Sustainable Arts Foundation for grants that support creators like me, who have to balance their creative energy and time with childcare duties.

My mother, Kaoru Sugiura, and my aunt Jun Kuroda for their invaluable contributions as research assistants and fact-checkers.

The real-life Emi, Mika, and Kai, whose intelligence, kindness, curiosity, joyfulness, and all-around lovability inspired their namesakes in this book.

Tai, whose countless imaginary childhood adventures inspired me to try going on an imaginary adventure of my own.

Kenzo for patiently listening to and workshopping every single early idea I had for those adventures, and for his wise advice to go with the one that led me to Momo.

Tad, whose quiet, stalwart, loving support in every facet of my life made this book a possibility.

Author's Note

One cool thing about the gods, monsters, and heroes of Japan is that they often come from a mash-up of several different traditions: a variety of religions and folktales, and even history. Japan's "native" religion, Shintō, stems from the indigenous religions of southwestern Japan. The Ainu in northern Japan have their own separate culture and religion. Then there's Buddhism, which originated in India and traveled through China before it arrived in Japan. The shared history of these religions and cultures in this relatively small country hasn't always been peaceful, but they've spent so long together that many of their stories have mingled and even gotten tangled up with folklore and historical facts.

For example, Daikoku was originally a Shintō god named Okuninushi who took on the identity of the Buddhist god Mahākāla—and Mahākāla is said to be connected to the Hindu goddess Kali. Daikoku is best friends with Ebisu, who was born to Shintō gods and raised by Ainu families. And then there's Hotei, a Buddhist god with links to a real-life Chinese monk, and Bishamon, a Buddhist god based on the Hindu god

Vaiśravana—and they all visit Shintō shrines to spread good luck on New Year's Day.

Because everything is so layered and blended, I had to choose which aspects of the various gods and demons I wanted to emphasize in this book. If your understanding of these legends and heroes is different from mine, I hope you'll remember that there are many ways to understand them and that this book is not a textbook—it is a story.

More than anything, I hope you've enjoyed spending time with these characters as much as I have, and I hope you'll join them for their next adventure together!

Glossary

Amabie (ah-mah-bee-eh) A glow-in-the-dark sea creature with a beak, long hair, and three fins (legs?) who emerged from the sea in 1846 and predicted a plague. She is part of a family of future-predicting creatures called amabiko. Kinda cute, but also kinda creepy.

Amaterasu (ah-ma-teh-rah-soo) The goddess of the sun and queen of the sky. She's kind of the boss of the Shintō kami, since all life depends on her. She's also the big sister of Tsukiyomi, the god of the moon, and Susano'o, the god of the seas and storms. But she's had big, huge fights with both of her brothers, so none of them really talk anymore.

Antoku (ahn-toh-koo) Emperor Antoku was an actual, real emperor of Japan about a thousand years ago. Born in December of 1178, he ascended the throne in 1180 and "ruled" until his death on April 25, 1185. Because a toddler can't *actually* rule a country, Antoku's grandfather Taira no Kiyomori ruled in his place. When Antoku was four, the Taira clan's rivals, the Minamoto, proclaimed their own emperor. After two years of fighting, the Taira were finally defeated in a sea battle. Antoku's grandmother Lady Tokiko took him in her arms and jumped overboard, telling him, "A kingdom awaits us under the sea." (Antoku's mom was on another boat and tried to jump, too, but was pulled out of the water before she drowned.)

Battle of Dan-no-ura (dahn-noh-oorah) That sea battle I was just talking about. It took place in a narrow passage between islands where the tides and the currents made it very difficult to navigate. The Taira were winning for a while because the tides were in their favor, but the tides literally turned, a traitorous admiral switched sides and pointed out Antoku's boat, and the battle ended with the Minamoto trouncing the Taira. The Taira samurai leaped to a watery grave rather than suffer the dishonor of defeat and, let's face it, probably be beheaded anyway. Lady Tokiko (holding Antoku) and her ladies-in-waiting also jumped, taking the Three Sacred Treasures with them. According to legend, the treasures are the kami's sign that you deserve to be in charge, so Tokiko's last act was basically a way of saying to the Minamoto, "You may have won the battle, but we've got the treasures, so *thbbbbt*."

Benzaiten (ben-zaai-ten) The goddess of music, language, creativity, poetry, knowledge, and rivers—basically anything that flows, if you catch my drift. You can visit her island home of Enoshima (where she lived with her husband, a five-headed dragon) if you go to Japan.

Bishamon (bee-shah-mon) The god of warriors, punisher of evildoers, healer (because he protects the body against invaders, get it?), guardian of the North, and one of the Seven Lucky

Gods. The original translation of his name is "the one who hears much." His colors are yellow and green, and most paintings and statues portray him as a scary-looking guy with his foot crushing a bunch of very unhappy demons. In my imagination, he loves Twix bars.

crane Specifically, the flying origami crane that Momo and her friends ride from her house to the Asian Art Museum in San Francisco. There's a fairy tale that involves a foolish man who rides a flying origami crane over the ocean in a rainstorm, and the crane gets all soggy and falls into the water. Don't worry, though: the man is rescued.

Daikoku (dai-koh-koo) One of the most popular of the Seven Lucky Gods, Daikoku is the god of farmers, commerce, wealth, and kitchens. He is almost always portrayed as male, but one of his/her original incarnations is the Hindu goddess Kali, the goddess of death and time (among other things), so sometimes she appears as female. (One translation of Daikoku's name is "the great black one.") Daikoku is usually portrayed wearing a farmer's hat, sitting on a big bale of rice, and carrying a wish-granting mallet.

Dōjigiri (doh-jee-gee-ree) The sword that Minamoto Raikō (a real person in history) used to cut off the demon king Shuten-dōji's head. The Tokyo National Museum owns a thousand-year-old sword named Dōjigiri that is said to have belonged to Minamoto Raikō.

Ebisu (eh-bee-soo) The god of fisherfolk, merchants, and luck. Ebisu is a hugely popular kami, maybe because he always has a big smile on his face. He's the only one of the Seven Lucky Gods to originate completely in Japan—his mom and dad are Izanami the Great Mother and Izanagi the Creator. He was born without proper bones, and his parents eventually put him out to sea in a basket—but lucky for him, the Ainu people on the northernmost island of Japan rescued him and raised him up into a full-grown kami.

foxes Foxes are everywhere in Japanese folklore and religion. They are the symbol of Inari, the god/goddess of the harvest, and are often seen holding magic wish-granting jewels outside Inari's shrines. Foxes love to play tricks on people, so you should never trust one. The more good deeds they do, the more powerful they become and the more tails they earn (up to nine).

Gozuryū (goh-zoo-ryoo) The five-headed dragon who terrorized a group of fishing villages until the goddess Benzaiten arrived and he fell in love with her and promised to stop terrorizing fishing villages.

heike-gani (hay-keh gah-nee) Crabs that still live in the waters of the Shimonoseki Strait, the site of the Battle of Dan-no-ura. Their shells have a pattern that looks like the furious faces of the drowned Taira samurai. ("Heike" is another name for the Taira clan, and "gani" [or "kani"] means "crab.")

hone-karakasa (hoh-neh-kah-rah-kah-sah) The literal translation is "empty bone umbrella." Hone-karakasa are ghostly old-fashioned paper umbrellas that are in such bad condition that you can see their wooden "bones." They appear before bad weather.

Hotei (ho-tay) The god of happiness and contentment. If you've ever seen a Laughing Buddha figurine with a big belly and a bigger smile, that's probably Hotei. His name, which means "cloth bag," comes from the bottomless sack of presents and food that he carries wherever he goes.

Island of Mysteries The local name for a teeny-tiny island off the southwest coast of Japan; its official name is Okinoshima. It is associated with Takiri-bime and is so holy that no one who sets foot on it is allowed to talk about their experience there—I'm not kidding! Technically, women aren't allowed on the island, but that's probably because someone's afraid that if women did go on the island, they'd become literally unstoppable.

Izanagi (ee-zah-nah-gee) The kami who started it all, along with his wife, Izanami. They came down the bridge from the Sky Kingdom and stirred the muck around and created land, and then Izanagi and Izanami had lots of babies that became more land, trees, mountains, animals—you name it.

Izanami (ee-zah-nah-mee) She gave birth to literally everything that became everything else. But when she gave birth to the god of fire, her body was burned so badly that she had to go down to Yomi, the land of the dead. Heartbroken, her husband, Izanagi, went down to rescue her, but . . . let's just say things got ugly, and he couldn't handle it. Izanami was *maaaaaad,* and she vowed to devote her life—I mean, her existence—to killing people to get back at her husband.

Kami-Con, aka Kami-ari-zuki (kah-mee-ah-ree-zoo-kee) The week around the tenth day of the tenth month, when all the kami in Japan gather in the region of Izumo for a general meeting to catch up with friends and make plans for the following year. The literal translation is "the month when kami are present." Elsewhere in Japan, this time is called kami-nashi-zuki, which means "the month without kami," for obvious reasons.

kappa (kahp-pah) They seem harmless from afar: funny-looking little green platypus guys with cute little duck bills and a waddly little walk. But don't be fooled! They're out for blood, and they'll pull you underwater and eat you up if you get too close. But if you can trick them into spilling the water from the little bowl on their head by bowing (they're very polite, so they often bow back) or beating them in a wrestling match, you can bargain with them. They'll do anything to refill their water bowl.

koma-inu (koh-mah ee-noo) These fierce creatures guard the entrances to Shintō shrines (and some Buddhist temples); sometimes called "lion dogs," they look like just that: a cross between a bulldog and a lion. They typically come in pairs—one male, the other female; one with its mouth wide open, the other with its mouth shut.

Kusanagi (koo-sah-nah-gi) One of the Three Sacred Treasures of Japan. Long story short, Susano'o got into a *huuuge* fight with Amaterasu that ended with him trampling her rice fields, killing her horses, and trashing her palace, so he was kicked out of the Sky Kingdom. While on Earth, he slew an eight-headed, eight-tailed dragon and found Kusanagi in one of the tails. Feeling bad for all the trouble he'd caused, he gave the sword to Amaterasu to show her he was sorry. Then he went to live in Ne-no-kuni, and his descendants ruled the Middle Lands. Later, Amaterasu regifted Kusanagi to one of her grandsons when another of her grandsons defeated one of *Susano'o*'s grandsons in a wrestling match—and then she claimed that this gave grandson #1 the right to rule the Middle Lands! You can see why Susano'o might want his sword back and why he and Amaterasu still don't get along. (Side note: If you were Amaterasu's grandson #2, who did the actual work, wouldn't you be really annoyed? I would.)

Lady Tokiko (toh-kee-koh) A person from history; her official name was Taira no Tokiko. She was Antoku's grandmother, and she was *very* proud to be a Taira. Also, she did *not* like losing. It was her idea for all the ladies on her boat to jump into the sea with the Three Sacred Treasures and Antoku.

Land of Roots Otherwise known as Ne-no-kuni. When Susano'o got kicked out of heaven for his anger issues, he spent a long time wandering the earth before finally retiring to a massive underground fortress. You know, where all the roots are.

Mikado-bashira/Gateway Pillars (mee-kah-doh bah-shee-rah) There are three tiny little islands—it might be more accurate to call them giant rocks—close to Okinoshima (the Island of Mysteries). I merged them into one island and called them by the name of the middle rock. Google "Okinoshima" and zoom *waaay* in to find them off the southern shore.

Minamoto (mee-nah-moh-toh) One of the two great clans that fought a legendary war (the Genpei War) for the imperial throne about a thousand years ago. They won.

Mukade (moo-kah-deh) "Mukade" means "centipede," and while there isn't an actual General Centipede in the legends and folktales, Susano'o did actually try to kill his grandson, who came to ask him a favor, by making him spend the night in a room full of centipedes.

Ne-no-kuni (neh-noh-koo-nee) Literally, the "Land of Roots," where Susano'o lives all by himself in his great fortress. That's really all anyone knows about it. *See also* Land of Roots.

oboroguruma (oh-boh-roh-goo-roo-mah) Back in the day when nobles rode around Heian-kyō (now known as Kyōto) in ox-drawn carts, the streets could get crowded. Sometimes there were traffic jams, and sometimes the nobles ordered their drivers to fight for a good spot to see a parade. The angry spirits of the nobles who lost those fights would turn into ghost carts with horrible scary faces that drove themselves around town at night.

oni (oh-nee) Demons. Ogres. Giant, evil, bloodthirsty humanoids with bad haircuts and horns (sometimes one, sometimes two, sometimes even three) on their heads. They typically have bright red, blue, or green skin. If you are really, really bad on Earth, you might become an oni in the afterlife; some exceptionally bad people become oni even before they die.

Rabbit in the Moon The Moon Prince visited Earth one day disguised as a beggar and asked some animals for a meal. Fox brought him a fish, and Monkey brought him fruit, but Rabbit didn't have anything, so he threw himself into the fire to make himself into a meal. I would have freaked right out, but the Moon Prince did not. Instead, he was so touched by Rabbit's sacrifice that he rescued Rabbit and took him back to the moon to live forever. You can see the rabbit when the moon is full—he's sitting on his hind legs, bent over slightly as he makes mochi cakes.

Raijin (rai-jeen) The god of thunder. When you hear thunder, that's Raijin banging on his drum.

Sea of Heaven We don't know a whole lot about the Sea of Heaven except that the *Takarabune* (the Ship of Treasures) floats around on it, and it's in the sky. If you sail for long enough, you will reach the Sky Kingdom, where Amaterasu lives.

Shuten-dōji (shoo-ten doh-jee) The demon king: the biggest, baddest, most bloodthirsty oni of them all. His mother was a human, and his father was an eight-headed dragon who terrorized villages by demanding that they sacrifice one maiden to him every year to eat. Shuten-dōji was such a bully as a kid that his mother sent him to a monastery in the hope that the monks would teach him to be nicer. (No one knows where his dad went—though I imagine that he wouldn't have been a great influence, anyway.) But Shuten-dōji was terrible to all of the monks and to his fellow priests-in-training, and he loved to get drunk and fight and terrorize people. One night, he put on an oni mask to scare the other priests-in-training, and when he tried to take it off, he found that it had become his actual face. You can visit the shrine where his head is supposed to be buried (*but is it still there?*) at the Kubizuka Daimyōjin shrine near Kyōto.

Susano'o (soo-sah-noh) The god of the sea and the god of storms. (I know, Raijin is the god of thunder. There's a lot of overlap in the kami-verse.) He was born when Izanagi the Creator blew his nose, so you could say that he's literally a big snot. He's not a *bad* guy exactly, but he has a terrible temper. He's the original owner of Kusanagi, and he lives in Ne-no-kuni, the Land of Roots, under the earth.

Taira (tai-rah) The clan that the Minamoto overthrew during the Genpei War a thousand years ago.

Takarabune (tah-kah-rah-boo-neh) or **Ship of Treasures** The Seven Lucky Gods sail this ship down to the Middle Lands on the first three days of the New Year so that they can spread good luck among humans.

tengu (ten-goo) I guess you could call them chaos demons. They're not super-evil, but they do love to cause trouble. They tend to be greedy, selfish, and impulsive, and they love a good fight. Sometimes, though, they're wise and good. The king of the tengu, Sōjōbō, trained Minamoto no Yoshitsune, one of the greatest warriors of all time.

Tsukiyomi (tsoo-kee-yoh-mee) The god of the moon. He's a middle child—younger brother of Amaterasu, older brother of Susano'o. He made Amaterasu *really* mad a long time ago, so the two of them never see each other anymore.

Urashima Tarō (oo-rah-shee-mah tah-roh) He was a fisher-man who rescued a sea turtle from a bunch of bullying boys and let it go back into the ocean. It turned out that the sea turtle was actually a beautiful princess in disguise—the daughter of the dragon king. She returned the next day, saying that her father wanted to thank Urashima for saving her life, and would he like to go with her to visit the palace? Of course he said yes, and after a few days of partying underwater with the princess, he thought he'd better be going back. The princess begged him not to leave, but finally she relented and gave him a box, telling him never to open it.* When he arrived back home, he discovered that he'd been gone for three hundred years. Distracted with grief, he opened his present (*NOOOOO*), and all the years he'd missed came out like smoke, and he um . . . died.

*Note: I will never understand why anyone would accept a present they were told never to open. You know there's nothing good in there. Just say no!

Uzume (oo-zoo-meh) The goddess of laughter, dance, and the dawn. Uzume invented both dancing and drumming by stomping around and shaking her booty on an overturned wooden tub.

Yomi (yoh-mee) The land of the dead, ruled by Izanami. It's cold and dark and full of demons, monsters, and ghosts.

GET LOST
IN A STORY

FOR MIDDLE-GRADE READERS

FOR YOUNG ADULT READERS

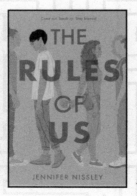

 LABYRINTH ROAD